Although Deanna's ... ep-
ing in them and her ha.... ...... loose from its pins and
cascaded down in a tumble of shining black curls, Matt
had never seen anyone so beautiful. She must have
noticed then how deeply he was looking at her for she
flushed slightly in embarrassment and raised her hands
to her hair and began to try to pin it up.

"Don't," he said quietly.

She hesitated, and the blue eyes widened a little as he
rose slowly from the chair and took the tray from the bed.
He turned away to put the tray on the dresser. Then he
looked back at her. She sat very still watching him. He
walked to the bed and sat on the edge. She did not seem to
be afraid of him, yet her hands trembled in her lap as her
eyes held his. He took one of her hands in his and raised
the fingers to his lips.

"Do you know how long I have dreamed of you?" he
whispered. "Night after night all that I can see is the
loveliness of your eyes."

She seemed mesmerized and he bent his head closer
and closer to hers until his mouth very gently took hers
in a kiss as soft as butterfly wings. Now he could feel the
trembling in her whole body, but it was nothing
compared to the reaction of his. . . .

BE CAPTIVATED BY THESE HISTORICAL ROMANCES

CAPTIVE ECSTASY (738, $2.75)
by Elaine Barbieri

From the moment Amanda saw the savage Indian imprisoned in the fort she felt compassion for him. But she never dreamed that someday she'd become his captive—or that a captive is what she'd want to be!

PASSION'S PARADISE (765, $3.25)
by Sonya T. Pelton

Kidnapped by a cruel and rugged pirate, a young beauty's future is suddenly in the balance. Yet she is strangely warmed by her captor's touch. And that warmth ignites a fire that no pirate's seas can put out!

AMBER FIRE (848, $3.50)
by Elaine Barbieri

Ever since she met the dark and sensual Stephen, Melanie's senses throbbed with a longing that seared her veins. Stephen was the one man who could fulfill such desire—and the one man she vowed never to see again!

TIDES OF ECSTASY (769, $3.25)
by Luanne Walden

Meghan's dream of marrying Lord Thomas Beauchamp was coming true—until the handsome but heartless Derek entered her life and forcibly changed her plans. . . .

TEXAS FLAME (797, $2.75)
by Catherine Creel

Amanda's journey west through a haven of outlaws and Indians leads her to handsome Luke Cameron, was wild and untamed as the land itself, whose burning passion would consume her own!

DEANNA'S DESIRE

SYLVIE F. SOMMERFIELD

ZEBRA BOOKS
KENSINGTON PUBLISHING CORP.

ZEBRA BOOKS

are published by

KENSINGTON PUBLISHING CORP.
475 Park Avenue South
New York, N.Y. 10016

Printed in the United States of America

In loving memory of my father
   Milo Finamore
Who opened the first book for me
      "I am a learner, a doer, a teacher
      Thinking,
      Reading,
      Listening,
      Observing others
         This is my learning.
      Adapting,
      Changing,
      Reconstructing,
      Adjusting these learnings
         This is my doing.
      Guiding,
      Sharing,
      Helping,
      Doing unto others
         This is my teaching."

Every man is a conquistador,
    The goals we seek like the land they sought.
Locate your goals early in life, set your
sails in their direction. Let no wind
blow you off course.
            Once you have reached them,
explore them, experience them, expand them.
            Whatever you do,
do it well—do it the best.
Then map your path for the other generations to follow.
Because, with no map to follow, no rudder to steer with,
How will the conquistadors of the future
            ever find their new worlds?

Prologue

The ship lay in the harbor rocking gently back and forth with the movements of the water. Her name was painted on her side in gold letters: *Destiny*. It was close to midnight, a moonless clouded midnight that lent an even greater depth to the dark shadows. There was no one on the docks and only few awake and moving about the ship. One was the captain who stood at the rail and watched the deserted docks as though he expected someone momentarily.

A carriage was drawn to a stop at the bottom of the ship's gangplank. From its dark interior stepped a cloaked figure. Only from the soft swish of the skirts against the cobblestones could the person be identified as a woman. She walked up the gangplank quickly, and the captain extended his hand to help her step aboard.

"Deanna, my child," he whispered, "is something wrong?"

"Everything," came a low whisper from the hood-shaded face. "All our plans have failed. We are at the moment being pursued. Mother and David are still captives. I must return home quickly and tell Father what has happened. We must find another way to get them free."

"Of all the inopportune times," he said.

"Why?"

"We have a passenger, and I have much news for you. Come below. We must talk."

They went below deck together and he ushered her into his small cabin carefully closing and locking the door behind him. It was only then that she dropped the hood from her head and sank wearily down on his bunk.

"Deanna, this trip is going to be quite difficult for you. I'm afraid you will have to remain in your cabin for the entire trip."

"Why?"

"Foxmore has been purchased and its new owner has booked passage with our owners to take him to America. There's nothing I can do about it."

"Foxmore . . . Who is he, this new owner?"

"Matthew Deverall, younger brother of Lord Jason Deverall. They are the sons of Lord George Deverall, who died a few weeks ago."

"Why would a wealthy man buy Foxmore and travel such a distance from his good life here, unless . . ." she mused.

"Unless?"

"Unless, the Governor is suspicious and is sending us a royal spy."

"If that is so, you absolutely must stay out of his sight. There is no way they know you are two."

"I'll keep to my cabin, but I must get home immediately. Father must be told and we must find a way to get Mother and David out of England."

"It is dangerous. If he is who you think he is, it is

10

imperative that he doesn't find out who you are."

"You needn't worry, my friend. I've no intention of being caught by any royal spy. Tell me about Matthew Deverall and just how this trip came about."

"Well . . . It began a few weeks ago, when there was a fox hunt at Deverall Hall . . ."

Chapter One

England, August 1776

Matthew Deverall, and his brother, Jason, sat side-by-side in the front pew of the Anglican church. Both men seemed to be intent on the words being spoken by the presiding clergyman, John Davenport.

John Davenport was a young man, and this was not only the first time he addressed the people of his congregation, but he was doing so at the funeral of one of the most renowned men in the area and one of the most beloved. This was not bad enough, but he was doing so in the presence of his two tall, strong sons who seemed to him at that moment to be staring holes through him.

John was a good and kind-hearted man, but he was extremely timid. Tall and slender, he had exceptionally large hands and feet. His blond hair was rather thin and hung just a little below his ears. His face was gaunt and his nose sliced outward like the sharp edge of a knife over thinly drawn lips. His Adam's apple bobbed continually in his nervousness. He had no way of knowing that the two men in question were not hearing or seeing him at all, but rather they were thinking of their father.

Lord George Carterett Deverall had been loved dearly by his two sons. Since the death of his wife when both boys were quite young, Lord Deverall was the center of the world for them. He was a tall, rather handsome man.

His nature was gentle and sometimes rather humorous, yet the hard hand of discipline came down quickly and heavily when necessary.

Jason, the older of the two, was just past his twenty-fifth birthday. He was taller than his younger brother Matthew's six feet by only two inches, and his hair, dark brown and thick as the mane of a lion, was only a few shades lighter than the deep black of Matt's. Where Matt had adopted a moustache and a short square beard, Jason was clean shaven. They were both extremely tanned from continual outdoor activity, for their father had allowed neither of them to loaf despite their great wealth. They were similar in many ways, yet sometimes they were completely different.

Jason sat quietly, thinking of his father. To Jason's mind the brass-handled coffin did not represent anything, for he wanted only to remember his father the last day he had seen him alive, strong, virile, laughing and happy. The sun had shone brightly that day, and the guests at Deverall Manor had been united to hunt, one of the favorite sports of the day. Matt and Jason were both enthusiastic for the hunt, because, at that particular time, they were in friendly competition over the favors of a dark-eyed, buxom young lady named Maurine, who lived close by.

Jason remembered his father's full, hearty laughter as they had mounted and the chase had begun. Less than an hour later, he and Matt had both been stunned to see their father's mount fail to make a jump, throw his rider over his head to land with a solid deadly thud on the hard ground. His neck broken, he had died before either of his sons could reach his side.

They went through the next few days numb from the

14

sudden loss. It occurred to neither of them to think about the issue of their father having a will or not. They had both supposed that their father's property and money would be divided equally between them. They were both wrong. The laws in England recognized Jason, the eldest, legitimate heir unless their father left a will saying it should be otherwise.

They sat now at the funeral, knowing that one week from this day, their father's lawyer would arrive at Deverall Manor to read the will. How they made it through the balance of the funeral and the long hours of receiving guests, neither of them knew. Words of condolence and sympathy were barely heard and they shook hands with friends and neighbors until both were exhausted.

For the next few days, Deverall Hall was a quiet place as they tried to adjust to life without their father's guiding hand. It was exactly one week to the day, that Frederic Townshend was announced to them, and joined them in their father's study. Frederic was about fifty, a little stout, but a jolly man with a benevolent glimmer in his blue eyes. After accepting a drink and a comfortable seat, he looked at them with a mild grin and said the words that put their whole lives on a new course.

"And now, what can I do for you gentlemen?"

Jason and Matt shared surprised looks; then Jason spoke for both of them.

"We thought you'd be anxious to read the will, sir, and get all the formalities over."

"Will?" he replied. "Why, Jason, my boy. There is no will. Deverall Manor, all your father's property and wealth belongs to you."

Both Jason and Matt were stunned. They knew the

laws of England, but they knew also their father had loved them both alike and had meant them to share his fortune equally.

"I tried to tell George that he should get a will written and done, but he always put it off. Said I was trying to rush him to his grave. Swore he was going to live another fifty years. Used to laugh at me and call me an old woman. So, there is no will, and under the law, you are Lord Jason Deverall, owner of Deverall Manor and all the wealth that goes with it."

"And Matt?" Jason asked quietly.

"I'm afraid . . . nothing," Frederic answered.

Matt felt the bottom fall suddenly out of his world. To have shared everything with Jason was their dream, but to be penniless, living off the charity of his brother was hard for him to comprehend. He felt a sudden desperate desire to run as far and as fast as he could.

"Matt . . ." Jason began, but he became quiet when he saw the hurt look in his brother's eyes.

"Not now, Jas," Matt replied softly as he rose from his seat. "Later, maybe, but not now." He left the room and the house, had his horse saddled and rode to the nearest tavern where he intended to get exceedingly drunk—and he did. The next morning, he woke with a tongue that tasted like the inside of the barn, red-rimmed eyes, a terrible headache and an unknown girl sleeping next to him in a bed whose owner he had no idea.

A few coins scattered about, and some mumbled words later found him back on the road to Deverall Hall still feeling as hurt and as empty as he had when he had left it. When he arrived home, he noticed the carriage in the drive and in his condition he did not want to run into anyone he knew. He skirted the house and went into a side door and made his way to his room. He removed his clothes after sending for a bath. He let the water soak away some of his misery, then dressed again and made his way down the stairs. Voices came from the drawing room; his brother and someone else were in conversation. He walked to the doorway and stood unobserved watching his brother as he seemed to be engrossed in what his visitor was saying.

". . . damnable situation," the man said. "The colonies actually believe in this rubbish about self-government. Why, they're like little boys tramping about in their father's boots, and they need the chastisement of a strong father to curb their waywardness."

Jason looked up suddenly and his eyes lit with happiness when he saw his brother. He almost leapt to his feet and walked quickly to Matt. He put his hand on Matt's elbow to urge him into the room, and at the same time gestured toward his guest who rose from his seat and extended his hand with a smile.

"Matt, this is an old college friend of mine, David Priestly. David, this is my brother, Matt."

The two clasped hands and Matt smiled the best smile he could muster.

"How do you do?"

"Quite well, now that I'm home," came the laughing answer.

"Home? Home from where?" Matt questioned.

"David owned a home in America, Matt. He's sold it and returned home. It seems the political problem over there is getting rather upsetting."

"Not sold yet, Jas," Priestly said, "but I hope to rid myself of it soon. I'm a good king's man, and I don't want to get involved with their traitor deeds."

17

"Is it really that bad?" Matt asked. "I've heard there's only a few colonies over there. What possible harm could a small group like that do? The King will probably put down this little uprising soon and it will all blow over."

Priestly shook his head negatively. "I don't think it will be that easy. These traitors are determined, if you will believe it, to liberate themselves from English rule."

"You're joking," Matt said in surprise. "How do they ever expect to survive without us? As small and defenseless as they must be, they wouldn't stand a chance of surviving alone."

"I know that," Priestly replied, "but these damn rebels don't seem to."

"Well, anyway, you're out of it," Jason laughed. "You will stay for dinner, won't you?"

"Yes," Matt said. "I'd like to hear about this place you're selling."

Priestly agreed, and they went on to talk of other things. A small germ of an idea was planted in Matt's mind as he watched his brother and Priestly in conversation, and it would not go away. "America," he mused. "I wonder what it's really like over there."

They had an enjoyable dinner together, then had brandy served in the library in front of a bright glowing fire. The conversation was easy and relaxed, and it was some time before Jason began to realize the way the trend of the conversation was going. He became alert to Matt's questions and David's answers. With a frown between his eyes, he watched the glow of interest begin in Matt and slowly develop.

They invited David to spend a few days with them and he readily agreed, for he and Jason had been very close friends in college. Matt took every opportunity he could to bring David's conversation around to the property he was trying to sell. Then the day before he planned to leave, Matt made David an offer for his property. Matt's mother had left both her sons a small amount of money. Matt had never touched his, for he had no need to. Now he felt it was his one and only chance for independence.

"That's a good offer, Matt, but what do you want with this property? I told you about the trouble that's brewing over there."

"I don't intend to get involved in the country's politics. I just want my own place, to build and to see if I can make something of my own."

"What's Jason going to say to this?"

"David, I'm my own man. Because Jason owns Deverall Manor does not mean he owns me. I want to do something with my own life besides live on my brother's charity."

David looked at Matt with the glimmer of respect deep in his eyes, then nodded slowly, his mouth curving up in a quick smile.

"Your offer is a good one, and I accept. And . . ." he laughed, "I hope this is not the end of a good friendship with Jason." He held out his hand and Matt took it with the sudden beginning of deep excitement. He'd just bought a house and a large piece of property, sight unseen, and was about to start out on a whole new life in a new country. He might have been a little afraid, but he would not admit that even to himself. He knew without doubt that Jason would be upset when he broke the news to him, but he also realized if he didn't take this opportunity, he might not ever get another chance like it.

The last evening dinner was relaxed and enjoyable, and Matt almost hesitated to tell Jason at all. They were laughing and talking over cigars and brandy when Matt leaned back in his chair and watched his brother through a haze of blue-white cigar smoke.

"Jas, I've some good news for you."

David watched both of them and was preparing himself for Jason's displeasure.

"Good news, what?"

"I've bought David's house in America and I've booked passage on the next packet. I'm going to see what can be done with it." Matt said the words quietly, and when he finished speaking the room was so still that David could hear their breathing. Jason stared at his brother in disbelief.

"You did what?"

"I bought . . ."

"Never mind, I heard you. Why, Matt? Why do a thing like that when this place is our home?"

"No, Jas. I don't mean to be blunt or cold, but this place belongs to you, and if I stay here it will be on your sufferance. Sooner or later it might cause some trouble between us and I don't want that to happen. I've used the money Mother left. There's enough left over to carry me along for a while."

Jason's face was pale, but Matt could see he was doing his best to control his emotions.

"Jas," David said softly. "I don't want any hard feelings between us. Matt made me a good offer, and I saw no reason to refuse him."

"I guess you're right, David," Jason said sadly, "but I sure wish you'd picked another time to visit. It's going to be a different world around here with Matt gone." He laughed rather shakily and stood up quickly. "Come on you two, let's go down to the Boar's Head and celebrate

20

David's sale and Matt's new home."

Matt probably felt more affection for his brother at that moment than he'd ever felt before. He and David agreed quickly and before long the three of them were riding down the road toward the tavern and their unhappy celebration. Many of their friends were already at the tavern when they arrived, and the news of Matt's new purchases and his planned trip was passed quickly around. Drinks were bought by many of their friends and soon the three of them were definitely in a mellow state of mind. They were laughing over some joke when a man came to their table.

He was a man of short stature, and his head was bald on top except for a fringe of white hair encircling it. Rather chubby, he had a merry twinkle in his eyes that smiled on them through the small square eyeglasses he wore perched close to the end of his nose.

"Gentlemen, I couldn't help overhearing the fact that one of you is leaving for America soon. Mayhap we are sailing on the same vessel?"

"I sail next week," Matt replied. "We'll be aboard the *Destiny*. Is that your ship also?"

"Alas, no, I'm sailing day after tomorrow on the *Reward*. May I stand you a drink?"

They accepted, and the older man joined them at their table. It was not long before they discovered that he was an enjoyable companion who had the ability to tell a story, the capacity for a great deal of drink, and even at the age of sixty-nine, an appreciation of the pretty girl who came to serve them.

Before dawn, the three of them wished their friend a good evening and departed, but not before Jason extended an invitation for dinner the next night. He accepted and watched them leave.

"Umm," he said to himself. "Foxmore, now I wonder just how that came about."

Jason and Matt, along with David, were discussing their friend the next evening before he arrived at their home. "He seemed to know a lot about the colonies," Matt said. "I hope he can give me more information. It would make it a lot easier on me if I knew everything there was to know about my place."

"Yes," David replied somberly. "Maybe he knows just a little too much. I wonder where he stands on this revolution."

"I don't really care about that. I told you I have absolutely no intention of getting involved in their politics. I just want to know about my own place."

Jason was about to answer when a light knock sounded on the door and the butler opened it.

"Yes, Michaels?"

"A gentleman has arrived, sir. Says he's been invited for dinner."

"Yes, Michaels. Show him in please. Oh, and wait a minute, Michaels." He looked sheepishly at Matt. "I don't know if I was too much in my cups, but I'll be damned if I remember the gentleman's name. Do either of you?"

"Why," David answered in surprise. "I don't believe he ever gave it."

"Michaels, when you show him in, get his name please. I'd hate to have him think we've forgotten it."

"Yes, sir," Michaels smiled as he left closing the door quietly behind him. Within a few minutes, he was back, and as he held the door open he smiled at Jason.

"Mr. Benjamin Franklin, sir."

Jason rose and walked toward Franklin with his hand outstretched and a pleasant smile as though he was greeting an old and dear friend. Throughout dinner he was found to be a charming and amusing guest, but his attention seemed to center itself about Matt.

"Tell me, my boy," he smiled. "What made you decide to make such a move as you are planning? It seems to me you have things much better here."

Matt hesitated for a few minutes. He did not want to say anything to upset Jason. In the most diplomatic way, he tried to explain to Mr. Franklin exactly how he felt about living off his brother, and about the independence he desired. He did not understand Franklin's faint smile and the agreeable nodding of his head with each sentence Matt spoke. Nor did he understand the twinkling eye as he seemed to absorb to his great satisfaction everything Matt told him.

"How do you feel about the situation as it is there now?"

"Sir, I don't understand what that little handful of colonies is trying to prove. They're certainly not big enough or strong enough to break away from us now. Why, they couldn't survive without our help."

"Are you so very sure of that, my boy?" he asked softly.

Jason chuckled. "Mr. Franklin, it's clear to every intelligent man. We're entirely too big and too powerful a nation. Why we would wipe them out in a few months. They would be much wiser and safer to stay as they are and follow the guidance of their motherland."

"You think they would be wiped out so very easily?"

"Most certainly!"

"Let me tell you something. Are either of you versed

23

in mathematics?"

"Yes." Jason answered.

"Well let me pose you a small problem to figure out before I leave. Britain, at the expense of $150,000,000, had killed one hundred-fifty Yankees in their last campaign, which is $100,000 a head. In another campaign she gained a mile of ground, half of which she lost again. During this time sixty thousand children were born in America. Can you calculate the time and the expense necessary to kill us all and conquer our territory?" He smiled at their surprised faces. "I'll leave you with that little problem and my thanks for a wonderful dinner and excellent company. I wish you the best of everything Matt. May you be lucky enough to find what I think you are searching for. Good night, gentlemen."

He walked to the door and it was Matt who regained his senses quickly enough to rise and see him out.

"Good night, Mr. Franklin. I hope when I've arrived in America and settled at Foxmore, you would be so kind as to visit sometime."

"Thank you, Matt, I should enjoy that very much. I tell you one more thing, Matt?"

"Of course, sir."

"It is better to have peace between our countries, better for both of us, but if peace cannot be maintained without honor, it is no longer peace. America is a young, strong and very vital country. It needs men like you to put their roots down and grow with it. I know that it is difficult for you. All I can say is I hope fervently the day comes when you not only understand my words, but are prepared to fight for them. Good night, son."

"Good night, sir."

24

Matt left the door and went back to join his brother and David who were talking together and laughing.

"It's ridiculous," David said. "I wonder where he got those figures. It's obvious he is one of them."

"Well, the mathematics problem dazzles my mind. If those figures were correct, and I'm not saying they were," Jason laughed as he put out a hand as if to ward off David's protest, "why, it would be impossible for England to win such a war."

Matt sat with them and listened to them laugh at Franklin's ideas, but he had suddenly gotten the feeling that someone had put a heavy hand on his shoulder. He wondered also if the name of the ship he was sailing on was to have any bearing on his future. It was as though fate seemed to be casting the dice and every roll led him in the same direction.

For the next few days, Matt began the procedure of saying farewells to long-time friends and neighbors. In some cases it was quite difficult for him, but in a few cases it was downright amusing. There were two lovely ladies that he and his brother had been in mild competition for and it was laughingly obvious to him that although the girls bid him a reluctant and fond farewell, the parents were quite relieved to know that it was he, the penniless one without a title, and not his brother Lord Jason Deverall that was leaving.

The closer the time for leaving came, the more upset Jason became, and he tried every way to talk Matt out of this "nonsense," as he put it. Not only did he try, but he enlisted the help of every friend they had.

Secretly, Matt felt fatalistic about this trip. He felt that everything that had happened lately, including the name of his ship, had pointed him in some preordained direction. He was anxious to see the property he had bought, and ignored talk about the war with the colonies. Because of their size he felt sure this was nonsense, and he put all such thought away from him.

Several good-bye parties were thrown for him by friends, and he laughingly declared he had best leave soon or he would be incapable of doing so. He hoped he was doing the right thing. To leave everything he had known and his easy way of life made him wonder not only if it was right, but if he would be able to do it alone. Despite the fact that his father had never allowed him to be lazy, he knew that everything he did was made easier by the fact that his father had already built his fortune by himself long before his sons were of an age to do anything. It worried him that when he did arrive in America it would prove too difficult a task. The idea of coming home a failure was the thing that preyed most on his mind; it came close to making him change his plans at the last moment and stay where he was secure.

The first thing he promised himself was that nothing in the world was going to induce him to get involved in the political situation. He was determined to stay neutral and to pay attention only to his own land. One way or another, he was going to make a success of his life. He knew that Jason, deep inside, felt the same way as he and that Jason's urging him to stay home was his way of trying to protect Matt from being hurt.

Jason, finally after days of arguing, forced more money on Matt to make sure that he could face whatever financial problem presented itself in America. They sat together the final night before Matt left. The meal was a silent one, for neither of them could put into words what they were feeling at the moment.

"What time does your ship sail, Matt?"

"Just after dawn. I think the Captain wants to catch the early morning tide."

"Well, brother, I hope all goes well for you there, but will you promise me something, Matt?"

"What?"

"If everything doesn't work out well, you won't let some foolish pride stand in the way of your coming back here?"

Matt grinned. "No, Jas. If it doesn't work out, I'll be back."

Jason nodded, both brothers too emotional to discuss it any further. Neither knew that fate had a different life in mind for both of them.

Chapter Two

Matt slept poorly the balance of the night, and dawn found him already putting his luggage in the carriage. Both he and Jason tried to find other things to talk of on the ride to the dock. Welcome activity of loading his belongings kept them both busy until it was time to leave. Then Matt turned to Jason and held out his hand. Jason ignored the hand and wrapped both arms about his brother, and for a quick minute they exchanged looks, each trying to control his feelings. Then, Matt turned and ran up the gangplank. He stood and watched as the gangplank was pulled up and the sails were slowly unfurled. With grace and ease the ship began to move slowly away from the dock. Jason walked along the dock and waved again and again. Then he could go no further, and he stood and watched the ship slowly recede until it was a small speck on the horizon. Matt never knew how desperately Jason had fought the urge to throw everything aside and go with him. He knew he had obligations to his father and to the title he bore, but at this moment he was having a very difficult time keeping them in perspective.

Then finally, he turned aside and climbed slowly back into his carriage.

"Back to Deverall Manor, Marcus," he said quietly to the driver who clicked at the horses and moved them slowly homeward.

Matt stood at the ship's rail and watched the coastline slowly recede. He loved his home and the pain of permanent separation showed plainly in his eyes. He was completely preoccupied when a voice at his shoulder brought him back to reality.

"We're on our way."

The voice belonged to a man called Cat. Matt had never known him by any other name. He was a huge black man Matt's father had brought home one stormy night, wet and bedraggled. He had been no more than ten then, a year or so older than Matt. They had grown up together, but Matt had never known anything about his past. Cat was the name his father had given him because he laughingly swore he had nine lives. He was so huge that he dwarfed Matt, who was not a small man. They stood together in silence; each knew and respected the feelings of the other.

The day had been slightly overcast when they had started for the ship. Now a slight drizzle of rain began to fall.

"We'd better get below," said Cat softly. "It's goin' to blow up a storm."

They turned from the rail and started for their cabin. The rain suddenly erupted into a drenching downpour. They ran for the shelter of the cabins below deck. As they reached the entrance to the companionway, Matt grabbed the door and jerked it open violently. A shocked scream sounded as the person with her hand on the other side of the door was pulled out into the decks, striking Matt full force on the chest and almost causing him to lose his footing. In self-defense, he threw his arms about the person, and they wavered together for a few minutes trying to keep from falling. When some semblance of balance had been achieved, Matt tried to look through the heavily falling rain at the girl in his arms. She wore a heavy cloak with the hood pulled over her head that shadowed her face. He could barely see the outline of her face, but his body told him she was young and very much a woman. She stepped away from him hastily.

"I'm sorry, ma'am. I didn't realize you were there. I must apologize for my clumsiness."

"It is quite all right, sir," she replied softly. "There is no harm done." The hood of the cape still covered most of her face and she stepped back in the shadows of the open door. "If you will permit me to pass, sir, I must see the Captain."

"Of course." He stepped aside and she moved to pass him. Her head was down so he still could not get the desired glimpse of her face. The soft scent of her perfume touched him with cloud-like fingers as she passed, and he stood watching her walk away, unmindful of the rain.

Cat's mild chuckle brought him around hastily.

"We'd better get below before we drown."

Matt laughed and they beat a quick retreat from the rain. When they had reached their cabin, they changed their wet clothes.

"I wonder who she was? There was no one on the docks this morning when we came down. Do you suppose she came aboard last night?"

"I don't know," smiled Cat. "But I bet you do before this trip is over."

Matt grinned at him. "A beautiful woman would sure be better company on a long trip than you, you great black ape."

"You don't know she's beautiful," said Cat. "But with your luck with women, I imagine she is."

They had stayed in the cabin until the rain finally ceased. It was late afternoon before they came on deck again. The Captain sent word for them to join him at the wheel. When they joined him, he greeted them warmly.

"Good afternoon, Mr. Deverall. Nasty morning, wasn't it?"

"It surely was, Captain," smiled Matt.

"I hope your quarters are comfortable?"

"Oh, quite satisfactory, sir."

"Will you join me in my cabin for dinner, Mr. Deverall? You and your friend would be quite welcome."

"Thank you, Captain, it would be a pleasure."

Cat merely nodded his head in silent acceptance.

"Good. Dinner is at seven."

"Thank you, Captain."

Matt suggested they take a walk about the ship. For a few minutes, they strolled in silence, then Cat gave a low throaty chuckle like ill-preserved laughter.

"What are you laughing about?"

"You, Matt. You're so obvious, it's downright funny."

"Obvious? About what?" questioned Matt but the light of suppressed merriment twinkled in his eyes.

"The lady ain't on deck. I think since it's our second time around, you can see that. Or were we goin' to keep on walkin' around until she shows up?"

"Well, she can't stay in her cabin for the whole trip. Maybe the Captain has invited her to dinner, too."

"At least, you hope so."

"That I do, Cat. That I do." He laughed again as they started another turn of the decks. After another half hour of nonchalantly watching for another appearance of his mystery woman, Matt finally gave up and they went below to prepare for dinner.

The Captain was a delightful host, making them comfortable with tales of the new country they were about to adopt. "It is quite beautiful there. You will love it as I do, I think young sirs. Where again did you say your home was to be?"

"It is in a place called Virginia. The estate is called Foxmore. Do you know of it?"

"Why, yes. It lies up river a ways. Between the Martin place and Dartmore Hall. Very beautiful, although a little run-down. It will take much work and no little amount of cash to repair it."

"Well, between Cat and I, we have the strong backs for the work and I have the cash. Is the place worth rebuilding?"

"Oh, definitely, sir. It's the most beautiful place on the river. Quite a few people would like to have gotten their hands on it. How came you by it?"

"Strictly good luck. Its previous owner was visiting my brother. It seems they were quite good friends at one time. Since he was desirous of staying in England and since it was important for me to leave, it seemed the right opportunity for both of us."

"Well, sir, you got a good bargain. The big house sets on a bend in the river. From the front door you can see both ways for miles. I've stood there myself. It's a lovely view."

Matt smiled in appreciation of his host's description. They sat after the meal and enjoyed their brandy, exchanging small conversation. Cat was watching Matthew with suppressed laughter as he tried to bring the

32

conversation around to the ship's passengers. Finally, after hinting about unsuccessfully, he became impatient.

"Tell me, Captain, who is the young lady who is our co-traveler?"

For several moments the room was completely silent. Matt was thoroughly amazed at the reaction his question had wrought on the Captain. His face turned decidedly white and he stared at the two men.

"Woman?" he said shakily as though he were suddenly short of breath.

"Yes, we bumped into her literally at the companion doorway. I could not see her face under the heavy cloak, but she seemed quite pleasant. Could we possibly meet her?"

"No!" The reply was given so vehemently that both men were startled. Then the Captain regained some of his composure.

"I'm sorry, young friends. It is impossible for you to meet the young lady. She is travelling incognito, an affair of the heart. I'm sure you understand." He smiled but his eyes were watchful and wary. The two younger men exchanged glances, not wanting to press the point since it was obvious the Captain intended to tell them nothing.

After some time of forced conversation, the two begged to be excused and left the Captain's cabin. As he closed the door behind him, Cat touched Matthew on the arm. Touching his finger to his lips, he pulled him aside to a small passageway. Within a few minutes the Captain's door slowly opened and the Captain stepped out into the passageway. Glancing in both directions, he started away from the door. They followed him silently, and he stopped in front of a cabin not far from their own. A soft rap on the door brought a muffled question.

"Captain Duprey," said the man quietly. The door was opened and the Captain slipped quickly inside closing the door firmly after him.

Cat gave a slow soft whistle and the two exchanged surprised looks.

"Seems we upset the good Captain," said Matt softly. "I wonder why? Maybe we better try to meet the young lady without the Captain's help."

Cat looked at him with narrowed eyes. "Maybe we should just stay out of it and mind our own business."

Matt laughed. "Where is your sense of adventure? A beautiful mysterious passenger we can't see."

"There you go again. How come you think she's so beautiful?"

Matt gave another smothered laugh as he turned to leave. "My eyes may not be able to see, my friend, but I know what my hands feel, and I'm saying she's beautiful. Come on, let's get out of here before we're found. Tomorrow's another day."

Cat heaved a sigh and followed him. It did no good to try to stop Matt once he desired to do something.

Chapter Three

Much to Cat's amusement they spent the next two weeks trying to find out who the young woman was. Matt was completely frustrated at every turn, as no matter how many questions he asked no one seemed to know anything. He would engage them in conversation and they would talk happily and openly with him until the subject of the mysterious lady traveler came up. Then their eyes would shift from his and they would mumble excuses to leave. It seemed no one on board the ship was going to tell him a thing about her. Matt was never given to a great deal of patience, and what little he had was slowly running out. He sat now on a chair tilted back with his feet propped on a table. His brows were furrowed in a deep frown and his deep brown eyes shone with an angry fire.

"What the hell do they think I'm going to do? Rape the lady right on deck? I only wanted to meet her. Damn, you'd think she was the queen, the way they act."

The slow spiral of his anger was halted by Cat's roar of laughter as he rolled on the bunk.

"Oh, God!" he laughed until he choked. "I never thought I'd see the day. Matt Deverall can't even get started with the lady." He rolled his eyes to the ceiling. "Matt Deverall, lady-killer, lover supreme, and he can't even get an introduction. Oh, I can't wait to tell Jas about this." He gave another howl of laughter that was cut short by the boot Matt threw at him.

"I'll make you a wager, you bastard. I'll know who the lady is and where she lives before we leave this ship." His eyes glowed a brilliant golden brown with anger.

"Done," laughed Cat. "We've got about three more weeks, my friend. You'd better start working fast."

Matt mumbled something incoherent as he slammed out of the cabin with the sound of Cat's laughter sounding in his ears. He climbed the steps to the deck and stood collecting his thoughts.

The night was calm, and there was a full yellow moon hanging just on the edge of the horizon. Millions of silver twinkling stars lit up the heavens and he inhaled the cool salty air. It was a beautiful night. He had taken to walking the decks in the evening, hoping for a glimpse of the lady. Trying to sleep did not help, as he had been having ridiculous dreams; dreams in which he had caught up with the lady and they had spoken together. Then as he reached to remove the hood, she had vanished. The dreams had added to his frustration even more. Tonight he was tired, and as he strolled about the decks he could feel the welcome lethargy overtaking him. He did not desire to return to the cabin until he was sure Cat was asleep, so he settled himself against the main mast and relaxed, stretching his long legs out before him. He watched the stars and slowly drifted into a half-awake, half dreaming state. He did not realize what it was that woke him. Finally it came, the soft whisper of voices. It took him several minutes to find where they were coming from. By the light of the moon he could make out two figures seated on the hatchway. It was her! She and the Captain were engrossed in what seemed to be an

36

argument. Matt hesitated to move. He did not want to be discovered eavesdropping. That was the reason he gave himself, but with his eyes glued on the woman, he realized that he was hoping she would remove the hood and let him see her. Their voices drifted toward him.

"You must not be seen, especially by the persistent young gentleman. I told you who he was."

"Captain," came the soft reply. "I've been enclosed in that cabin for weeks. I must have some fresh air. You checked their cabin, they are asleep. If anyone should come, believe me, I shall return to my cabin."

The voice became pleading now, and a small white hand reached out to touch his arm.

"Just let me have a few minutes, then I shall be satisfied and return obediently."

The Captain looked at her, and to Matt's amazement, a soft look of pity came into his eyes.

"All right, my dear. It's just that it's your life. If you're discovered, I don't want anything to happen to you."

"I know, and I appreciate your concern. I shall be very careful. I shall only take a few minutes then I shall return."

"Shall I stay with you?"

"No, please, I want to be alone for a while."

After the Captain had reluctantly left her she sat quite still, her eyes lifted to the stars. Matt could barely breathe, he was so tense. He had definitely decided not to let her know he was there. She rose now and walked slowly to the rail. Silhouetted by the moon, he could see her quite clearly from his position, and he inhaled a breath and held it as her two hands rose to lift the hood from her head and drop it over her shoulders. Matt could feel himself shaking and felt rather foolish at the effect this was having on him. She turned slightly and stood almost facing his hiding place. Matt stared in fascination. She was beautiful, with long black hair that was loose and fell almost to her waist. Her face was heart shaped with large, wide-spaced eyes. She had full, sensuous lips that were slightly parted now in pleasure at the soft sea breeze. She turned a little more, and as a soft sigh escaped her, her face came more into the moonlight, and he could see the glistening of tears on her cheeks. He fought the desire to stand and let her know he was there, then he remembered what the captain had said to her: "It's your life." Why was it that she was so afraid of discovery?

Then he remembered something else the Captain had said. "I told you who he was." They were hiding her from him specifically. Why? Why? He continued to watch her for several minutes. She must have felt uneasy for she looked about her as if she knew she was being watched, then she lifted the hood over her head again and turned to leave. Matt continued to sit still long after she left, with question upon question hurled about his brain. It was quite some time before he rose and went back to his cabin. He removed his clothes and lay back on the bunk and slept.

Cat was surprised at his sudden moodiness for the next few days. Matt seemed to have given up trying to find out who his mystery woman was. He paid the money he had wagered Cat, then refused to discuss it any further with him. Instead he took to spending much time alone, mostly in the evenings, and Cat feigned sleep many nights when he heard him slip from the cabin. Now he lay curled with his back to the room. He was trying to breathe evenly as if asleep. Within a few minutes he heard Matt slip from his bunk and don his clothes. Then

38

came the quiet click of the door as it closed softly behind him. He rose immediately and hastily put on his clothes, then he too slipped quietly from the room. He moved slowly, for he was not sure of the direction Matt had taken. Reaching the companion doorway, he stood in the shadows while his eyes searched the ship. Presently, he saw Matt. He was standing mostly in the shadows by the main mast, and he appeared to be trying to keep from being seen, although as far as Cat could see, there was no one else on deck. He slipped out the door, circled around behind him, and was almost at his side when he spoke.

"What is it, Matt? What are you waiting for?"

Matt gave a startled jump as though he had been caught stealing.

"Cat, what are you doing here?" he whispered.

"I wondered what's been the matter the last few days. Since you wouldn't tell me, I decided to follow you and see for myself."

Matt had been shifting his gaze about rapidly, watching all directions. Now he grasped Cat's arm and pulled him into the shadows. Cautioning him to silence, he pointed to the dark companionway.

Cat stared at the dark doorway for a few minutes, then the soft flutter of movement caught his eye. Someone was standing just inside the door.

"Who is it?"

"Shhh, watch!"

Presently, she slipped from the doorway when she was sure no one else was on deck. She repeated her actions of the nights before. When she removed the hood, Cat gave a startled jump. For the few minutes that she enjoyed the warm sea breeze and the silver stars, the two men watched in silence. Then she again replaced the hood and returned to her cabin:

"She really is beautiful. Have you found out yet who she is and why all the secrecy?"

Matt explained the Captain's words from the previous evening and Cat shook his head in doubt.

"Why should they be afraid of us seeing her? I don't know her, do you?"

Matt gave a negative shake of his head.

"No, but when she leaves this ship, I'm going to follow her and find out. I figure when we dock she'll leave the night before we disembark. I intend to be up to find out."

"You better watch out, Matt, you don't know what might be going on. You might be asking for more trouble than you can handle."

But Matt was beyond listening to him now.

"I've got to find out why it should be us she's afraid of. What's the connection?"

"And you've got to find out who the beauty is, and how you can meet her."

Matt smiled. "That, too. From now on we ask no more questions, just keep our eyes open. We're going to take turns sleeping so if she leaves her cabin we will know. I wouldn't want her going over the side in a small boat and get ashore before I had a chance to follow."

"All right, Matt. Now can we get some sleep. I'd say it's near dawn and I'm tired."

They returned to the cabin and Cat fell immediately into a deep sleep. Not so for Matt, who lay with his hands behind his head drifting with a relaxed smile into what had now become his favorite dream.

Chapter Four

They had carried out their plan well, and had not mentioned the lady again, much to the relief of the Captain and crew who enjoyed the company of these two pleasant young men. They sat now in the captain's cabin after an excellent dinner, drinking brandy and relaxing.

"How much longer will we be at sea?" asked Matt.

"Oh, I think another two weeks will see us safely berthed at Yorktown."

"Good, I'm anxious to see my new home. Tell me some about my neighbors."

The Captain settled himself back more comfortably in his chair, pleased to be able to give the necessary information. "Well," he began. "About six miles this side of Foxmore you'll find Vern Markham's place. Quite beautiful, knows his business well and runs a well-paying place. He raises some of the best thoroughbreds in the state of Virginia. His home is really a showplace now, since he's redone it. On the other side of Foxmore is Paul Martin's place. Martin is a widower with a daughter named Deborah. Beautiful girl with long black hair and green eyes. She and Vern have been working on Dartmore Hall for over three years."

Matt caught back the words he was about to speak, for the Captain had described his mysterious passenger. Then the lady below must be Deborah Martin, daughter of his closest neighbor. He had caught Cat's eye and gave a slight negative shake of his head. It was a good thing, for the Captain's next words again left him mystified.

"Vernon and Deborah will be at the dock to meet us. Most of our cargo belongs to them, and we also carry Deborah's wedding trousseau. She's to marry young Markham in six months. A perfect match, bringing together two of the biggest plantations along the river. They are probably quite anxious to meet you, too, Mr. Deverall, since you form the link between their two places. I'm sure they expect to be good friends of yours."

Now Matt was completely engrossed in the Captain's words. Why should he be expected to be good friends with the Martins when they had gone to such pains to keep him from seeing her on board ship. It made no sense to him, and Matt's muddled thoughts could find no avenue of solving the mystery. He shrugged away his uneasy feelings and changed the subject. They talked of tobacco and planting for some time, then the two thanked the Captain for an excellent dinner, excused themselves and left.

"Matt, how the hell is it going to be possible for that girl to meet us at the dock when she's stowed away on board right now?"

"I don't know, I can't figure out what's going on. But for the next two weeks I'm going to watch every move they make. There's something odd going on around these people, and I have a feeling somehow that I'm in the middle. I don't mind playing the game, but I'd like to know the rules."

They did watch, taking turns sleeping. But nothing unusual could be seen. The Captain and crew continued their business and as far as they could see, there was no

42

contact between the lady in the cabin and anyone on board ship. They were as much in the dark two weeks later when the lookout shouted that they were approaching land as they were at the beginning.

"From now until we dock keep your eyes open, Cat, and stay alert. If she goes ashore, I want to know about it."

"We should be docking in about two hours. If she's going ashore beforehand, she'll have a hard time doin' it without us seeing her."

Matt simply nodded his head. The whole thing had him completely mystified. For the remaining time, they stood at the rail and watched the Captain bring his ship gracefully up to the dock. They were joined at the rail now by the Captain who seemed to be in an extremely good humor.

"Ah! Young fella, we're home!" he said with a smile. "It always brightens my spirit to come back here. No matter where I travel, this will always be home." He stretched his arms out to expressively include the entire surrounding countryside.

"It is beautiful, Captain, I must admit. I've never seen a more lovely place."

"Wait until you see the view from your own front porch. You will immediately become a native," the Captain chuckled.

Their attention was hailed by a group of people standing on the dock. A young man, just a little older than Matt, had his arm raised in a wave and had just shouted the Captain's name. The young man hailing them was Vernon Markham. Vernon would have attracted the attention of anyone, anywhere. He was a huge man. There was not an ounce of fat on his body. He was tall, standing well over six foot and must have weighed two hundred-forty pounds. His hair was black and worn slightly long and his skin was tanned a deep golden brown, telling of many hours in the hot Virginia sun. It was not this striking man who caught Matt's attention however, and caused a sharp intake of breath. It was the lovely girl on his arm. She had turned with a smile and taken Vernon's arm when he shouted at the Captain, and now she looked directly up at Matt.

Cat's mouth dropped open and a look of sheer amazement crossed his face.

Matt was too surprised for a moment to utter a sound. Then he looked at Cat. For several seconds, the two men exchanged shocked looks, for the girl on the dock was the mystery lady from the cabin.

"Cat!" Matt whispered. "Slip below and see if she's still in there."

Cat left his side silently and went below. He quickly went to the girl's cabin and gave a light tap on the door. There was no answer. Trying the knob he opened it slowly. There was not only no one there, there was not a sign of anyone having ever been there. The mattress to the bunk had been rolled and tied in a small bundle. Other than that, there was not a single thing in the room except a small chest. A quick look told him that too was empty. He shook his head in disbelief and went back on deck. In a soft whisper, he told Matt of his findings.

"How could she have gotten off this ship?" whispered Matt. "We've been watching every minute. I would swear it was impossible."

"It is impossible. There must be two of her. Twins! That's it! There's two of them."

"But the Captain never mentioned anything about

44

twins, just the Martin father and daughter."

"Maybe for some reason they don't want anyone to know."

"That doesn't make sense. How do you hide twin daughters?"

Cat shrugged. "Let's just play along like we never saw her. Now that we know we can keep an eye out, if there's two of them, some way they'll slip and we can clear up this mystery."

They stopped speaking when the Captain called them to come and meet his friends.

Matt bowed low over Deborah Martin's hand, but his eyes gave her a thorough appraisal. There was something that struck him instinctively as different between this girl and the one on board ship. He could not find what the difference was, and his serious gaze flustered her slightly.

"Is there something wrong with my face, sir?" she laughed hesitantly looking up at him. There was the sparkle deep in her green eyes.

"That's it," he said. He had been thinking so strongly that he spoke the words aloud. Even Cat looked at him dumbfounded.

"That's what?" questioned Vernon Markham, whose face was slightly flushed with the beginning anger.

"Oh, I am sorry, Miss Martin," Matt said very sincerely. "I was thinking out loud about how much you resemble someone I know. But now I see you are much lovelier than anyone I've ever met."

His sincere look and apology broke the strained atmosphere and Deborah laughed again. Leaning on Vernon's arm, she forgave him pertly and urged Vernon to a smile and an offer of his hand.

"You have just bought Foxmore. Have you not,

Mr. Deverall?"

"Yes, I hope to get you to help me bring it back to a workable plantation. I hear you are the best tobacco planter in this part of the country."

Vernon smiled with pleasure at the compliment. "I should be glad to help you in any way possible. Foxmore should be one of the best producers in this area, it is neglect only that has put it in the condition it is now. You know, of course, that the house is not even liveable?"

Matt looked slightly startled and turned to Cat, who also gave a surprised look.

"Not liveable! But I thought to move in right away."

Deborah and Vernon exchanged a look that said more than Matt could understand.

"You will of course, accept the hospitality of my father's house, Mr. Deverall, just until you get your own home ready."

Vernon tried to interrupt, but Deborah silenced him with a smile.

"We must keep Mr. Deverall where we can help him, must we not, Vernon? And I'm sure my father would be upset if we did not extend every possible courtesy."

"Of course, my dear," chuckled Vernon. "I should not want your formidable father upset with me."

"Then it is settled. Mr. Deverall, you shall stay with us and I should be happy to show you about and help you meet all our neighbors and friends."

"Thank you, Miss Martin, I shall be delighted."

"If you will join us in our carriage, Mr. Deverall, we shall proceed to Clearhaven."

"My friend, Cat?"

46

"If he will stay to see to the baggage, he can come along later with Captain Duprey."

After all the arrangements were agreed to, Matt left with Deborah and Vernon. Cat stayed behind ostensibly to see to the baggage, but his intent was to find all the information he could.

Chapter Five

The carriage moved slowly down the road from the docks. It was a poor road at best and today had been their first day free of rain in the last three days so the road was muddy and rutted, causing them to pick their way slowly. It gave Matt a chance to study his two companions. The girl was very lovely and chatted with him gaily, her sparkling wit bringing the two men together in conversation.

His startled exclamation on the dock had been drawn from him involuntarily. But now that he was sitting so close to her he could see the difference that had caused it; her lovely green eyes. Lovely they were, and decidedly green they were. But the girl on the ship had eyes of the softest blue he could imagine. There was no mistaking it, for they had floated above him in his dreams night after night. He remembered the soft glint of tears in them and wondered again why she should be kept such a secret when Deborah could move about obviously quite free and happy. He thought determinedly, "I'm going to find out the reasons. Whatever they may be, I've got to release her from whatever is holding her prisoner. I've got to see those blue eyes smile."

He didn't realize that Deborah had been talking to him until she repeated his name a second time.

"Oh, I'm sorry, Miss Martin, I was watching this

beautiful place and daydreaming."

"We'll be coming to Clearhaven soon. It's the first plantation along this road. Your Foxmore is next. Do you ride, Mr. Deverall?"

"Yes, Miss Martin, and please call me Matt, if we're going to be neighbors."

"Of course, . . . Matt. Maybe tomorrow, we'll ride out and you can look over your place. I'm sure Vernon can give you a good bit of help in repairing what is necessary." She smiled at Vernon, who agreed immediately to ride along and help Matt.

They turned off the main road and entered the long tree-shaded drive that led to Clearhaven. The house itself sat upon a slight rise of ground. It was a two-story house that gave the impression of having been added on to at random. They arrived at a circular drive that curved under an overhanging roof held up by large white pillars. There was a short flight of stone steps leading to a long enclosed porch surrounded on two sides by the rooms added on to the center square of the house. They were met at the door by a man of undetermined age.

"Good afternoon, Jake," said Deborah. "This is Mr. Matthew Deverall, the new owner of Foxmore. He'll be spending a few days with us. See to his room and his luggage when it arrives. A friend of his will be bringing it. Send him into the study when he arrives."

"Yes, ma'am," the old man said, and went hastily to carry out the orders he had been given.

"Did you eat on board ship, Matt?" questioned Vernon. "Or could you do with a little lunch?"

"No, we didn't eat before leaving the ship. I'm afraid we were preoccupied with another problem and forgot all about lunch."

"I'll send for something, and after we've eaten we'll show you about Clearhaven and then we'll go on to my home. On the way back we can stop by Foxmore since it lies directly between our two places."

"Good. I should like to get an idea of what I need to begin work, since I would like to go in as soon as possible."

"Do you have any servants, yet?"

"No. The only person I brought with me was Cat, and he is not a servant. He is more my right arm. What I cannot learn or accomplish, I'm sure Cat can."

"Well, you'll need quite a bit more than just the two of you. I'll lend you some of my boys for a few days until you can get some of your own."

"I'll be very grateful for your help, and any suggestions you have."

"Oh, Vern will be full of suggestions, and if I don't get you two men in to lunch, he'll begin making them and I'll starve to death," laughed Deborah.

Vern smiled at her and dropped his arm about her waist. He looked at her in a way that left no doubt about how he felt for her.

"We wouldn't want that to happen, my dear. Shall we feed Matt and then show him about?"

"Decidedly," she said.

They sat down to a hastily prepared lunch of cold sliced roast beef and fruit with a chilled bottle of wine.

They had barely finished when Cat's arrival was announced. He stepped into the room and Matt could feel the slight change in the atmosphere of the room. Although he was not a slave, a man of color had never sat at the Martin table before. If Matt was conscious of the mood Cat was even more so. A slight hint of a smile

50

played about his lips and the glint of laughter in his eyes relieved Matt's tension.

"Our baggage is here, Matt. They've taken it upstairs. If you'll excuse me, I'm having lunch in the kitchen."

He turned to leave and Matt hastily left the table; he caught up to him in the hall. "Cat, what are you trying to prove?"

"Don't be stupid, Matt. What better way to get information than from talkative servants. This will be perfect since I fit in there so well." He smiled at Matt. "Don't be so upset, Matt. It doesn't bother me. I'll see you at home in a few days. In the meantime, I'll find out all I can about our mystery lady."

Matt watched the huge man saunter toward the kitchen whistling softly. If there was anything to be found out at the Martin place, Cat would find it. He re-entered the room and smiled at his host.

"Well, shall we get on with our tour?" asked Vern.

"I'm ready," Matt replied.

Vern sent for the carriage, and soon they were on their way again. The road did not improve with distance but the surrounding view did. Matt gazed about him in admiration. He was glad he had bought the property here, now; it had to be the most beautiful place he had ever seen. Vern and Deborah sat quietly smiling while Matt was engrossed in the countryside. Travelling the winding scenic road gave Matt the first sense of peace since his father had died. Here is where I belong, he thought. This is home.

He had never felt this type of feeling before, this feeling of belonging to something, the urgent need to begin something here in this beautiful country. Huge green trees lined the road and the air smelled fresh and cool. He sat back against his seat and let himself completely enjoy the new beauty surrounding him.

They arrived at Vern's home, Dartmore Hall. It was a smaller version of Clearhaven. Vernon had taken up raising a strain of the most beautiful horses in the county. He took a great deal of pride in his thoroughbreds. After their arrival and introduction to Mr. Martin, who was at that time visiting Dartmore, he had taken Matt on a short tour of his holdings. Mr. Martin was a tall, slender, rather handsome man who carried his years well. The light touch of gray in his hair, merely enhanced the black color. It was easy to see the resemblance between him and Deborah, and it was also easy to see the resemblance to his mystery lady, for he had deep velvet blue eyes. There were soft smile lines at the corners of his eyes, telling of his humor. But there was also a deep unexplainable sadness Matt caught lurking in them when he thought no one was watching him. Together they strolled back from the stables, as the three men returned from examining some of the horses.

"So you are now the owner of Foxmore?"

"Yes, sir," replied Matt.

"You have a magnificent piece of property there. I have tried to buy it several times. You wouldn't consider selling would you?"

"No, sir," laughed Matt. "I intend to make Foxmore my permanent home. I love this place already, and I've only been here less than a day." The quick look exchanged between Vern and Mr. Martin did not go unnoticed by Matt. So whatever was going on, they were both together in it.

"Well, if we're going to stop by and take a quick look at Foxmore before supper, we'd better be on our way, Matt.

Tell Deborah to ride over tomorrow, will you, Mr. Martin?"

"Of course, Vern. We shall see you again soon, Matt. Good day."

"Good day, Mr. Martin."

The two men talked of planting and tobacco crops on the way to Foxmore. Although Matt had a million questions he would really have liked to ask, he kept silent. With Cat's help and his determination, he would find the answer to the mystery. Stepping down from the carriage, Matt gazed at his new home. Foxmore had at one time been a lovely house. It sat on a rise facing the river. The long green lawn extended in a gradual grade down to a dock on the river bank, surrounded by cypress trees. They arrived at the side entrance that had a tree-shaded border. It had a double set of wide French doors that opened into a large, bright foyer.

"The sun rises from this direction," said Vern. "I think that's why they put the huge glass doors there. In the morning it's filled with sunlight."

The doorway to the left opened to a large, well-lighted kitchen. The hearth took up one whole wall, and whoever had worked there last had cleaned the place well. Everything was in its proper place. "Almost as if they had just left it today instead of months ago," thought Matt.

They left the kitchen and went back across the foyer to the double doors. Swinging them open, Matt faced a long spacious dining room with wide windows that faced the river. It could be changed into a small ballroom for parties, and Matt decided he would do just that when he had finished doing the house over. There was also a roomy study, filled with books. This room looked also as though its owner had just left. There were two more rooms downstairs, a morning room and the other what must have been a small dining room with doors that opened onto a small garden. The garden was unkept and overgrown, but must have been very beautiful. Matt went upstairs himself as Vern decided to sit down and let Matt wander about. There were five bedrooms upstairs. Four of them were quite large and partially furnished. The other was a small corner bedroom, and when Matt opened the door he felt the hairs on the back of his neck prickle. On the table was a candle that gave a small waft of smoke as though it had been extinquished within the last half hour. The bed was covered with clean bedding which bore the clear imprint of a body. Matt sat down on the bed and his eyes fell on a book on the nightstand. He picked it up, and when he did the soft scent of perfume reached him—the same perfume she wore on the ship. The book was a book of love sonnets. She had lain here and read within the last hour. He opened the book to the first page and the words, in a soft feminine handwriting claimed, "This book is the property of Deanna Martin, June 1, 1771."

Chapter Six

Cat rubbed the horse briskly, whistling softly through his teeth. Tomorrow he and Matt were finally leaving Clearhaven and going home. It had taken many men and Vernon several weeks to get the house in order. Although it was only the beginning, Matt insisted it was liveable. Cat knew of the book Matt had found in the small bedroom at Foxmore, but they had not had much time together since then for Cat to tell him of the things he had discovered. He had spent the days helping the servants with odd jobs and making himself generally pleasant until they began to accept him and relax in his presence. It was only then that he had begun to ask questions. One of the serving girls that worked in the kitchen was a laughing beauty who had captured Cat's attention. It had not taken the handsome Cat long to attract hers also. They had spoken the first time when he had eaten his first meal in the kitchen. Placing the plate in front of him she had smiled at him, her dark eyes glowing with knowledge. After he had eaten he had looked for her, but she was gone. It was two days later before he saw her again. She was carrying buckets to the well for water. He came to her and took the buckets from her, smiling down into her dark eyes. She was excitingly beautiful and he resisted the urge to try to get her into the barn. For some reason unknown to him he wanted more from her than a quick tumble in the hay.

"You've been here long?" he asked nonchalantly as he slowed his long stride to her short ones.

"No," she smiled up at him. "They bought me two years ago."

Cat clenched his teeth at the word bought, bringing a soft chuckle from the girl.

"That does no good, big one, I too clenched my teeth when I was taken from my mother. But it does no good to fight for anything you possess, anything . . . They are free to take all but your soul, and they try for that."

"And you?" He turned to her and looked into her eyes. "And you, what do they have of you?"

For a long time she looked at him, then they both smiled with the same understanding.

"Nothing more than they have of you. Nothing. I am my own just as you are your own."

"I know," he smiled. "I knew it when I first met you. I would like to know you. Not the you that you show them, but the real you."

"Would you really? Maybe you would not like what I've been."

"I said the real you," he said softly.

They had talked together often in the past few days. She felt comfortable with Cat and he with her. It did not take long for Cat to realize that his attraction to her was more than a casual friend. He found himself seeking her out on every possible occasion just to be near her for a few moments. He sensed that her life had not always been easy and that the men in her life had not always been kind. It took him many days before he could even sit close to her without feeling her quiver with some kind of fear and draw within herself. He took his time, speaking

56

softly and using no overt actions, to woo her away from her fear and to develop trust in him. It almost made him shout with happiness the first time she smiled directly at him without the guarded fearful look in her eyes. But it was longer still before he gently reached for her tiny hand and held it between his huge ones as he spoke to her. Then came the magical day when he kissed her for the first time and felt the warmth of love seep through his body at the touch of her soft lips. He realized he had fallen in love with her, but he was not about to damage it in any way by reaching too fast. It was more days and nights of gentle persuasion before he began to see the look in her eyes he wanted to see. She had begun to depend on seeing him every day, and sometimes would wait for him at the well if he was late. Today he was whistling because he had decided to ask Matt to buy her and set her free. He wanted to ask her to marry him.

Finishing up the grooming of the horse, he washed himself and slipped his shirt back on. Then he left the barn and headed for the well. She was there sitting on the edge of the well. For a moment he stood and looked at her before letting her know of his presence. She was very beautiful, he thought. Her hair was black and shiny and hung straight. Her skin was the color of coffee with heavy cream. Her large dark eyes were wide spaced and clear under straight brows. Her mouth was wide and full and softly pink. She was sitting in profile to him and the soft round curves of her body caught his breath in his throat. He could feel the warm stirring in his loins that she always caused.

"Deeta." He said her name quietly.

She turned to look at him rising slowly. The light that sparked in her eyes caused him to tremble slightly, and without a spoken word he held out his arms to her. She moved slowly, keeping her eyes locked on his, and stepped into the circle of his arms. As his mouth came down to meet her upraised lips, he murmured her name again. Then he gathered her into his arms and held her tightly against him. Her warm soft lips parted under his searching mouth and she lifted her arms about his shoulders caressing the back of his neck with one hand. She brought her body tightly against him in a giving surrender he could feel through every muscle of his body.

"God, I love you, girl," he said with his face pressed against her hair. "Deeta, I've got to talk to you."

She stirred in his arms and held him more tightly.

He gave a soft laugh. "If you keep doin' that, girl, I'll forget what I got to say to you."

She laughed happily and tried again to move closer. He grasped her by the shoulders and held her away from him with an effort.

"Listen to me, Deeta. Do you want to be free, and live with me?"

The question took her so much by surprise that she could only stare at him.

"Free?"

"Yes, free," he said. "I'm goin' to ask Matt to buy you. He'll do it for me and set you free. Then we can marry. What do you say to that, girl?"

"Oh, Cat, if I could only be free, free!" she cried. "Even if it was just for a while. To be free after being a slave all my life, oh, Cat!"

"If you were free, girl, would you chain yourself up again . . . to me?"

She smiled up at him and gave him her answer in a way

he could not doubt. Holding him tightly she moved her body against his until he gave a soft groan and crushed her against him again lowering his head to take her mouth with his.

"We'll ask Matt, later," he said quietly. He took her by the hand and they walked toward the barn. He swung the big door open and she stepped inside. Closing it after them, he pushed the lock in place. It was cool and dark inside. He could just make out her small form and he stepped toward her.

"Deeta," he said huskily as he pulled her close, gently caressing her body with his hands. They dropped together on the fresh hay and she moved her body tightly against him. He was fumbling with her clothes and she had to help him remove the blouse she wore. Gently he kissed her again and again. Dropping his mouth to her throat, then her shoulders, he caressed her breasts and kissed them softly until the nipples rose hard and firm against his lips. He was lost in her and he wanted to stay lost forever. The remains of her clothes seemed to melt away under his fingers and his hands explored all the soft valleys of her body until he brought a soft sigh of pleasure from her. He could stand it no longer and he rolled above her and brought himself into her with long firm strokes. Her body lifted under his and she cried out his name as she moved to meet him in the age-old rhythm. They moved together as one until they stood on the edge of their passion. It exploded with a fury he had never experienced before, and with a trembling in his great body he grasped her to him and molded her body to his in a devouring flame.

Afterward, they lay together in the hay. He supported his head on his hand and lay on his side facing her. As they talked he ran the tips of his fingers over her body as though he would never get enough of touching her.

"We'll talk to Matt. We can be married soon. I want you for always, Deeta. I love you."

"And I love you, Cat. Even if it doesn't work out and they won't give me my freedom, I shall always love you."

"Don't say that, it will work out. Matt is a great friend. We have been together since we were children. He would do this if I ask him."

"Of course, he would, but he is not Mr. Martin. Maybe Mr. Martin will not want to sell me."

She wrapped her arms about his neck and lay her head in the hollow of his shoulder. He could feel the warm tears on his skin.

"Deeta, one way or another, I'll get you. If he won't sell you, I'll take you away. We'll be together."

"No, Cat, that would make a slave of you also. Do you know, Cat, that if I were to have a child it would be a slave? The only hope we have is that your friend buys me. If not, we must forget about each other. It is a luxury we can't afford."

"I could no more forget you than I could forget my own heart-beat. I'll find a way. Trust me, I'll find a way."

"I do," she sighed. "I do trust you, Cat."

When he kissed her again it was a gentle tender kiss, and she almost cried at the beauty his love had shown her.

Chapter Seven

Cat rapped on the bedroom door and walked in. Matt pulled himself reluctantly from bed.

"What time is it?" he mumbled.

"After six."

"Six! What are you getting me up at this ungodly hour for!"

"We're leaving for home today."

"I know we're going home, but don't you think we ought to wait for everyone else to get up first?"

"I've got to talk to you, Matt."

For the first time, Matt noticed the serious look on his friend's face, and the unnatural nervousness he was showing.

"Matt, I ain't never asked you for anything before, I've been with you a long time."

"Cat . . ."

"Let me finish first, Matt, while I still have the courage. You know it goes against me to ask anyone for anything. But there's something I want more than anything else in the world and the only person that can do it for me is you."

"Cat, if there is anything I can do for you, you know you only have to say so."

Cat gulped hesitantly. "There's a girl . . ."

Matt stared at him in amazement. This was Cat who

never took an interest in women except for casual physical relief. He had used more than one and walked away without any sign of ever being touched by it.

"A girl . . . who?"

"She belongs to Mr. Martin."

"Belongs, you mean she's a slave."

Cat's face flushed slightly with suppressed emotion.

"I want you to buy her, and set her free, Matt . . . I want to marry her."

"I never thought I'd live to see the day. I've got to meet this girl. She must be quite a woman."

"She is, Matt. She's beautiful. Will you ask Mr. Martin, Matt? Her name is Deeta, she works in the kitchen."

"Of course, I'll ask him. I'll buy her no matter what the price is."

Cat expelled a long sigh of relief and dropped into a chair.

"Have you found any clues to my mystery, Cat?"

"Well, I've nosed around quite a bit. Couple of things go together. The people here are afraid of your place. Ever since the old owner left, which was quite a while ago. They say there's been something goin' on over there. From the way they act, I think they think the place is haunted. You finding that book kind of fits in. Someone's been staying there, and I think we know who it is. The question is, why? Why don't she live here with her father and sister? Why the secret trips from England to here? And one more thing, Matt."

"What?"

"Since we've been fixing up the place and travelin' back and forth to the house, haven't you thought of one more thing? Since she can't be stayin' there, and she ain't stayin' here, where is she?"

"Yes, I've thought of that. She's definitely not at Markham's place. I've been riding with Deborah several times since we got here. She shows no sign of anything being wrong. I just don't understand all this."

"Well, we'll be moving in tomorrow, then we'll be free to really look around. There's two cabins up in the woods behind your place. Maybe we can start there."

Cat heaved his large frame to his feet and walked toward the door. With his hand on the latch, he turned to face Matt.

"You won't forget Deeta, will you Matt?" he asked softly.

"No, my friend, I'll not forget. You'd better get the rest of our things together. I'll go down to breakfast and talk to the Martins. Let's try to get on our way right after breakfast. I'm anxious to get to my own place."

"Yes, so am I," smiled Cat. They exchanged understanding glances and Cat left the room.

Matt washed and dressed, then went slowly down the curved stairs to the dining room for breakfast. Deborah Martin was already seated at the table. It was only a few minutes after Matt's arrival that Mr. Martin appeared.

"Good morning, Deborah." He dropped a light kiss on top of his daughter's head.

"Good morning, Father. Did you sleep well?"

"Yes, my dear," he said as he dropped into his chair. "Good morning, Matt."

"Good morning, Deborah, Mr. Martin. It is a beautiful day. I'm kind of anxious to get home. Cat and I will be leaving right after breakfast."

"Do you mind if I ride over with you, Matt?" asked Deborah. "I'm going to invite Vern to my masquerade ball. By the way, it's next week. Would you . . . and your

63

friend care to come?"

Matt smiled at her for her attempt at consideration of Cat's feelings.

"I'm sure I can speak for Cat. We'd love to come. There is something I would like to speak to you about, Mr. Martin."

"Yes, my boy, what can we help you with?"

"You have a young girl working in your kitchen. A girl named Deeta."

"Yes, I remember her, beautiful girl. I picked her up about two years ago."

"I'd like to buy her, sir, if you'd sell."

"Buy her? Well, I'd like to sell her to you, Matt, but I can't."

"Can't? If it's a matter of price, sir, I'm willing to pay anything you ask."

Mr. Martin inhaled deeply in the beginnings of ill-concealed anger.

"Money is not the object."

"I'm sorry, sir. I didn't mean to upset you. If you knew how important it was, you'd understand my anxiousness."

"Be that as it may, Matt, I can't sell her to you."

"Can you tell me why?"

"Surely. She's not mine to sell," he smiled.

"Not yours, whose is she?"

"She's part of Deborah's trousseau, so I guess you'd say she belongs to Deborah now."

Matt turned to Deborah. "Well, Deborah, will you sell the girl to me?"

Deborah looked up at him through eyes that gave him no idea of her thoughts.

"Will you tell me why you want her so badly, Matt?" she asked softly.

He looked at her silently for a few minutes trying to figure the best approach to her. Finally he decided direct honesty was the thing.

"Cat is in love with her, and she loves him. They want to marry. He doesn't want her to be a slave and more important he doesn't want his sons to be slaves. Is that a good enough reason?"

"It is a most excellent reason, Matt," she answered. "And you most certainly cannot buy her from me."

Matt gazed at her with a stunned expression. He could not believe his ears. "You mean you refuse to let those two have any happiness?" he said coldly. "You have everything and you will give them nothing. I hardly thought that of you, Deborah."

She smiled up at him again; this time there was a wicked look in her eyes.

"You can't buy her, Matt, because it is going to be my pleasure to give her to Cat personally." Still he stared at her dumbfounded.

"Close your mouth, Matt," she laughed. "You're not the only one who can care for a friend. Deeta may be my slave, but it is an institution in which I do not believe. It would give me a great deal of pleasure to give her to Cat and see her happy."

Mr. Martin laughed now at Matt's speechlessness.

"Consider it done, Matt. Deeta belongs to Cat now."

"I'll not forget this," Matt said softly. "If I can ever do anything for either of you, no matter what it is, consider it done. That is from Cat and I. You have two friends you can count on no matter what."

Mr. Martin looked deeply at Matt's face and saw the sincerity of his answer. He and Deborah exchanged glances.

"Maybe someday we will need your help, Matt. For now let's go tell Deeta and you can take her home with you."

Cat was seated on the wagon that carried the last of their belongings. He had never felt so helpless in his life. Mentally he was figuring ways of taking Deeta away even if they refused to sell her, although he knew it was almost impossible.

When the door opened and Matt and Deborah came out on the porch, there was no sign of anything on their faces. Cat held his breath and watched them. Matt could see the tension and fear in the big man. He could hold back the good news no longer.

"Cat, Mr. Martin is making out Deeta's papers now. We didn't have to buy her, she's a gift from Deborah to you."

Cat leapt down from the wagon and walked to Deborah's side.

"You'll never regret this, Miss Deborah. You have my undying gratitude," he said softly.

Deeta came to the door carrying in her hand the papers of her freedom. The happy glow on her face and the tears in her eyes made both Matt and Deborah smile. But Deeta and Cat had eyes only for each other. She came to his side and he put his arm about her.

"I'm free, Cat," she whispered. "I'm free."

"I know," he replied with a gentle smile. "But you're not free for long."

"Well, if you think you're taking her tonight, Cat, you're wrong," said Deborah with a small laugh. "I've

66

some clothes I want her to have and I've a beautiful dress for her to be married in . . . tomorrow."

"Tomorrow," said Cat in a disappointed voice. "You mean . . ."

Deeta giggled in embarrassment, and Matt and Deborah laughed loudly at Cat's disappointment. Cat smiled sheepishly. "Tomorrow's fine. The sooner we get married, the sooner we can get home to Foxmore."

Deeta's face became still. "Foxmore? Cat, do we have to live at Foxmore?" There was almost a sound of fear in her voice. Matt was watching Deborah also and her face suddenly lost its glow and became unreadable. Cat was taken by surprise.

"Where else could we live? I certainly can't live here. I belong at Foxmore."

Deeta nodded her head in agreement, but Matt could still see the touch of fear in her eyes.

"The cabins behind my place, Cat, are they liveable?"

"Yes, they're very well made. All they need is more furniture."

"Well, how about me giving you and Deeta one of the cabins and a piece of ground. Then you could fix it up and have your own place."

Deeta gave a gasp of delight and threw her arms about Cat, who laughingly took advantage of the situation to hold her tightly. When he finally let her go they were both shaking with the sudden happiness of the day.

"Come on, Cat, let's get home. We've a lot of things to do."

Cat reluctantly agreed, and they climbed aboard the wagon. Waving good-bye to the two women, they started toward home.

"Matt, did you see Deeta's face when I mentioned

67

living at Foxmore?"

"Yes, and I watched Deborah, too. There's something strange going on and it all settles around there. Well I'll be living there from tonight on, so maybe we'll find out. By the way, we're invited to a masquerade ball at the Martins."

"No, Matt, you go. It's too soon for me and Deeta to try that. Besides," he said wickedly. "I'd rather stay home anyway."

Their laughter filled the morning air, as they headed home.

Chapter Eight

Matt had arrived at the masquerade ball a little late. Dressed as a buccaneer, he attracted the appraising glance of every woman—married or single—in the place. The white shirt with its full sleeves open to the waist, the tight-fitting pants and high black boots accentuated his lithe form. He had his hair, worn long, tied back with a piece of black ribbon, and his tanned face and black beard gave him a dashing appearance. He was approached by a glittery dandy, whom he soon recognized behind the mask as Vern.

"Good evening, Matt," he laughed.

"Could you tell that easily it was me?"

"Even behind the mask, my friend. There is no way of you ever hiding."

"Where is Deborah and her father?"

"Mr. Martin is about here somewhere. Deborah has not yet arrived. I do believe the lady loves to make an entrance." He laughed. "In the meantime, let me introduce you to our illustrious Governor," he said with such a dry expression that Matt turned to look at him.

"I'm sorry, Matt, but you may as well know right now. My sympathies are with the American cause no matter what my birth. The Governor does not hold me in great esteem and I feel the same about him." Touching Matt's arm he guided him in the direction of a small group of men who stood talking.

"Excuse me, gentlemen," said Vern. "I should like to introduce our new neighbor. This is Matthew Deverall. Matt, may I introduce Governor Rosemond and Colonel Bartly, Lord Morrison and Lieutenant Simmons."

"Gentlemen," said Matt in a firm voice. "It is my pleasure to finally meet my neighbors."

"Good evening, Mr. Deverall," said Governor Rosemond, extending his hand. The handshake belied the looks of the man. To all outward appearances, he looked like an emaciated, fragile man. But the handshake startled Matt with its strength, and the eyes were brilliant and penetrating. They missed nothing and gave Matt the impression that he was being read like a book.

The others expressed their greetings.

"You have just recently come from England, have you not?" questioned Lord Morrison, a rather pompous, ruddy-faced man.

"Yes, my lord."

"And how are the feelings now at home over this confounded rebellion?"

Matt could feel Vern's scowl of displeasure more than see it. He laughed rather shakily.

"Well, I really don't know, sir. I have not taken much of an interest in the situation since it did not affect me."

"Not affect you!" said Colonel Bartly, and both he and Lieutenant Simmons exchanged exasperated glances. "You've bought land here. How could it not affect you?" questioned Lieutenant Simmons rather sneeringly. Matt clenched his teeth together and caught a merry twinkle in Vern's eyes as he answered somewhat coldly.

"I've bought land here, sir, and I intend to live on it in peace. I know nothing of the American cause, as you put it, and I do not care to get involved in it. I've come here to be a quiet country planter and I shall remain so."

"And what will you do if they decide to throw you off your land and out of their country?" Again the disdainful look from Lieutenant Simmons as though he thought Matt a thorough coward.

Matt turned to look directly into the lieutenant's eyes. His eyes had taken on a hard cold glow. "Lieutenant Simmons, no one takes from me what is mine. As I said before, I intend to be a quiet country planter, to live my life as I see fit. Up to this point no one is challenging either myself or the way I choose to live. If the occasion arises, I shall fight for what is mine."

"Fight whom?" questioned the Governor quietly.

"Whoever tries to stand between me and what I want. As I said before, I know nothing about the political situation here, and have not taken sides—nor do I intend to. I have no argument with either side as long as they do not meddle in my life."

"What loyalty do you feel toward your own country?" questioned Lord Morrison.

"England? England has been my home all my life. It has given my family wealth and position. I received, with my brother, a good education. I would say I owe her love and gratitude. But there are two sides to this political coin and having never been a politician, I'm afraid I don't understand either. One cannot do battle with someone over a cause one does not understand. I need more time to live here, to meet the people and to listen to their side of the coin. Until then I intend to keep my nose to myself. Out of the King's business, and out of the Americans' business."

Vern was almost overcome with silent hilarity at the

broiling tempest over Matt's words. He wished that Paul were here to listen. Deliberately, he edged things along. "How do you feel about taxation?" he questioned Matt.

"Vern, no one can run a country without some form of taxation. Fair taxation is a necessity and every man who wants to be represented in his government should be agreeable to paying for the privilege."

"Ah, representation . . . but what if . . ."

Governor Rosemond interrupted in a cool deliberate voice. "These colonials need to be taught a lesson. They could not exist without us. In time they will learn that fact one way or another. We must teach them this lesson firmly and without mercy. Then when we have reduced them to their proper place, we can get things back to normal. America is a colony of England. It must remain so. I'm afraid, sir," Governor Rosemond said quietly, "unthinking people seem to believe that the majority of the people are in favor of this revolution. This is not true. We have a great many people in this country with enough sense to realize that they should be loyal to the country that gave them birth." He stared pointedly at Vern, who hid his smile behind the rim of his glass. "I am governor here, and I am loyal to my king and my country. If I come across any of these revolutionaries or 'patriots' as they call themselves, I shall show them who is the power here. Their land will be confiscated to the crown and, if possible, I shall have them hanged."

The Governor had spoken quietly, but his words had fallen clear and cold on the ears of the group. Matt could understand Vern's feelings, although he was not a loyal defender of the American cause, since he did not understand what was happening. Still he bristled at the attitudes of the men in the group.

There was a stiff cold silence for a few minutes while the men sipped their drinks. Matt's eyes drifted over the crowd. He did not really know what he was looking for. At that moment a lovely vision descended the bottom of the steps. A Grecian goddess with lovely black hair piled high upon her head in a cluster of curls and one long lock hanging over a creamy white, bare shoulder. The soft folds of the white Grecian gown clung to her lovely rounded form. She wore no jewelry, but a thread of fine white pearls was strung through her hair. She stood still, searching the crowd until her eyes met his across the room, and a slight smile lifted the corners of her mouth.

"Vern, your lady has arrived."

"Oh, Matt, be a good fellow and entertain her for a moment, would you? I must discuss something of great importance with her father."

"Of course, it is my pleasure," laughed Matt as he headed for Deborah's side.

He did not see the look on Vern's face as he left him or it might have caused him considerable surprise. There was a gentle smile on his lips and a friendly glow in his eyes as he watched Matt walk to Deborah's side and speak to her. In a few more minutes, Vern slipped silently from the room and climbed the stairs to the upper floor of the house. He tapped gently on the door and stepped unhesitantly inside.

Matt reached her side and bowed with a smile.

"Can a buccaneer pirate you away, mademoiselle, for a few minutes?"

There seemed to be a slight tenseness in her as he straightened up and looked at her. The mask she wore was of soft white and shielded her eyes from him momentarily. Then she turned and faced him. The shock caused him to stop speaking and stare at her. Blue! they were BLUE. This was not Deborah. He felt his hand shaking, and for the life of him could think of nothing to say. He had wanted to find her for so long and now he could say nothing because everyone would think he was crazy. The music started a slow waltz.

"Dance with me, Matt," she said softly.

Wordlessly, he took her hand and led her to the floor. When he faced her, she lifted her arms to him and he placed his hand on her waist and held her other hand in his. Slowly they moved to the soft strains of the music. He wanted to shout something, do something to make her know he knew, but still the words did not come. They had made several turns about the floor before his wits began to return to him. He smiled. "Deborah, you look exceptionally lovely tonight."

She seemed suddenly to relax. "Thank you, sir."

"If you were not engaged to Vern, I should give the gentleman some competition," he laughed. "But I do believe having Vern angry with me could make me quite a coward."

She looked up at him and her face took on a sad, rather shaken look. "I could never think of you as a coward," she said softly.

He watched her for another few minutes, then gathered her a little closer in his arms. He met with no resistance as her body swayed with his in the slow movements of the dance. Then suddenly, the realization came to him. This had been planned. She had wanted to meet him, see and talk to him, to decide what? He no longer cared. With firm steps he guided her toward the open doors and out onto the patio. It was very dark, and they did not speak a word. Now he pulled her even closer to him and held her as he had wanted to do all those weeks. He would play their game, but he would also take advantage of his opportunities. They were no longer dancing, and he slid his hands up from her waist to her shoulders and very gently pulled her into the enclosing circle of his arms. Dropping his head to her upturned one, he gently took her mouth with his. The fiery shock of the kiss set his head reeling, and he put his arms tightly about her and held her body close to him. He forced her mouth open and touched the inside of her lips with his tongue. She responded with a warmth that matched his own. She had lifted her arms about his neck and held one hand on the back of his head while she caressed his back with the other. There was no resistance to her body, and she molded herself against him as his hands caressed her. He felt as though he were falling off the edge of the world, and she was the only thing to which he had to cling.

When he finally, reluctantly, lifted his head from hers, they were both breathless. She dropped her head to his shoulder and he held her, feeling her soft hair against his face. The soft scent of her stirred his blood as he remembered the times he had smelled the familiar odor before and the dreams it brought to him.

"Deborah," he said huskily, wanting desperately to call her by her right name and end the charade.

"No, don't, Matt. Don't talk, just hold me for a moment more." She sighed a rather lost, hopeless sigh.

"I'll hold you forever," he said.

"No, Matt. That's impossible for us. I wanted at least this moment to remember. Our destinies are planned and we cannot control them."

"I control my own life," he said fiercely, gathering her even more tightly against him.

"But I don't control mine," she sobbed. Now she moved away from him a few steps and looked at him. "There are some things that cannot be."

"Let me help you," he said softly. "Trust me."

He gave her every opportunity to tell him, and for just a few moments he could see the desire on her face. Then, with a sob, she turned and ran back into the ballroom. He followed her rapidly but still was too late to catch her as she ran up the stairs and away from him. He groaned inwardly. Why hadn't he told her and demanded an explanation? But he knew the answer as he remembered Captain Duprey's words. "It's your life." He could do nothing to jeopardize her life. He had to wait until they trusted him enough to tell him. He was still watching the stairs when he saw her descend again. But this time, he knew it was Deborah and that the masquerade was over for tonight.

Chapter Nine

Matt sat on his front porch with his chair tilted back and his feet propped on the railing. The night was quiet except for the trilling call of the chickadees. There were millions of tiny diamond-like stars trailing across the black velvet sky. Matt had never felt so contented and at peace in his life. The wedding of Cat and Deeta three weeks before had been simple but beautiful. She had worn a soft green dress that Deborah had given her, and the love in her eyes for Cat had brought moisture to the eyes of all involved. They had given a beautiful dinner for Deeta, with all her friends there, and had sung and danced until Cat's desire to get Deeta away had become laughingly obvious. The two had gone to the cabin Matt had given them. Now that Cat was gone he felt the urge to share his happiness with someone close. Matt had said good night and had left for a large home that felt quite lonely now. He enjoyed his last cigar before going to bed. His thoughts were drifting contentedly. He planned to write his brother Jason in the morning to tell him how happy he was here. It even entered his mind to suggest that Jason might pay him a visit. He supposed, deep in his heart, that he would be even happier if Jason were living here too. Between the two of them they could build Foxmore into a beautiful estate that would rival Deverall Hall. His mind was a jumble of thoughts. He had vowed he would not get involved in the political situation here, yet he knew if it meant contact with Deanna Martin again he would have a difficult time keeping them.

It frustrated him that he knew about her and was unable to say anything to anyone. He refused to question himself about his keeping silent. In a way he knew it was some type of involvement. Putting aside any political reasons he could not deny one blazing fact. He had fallen in love with Deanna at first sight, and holding her, kissing her at the ball only made him want her more. Where was she tonight? he wondered. Both he and Cat had kept up some type of secret search, but it seemed as if the ground had opened up and swallowed her. If he could find her, make some type of contact again, he was going to do everything in his power to hold her, to stop her from this folly she was involved in.

The flickering fireflies danced about the lawn and he was watching the river when a soft light flickered on the opposite bank. He thought it was his imagination at first, then suddenly the light reappeared. Its flickering on and off was not an accident. It was a signal to someone. Slowly he rose to his feet, still watching the light. On . . . off . . . on . . . off . . . Definitely a signal, but to whom? Did they expect someone else to be in the house? Now he moved swiftly. Counting on a sudden idea, he dashed up the steps and into the small corner bedroom. From the window he looked directly across at the blinking light. Then he lit the lamp and held it in front of the window. Taking a pillow he covered and uncovered it in what he hoped would be an answering signal. Another flicker from the river then all was dark. He darkened the light and sat down in the dark room to wait. It seemed to

78

him hours before the first quiet stirring appeared at the edge of the lawn. Then a dark form moved hastily but quietly across the grass. He held his breath and waited. If the person coming was the one he thought it was going to be then he was about to see Deanna again. The interminable time before the door moved set his teeth on edge and caused soft beads of perspiration across his forehead. He wanted desperately to get her inside the room before she discovered the one in the room wasn't who she was expecting. Quietly the latch turned and the door opened a few inches. "Father?" she whispered softly as she moved away from the door toward the bed.

"Yes, my dear," he answered in a soft whisper. She stepped inside and closed the door behind her. The only light in the room was pale moonlight that created black shadows. She slowly groped her way toward him. He held his breath, hoping she would not become alarmed and run before he could get himself between her and the door. He was standing within a couple feet of her now but she still had not recognized that she had the wrong person.

"Oh, Father," she sighed and crossing the few feet that separated them threw herself into his arms. He wrapped both of his arms about her tightly, and at that moment she realized her mistake. She jerked violently and began to struggle in his arms. Without making a sound, she fought him with all her strength, but she was no match for him and soon he held her in a grip from which she could not move. He could feel her body trembling and knew she was crying softly.

"Don't be afraid, Deanna, I'm not going to do you any harm," he said gently.

"You know me?"

"I know you. I met you on the ship. Do you remember

the man you bumped into at the companionway?"

"Yes, but you did not see me. I made sure you did not see me," she said in a voice cracking with panic.

"But I did. I also made a point of doing so. You are the loveliest creature I've ever seen. I can't be faulted for wanting to see you again, for wanting to meet you, to know you." He went on to explain about all the nights on board ship when he had waited for hours in the shadows for a brief glimpse of her. How he had wanted to reach out and comfort her when she had cried. He told her how he had kept his silence and had Cat do the same when one word from either of them would have put an end to her plans and possibly her father's life. He wanted to exact a little gratitude from her, and a little dependence. "One emotion," he thought, "might possibly lead to another."

Her body sagged a little in his arms. He realized that he had never enjoyed holding a woman as much as her. He held her tightly with one arm and maneuvered the lighting of the lamp with the other. When the room brightened, he looked down again into her soft blue eyes. "I was right," he smiled at her. "Your eyes are blue, and your sister's are green. I've seen those blue eyes in my dreams for weeks."

"Please let me go," she pleaded.

"Will you promise not to run? I've waited too long to see you to have you get away now."

"I promise," she said quietly.

He relaxed his hold on her, but kept himself between her and the door. Very reluctantly, he dropped his arms from her. She stepped back from him.

"I thought you were still at Clearhaven. How did you know where and how to give the signal?"

"It was just a guess." He explained how he had found

80

the book there and knew she had been using the room. "When I saw your light I just took the chance."

Her face was pale with fright and she was trembling a little. There was such a look of defeat and despair in her eyes that he could not stand it.

"I'm a friend, Deanna. I owe your father and sister a debt I cannot begin to repay. I would like to start repaying it by helping you if I can. You look as though you need a friend. Let me help."

Her mouth began to tremble and tears started in her eyes and dropped down her soft cheeks. He stepped closer to her again and this time he pulled her gently into his arms. Holding her head against his chest, he let her cry until she had released some of the tension. He could smell the soft fragrance of her hair. It was the same perfume he had smelled on the bed when he found the book and also at the masquerade ball. He would contentedly hold her for hours if she had not gathered herself together.

"Now can you tell me what's going on? If I were going to betray you I could have a long time ago. I've known there were two of you since I arrived. Who is it you're hiding from and why? Maybe there is something I can do."

She sat on the edge of the bed and clasped and unclasped her hands anxiously in her lap as she began her story.

"My father bought Clearhaven about five years ago. When he first came here he was alone. My mother and my sister, brother and I stayed in England. Father had been here for a short time when he became sympathetic to the cause of the Americans. Although he loved England, he came to love America more. Alexander

81

Rosemond, who is the governor, is a hateful vile man," she said fiercely. "He hated my father for all he had accomplished—and the honor. He came into information that linked my father to the American cause without Father's knowledge. He realized how useful Father could be as a . . . spy. Then my father sent for the rest of us. But Governor Rosemond had other plans. He attempted to have us abducted and held to get my father to do what he wanted. His plan was half successful. My mother and brother are still in his power. My sister and I escaped. He had no idea that there are two of us. I just returned from England when you saw me to tell my father that I was completely unsuccessful in finding anyone to help us get my mother and brother free. Father will have to give in to his demands and betray the men who trust him. Since Deborah has kept herself clearly visible to the governor and his friends, I have been able to travel back and forth freely. When you bought Foxmore, we thought it was another, sent to spy on us. I could not let you see me and connect me to Deborah and Father."

She covered her face with her hands.

"Oh, I have failed so miserably in everything. I cannot help Mother and David, and I cannot help myself."

He went to her and knelt by her feet. He took hold of her hands, and lifted them away from her tear-stained face.

"Then let me help you, Deanna," he said softly. "I have many friends in England including Lord Jason Deverall . . . my brother. Together we'll bring them home."

He was looking directly into her eyes now, trying desperately to convince her. She looked at him intently. He waited, holding both her hands in his. Then he felt her

82

body relax. "Yes, I'll trust you. I've done no good, maybe this is our one last chance. I feel if Father were forced against his honor to betray his friends it would kill him."

Now for the first time he could see the exhaustion in her face.

"Where have you been staying?"

"Until you started to repair Foxmore, I stayed here."

"And then you used the cabin in the woods, right?"

"Yes, until your friend came along. He almost found me one time," she laughed in remembrance. "I was hiding in the room when he came. I spent a most uncomfortable few hours while he was there."

"You must be very tired?" he questioned.

She gave a soft exhausted sigh. "Yes, very."

"Why don't you lie down and sleep for just a few hours? I'll fix us something to eat in the meantime."

She hesitated for a few moments but the idea of the comfort of a soft warm bed beckoned her. "Just for a short time," she said. "Captain Duprey sails soon. There are messages I must carry."

He wisely kept his mouth closed and offered no advice, but he was determined not to let her travel again. Another plan was forming in his mind. He mused on his ideas for a time until a soft contented sigh caught his attention. She had lain back on the bed and her exhausted body had given in to the rest she so badly needed. He went to the side of the bed and looked down at her small curled form. Then he reached out and gently loosened her shoes and removed them. Covering her with a blanket, he touched her soft hair gently. She stirred under his hand and moved more deeply against the pillow. In sleep her face softened from the tired lines. She looked so young and vulnerable, his heart stirred violently against his ribs and a lump formed in his throat so that he found it difficult to swallow. He could not deny to himself the desire that welled up in him, and he wanted desperately to cradle her in his arms and protect her. It took all his will to turn away and go downstairs to see what in the house was edible.

Chapter Ten

She sat cross-legged on the bed with the tray of food in front of her and ate with a ravenous appetite, casting quick, bright smiles in his direction between bites. He was sitting on a chair beside the bed watching her, and enjoying it almost as much as she was.

"I'm sorry about my lack of manners, but I am ravenously hungry."

"Enjoy it! I'm just sorry it isn't a better meal. The next time I hope I have something better to offer."

"This is marvelous," she laughed as she licked her fingers delicately. "I never realized how good a piece of cold chicken could taste."

"Would you like a little more wine?" he asked and began to rise from his chair.

"No . . . no thank you. I've had much more than enough. I'm not much of a drinker. My head is spinning just a little, already."

He sat back in his chair and watched her. Her eyes were bright from the wine and she was so very lovely he could have spent the day just sitting and enjoying her. He felt as though he had known her always, as though their meeting, like many things in his life lately, was some kind of predestined thing. He didn't know why he felt so; he only hoped the feeling rubbed off on her. He wanted her to be a part of his life . . . permanently. He was also aware that he was physically reacting to her nearness. He had stayed in the room after she had fallen asleep. Pulling a chair close to the bed, he had sat and put his feet up on the edge of the bed. She lay, so beautiful, so vulnerable and yet she had seemed to feel secure. It was then that the thought came to him that she and her family had been observing him in the months that he had been here. They must have told her somehow that they approved of him. At least he hoped so, for he had tried in every way possible to prove to them he was no threat to their cause. He wanted her completely and irrevocably, no matter what she was involved in. "Somehow," he thought, "I can get her away from this dangerous involvement." To make her see what a wonderful life they could have together. He was wealthy enough to give her everything she could want. He thought he could convince her. It never occurred to him that at that moment her mind was contemplating the thought of convincing him otherwise.

Although her clothes were rumpled from sleeping in them and her hair had come loose from its pins and cascaded down in a tumble of shining black curls, he had never seen anyone so beautiful. She must have noticed then how deeply he was looking at her for she flushed slightly in embarrassment and raised her hands to her hair and began to try to pin it up.

"Don't," he said quietly.

She hesitated, and the blue eyes widened a little as he rose slowly from the chair and took the tray from the bed. He turned away to put the tray on the dresser. Then he looked back at her. She sat very still watching him. He walked to the bed and sat on the edge. She did not seem to be afraid of him, yet her hands trembled in her lap as her eyes held his. He took one of her hands in his and raised the fingers to his lips.

"Do you know how long I have dreamed of you?" he whispered. "Night after night all that I can see is the loveliness of your eyes."

She seemed mesmerized and he bent his head closer and closer to hers until his mouth very gently took hers in a kiss as soft as butterfly wings. Now he could feel the trembling in her whole body, but it could not match the violent reaction of his. Softly he murmured her name. "Deanna." He slid his hands up her back and across her shoulders. Cupping her face in his hands, he kissed her forehead, then her eyes, her cheeks. When his mouth found hers again it was no longer soft, but sought hers in a demanding probing kiss that left them both breathless. He lifted his face from hers, and with slow gentle fingers let his hands slide down the white column of her throat to her breasts. Gently he caressed her for a quick moment, then moving his hands about her, he pulled her against him. There was no reality but him in her dizzy spinning world. She lifted her arms about his neck as he brought her body against his. He could feel the soft roundness against his chest. Now the desire for her climbed to a wild beat. Holding her against him tightly he again sought her mouth. It lifted to his, slightly parted. He probed the soft corners with his tongue, then forced them further apart. The darting response of her tongue blended with his, and was as demanding as his own. The kiss left them both shaking and clinging tightly to one another.

Without saying anything he rose from the bed, drawing her with him. Holding her eyes with his he drew her close and began to loosen the buttons of her dress. Unbuttoning it to her waist, he gently pulled it down from her shoulders. The thin chemise she wore under it

87

did nothing to hide the beauty of her soft round breasts as they pressed upward against the soft material. He maneuvered the chemise down from her shoulders and trailed his fingers over her warm body. Cupping both breasts in his hands, he lowered his head and took them with his lips, first one then the other, caressing the taut nipples with his tongue and fingers until they rose firmly under his hands. She held his head gently against her, running her fingers through his hair and across his broad shoulders. Softly she sighed his name as his mouth found hers again and again. He had dropped her dress and chemise to the floor and now he held her naked body tightly against him. Running his hands from her waist down over the soft curve of her hips, he grasped her and held her firmly against him. She gave one small gasping sigh as she felt the hardness of him rise against her body. Then her hands went to the buttons of his shirt and one by one she released them and he shrugged the shirt from his body. Within a few seconds, the rest of his clothes followed. Now, he held her against him, breast to breast, thigh to thigh. She ran her fingers up over his shoulders and grasping the back of his head pulled his mouth again to hers. "Matt," she said softly against his lips. "I've never . . . please, Matt." It was almost a sob.

"I know, I know," he said. Holding her away from him for a moment, he looked at her frightened face. "Trust me, Deanna, I won't hurt you. I love you. I love you," he repeated softly as he drew her tightly against him again. This time his mouth took hers in a demanding passion that swept away all her resistance. He lifted her from the floor with a slight bend of his knees and laid her on the bed. Without releasing her even for a moment he lay beside her. Now, his hands sought her body again, the tips of his fingers wandering, probing every soft curve of her. He could hear her soft moans of pleasure as she trembled under his searching hands. His mouth travelled after his hands in gentle kisses over her body until she gasped his name.

"Matt, love me, love me," she sighed. Now he was over her and could hold back the flood of his desire no longer. He tried to enter her gently, but still heard her soft stifled cry of pain. Then her body rose to meet his. He released his passion now, fearing no more. Pulling her tightly against him they moved in rhythm together, each giving and demanding the same until with a sobbing cry, she arched herself against him as together they faced the explosion of their passion.

Afterwards, he held her close in his arms, her head lay against his shoulder, and he buried his face in the soft mass of her hair. For a short time, they slept. After a while, Matt awoke and lay very still. He was contented to hold her lovely body close to him. He was touching her very softly just running his fingers over her when her blue eyes opened and looked up into his with so much trust and love that he could feel the lump rise in his throat constricting his breathing.

"I love you, my lovely blue-eyed witch," he smiled. "I guess I've loved you from the first moment I saw you on board ship. You have no idea how hard I tried to meet you then, but it was like running up against a stone wall. You certainly have loyal protectors in Captain Duprey and his crew."

"Captain Duprey is my very dear friend. He and his crew are freedom-loving people who are deeply loyal, but more to a cause than to me."

Matt wanted to shy away from political conversation.

It was shaky ground for them and he knew it. It was possibly the only thing that could come between them.

"Why did you run away from me the night of the ball? I knew the moment I looked into your eyes that you were not Deborah."

"I didn't think you had seen me before and I also didn't think you would notice the difference in the color of our eyes."

"I've not missed a thing about you. I would know you in the darkest night. You may be a twin, my love, but to me, you are one of a kind. There is no one who can compare. I'm so very glad I've finally found you. Let me warn you that I have no intention of ever letting you go again."

"I don't regret coming, Matt," she whispered, "but you must understand there are things in our lives that are bigger obligations than to ourselves."

"Not for me. With Foxmore and finding you, my world is complete. You felt it from the beginning just as I did. Admit it, at the ball you deliberately chose to come to me."

"Yes, I wanted to see and talk to you. Vern and Deborah wanted to trust you. So did Father. But I wanted to see for myself. The situation got away from me when you held me in your arms. All I knew then was that I wanted you so much it made me ache. I knew then I could not judge realistically so I ran away."

"If you had given me a chance, I could have proven you could trust me."

"I know," she said wryly. "Deborah told me so, again and again and again."

He laughed and pulling her body tightly in his arms, he kissed her over and over. "Now that you trust me a little," he said, "how about telling me what you are up to?"

"There are a group of men coming down from Boston to talk to Father," she began. "He is supplying them with money and a few arms. All he can smuggle in on Captain Duprey's ship without being caught. They bring the ship up river and anchor in a small inlet right across from your dock, and when the way is clear the cargo is unloaded there and stored in the two cabins in the woods. From there they are broken down into small shipments and smuggled to General Washington's army. You don't know how desperately he needs those supplies, Matt. He is holding together an army by the sheer force of his will. He is a very great man. I admire his courage in the face of all his adversity. You can see why we were so upset when you bought Foxmore. Being an English lord, what were we to think? That someone had found out what we were doing and sent you there to find out."

"I'm not an English lord," he said absently. He was concentrating on the kiss he was depositing on her throat. "My brother is the lord, I'm only the second son. I inherited nothing. All I have is Foxmore and some money my brother gave me, and I'd like you to admire me for my courage in the face of all my adversity. Do you know the great battle I have fought to get you where you are. I, madam, have faced unmentionable odds, and . . ." he chuckled, "I think I deserve my just reward."

She wriggled away from him long enough to look up into his face. "Matt, where do you stand in this affair?"

He sighed resignedly. "Deanna, I know nothing about your so-called revolution. But I really don't see how you think you stand a chance. I've been asking questions and listening. You're too small and too young a country to

91

break away on your own."

Deanna's face became a study of suppressed anger. "You don't understand, Matt! Give us a chance to prove our need for independence to you. Let my father explain our needs to you. We're over-taxed and burdened with unnecessary royalty like . . ."

"Like me?" he smiled at her and kissed the tip of her nose. "Why can't you just live here with me and let the rest of the world take care of itself?" His hands had begun to drift over her again and he pulled her closer to him and began to nuzzle her throat.

"Matt, stop!" she said forcefully. "How can you love me when you won't even try to understand how I feel and what I believe in? I'm a complete woman, Matt. I want you to love me for more than just a romp in bed. I want you to understand, I want you to share my home and my country with me. I want you to share my life with me and my life is here. This country may be young, but it is stronger than you think. We have a will, Matt. A great desire for freedom and the chance to grow strong in our own right."

He had not taken it seriously until now. But watching her face and seeing the deep fire of dedication blazing in her eyes, he began to change his mind.

"All right, Deanna. I'll talk to your father, and I'll help you in every way I can."

She smiled and he noticed there were tiny crinkle lines at the corners of her eyes. He maneuvered a kiss at the corners of each eye. From there his mouth drifted down her face to her mouth and quieted her in the most effective way. She gave a soft little cry, either out of exasperation at him or at her own weakness. But all her other emotions were drawn into her growing desire for him. Slowly, she ran her fingers through the hair on his chest and up over his shoulders. She clasped them together behind his head and leaned her body against him, lifting her mouth to his in her own seeking kiss. "Oh, Matt," she sighed against his lips. "I do love you so very much."

Now his mind slipped from every other thought but her. He wanted to dive into her and never come up. His mouth took hers with such blazing force of desire that it left her breathless, and she surrendered completely to it, letting it wash over her in crashing waves. Again he came into her with the warm hardness of his body, depositing his soul as he did and giving her all his life, love and desire forever.

When the first ray of the morning sun tiptoed across the floor to bounce happily on the bed, he stirred and came immediately awake. He was not used to waking in the mornings with the weight of someone's head on his arm, and it took a few minutes to recall his thoughts. When he did, he turned to look at her sleeping face. "She is so beautiful," he thought. Slowly so as not to waken her, he pulled the covers away and looked at her. She must have felt the chill as she gave a soft sigh and curled against him for warmth. He pulled the blanket up over them both and with a contented sigh held her in his arms and went back to sleep.

Chapter Eleven

When he awoke again, she was no longer at his side. The sun was high in the sky. "It must be noon," he thought sluggishly. Then he yawned and stretched and rose from the bed. Matt was an exceptional-looking man. Standing over six feet tall, he was muscular yet slender in build, narrow-waisted and hipped with broad shoulders. There was a mat of black hair on his chest and his beard and hair were no less black. He had a strong face. There was a golden glow in the depths of his brown eyes, widely set and piercing. His nose was a little long but straight, giving him a slightly hawk-like look. The broad mouth when he was serious was straight and full, but when he smiled it lit his face like a flame.

He stood by the window now and looked out over his property. He was contented. If he could follow the plans he had he was going to keep Deanna at his side permanently and never let her away from him again. Thinking of her now made him warm all over. It also made him wonder where she was. Slipping into his pants, he left the room and went downstairs. He could hear the soft sounds from the kitchen and the smell of food came to him. When he swung open the kitchen door, she was working over the stove, humming to herself. He stood for a while and just watched her move gracefully about the room. "How much I love her," he thought. It brought a tightness in his stomach and a warm glow to his eyes.

She turned then and saw the look in his eyes, and with a slight flush of pinkness to her face, she came to him laughing. "You must eat first, Matt. You'll be all worn out."

He laughed with her. "If I'm going to die of exhaustion, I can't find a better way to die myself!" He reached for her but she moved just out of his reach.

"You are insatiable, sir! Sit down and eat, for I must talk to you."

Again he reached for her, this time catching her by the arms, pulling her against him. "I don't want to talk," he murmured against her hair. "I just want to keep you here in my arms, safe."

"Matt, you know it is impossible for me to just stay here with you. As much as I want to, and I do. There are obligations that I have to see fulfilled."

"You mean your mother and your brother?"

"Yes, I must help Father until he gets them safely away. If Governor Rosemond finds out now, he would stop Father and maybe do harm to my mother and brother. Don't you see, Matt, we have other things to think of than ourselves."

"Deanna, I can't let you go away from me again. I may never see you. Something may happen. I couldn't stand it. Now that I've finally found you, I'll not let you go."

She placed her fingers over his mouth. Then when she had silenced him, she put both hands on his shoulders and gently dropped them down over his chest. She looked up into his eyes and said very quietly but very seriously, "Matt, we can never find happiness at someone else's expense. Don't you see, my darling? We must do everything we can to help my father, for if anything happened to my mother and brother because of my selfishness, I couldn't bear it. I would shrivel up inside and die. I would be no good to myself or to you."

There was the hint of tears in her blue eyes and a soft trembling about her lips. He touched her lips with his in surrender.

"I'll do what I can, and we'll work it out together. But Deanna . . ."

"Yes, my love."

"I'll not let you go to England again. I'll not let you away from me. Whatever we decide to do we'll do together."

She gave him no answer, merely laid her head against his chest. With their arms wrapped about each other, he accepted her silence as agreement. While she knew deep inside that they would eventually both do what they had to do. She could feel the desire for her rising in him but she pushed him gently away.

"Eat, Matt, we've things to do."

"What?"

"First, I must see Father and find out why you were here instead of him, and why he didn't warn me not to come."

"Are you sorry you came?" he asked.

"No! No, Matt. But I must know what happened. We've a line of communication that must remain unbroken."

"Shall we ride over and see what happened?"

"No, I cannot ride out until I know where Deborah is. We cannot be seen in two places at one time. I think if you rode over and brought Father back we could talk."

"Good idea. I'll go right after . . ."

"After you eat!"

"That too," he leered at her.

She laughed happily. "Eat, we've plenty of time tonight."

"You'll stay here? You won't disappear on me?"

"No, I'll be here until you return. We've some time to ourselves. I'm staying here, remember?"

He looked deeply into her eyes, trying to read the mysterious things he saw there. For some reason he felt this was just the beginning of something. Something he would not like and something he was powerless to stop. He ate a little, but the tiny knot of fear in his stomach hampered his appetite. When breakfast was over he dressed and went to the barn and saddled his horse. Bringing him to the front of the house, he tied him and reentered the house.

"I'm ready to leave," he said. "I'll bring your father back as soon as I can. Do you want me to bring Deborah, too?"

"No, just Father. After we have talked things out will be time enough to speak to Deborah."

He chuckled deep in his throat.

"What's so funny?" she smiled.

"I can just see your father's face when I tell him Deanna wants to see him. I wonder what he'd say if I told him we spent the night together?"

She looked shocked. "Matt, you wouldn't."

He laughed out loud and squeezed her until she was almost breathless.

"No, but if I thought he'd be an old-fashioned father and make you marry me with a shotgun, I might give it some serious thought."

She pounded him gently on the chest with her fists, laughing with him. "You are a monster with a mind that falls only in one direction."

"Of course, just look at yourself closely some day, Deanna. You'll see why it takes all I can do to keep my hands off you."

"You don't succeed very well in keeping them off me," she said in mock anger, pushing him away. "Now, go and get my father." Then she added softly, "Tonight we will see to you, monster."

With a feeling close to sheer jubilation he mounted his horse and headed for Clearhaven. She watched from the door until he was out of sight, then she went inside and up the stairs to the small room they had shared. She stood inside for a few minutes without moving, for the room was full of the feel of him. She could still feel the heat of his passion. Shaking herself free of her dreaming, she picked up the lamp and walked to the window, and lighting it, she lifted and lowered it in a signal to someone on the opposite bank of the river.

Matt rode as rapidly as he could push the horse, but it was still almost an hour before he reached Clearhaven. When he gave over his tired horse to a groom, he had himself announced to Mr. Martin. Standing in the entrance hall, he was half smiling to himself as he thought of several different ways to tell Deanna's father what had happened, or at least, most of what had happened. When the butler returned, he told Matt that Mr. Martin was entertaining Governor Rosemond and Lieutenant Simmons in the library and would he please join them there. Matt thanked him and walked to the library door. There was a small lighted fire in the fireplace and Mr. Martin and his guests were seated beside it. When Matt came in, Mr. Martin rose and extended his hand in greeting. "Good afternoon, Matt.

How are you? What brings you over here on this lovely afternoon?"

There was a smile on his lips but his eyes were worried and solemn. They questioned him in silence.

"Oh, I was just out riding, sir, and I thought I would stop by and see if Deborah would care to join me."

Mr. Martin motioned him to a seat and returned to his own. He was about to answer when Governor Rosemond interrupted in his chilled voice. "We were just about to ask after Miss Martin ourselves, sir. It seems the young lady is already out and about."

The voice was nonchalantly quiet, but the icy piercing eyes watched constantly for every reaction.

"Yes," said Mr. Martin. "She went over to Vern's place this morning to discuss some of their wedding plans. Most of her things have arrived from England."

"Most!" exclaimed Lieutenant Simmons. "The young lady must have spent a fortune, since it has taken two trips to bring only most of her things over."

"Oh, yes, Mr. Martin," said Rosemond softly. "How many trips do you think will still be necessary?"

Mr. Martin stiffened slightly and Matt felt the tingling of fear climb up his spine. Thank God Deanna would never be travelling on that ship again.

"I doubt if my daughter will need many more things. I'm sure we are now well prepared for any emergency," answered Mr. Martin in a tight, subdued voice.

"Good, good. I'm looking forward to this wedding. How soon is it to be?"

"In three months. If all goes as planned."

"Well, sir," said Rosemond with a mirthless chuckle, "I do hope everything goes as you plan then."

There were several seconds of silence; then the

governor rose. "Come, Lieutenant, we have a great deal of work to do. Good day, Mr. Martin. Good day, Mr. Deverall."

When Mr. Martin had shown out his two guests, he returned to the library. His face was ashen and his hand trembled as he poured himself a stiff drink. It seemed to calm him slightly and he turned to Matt.

"Well, I'm sorry Deborah is out, Matt. She will be sorry to have missed you."

"There is no more use of pretense for my sake, Mr. Martin," he said softly. "Deanna came to my house last night. She wants to see you; that's why I'm here, to bring you to her."

"Then you understand," he said, and with a deep exhausted sigh he dropped into a chair. "You will help us. I told her you would."

"Don't misunderstand, Mr. Martin. I won't betray you, but I won't help you either. All I want to do is get Deanna out of this whole mess. Then we can forget all this and start a new life . . . together."

Chapter Twelve

The two men contemplated each other in silence. Matt faced him with a grim determination which the older man understood and sympathized with. There was a closeness between father and daughter that was extraordinary. He knew how Deanna felt about her family obligations, and her deep and abiding love for her country. He also knew that Matt did not understand these things yet.

"Matt, tell me, why did you leave a comfortable home in England to come here?"

The sudden change of subject caught Matt by surprise, and his face lost some of its fierce determined look as he answered.

"I was the second son in the family. Although my father loved me, there was no way he would alter tradition. When he died, he left everything to Jason."

"Well, why didn't you stay and let your brother support you? After all, it should rightly have been shared, should it not?"

"I don't want any charity from my brother. What I do and what I become depends on me, and me alone. I want to build something with my own hands that belongs to me."

"And if you have sons, Matt, what do you want for them?"

"I want them to be able to achieve whatever they are

101

capable of. Why are you asking me all these things, sir? If you think I couldn't do well for Deanna, I assure you I will."

The older man chuckled. "I have no fears for Deanna. She is an independent girl with excellent judgment. If she chose you, I would never question her. She would have my sincere blessings. How long have you known her?"

Matt became hesitant. Then he began at the beginning and told him of falling in love with her on the boat and the subsequent meeting at the ball, at which the twinkle in Mr. Martin's eyes became mirth.

"Deanna was so sure you would never know who she was. We had been telling her so many things about you, she wanted to meet you. It seems you upset her slightly and she forgot the questions she was going to ask."

Matt smiled, thinking of the feel of her in his arms the night of the ball, and the more recent feelings.

"I'll take good care of her, Mr. Martin. Be assured of that."

"Matt, talk things over with her. Find out her feelings. I'll go along with whatever she decides. If you will agree to do the same."

"I will. We can get married and this game will be over for her."

"It's not a game, Matt. It's a matter of life and death. The life of a country and an ideal."

"All the same, if you'll forgive me, sir, I want Deanna out of it and safe."

"Then you'll abide by Deanna's decision?"

"Yes, sir," Matt said firmly, sure in his heart that she would be with him forever.

"Well, I guess we'd better get over there. I'm sure

Deanna must be impatient by now."

They rose to their feet and went out to the stables. They were waiting for Mr. Martin's horse to be saddled when the sound of approaching hoofbeats cut the air.

Deborah rode up and dismounted. Approaching the two of them she smiled brightly.

"Good afternoon, Father. Matt. How are you all today?"

"Much relieved, Deborah," answered Matt rather laconically.

Deborah cast him an inquisitive look. "Relieved?"

"Yes, I'm glad Vern isn't angry with me."

Now she was completely at a loss.

"Why should Vern be angry with you, Matt?"

"After the ball I was sure I would be challenged to a duel, at least."

Deborah swallowed with difficulty and became embarrassingly flustered. "Oh, the ball."

Not being able to hold back their mirth any longer, both men laughed loudly.

"Matt has Deanna at Foxmore, Deborah." Her father came to her rescue.

Deborah smiled with relief, "Oh, I'm so glad she finally came to see you. Is everything all right?"

"It couldn't be better," he said so heartily that both father and daughter exchanged laughing glances.

"We're on our way now. Deborah, do you want to come along?"

"Yes, I should like to."

They mounted their horses and made for Foxmore. When they arrived at Foxmore, Deanna was waiting for them on the porch, but she was not alone. Two men were there also. One sat on the porch step with a rifle laid across his lap. He was fairly young, about thirty. He was slight of build, but wiry. His eyes were bright and intelligent. He did not speak, and Matt watched him closely with rising curiosity and a sudden feeling of dread. The other man had been deep in conversation with Deanna, and stopped speaking in mid-sentence when they rode up.

Deanna's face brightened with an inner light when Matt walked toward her. She extended her hand to him and he took it tightly in his. He had the sudden feeling that if he didn't hold tightly to her now, he was going to lose her. Deanna's father walked up the steps and stood beside her. She moved to him and kissed him on the cheek with a light touch of her lips. "Father, I must speak to you." She whispered so that only he could hear. With a quick nod of his head, he turned to face the two men.

"David, John. It is good to see you safely here. How goes everything?"

Both men looked at Matt and did not answer.

"It's all right," Mr. Martin said. "He can be trusted. He may not exactly be one of us but he will not betray us. Right, Matt?"

Matt nodded his head, but still the men hesitated before they spoke. Then finally the older one said. "You're the new owner of Foxmore, aren't you?"

"Yes, I am," answered Matt.

"You've a lovely place here. Do you really appreciate what you've got?"

"I think so. This is going to be my home from now on. I intend to stay here and rebuild Foxmore to what it should be." Matt bristled slightly at the man's questions. "Why is it that you all feel I should be enthusiastic about this just because I have a respect and appreciation of my own possessions. I have no intention of betraying you and my word has always been good, but I have no intention of joining you. I don't understand and I have no intention of trying to. Foxmore is a home I intend to build on and live in peace and raise my family. I want no help from anyone, and I don't want to get involved in local disagreements."

"Local disagreements!" The man's eyes glittered with amusement. When he smiled at Matt his pained features took on a sudden change that made him look suddenly young and friendly. He extended his hand, "I'm John McMahon, Mr. Deverall. I'm pleased to meet you."

Matt smiled in return a little sheepishly and extended his hand. The handshake was firm and strong and Matt suddenly found himself warming to the man. Then John turned to Mr. Martin. "Things are going passably well, sir. We've brought some dispatches down. I was told we'd have to wait here for answers. We also heard some more rumors about Rosemond. I think he's going to try to move in on some places around here. If he had any suspicion about you and the girls, you're going to be the first."

"Don't worry, John," smiled Mr. Martin. "We're watching his every move closely." He began to chuckle again. "You might say we have spies on his spies. Now, if you gentlemen will excuse me for just a few minutes, I'll read those dispatches and give you your answers. Deanna would you come in with me, please?"

"Of course, Father." She disengaged her hand from Matt, who let her go very reluctantly. Then she entered the house with her father and shut the door firmly.

Deborah gave Matt a strange quiet look, but none of them spoke for quite some time. It was Deborah who finally broke the strained silence. "Did you have any trouble this trip, John?"

"No, ma'am, Miss Deborah. We slipped in real quiet-like. The only times I worry about getting there and back is when we have Miss . . ." He caught himself and closed his mouth firmly, looking in Matt's direction.

"You mean when you have Deanna with you, right?" questioned Matt.

The two men looked at each other and then cast a helpless look at Deborah.

"Matt," Deborah said reproachfully. "Deanna has made several trips north, as have I and my father. We may have to make several more. If it is necessary for us to do so, we will."

"I want Deanna out of this. She's been through enough. I know about your mother and brother. If I get the help of my brother, Lord Jason Deverall, we can get them out of England. Once they're home, Deanna and I can marry and stay at Foxmore. I want Deanna out of this," he added vehemently.

"Matt, there's more to this than Mother and David. We believe in this country. We believe in being free. Isn't there some way we can make you understand?"

"No, not as long as Deanna's happiness is involved."

"Do you think Deanna could ever be happy if she turned her back now when she's needed? If you do, you don't understand her very well. We do more than look alike, Matt, we think alike. Deanna loves her country and to win our freedom she would sacrifice herself willingly, as would my father and I and these men. There is freedom for ourselves and our children at stake, and we will fight for it with everything in our power."

Somehow the words seemed to echo the ones her father had spoken to him earlier. "And what do you want for your children, Matt?"

Matt remembered a document Deanna had given him to read. She had called it their Declaration of Independence. It was a remarkable document, all things considered. Its style terse and its reasoning direct. There were some generalities in it that he was sure could be challenged. "It is certainly strange," he thought, that men should declare it is self-evident, "that all men were created equal" and that among their inalienable rights are "life, liberty, and the pursuit of happiness," while at that time there were some six-hundred thousand slaves in the country. "But in spite of this," he thought, "the Declaration was a powerful document." It appealed directly to the people in a way he could understand.

Ideas began to writhe about in his head. He did not know enough of the situation yet, but he could feel the dedication of these people and he wanted to try to understand. He wanted so badly at that moment to have Deanna alone and feel her arms about his neck, to feel that everything was going to be all right. Somehow, the feeling of dread settled itself on his shoulders. And refused to be shrugged away.

At that moment, the door opened and Deanna and her father came out onto the porch. Mr. Martin handed a packet of papers to John McMahon.

"Here are your answers, John. You and David stay here tonight and tomorrow. By tomorrow night, you can get ready to leave. Everything you will be taking along

107

will be ready to go by then."

Matt's eyes had not left Deanna's face for a moment, but her eyes were downcast and did not meet his. He knew the reason for his feeling of dread. She was going with them. He knew this with the same sureness as he knew he would try everything in his power to stop her.

Chapter Thirteen

Deborah and her father, after giving instructions to John and David, left again for Clearhaven. The two men melted away silently with a whispered final word to Deanna. Then they stood alone on the porch. He walked up behind her and put both arms about her waist, pulling her back tightly against him. She leaned against him, holding her hands over his as he buried his face in her hair. They stood this way for a few minutes before either of them felt safe to speak.

"Deanna." It was just a quiet whisper of her name.

"Matt, we have to talk. I must try to explain to you."

His stomach became a hard knot and he suddenly found it difficult to breathe. He wanted to cry out to her, "Don't go Deanna, I love you. I need you here where I know you're safe." But he also knew deep down that if he demanded she stay and would not listen to her she would fade away as quietly as she had come into his life and he may never see her again. He was determined to try to understand what she was going to say. Maybe there was something he could do to keep her from going.

They went inside and sat together on the couch. He tried to take her in his arms again but she put both hands against his chest. "Wait, Matt. Let me talk to you, please. It's so important to me for you to understand."

He moved slightly away from her and dropped his

hands in his lap. "All right, Deanna, I'm listening."

"Are you really, Matt, really listening. Listen with your heart, Matt," she pleaded. She slipped to her knees in front of him and looked up into his eyes. "I want to try to explain so much to you in such a short time," she began. "My father belongs to the Committee of Correspondence. He is part of a chain of patriots that are devoted heart and soul to the freedom of our country."

"Don't you see the impossibility of all this, Deanna?" he said seriously. "There are so very few of you, and you are so ill-equipped, so poorly led. It could only end one way."

"Matt, you're taking into consideration only the material things. Can't you feel the strength beneath all this? Can't you sense the desire for freedom, for being the guardians of our own destinies? Look at yourself, Matt. Without realizing it, you are the greatest example of what we're fighting for. It would have been so easy for you to stay in England at your wealthy estate and live off of your brother, but you have an independent spirit. You must guide and control your own future. Can't you sympathize with us? Can't you feel what we feel? Can't you try to put away all your old way of thinking and listen to the beat of this new flame that's beginning to burn so brightly?"

He wanted to understand, he desperately wanted to, but his logical thinking mind could not let him accept the success in such an unevenly balanced confrontation. She realized this and her eyes grew sad, but her chin lifted.

"I have to go, Matt."

"Why, Deanna, why you?"

"Word must be kept moving so that all our leaders know what is happening. There is a meeting in Philadelphia. I must inform the next link in our chain. It is impossible for Father to go. Governor Rosemond watches his every move. He is trying to confiscate our property for being traitors. Also as long as Mother and David remain in England, Father's hands are hopelessly tied. They know me. They cannot trust anyone now. It has to be someone they know."

"Couldn't I carry some form of identification from you and go myself?" asked Matt desperately. He was beginning to understand, and she was slipping away from him.

"No, Matt," she said softly. "There is another thing I would ask of you. Something very dear to my heart."

"What?"

"I want you to go back to England."

He gave a sudden start. "No! Never, while you're still here. This is my home."

A slight smile played about the corners of her mouth.

"Not to stay, Matt. I'm too selfish for that. But to see if you and your brother can bring the rest of my family home. If my mother and brother were here it would release me for my father would be free to move and he could make these trips himself."

"I can't do it, Deanna, I can't just leave you here not knowing where you'll be and what you'll be doing."

She placed both hands on each side of his face and touched his mouth gently with her own.

"I shall make this one final trip, then return here. I promise you it will be the last one and I shall wait here for your return. Matt, I love you, and I want to be your wife so desperately for all the world to see. But I cannot sacrifice others to my desires. The others that I sacrifice might be our own sons. If we give them nothing else along

111

with life, Matt, let us at least give them freedom."

He was beaten and he knew it. With a small choked sound he gathered her into his arms. There was no exultation in her winning, for she also felt a desperate desire to remain in his arms and forget everything else.

"We still have the rest of today, tonight and tomorrow," she said softly. "There is a ship waiting in a small hidden cove across the river to carry you to England. David and John will not leave until tomorrow night."

"You'll stay with me?" he asked huskily.

"Oh, yes, Matt, my love," she sobbed as his mouth claimed hers in an agonizing kiss. She was weak and filled with desire for him as he was for her. There was no necessity for words. Together they climbed the stairs to their small sanctuary. There they made love, first with a demanding passion and later with a gentleness that made her cry. They slept for some time and the black night was filled with a million stars when they awoke. Matt woke first. The room was very dark and he would have been happy to have it remain so for as long as possible. He could feel Deanna's soft breath on his arm. She was lying with her back to him and her soft warm body lay curved to fit his. His left arm was under her head and his right arm circled her waist. He closed his eyes and let his thoughts drift, content to hold her as long as possible. It was some time before he noticed the slight change in her breathing. She was awake and trying not to waken him.

"I love you," he whispered softly.

She turned about so that she faced him. He could not see her in the dark but he could feel the warmth of her. She raised her arms and clasped them about his neck bringing his head down to hers. Her lips were warm and moist under his and he kissed her slowly and thoroughly. She moved against him and his hands sought her, exploring and caressing until he brought a soft sighing gasp of pleasure from her. Then his lips completed what his hands had begun. Soon they moved together and he entered her moving slowly. He wanted to savor every moment of her for as long as possible. Then suddenly they were both lost in the magic of the moment and she thrust up to meet him in an engulfing passion that left him breathless. He held her to him and they shared a moment of blinding fury and all-possessing love.

They lay together and talked for the remaining hours until dawn. He told her of his life before her and she told him of hers. They laughed and cried together and tried to push a lifetime of memories into a few short hours. Then long before either of them were ready to greet it, the sun sent its long exploring tentacles into the early morning sky.

"What shall we do with this day, Matt?" she asked. "Let's not waste a precious moment of it."

"Why don't we pack some food and ride to the hills. We can travel up there in safety. We'll picnic there, then maybe stop at the cabin and see Cat and Deeta. I want them to meet you. They're a very important part of my family."

"Wonderful idea, Matt. I'll get up now and make you something to eat and pack a lunch. We can leave in an hour or so. By the time we get to the cabin, it will be lunch time. We'll share lunch with Cat and Deeta."

"If we skip breakfast," he said wickedly, "we could stay in bed another hour."

"Insatiable beast," she said in mock horror. "Do you want to spend our last day in bed?"

113

"Sounds like a wonderful idea to me," he said suggestively. "I'm sure we could find something to do?" She laughed and wriggled free of his arms. He watched her rise from the bed and pick up her hastily scattered clothes. She moved slowly and gracefully, unashamed of her nakedness, knowing he was watching her and happy in the pleasure it brought him.

"Madam, you had better dress or leave this room shortly or you'll find yourself flat on your back again," he grinned. She stuck out her tongue at him as she wriggled into the last of her clothes.

"You would have to catch me first," she laughed, "and frankly, I don't think you have the strength."

He gave a mock shout of anger and made as if to leap from the bed. She gave a light shriek and ran from the room. His laughter followed her down the stairs. She was humming softly to herself when he finally came downstairs. He had slipped on only his pants. Now he sat down at the table. "I'm famished," he said.

"I can imagine," she said. "You've certainly used up any reserve energy you must have had."

He leered at her evilly. "Madam, I've only begun. I've a vast reserve of unused energy I'm simply dying to use."

"Eat, Matt," she laughed. "I may take you up on that threat later."

He moved to stand up and she came and placed both hands on his shoulders, pushing him back down in the chair.

"I'm going to fill the tub and take a bath," she laughed. "If you eat quickly, beast, you could join me."

He was absolutely certain that he had never eaten a meal so quickly in his life or with such a rapidly diminishing appetite. It couldn't have been fifteen minutes before he rose from the table and went to the bottom of the steps. He climbed them quickly, two at a time and entered the room. She had filled the large wooden tub with water and was busy soaping herself when he came in. She made a lovely sight, her round creamy breasts with the taut pink nipples standing just at the water line. He watched as a soft pile of soapy bubbles cascaded down her shoulders and floated slowly to the water. Her hair had been pinned up on her head in a knot and a few tendrils lay wet against her neck. She smiled at him. "I'll be out in a moment and it's all yours." But by the time the words had left her lips, he had already dropped the pants and was climbing in beside her. She giggled with delight as he took the bar of soap from her and began to lather his hands. Then he dropped the soap and slowly moved his hands over her shoulders and breasts, lingering on the nipples with the tips of his fingers. She looked up at him in amazed delight and reached for the soap. She lathered her hands as he had done and began to play them over his body. By the time she had covered most of his large frame with soap they were both past worrying about the cleanness of the bath. He sat down in the tub and pulled her over onto his lap. Now his hands covered her body in a slippery eagerness and she let herself lay against him. He sought her mouth again and again leaving her gasping and weak. When he knew he could stand the beautiful agony no longer, he rose from the tub and lifted her with him. They stood together for a moment, then with a quick bend of his knees, he lifted her dripping body from the water and stepped out of the tub and walked to the bed.

"Matt, you'll ruin the bed," she whispered as he lowered her on it.

115

"To hell with the bed," he groaned as he brought her body firmly against his. His hands kneaded and caressed her until she cried out. Never had they reached the heights as they now did. Theirs was a giving and sharing that neither had ever experienced before, and it left them breathless and amazed at the wonder of it. When they finally rose from the bed, there was a gentle quietness between them. They had shared a miracle between them and they were so in rhythm with one another that words were unnecessary. They took the packed lunch and rode toward the hills. They would be on Matt's property all the way to Cat's cabin. As they climbed higher the air became fresher and a scented breeze floated down from the deeply forested hills. Cat's cabin sat nestled against the hillside surrounded by trees. If Deanna had not known the way they could easily have been lost. They tied their horses in front of the cabins and gave a shout. Within a few minutes the door was flung open and Cat emerged.

"Matt!" he shouted happily. "I thought you'd forgotten I was alive." He stopped shouting when he saw who was with him. For a few minutes he stood dumbfounded, then he gave a wild shout of pure joy. Deeta came to the cabin door and smiled, watching her husband and Matt pounding each other on the back and laughing. After they had finally settled down, Matt walked over and helped Deanna dismount. They entered the cabin and Matt whistled with admiration. Deeta and Cat had been working hard every day. He had put together furniture which they had rubbed and polished to a high glow. The floor was the same, reflecting the light of the fireplace. There were bright covers over everything and flowers in profusion. It looked like the home of a very happy woman.

The camaraderie that existed between Matt and his friend made it easy and comfortable for the two women to get acquainted. In a very short time, they were discussing and chattering over everything in the house, becoming friends. Cat motioned to Matt with a slight twist of his head and both men excused themselves and left the cabin. At the side of his porch was a deep well, and grasping a rope that was attached to the side with a grin, Cat pulled up a jug. Producing two cups from inside his shirt, he poured a drink for each of them. Matt lifted his to Cat. "Here's to you and Deeta."

Cat lifted his cup also. "Here's to the story you're about to tell me, and it better be good." They laughed and drank together then sat down on the steps as Matt began talking.

Chapter Fourteen

Cat watched his friend very closely as he talked, shaking his head now and then, but not interrupting. Finally when Matt had brought him up to date, he heaved a sigh and leaned back against the wall.

"Well, Matt, what are you going to do?"

Matt shrugged helplessly. "When we go home tonight I'm boarding the ship for England to get Jason's help. I've no doubt we can get her family home. There is only one thing I'm afraid of."

"What's that?"

"It should take Deanna about three weeks to make the trip to Williamsburg and back. She'll return home at least two weeks before I get back. I don't want her to be there alone . . . Cat . . . would you and Deeta consider staying at Foxmore for a short time? I can't trust anyone else. If Rosemond finds there are two girls, he'll be on Mr. Martin before he can get to her. I need someone to protect her for me."

"Matt, you know you can count on Deeta and me. There isn't anything you could ask that we wouldn't do. You know we're only here and happy because of you. If Deanna needs protection, she'll get all she needs. We'll move in the day she comes home."

Matt gave him a quick look of gratitude. "Thank you, Cat. I knew I could depend on you."

"Well, we'd both better get back inside or I have an idea it'll be me that'll need protection." Cat laughed but it was the easy laugh of a man who was sure of his life. For a few minutes, Matt looked at his friend in envy. This is what he wanted for himself and Deanna. This freedom to live as he chose; to ask no one for anything; to have the ones he loved close at hand. He felt he was on the edge of a great discovery, but it slipped away from him leaving him strangely empty and filled with gnawing desire.

They both rose hastily as the door opened and Deeta stuck her smiling face out. "If you gentlemen are hungry, come in and eat. If you want to get drunk stay out there."

"Used to be, I could have a little drink in peace," grumbled Cat with a twinkle of laughter in his eyes. "Now you see, you get attached to a woman, and first thing she does is take away your pleasures in life."

"If that's your greatest pleasure, Cat," giggled Deeta, "you can sleep out there tonight by your jug." She ended the last word with a shrill squeal as Cat grabbed her up in his arms and swung her around laughing.

"No, thanks, woman, in your bed is where I belong and in your bed is where I'll stay."

He sat her down reluctantly and Deeta knew if it weren't for Matt and Deanna's presence, it would have ended a different way. She cast a flustered embarrassed look at Matt and Deanna, who laughed heartily in return, sharing a promising glance of their own.

The rest of the day was filled with laughter. They had gone walking in the woods and Cat had shown them a beautiful view of the river from the top of the hill. Deeta and Deanna had gone on ahead to prepare for their departure while the two men walked slowly back.

"Matt, you've been very quiet. What's troubling you?"

Matt shrugged. Then he answered slowly after much thought. "I wish I understood and could give Deanna the support she really needs, Cat. I just can't feel so fired up about a little group of colonies that in all probability would be better off if they stayed as they were."

Cat nodded in response. There was no way for him to explain to his friend a lack of freedom since he had never felt it. Cat felt slightly sorry for Matt.

"Give it time, Matt. Try to help her as much as your conscience will allow. Maybe when you least expect it, it will come to you."

Matt shook his head slightly. "I hope so, I hope when she really needs me, I'm there."

When the evening sun was just nestling comfortably behind the hills and gently releasing its hold on the day, the four of them sat on Cat's front porch silently watching the beauty of it. Both Matt and Deanna were reluctant to move. They had sat close to one another and now she dropped her head on his shoulder with a sigh. He slipped his arm about her waist and pulled her close to him. They sat quietly for some time until the bright flicker of fireflies could plainly be seen through the trees.

"We have to go, Matt," she said softly.

"I know, I know," he answered.

They both stood up and turned to Cat and Deanna.

"I want to thank you for one of the loveliest days of my life," said Deanna.

Cat smiled at her. "We enjoyed having you. When you can, whenever you're free, come back."

"Thank you, Cat. I will."

Deeta placed a shy kiss on her cheek and turned to

120

Matt, rising on tiptoe she kissed his cheek also. "I wish you both as much happiness together as you've given us. May God keep you and bring you back."

"Thank you, Deeta," said Matt. Then he extended his hand to Cat, who grasped it and held it firmly.

Matt helped Deanna mount and they rode most of the way back in silence. They were almost down from the hills and on the fringe of the forest when he realized that they had not spoken a word for over an hour. He reined in his horse for a moment and stopped to look at her. When they got home there would be no more time to talk, they would be separated for weeks. As he turned to look at her, the moon moved from behind the clouds and cast a golden glow over her face. She was crying softly so that he would not know. The look in her eyes when she found him watching made the sharp pain in his chest even worse. Without saying a word, he dismounted and walked to her side. She looked down at him. Then he lifted his arms to her and she leaned into them, allowing him to bring her slowly to the ground.

"There is no time, Matt," she murmured through her tears. But still he brought his mouth to hers, and cupping her face in his hands, he kissed away the tears and found her trembling lips again and again.

"Remembering this might make the waiting a little easier. I'll be back as fast as I can. Remember you promised to wait for me at home. Deanna, if you aren't there, I'll come after you no matter where you are, do you understand?"

"Yes, Matt."

"I love you, Deanna."

"And I love you, Matt."

He lifted her again to her horse and they rode the rest

of the way home in silence.

David and John were already waiting for her. She dismounted and bade them wait until she changed and ran into the house. Within a few minutes, she was back wearing a shirt and pants, strong boots and a rather large black hat with her hair stuffed under it. Matt smiled at the picture she made.

"My darling," he laughed. "There is no possible way on God's earth to make you look like a boy."

She gave a throaty chuckle, and placing her hands on her hips she tilted her head to the side and looked at him, "For your information sir, this outfit is for riding purposes. Don't you think I'd even pass as a boy in the dark, Matt?"

He stepped closer and whispered quickly in her ear. "I'd never mistake you for a boy whether it is dark or light. Try me and see."

She pushed him away laughing. John McMahon helped her on her horse and she leaned down to kiss Matt gently.

"Captain Duprey will be here to pick you up first thing in the morning, my love," she said softly. "I'll see you in a month. I'll be waiting."

"I'll be here. One month from tonight, and you'll never get away from me again. That I promise you."

One more fleeting smile and she was gone. He watched them ride away until he could not even hear the sound of their horses. Then he returned to their room. He stood in the doorway and looked at the room. The tub of water was still sitting there, and the bed was still damp and rumpled. He knew it would be impossible for him to spend a night in this room without her. Taking a blanket he went to the parlor and stretched out on the couch to face the dream-filled nightmare of the night.

He was up very early the next morning after having tossed and turned through the few short hours. Captain Duprey had arrived at dawn and they had left wordlessly for the ship. There was a small boat moored at the Foxmore dock. Matt questioned Captain Duprey. "We're not going to row clear to the ocean, are we?"

Captain Duprey smiled. "Didn't Deanna tell you about the cove?"

"She may have, I've forgotten."

"There's a cove across the river and down a couple miles. You can't see it unless you know it's there. Its entrance is covered with hanging trees." They rowed in silence. The Captain began to inch his way toward shore, and when he was a few feet away he gave a soft low whistle. As if by magic the branches of the trees along the side of the river raised and allowed them to slip through to a large cove where the ship lay drifting at anchor.

When they were on board, Matt watched in fascination as they gently maneuvered the ship out of the cove by attaching it to the small boat, and with six men rowing, literally pulled it out. They drifted slowly downstream. The Captain seemed to know the depths of the river very well.

At Matt's inquisitive questions, the Captain laughed. "My boy, I know this river like the back of my hand. I was born and raised around here, lived on the riverbank almost all my life. I could probably take you up and down with my eyes closed. We're going to lie at anchor just this side of the town so we can't be seen. When night comes we'll slip through and old Rosemond won't even know we've been here."

It was almost noon when the Captain gave the order to drop the anchor. If his calculations were right they should be about ten miles from town. There was a curve in the river and all Matt could see was an abundance of trees.

"Care to join me for some lunch, Matt?"

"Yes, sir." He realized he had not eaten since they had shared a meal at Cat's cabin. They went to the Captain's cabin where the meal he had ordered was waiting. For a few minutes, they ate in silence. Then Matt began to question him. When the questions began he found he could not stop. He was hungry for anything that would help him understand Deanna and her cause. The Captain was only too happy to give him all the information he wanted. They sat opposite each other over the table, with good wine and cigars, and the Captain began to fill in the answers he knew Matt was seeking. "It should be remembered, Matt," he laughed, "that in all his history, the Englishman has hated nothing more than taxation. The struggle with the kings over the right of taxation has lasted for centuries. Also remember that the colonists are Englishmen. They claim the rights, privileges, and immunities of Englishmen under their charters. They object, for one thing, to the exercise of the taxing power in a body which in no sense represents them."

Matt watched the Captain's face and heard his voice deep with conviction, and the logical part of his mind could accept this idea.

"Our legislators opposed this. Unfortunately, the opposition was not wholly dignified or peaceable. In places there were riots, property was destroyed, officials threatened."

"There have always been unwelcome taxes, even at home."

"Agreed. The struggle that came with the colonies

benefitted the English people as much as our own, for reforms were gradually acquired. The stamp act here was a failure not only because the people objected to taxation in the form laid, but also because in cases arising out of it trial by jury was denied, probably because it was feared local sentiments would prevent convictions."

"Is that all that started this?"

"No, in '67 Parliament passed three acts. These did more to start everything than any other laws. The worst of them was the one that laid direct taxes on tea, glass, paper, paints and some other articles that were imported into the colonies. Then, another was that we had to quarter the royal troops." The Captain poured another drink and began to chuckle. "I must tell you a story about one of the incidents involving the tax on tea. It was a jumbled affair because just before it happened, Parliament repealed all taxes except three pence per pound on tea. Now the previous export duty of twelve pence per pound was taken off so that tea was actually nine pence cheaper than formerly. Some leading men in the town, disguised as Indians, boarded a vessel in '73 and threw all the tea overboard."

Matt laughed along with the Captain at the vision constructed before his mind's eye.

"Well, it's funny now but it sure damaged the dignity of the crown. Officers came to search, carrying their search everywhere, even beyond the limits described in their warrants. This, my friend, was an invasion of the cherished belief of the Englishman that his house is his castle."

Matt went on listening, more and more attentive as the days passed. By the time they picked up the English shoreline, Matt was as well informed as any man could be and he was also feeling the stirrings of something in his own freedom-loving soul.

After they docked, he hired a carriage and within an hour he was at his brother's home. The greeting he received almost knocked him off his feet. His brother Jason had seen him coming and threw open the door. Throwing his arms about him, he had shouted and pounded him so hard that Matt was gasping for air. "Jas, for God's sake," he laughed.

"Matt," shouted his brother. "It's so good to see you home. Are you staying? How was America? Where . . ."

"One thing at a time, Jas," he laughed. "No, I'm not staying. America is wonderful. I love my home there, and yes, it is good to see you."

"Come on in, let me get you a drink. Damn, but it's good to see you, Matt."

They went into the study and after they had shared a drink, Matt said seriously, "Jas, I can't stay long, only until Captain Duprey picks up supplies. Sit down and listen. I've got a long story to tell you and I desperately need your help."

Jason looked at his brother closely for the first time since his arrival. He had changed somehow; become more serious. There were worry lines between his dark, shadowed eyes. Jason dropped into a chair and waited patiently in silence. He wanted to know what could cause such a change in this fun-loving brother.

Chapter Fifteen

Deanna was exhausted, but she uttered no complaints. They had been travelling for over a week, pushing harder than they ever had before. If all went well, they would reach the outskirts of Williamsburg tonight. Then it was only a matter of a few hours before they made contact, left their information and started for home. She had never been so anxious to complete a mission in her life. She missed Matt so much that the thought of him made her ache and left her tossing and turning in wild dreams at night. John finally pulled in his horse. With a quiet whisper he said, "We'll stop here. You two stay here, and I'll ride on in and see how everything is. I should be back in an hour."

As quiet as a summer breeze, he was gone. Deanna and David dismounted and tied their horses in the shelter of some trees. They were both too tired for conversation and merely sat on the ground with their backs against the tree and closed their eyes to rest. It seemed to her that she had just closed her eyes when the soft clop of a horse came to her. They waited sitting silently until they heard a low whistle. David gave an answering whistle and they remounted their horses and met John on the road. "They're waiting for us," whispered John. "We'll leave the main road now. You both know the way across the fields. Keep a close eye now, the place is overrun with British."

"What's going on, John?" she asked softly.

"I don't have time to explain now, Deanna. You'll hear it all when we get in. Seems all hell broke loose. Let's get started."

They cut across fields and followed paths that only they knew. After an hour of heart-stopping travel, they arrived at the back of a small house that sat on the edge of town. The house was dark, but John's soft whistle was answered almost immediately. They left their horses under the trees and moved swiftly to the door that was opened on their arrival. They slipped inside and for the first time in hours, Deanna breathed a sigh of relief.

Curtains were pulled across the windows to make the house appear dark from outside. Inside there was a fire burning in the fireplace, which gave the only light in the room. A short, plump woman rose from a chair beside it and went to Deanna. It was plain to see the effects of sorrow on her face, for her eyes were puffy and red with weeping.

"What has happened, Mrs. Monroe? Where is Paul? Where is Steven?"

Fresh tears rolled down her face and she sobbed softly in her throat. "Dead. My son, my husband . . . dead . . . both dead."

Deanna gasped in painful sympathy. "Oh my God! When, where, how?" she asked.

Another woman had been seated before the fire, unspeaking. Now she rose and went to the older woman. "Come, Mama, let me put you to bed. I'll take care of things here." She put her arm about the older woman's shaking shoulders and led her out of the room.

Now they turned their attention to the one remaining

128

person in the room. "What happened?" asked Deanna.

The man's face was gray from fatigue and he slumped into a chair before he spoke.

"Me and Paul were goin' up to Lexington to carry some dispatches. It was just a routine trip so Paul decided to let Steven come along since he always wanted to go so badly. When we got there, there was a big stir goin' on. We didn't know exactly what was happenin'. When we started circulatin' we found all the men gathered, they was expectin' the British any minute. Then they came." He paused for a moment and she could see by his eyes that there was pain in the remembering. When he resumed speaking his voice was low and hoarse. "I swear to God, ma'am, nobody meant to fire on 'em. I don't even know where the shot came from. I only know what come after was horrible. We had to keep fallin' back and firing. Me and Paul grabbed Steven, all we wanted was to get back home. Get the hell out of there. We was runnin'." He sobbed. "We was runnin' when they got hit. I seen 'em go down and I knew they was dead before they hit the ground. I ran until I didn't have any strength left. Then I waited. After dark, I went back. The British had swept on through toward Concord. I searched until I found where they took Paul and Steven. Then I got a wagon and brought them home. I just got here a few hours before you."

The man dropped his face in his hands and his body shook with the shock and pain of what had happened.

"What about the dispatches?" asked John quietly.

The man raised his head with a surprised look on his face. He reached in his pocket and withdrew a packet wrapped in oilcloth.

"My God, who do I deliver these to now? Our contact

129

is broken in Lexington. What do I do with these?"

Deanna reached out her hand with a gentle smile on her face. "Give them to me. I'll see they're delivered in Boston where these I'm carrying are also going."

He looked at her with doubt in his eyes for several minutes.

"You're exhausted and they need you here for a while. We'll go on to Boston and deliver both packets." She spoke softly but with such confidence that he handed the packets to her.

As she rose from the man's side, John dropped his hand to her shoulder. "What about your man? Ain't he going to expect you to be home when he gets there? How you going to get word to him?"

She faltered for a moment, then she looked at him with moist eyes.

"I love him, John, but he must understand. This is a thing I must do. I could not face myself again if after men had died, I turned away for my own selfishness."

She smiled gently at him and touched his arm. "And I believe that Matt will understand, I love him. I believe I know him, maybe better than he knows himself. But whatever happens, I must do this. You understand, John?"

He nodded his head and patted her gently on the shoulder with a gruff gentleness that brought fresh tears to her eyes.

"I'll go see to the horses. If you want, we can leave just before daybreak. We'll have to take it a lot slower now after what's happened."

She nodded her head and went to the chair by the fireplace. She leaned her head back against the back of the chair and closed her eyes. John stood and watched

130

her for a moment, his eyes filled with pity. Then he went out with David and closed the door behind them.

She dropped into a semi-sleep. The dreams came as they always did when she had a quiet moment. She wondered if she would see Matt soon again, if she would be able to explain so he would understand. The thoughts drove themselves around in her mind so furiously that she woke with a start and for the rest of the night remained watching the fire.

John came back in just before the first streaks of daylight could extend into full day. Deanna was still seated beside the now cold fire. It seemed to him she hadn't moved since he had left. It hurt him to see her like this but he said nothing.

"Are we ready to leave, John?"

"Yes, it's time. We have to be away before full day."

"I must say good-bye to Mrs. Monroe."

"She's asleep finally, Deanna," he said. "Best leave her sleep as long as possible. They're goin' to bury Paul and Steven today. She needs her rest."

Deanna nodded and her eyes filled with tears. It was the first time in her life she felt almost unable to go on, and it was her first doubts of the rightness of what she was doing. She shook herself free of the mood and stood up. She could go back now and meet Matt and her life would be good. The temptation was so great that she turned to look at John with the words on her lips. Then she thought of Mrs. Monroe and her sacrifices and she straightened her shoulders and with a slight smile at John passed him and walked out the door toward her horse.

They rode in silence keeping away from the main roads. John knew the country well and they had no trouble. There were houses set up along the way for them to stop and rest and eat. Deanna travelled as rapidly as possible. When they did stop, she could not seem to rest but paced back and forth. John was worried about the small amount of food she ate. After a week of this he finally approached her.

"Deanna, I don't mean you no wrong, you know that. But you can't go on like you're doin'. You won't be any use to anyone especially yourself if you push until you collapse. Besides," he chuckled, "your pa will string me up like a side of beef if I let anyone hurt you—even yourself."

It was a long speech for John, but he looked resolutely into her eyes the entire time he spoke. For a while she just looked at him; then her numb mind accepted the words he spoke. She nodded her head and he reached up and helped her down from her horse. They had stopped at one of the designated places. The house was a small cabin outside of town nestled among some trees.

"You rest for a while, and I mean rest. I'm goin' to rustle you up something to eat and you're goin' to eat it. You're gettin' skinny," he smiled and patted her arm. She sat down on the porch and leaned her head back against the railing. It took some time before he had the food ready, but when he came back with it she was curled against the rail sound asleep. He set the dish down and lifted her slight form in his arms and carried her inside. He laid her gently on the bed and pulled the cover over her. "She's just a baby," he thought. "This goddamn war is goin' to ruin everything."

He went outside and sat on the porch eating the food he had made for her and waiting for her to waken. He allowed his thoughts to drift, mostly to the origin and reason for his involvement in this revolution. The whole issue, in his opinion, was one of method and had no reference to the "divine rights of kings." He hated the clash of opinions in America because, despite what most people in England, like Matt Deverall, believed, all people were not united in the revolution. This, he knew was true, and sometimes gave him serious doubts about their ability to win. The unanimity of feeling that existed before the first Continental Congress never existed afterward. It offered proof of the smallness of the Patriot army. Sometimes, like now, he felt that all their struggles could come to no good end. He wondered if Matt were right. Were they too small, too ill-equipped to win? He thought these things while he knew he would continue his struggle for what he believed in.

Chapter Sixteen

Matt stood at the rail and looked out over the waves toward home. The ship moved rapidly, as she was unladen by cargo and was sailing before the wind with all sails unfurled. Still, to Matt, it seemed they were barely moving as his heart raced on ahead to Deanna and to home. He suspected he hadn't felt happier in a long, long time. He chuckled to himself at the memory of his short time at home and what they had accomplished.

Getting his brother Jason to help him rescue the Martins was not difficult. Jason had always risen to this type of escapade. Their first job had been to locate exactly where they were held and how. It did not take Jason long to uncover this information. Then they began to plan just how they were going to get them out from under the noses of their captors.

Margaret and David Martin lived in a large home just outside of London. Because of his social position and his eligibility as a wealthy bachelor, Jason found every home open to him. It did not take him long to find a mutual friend who could arrange a meeting between himself, his brother, and Margaret Martin.

Jason and Matt rose to their feet as Margaret walked into the room. Matt was stunned at the resemblance between herself and her daughters. She watched both men closely, curious as to the reason for their visit, and wary enough to be careful of what she said. She had been under surveillance for so long that she no longer trusted anyone. Jason knew he had to quickly do something to make her understand why they were here and what their future intentions were.

"Good afternoon, gentlemen," she smiled. "I'm very pleased that you should call on me, Lord Deverall. But I can hardly understand why such a handsome young man would take the time to call on a poor old woman like myself."

Jason chuckled and Margaret's eyes sparkled in response. At possibly thirty-nine or forty, Jason thought, "poor or old" were two words that definitely did not describe Margaret Martin. Both of them knew that servants watched their every move and listened to every word they spoke. It was impossible for either Jason or Matt to tell her in these surroundings the real reason they were there.

After several compliments from them and some inconsequential conversation, Jason casually invited Margaret and her son to an afternoon of riding and an early supper at Deverall Hall on a day early in the following week.

Margaret accepted, and after they exchanged more pleasantries, Margaret was surprised that Jason lifted her hand to his lips and brushed it with a light kiss. Surprised until she felt the paper pressed into her palm by him. She smiled and bade them both farewell, clutching the message he had given her tightly in her palm and holding it against the folds of her gown. She could barely wait until night, when she was sure she was alone. Lighting one candle, she unfolded the piece of paper and read. Then with tears in her eyes, but a soft

135

smile playing over her lips, she touched the paper to the candle's flame and watched as it slowly disintegrated to a small pile of white ash.

When the day arrived, Margaret and her son, David, arrived at Deverall Hall in an open carriage so that anyone who wished could watch their every move. After they had been welcomed, they were shown into the small library where they came face to face with Matt and Jason's other guests. A woman and a young man who bore so close a resemblance to Margaret and her son that unless one was right beside them, they would be mistaken for David and his mother.

"Mrs. Martin," Jason laughed, "meet Mrs. Martin."

The woman extended her hand to Margaret. "I'm Ellen Macquire," she laughed, "and I'm as surprised at our resemblance as you are. Jason asked me to do him a favor, and I imagine I'm to pose as you temporarily."

"Just for this afternoon, Ellen," Jason replied.

"You'll ride with us and dine with us while they smuggle Mrs. Martin onto Captain Duprey's ship. Tonight you will leave here in the Martin carriage. From there on, the money I gave you and the carriage are yours."

The plan worked like a charm, and while Matt, Jason and Ellen and her son were riding under the eye of their watchers, David and Margaret were smuggled on board ship. Later that night Ellen left, and a few minutes after her departure Matt and Jason headed for the ship. Once there, Matt got another pleasant surprise.

"I'm going with you," Jason laughed. "It's dull around here, and you seem to be having all the fun. I've put everything up for sale and our attorney will handle it all and send the money. Now we both are making a

136

new start."

Matt was delighted, and he and Jason stood at the rail and watched England fade to a small line on the horizon with no regrets.

"I can't wait to meet Deanna. She must be a very beautiful woman and something very special to tame you."

"Oh, she's special, Jas. She's the most beautiful woman I've ever seen in my life."

"There speaks an unbiased opinion," laughed his brother. "I really think she must be if she looks like her mother, though."

Matt agreed Margaret Martin was simply an older version of her daughters, but she had the soft blue eyes of Deanna. Looking at her had made him long for home even more. As if in answer to his thoughts, Margaret Martin stepped through the companionway onto the deck. Seeing the two men at the rail she joined them.

"Good afternoon, sirs."

"Mrs. Martin," said Matt bowing slightly toward her. "Is everything well?"

"I'm a free woman going to join my husband after years of separation thanks to you. Everything could not possibly be better."

She smiled up at him and he remembered the soft smile on Deanna's lips the night they had parted. "I'll be waiting," she had said. He felt as though the ship were barely moving.

"I do hope we make the coastline by nightfall. I should hate to have to be out here at anchor for another day."

"What would happen if we are too early to go in?" Margaret questioned.

"Well," Matt said, "the Chesapeake is about one

137

hundred and ninety miles long and about twenty-five wide. We can just stay out far enough and drop anchor so they don't see us. Then, after nightfall, we'll slip past the town and up the James River before they can do anything. You'll be with your husband and daughters by daylight tomorrow."

"Ah, Mr. Deverall, you have no idea what that means . . ." She looked at him closely as his gaze lay on the horizon. "Or do you?"

"I do, Mrs. Martin. Believe me, I do. I have never had such a desire to be home in my whole life."

The hours passed slowly and Matt greeted the setting sun with enthusiasm. Now as the first stars began to glitter, the three of them watched as the crew skillfully maneuvered their black-sailed vessel through the mouth of the river. Within a few more hours, the soft whistle brought the lifting of the branches and they were safe in the cove once more. Without wasting any time, the small boat was dropped and the passengers were rowed back downriver toward Clearhaven. Mr. Martin's figure could be seen from a distance, pacing back and forth on the dock. When the boat finally came alongside he gave an exclamation of joy and reached for his wife and son.

The tearful reunion was a joy for Matt to see, for to him it meant Deanna's release and his happiness. He did not question the fact that Deanna was not there with Deborah and her father. He had wanted her to be at Foxmore when he came home and he thought that was where he would find her.

Deborah had remained strangely quiet and watchful. Seeing her made him long for Deanna even more. After their greeting of each other, Matt introduced his brother to Mr. Martin and Deborah.

"I don't know how I'll ever repay you for what you've done, Matt," said Mr. Martin. "You've given me a new lease on life. With Margaret and David here, we're free to do as we choose from now on."

Matt smiled and was about to speak when Jason interrupted him. "I imagine you have something Matt wants very much and I don't think he'll hesitate to ask for her."

Matt's face flushed slightly at Margaret Martin's quick look, but her smile eased him. "You and Deanna?" she asked.

"Yes, ma'am, I love her very much. I want her to be my wife as soon as I get home."

There was a silence that raised an alarm in Matt. Even his brother noticed the hesitation and the swiftly exchanged look between father and daughter. A sinking sensation struck him in the pit of the stomach and he felt a weak trembling in his knees.

"What is it, Mr. Martin? Has something happened to Deanna? Is she safe, where is she?" His voice cracked slightly in his fear. Somehow he knew what Mr. Martin was going to say and he didn't want to hear it.

"We can't talk here. We'll go home. Then Deborah and I can explain all that has happened."

Matt shook his head negatively. "Just tell me, is Deanna at Foxmore?"

"No, Matt, she isn't."

"She said she'd come right home, that this would be her last mission. She said she'd wait for me at home."

"Matt, believe me that was her greatest desire, but there are unforeseen things that happened. Things beyond our control. Matt, she would have been here if she could. Come home with us, let us tell you what happened. Together maybe we can do something to bring her home."

Mr. Martin took Matt's arm and guided him and the rest of the group toward the carriage. On the trip to Clearhaven Matt was silent. His mind was in a turmoil. The disappointment he felt was a physical thing. He could feel the tight ball of pain centered somewhere in his chest. It gave him a choking feeling in his throat so that though he had a million questions tearing apart his brain, he could not put words to any of them. He did not even notice the movements or conversation of the people around him. Mr. Martin was so engrossed in the presence of his wife and son after an absence of so many years that he almost totally ignored Jason. At any other time, Jason may have been verbally upset, but not tonight. Tonight he was completely absorbed in the presence of the black-haired, green-eyed, voluptuous beauty who sat opposite him and tried desperately to keep him from being insulted at the apparent rudeness of the rest of the passengers.

"Mr. Deverall, I do hope you enjoy your stay here in Virginia." She tilted her head to the side and looked up at him.

"Why, Miss Martin," grinned Jason, "I have already begun to enjoy it, very much."

She dimpled prettily at the compliment, and for the first time since she was a child, Deborah Martin became confused and speechless.

"Do you plan on staying long, Mr. Deverall?"

"I plan on staying permanently, and would you please call me Jason. Since we're going to be neighbors."

"Ah, you're going to live at Foxmore with Matt?"

"Yes." He proceeded to explain to her that Matt's

description of Foxmore, of Virginia and his neighbors especially had helped him to make the decision. "Since my brother left home, life there was completely different. It seemed I had nothing for which to work, since Father had built everything we had. Do you understand? There was nothing for me to do. When Matt explained the opportunities here it did not take me long to make the decision." He looked directly into her eyes. "You have no idea how glad I am that I did so."

Again the bright flash of her dimpled smile. For the rest of the trip, they discussed unimportant things strictly for the benefit of conversation. They arrived at Clearhaven and disembarked. Matt and his brother were asked into the study while Deborah took her mother and David to their rooms.

"Matt," said Mr. Martin, "will you please sit down and have a drink?"

"I can't sit down, and I don't want a drink. I'm sorry, sir, but can we skip the small talk and all the amenities. Where is Deanna?"

Mr. Martin sat down with a sigh and began to speak softly. "The last time we heard of her, she left Williamsburg for Boston," he began. Quietly he narrated the story of what had happened at Lexington and why she had gone on to carry the rest of the messages to Boston. "If everything had gone well," he said, "she should have been home yesterday. There had been no word until tonight. A courier came through and gave us word. She is still in Boston, but for all intents and purposes, she is a prisoner of the British."

"A prisoner! Locked up in jail?" Matt shouted.

"No, not locked up, Matt, I don't even think they know they're holding her prisoner."

"I'm sorry, Mr. Martin, I must be dense. How could they hold her prisoner without knowing they're holding her?"

"Now will you sit down, Matt? It's a long, long story."

"Yes, Matt, sit down," said Jason. "We can't do anything constructive until we know what the situation really is and all the circumstances."

Matt looked at the two men and realized that what they said was true; he could do nothing until he knew all the story. He sat down opposite Mr. Martin.

"All right, start at the beginning. Leave out nothing. I have to know everything if I'm leaving for Boston tomorrow."

Mr. Martin looked at Jason who shrugged his shoulders. Then he started his story.

Chapter Seventeen

Mr. Martin talked for over an hour, but when he finished, Matt and Jason knew everything from the beginning to that very moment.

"Matt, what do you plan to do now?" asked Jason.

"I intend to go home to Foxmore, pack a few things, saddle my horse and be on my way to Boston by dawn. I'll bring Deanna back one way or another."

"Well, I'm going with you," his brother said quickly.

"All right, Jas."

Mr. Martin interrupted, holding up his hand.

"Wait, Matt. This is impossible. You don't know where you're going. You'll be stopped and held before you can ever get near her. You need someone to guide you. Give me two days, and I'll find a guide who knows the way."

"Mr. Martin, in two days they may find out just who she is and what she's been doing. Anything can happen. I can't let her be alone there one more day than necessary."

"Maybe Mr. Martin's right, Matt. We don't know where we're going and how to get there. Maybe we better wait the two days and get a guide."

Matt turned his distressed eyes to his brother. "I can't, Jas," he said softly. "I can't wait, wondering if she's all right. Don't you understand, Jas? I can't wait."

143

Jason touched his brother on the shoulder. Through his fingers he could feel the hard tense trembling along the muscle in his arm. He was beginning to realize just how afraid Matt really was.

"All right, Matt. Give me a half hour and I'll be ready. We'll leave right away."

"Thanks, Jas. I knew I could depend on you."

His brother flashed an answering smile. Before anyone else could speak again, there was a tap on the door. Jas walked over to get it. Before he could reach for the handle, it was opened from the outside. Deborah stood framed in the doorway.

"I'm sorry, Father, I couldn't help overhearing. Matt, you don't have to wait for a guide. I know the way quite well. I know all the houses that are safe to stop at. I'll guide you."

"Deborah!" her father groaned the name. The thought of losing another daughter after bringing his family together finally tore him apart. "You can't! I won't let you."

She walked to his side and laid her hand gently on his chest. Rising she kissed him softly. "Father, you know we will do whatever is necessary, you and I. I will go, and you will let me. We cannot leave Deanna there. And Matt is right, we must hurry because every moment counts for her. Can you imagine the fear she is living in now?"

Although his eyes were filled with pain and he desired with all his heart to refuse her, he knew that without her Matt and Jason did not stand a chance of reaching Deanna. "What will I tell Vern tomorrow?"

"You will tell Vern the truth. He was contented when it was Deanna who was taking the risks. Now he will have to be as understanding when it's me."

"Deborah," Matt interrupted her. "If Vern will be that unhappy about it, maybe you'd better not."

The anger that flashed from Deborah's eyes startled him.

"Matt, when Deanna told you how she felt and what she had to do, because you loved her you understood and let her go. Can I expect less from Vern than the sacrifices all of us are willing to make?"

She turned to her father and asked quietly, "You understand, Father. Can I ask any less of him?"

"No, my dear. You are right. You must do what you must do. You have my blessings. When you are prepared to leave come to me and I will go over the route again with you and make sure."

"Thank you, Father," she whispered. Silently, without again looking at any of the men, she left the room.

There was a silence for a few minutes, then Matt turned to Jason.

"We'd better get going home."

Jason nodded.

"We'll be back in about two hours, Mr. Martin. Can Deborah be ready by then?"

"She'll be ready, Matt."

"May we borrow your carriage, sir? We'll leave it at Foxmore and ride back here."

"It's yours, Matt."

The two men left and Mr. Martin slowly lowered himself in the chair. There were small beads of perspiration across his forehead. "Keep my children safe. Please keep my children safe," he prayed silently.

His were not the only prayers said that night. During the ride home Matt was grim and silent riding beside a brother who knew and felt his emotions. When they rounded the driveway and faced Foxmore, they were amazed to find lights glowing in the windows. For a moment they stopped the carriage and looked at it in amazement. Then the realization came to Matt.

"It's Cat. Cat and Deeta. I asked them to stay here with Deanna until I got back. They must be frantic with worry."

They brought the carriage to the stables and woke the stable boy who took care of the horses. They then moved swiftly to the front door.

"This is a beautiful place you have here, Matt. It needs a little work, but it has great possibilities."

"I've not had the time to really get started, Jas. But I hope we can make this place as beautiful and productive as father made our old home."

They entered the house and Matt shouted loudly for Cat. It was only a few minutes before a half-dressed, foggy-eyed Cat came down the step.

"Matt, when did you get back?"

"Just about an hour ago."

"Matt . . ." the big man hesitated.

"I know she's not here, Cat. I know the whole story. I thank you for being here when I got home though."

Cat's look of relief brought a laugh from Matt.

Cat sagged wearily into a chair. "I've been watching for you for the past three days. Tonight I was so tired, I decided to skip a night, and when do you get home . . . tonight."

"I'll bet you decided to skip a night just because you were tired," laughed Matt. "By the way, Deeta is here with you, isn't she?

"Jas, you've got to meet Deeta, she's the second most beautiful girl in the world. And she's definitely much too good for this big gorilla."

Cat smiled lazily. "You go to bed. I'm goin' back to bed myself. You can meet Deeta in the morning, Jas."

"We won't be here in the morning, Cat."

"Where are you going? Matt, you can't go up there after her!" His voice held a note of alarm. "You don't know where you're going or what you're doing. This ain't our war, Matt, you said so yourself. Sure as hell, you'll get yourself killed . . . damn you, Matt. I'm goin' with you."

"No, Cat. I need you to stay here. I'm turning Foxmore over to you until I get back. If I don't get back, it's yours."

"Goddamn it, Matt!" He rose from his chair with a shout. Matt put his hand on Cat's shoulder and gave him a gentle push back into his chair.

"Easy, Cat. The only reason I can't take you along is that—number one, Deeta would kill me, and number two—and most important—we'll travel safer and faster in a small group. We have a guide."

"Who?"

"Deborah."

"How's that gonna set with Vern?"

Matt shrugged. "It's her sister, and it's her decision."

Cat nodded speechlessly. Jas and Matt began their preparations. After almost forty-five minutes, they were standing in front of the stables while their horses were being saddled.

"When I get back, Cat, we have to have a long talk about this war. And where we really stand."

Cat extended his hand to Matt who grasped it firmly. "Take care, Matt."

"I will."

147

They mounted their horses and with a final wave to Cat were on their way to Clearhaven to pick up Deborah.

It took them a little over an hour of rapid travel to reach Clearhaven. Deborah was standing outside by her house waiting for them. The sight of her brought a fresh agony to Matt's mind, for she was dressed in pants and shirt with a wide-brimmed hat pulled over her hair. The memory of Deanna as he had last seen her was brought to his eye. He could hardly keep himself from crying out her name. They did not dismount, merely waited for Deborah to mount her horse. The three of them waved good-bye to Mr. Martin and began their long journey.

Chapter Eighteen

Deanna stood by her horse deep in the shadows of a crop of trees. She had waited almost a half of an hour for John and was becoming quite nervous. They had travelled by night and rested by day for the past week. They were four miles outside of Boston. John had told her it was still too light for them to get any closer. He had slipped closer himself to scout the area and now she waited impatiently for him.

A soft rustle and a long loud whistle eased the tension of her waiting.

"John," she began as he walked toward her. "How is everything?"

"The town's overrun with soldiers. Gibson's house can be got to but we have to be careful. It's best to leave our horses here and send someone for them when we find out how the situation is."

"Good," she said. "Let's get started right away. I'm starved, and I'll sell my soul for a soft bed."

He smiled at her. "Hobble your horse so he don't drift away too far and they can find him. We'll get started."

She followed his instructions, taking care that the packet of papers she was delivering was tucked away firmly and safely. Then she followed John as he eased out of the trees and started across the fields toward the town. It was almost three hours before they came behind the house which was their goal. The signal was again given and in a few minutes the back door opened slightly. A signal from an old man waved them over and they crossed the back yard quickly and entered the house.

They entered the kitchen where there usually was a bustle of activity in the Gibson house. Tonight it was dark and quiet. Deanna and John exchanged worried glances, which were not overlooked by the old man.

"Things ain't right," he whispered. "But we're managing okay. Miz Gibson wants you two to take the back steps up to the big bedroom. You know where it is, John, you slept there enough times. You're to stay there until she comes up." He turned away to leave when John caught hold of his sleeve. "What's wrong, Bert?"

"Seems we got to let a couple of those British Army bastards stay here. Seems they're scattering their officers all over town in almost all the houses, and we got two of 'em. Miz Gibson's been scared stiff she wouldn't be able to warn you two before you walked in. The soldiers is out for a while, but they'll be back. You two get upstairs until Miz Gibson can figure out what's best to do."

They went up the steps and into the large bedroom. Deanna found herself shaking. She did not know if it was the fact that she was so tired or the presence of the two British soldiers in this supposedly safe home. She removed her hat and sat down to take off her boots.

"John," she laughed. "I'd do anything for a bath right now."

He smiled in return and slumped down into a chair. Removing his boots, he propped his feet on a small table and released a sigh of pleasure.

"I'm just happy to get out of that saddle. I swear I thought I was growing to it."

150

Deanna lay back on the bed with her hands behind her head.

"John," she said softly. "Do you suppose David got the message to my father by now?"

"Sure, he's had plenty of time." He looked at her through narrowed eyes. "Don't worry, Deanna. I think Matt will understand. Everything will be all right. He'll stick with you and once this damn war is over, you two kids can get back to what you should be doin', raisin' babies."

She smiled, casting him a grateful look for his understanding and his confidence in Matt. They settled themselves contentedly, and within a half hour Deanna was asleep. John sat for a long time watching her and waiting for what he soon heard. There was the tiniest tap on the door. He rose and gave a light tap in the inside. The responding whisper moved him to hastily open the door. A woman slipped inside and told him in a soft whisper.

"Close it quickly, and lock it."

He did so immediately. Sarah Gibson was about thirty-seven years old, although she had the type of face upon which age had no effect. Her hair was parted in the center and pulled to a tight bun at the nape of her neck. Her figure was still that of a young woman and her skin was soft and slightly golden. Her eyes were large and dark and had captured the attention of many men. No one knew her past life and she had encouraged no one to any close relationship. Although there was an understanding between herself and John, he still did not know too much about her. He knew that she was completely trustworthy and was more loyal to the American cause than anyone else he knew.

"John, we've two British officers quartered here."

"I know, Bert told me. Why?"

"They say they need quarters for their men and there's not enough room so they've made use of some of the houses. I don't know how they chose them but I do know we have to be very careful. The two I have here seem to be uninterested in anything but quarters. I've told them I live with my niece who's been sick in bed. If they should find Deanna here that's the story that will cover for her."

"What about me?" he smiled. "What kind of story have you created for me?"

She chuckled lightly. "Why, you're my husband, John, didn't you know?"

Now his smile turned to silent laughter. "And why would a good husband like me be away from home when they arrived?"

"Well, it seems you've a brother in Philadelphia and we've been contemplating moving. You just went down to see about work. You've just returned."

"You're quite a lady, Sarah."

"Thank you, John."

He gave a quick glance over at the sleeping form of Deanna. Then he turned back to Sarah and with a slight smile touching the corners of his mouth he reached for her. She came into his arms willingly and raised her mouth to his. After a few moments, she pulled away from him.

"When she wakens, tell her what to expect and explain our situation. When everything is clear to her, let me know." She looked up at him with a slightly wicked smile. "After all, I can't have my niece and my husband sleeping in the same room now can I?"

With soft laughter following her, she slipped as silently from the room as she had come. When Deanna awoke, John explained what had happened and how the situation now stood.

"We're safe as long as we make no slips and let them know who we really are."

Deanna rose and took the long-desired bath. Then she put on a dress that Sarah had put out for her. When she was prepared, she went downstairs. Sarah was seated in the drawing room with two men in uniform. Deanna felt her heart pounding, but she entered the room smiling.

"Good morning, Aunt Sarah, I'm sorry. Am I interrupting you?"

"No, my dear, come in, come in." Sarah smiled at her.

The two officers rose and waited for an introduction to the beautiful creature that had brightened their day.

"Deanna, may I introduce Colonel Mark Severn and Captain Daniel Webster. They will be sharing our house for a while. Gentlemen, my niece, Deanna."

Both men bowed to Deanna, who smiled warmly at them.

"Good morning, Colonel, Captain. I am very pleased to meet you."

Colonel Severn was a man of about her father's age. He was tall and slender with a bearing of a man who had spent all his life in the military. He had deep piercing brown eyes and a face that hinted at humor. He seemed an altogether pleasant man and Deanna found herself rather liking the bright smile he gave her.

Captain Webster was a much younger man and the glance he gave was one of open admiration. He bowed toward her and his eyes never left her face. It was obvious that the man was completely captivated. It caused a small worried drawing together of Sarah's brows as she watched. They went to the dining room for breakfast.

153

Captain Webster engaged Deanna in conversation as much as possible. The meal was uneventful and Deanna breathed a sigh of relief when Colonel Severn said they must be on their way.

"We will see you at dinner?" questioned Captain Webster of Deanna.

"Oh, yes, Captain. I shall be here."

She warmed him with another sunny smile. A harsh clearing of the throat by Colonel Severn brought the reluctant captain away from her. When the door had closed behind them, both women sighed with relief.

"Do you think they accepted me?"

Sarah laughed aloud. "My dear, if Captain Webster had accepted you any more than he did, you would be upstairs by now."

Deanna's face flushed a bright crimson.

"Sarah!"

"It is not him I'm worried about. It's Colonel Severn. The man is quick and very intelligent. We will have to be careful what we do and say with him."

"I'll be careful, Sarah. What about John?"

"We'll find out tonight if that goes over. I've told them about him already. We'll see what happens at dinner. In the meantime, I would like you to stay in the house as much as you can while you're here. The fewer people who see you the less chance we take of someone knowing you."

"All right, Sarah. I'll do whatever you say."

If Sarah and Deanna had been with Colonel Severn in his office after he was alone, they would have been more frightened than they had ever been in their lives. He had closed the door firmly and pushed home the lock. Then he had hastily moved to his desk from which he took a small box. He opened it and removed a small likeness of a very beautiful woman. For quite some time he sat and stared at it. "Well, well, well," he finally said softly to himself, and a quiet smile played over his lips. He returned the picture to its box and stored it away again in his desk. Then he sat back in his chair and for a few minutes closed his eyes in remembrance of a beautiful dream.

Chapter Nineteen

Dinner that night was a very pleasant affair. Captain Webster was absolutely beside himself trying to win smiles from Deanna. They were watched contentedly by the two older people. Sarah had shifted her glance again and again to the face of Colonel Severn, but could read nothing in his eyes. His manner was completely relaxed as he joined the rest in trivial conversation. After dinner they went to the drawing room. After asking permission to smoke, Colonel Severn relaxed in a chair and contentedly lit a pipe. There was a small music box on the table beside him and he gently lifted the lid. The soft tinkling sound of the music was all the incentive Captain Webster needed.

"Madam, may I have the pleasure of this dance?" he asked laughing as he bowed to Deanna.

She cast a quick look at Sarah who smiled, and in a moment she was on her feet. They swayed slowly to the music of the waltz, and Captain Webster was wearing his heart in his eyes by the time it was over.

Colonel Severn raised his hands in gentle applause and Captain Webster and Deanna laughingly acknowledged his salute.

"Would you care for a walk in the garden? It is a beautiful evening," Captain Webster questioned Deanna.

For a moment, Deanna hesitated, then her eyes caught

Sarah's, who gave an almost imperceptible nod of her head.

"I should love to, Captain." She gave him a demure smile and tucked her hand into his arm.

For a while, Deanna and Daniel strolled in silence, she enjoying the beauty of the surroundings and he enjoying the nearness of the beauty on his arm. Sarah had been watching Colonel Severn all evening. With her sensitive instincts, she felt something was wrong. She sat down opposite him, and their eyes met. He smiled and his eyes crinkled at the corners. "You need play your game no longer, Sarah. I not only know who Deanna is, I probably know her family far better than you do."

Sarah sighed. "I felt there was something in the air, Colonel. Let me talk to you before you take any action. This war is damaging everyone's life. It is one thing for me, who has seen more of it. It is another for this child. Please, if someone must be taken, take me. Don't destroy a life as young and innocent as Deanna's."

"Do you really think I haven't been giving that some consideration all week? Do I appear such a monster to you that I would hurt that child?"

There was more to this, Sarah thought, but she could not put her finger on what it was. "What are you going to do?"

"I'm going to arrange for every move you make from now on to be watched," he laughed. "Not that I really believe you are foolish enough to do anything that will jeopardize your freedom . . . or Deanna's."

"You know I wouldn't."

"Then you will consider that from this moment on you and Deanna will be under constant surveillance. I'd suggest that you did not try to contact anyone else. It would mean my having to put you under lock and key and I should hate to do that. You are such charming company."

Colonel Severn rose from his chair and paced the room for a few minutes. Sarah watched him, a worried frown between her eyes.

"Colonel . . ." she began.

He stopped pacing and smiled at her. "You needn't worry. Believe me, I intend the child no harm. You may retire now, I shall explain to her when they return." He held up his hand when Sarah began to protest. "I should hate to insist," he said, his eyes becoming shuttered, "but I will if necessary."

Sarah realized that there was nothing more she could say or do. She rose slowly from her chair, her eyes holding his. "I trust you to make things as easy on her as you possibly can, Colonel," she said softly. "Don't . . ."

He interrupted gently. "Sarah, you may rest assured, I'll do nothing to harm her, I merely intend to curtail her activities until this conflict is over . . . Goodnight."

She went up the stairs quietly. Colonel Severn sat back down in his chair, a half-smile on his face, and awaited Deanna's return.

"Miss Gibson," he began hesitantly. "May I call you Deanna?"

"Yes, Captain Webster," she said.

"Would you please call me Dan, it should be very uncomfortable seeing you every day and having you call me Captain Webster all the time. You will be staying here permanently, will you not, Deanna?" he asked hopefully.

"I really don't know, Dan. My plans are quite indefinite, since the war . . ."

158

"Confound this war. We should get these filthy colonials settled down shortly. It's all such a stupid business. They belong to England, they should be grateful to remain so."

It took concentrated effort on Deanna's part to stifle the words that were on the tip of her tongue. She suddenly wanted nothing more than to see Matt again and feel his arms about her.

"I think it's time we went inside, Dan. My aunt will be worried about me."

He agreed reluctantly and took her inside. Colonel Severn was sitting in front of the fireplace placidly smoking, but Sarah was nowhere to be seen.

"Where is my aunt, Colonel?" asked Deanna.

"She told me she had something upstairs to which she had to attend. She will return in a few minutes."

Deanna sat down opposite the Colonel in a chair facing his. Being alone with both officers made her extremely nervous, and she began to admire the courage Sarah displayed.

"Captain Webster, I believe we should retire early. We have a great deal of work to do tomorrow and I should like to get an early start."

Dan Webster realized he was being gently told to remove himself from the room. He had no idea why, but not obeying a demand of Colonel Severn had cost him a severe tongue-lashing before and he had no desire to have it happen again.

"Yes, sir, I believe I shall retire right now. If you will excuse me, Deanna, I shall see you at breakfast?"

"Yes, Dan, good night."

When he had gone she watched the Colonel closely under lowered lashes. He continued to stare at the fire for some time and when he finally spoke it was in the gentlest of voices.

"I must tell you a story, Deanna, I may call you Deanna, may I not?"

At her silent nod, he continued talking.

"Once upon a time," he said with a smile, and she smiled in return, "there was a handsome young Captain who thought of himself as a great defender of his country. Dressed in his military finery, he was a dashing figure who caught the eye of many a lovely lady. It was very sad, for the handsome young Captain could really see no one except himself. Then one day he met and fell in love with a beautiful princess. The princess was a lovely lady with long black hair and very soft blue eyes."

The Colonel's voice was almost a whisper, but he held her completely spellbound as a small tingling of fear curled up her spine.

"It was unimaginable to the handsome captain that the beautiful princess did not love *him* as much as he did her. It seems she was in love with what he considered a not-as-handsome, rather ordinary man. The Captain coaxed and pleaded, but to no avail. The lady married her ordinary man, and they had children. No matter how he tried, the Captain could not forget his princess, then the truth finally came to him and he began to see himself as others saw him. But it was too late and the princess was already lost to him. He never took another woman because he held in his heart the love he felt for his lost princess. Then the ordinary man took the princess and her children away to a strange land, and he thought he would never see her again. But he was wrong. The leader of his country sent him to the same land to make it theirs."

She was watching him openly now, for his eyes had

caught hers and held them. Deanna clasped her hands together in her lap to keep them from shaking.

"He came to that land a very unhappy man, for he still loved the princess with his whole heart. And who do you think he met when he arrived there?"

She shook her head for her throat was too constricted for her to talk.

Colonel Severn's voice was so quiet now, she found herself leaning slightly toward him to hear his words.

"The lovely princess had twin daughters, and he had the good fortune to find one of them. Tell me, Deanna . . . how is Margaret?"

"My mother?" she said very softly.

"Yes, your mother."

"Then you know all about me?"

At the slight nod of his head, she leaned back in the chair, not because she was tired but because her whole body was shaking and she needed support.

"What are you going to do?" she asked.

He contemplated her silently for some time before he spoke. "I have been thinking about nothing else all day. I believe I know just what I'm going to do."

"What is that, Colonel?" The words came out strained through stiff dry lips.

"I'm going to keep you here where I can keep an eye on you. That way I shall render you inoperable. I have already made plans to keep Mrs. Gibson locked safely away. You shall be of no more use to them, and anyone who comes here to contact you or her shall be immediately arrested as a spy and shot."

She swallowed with difficulty and her voice cracked with fear when she spoke.

"You could have been my father?"

161

"I should have been your father."

"Do you still love my mother very much?"

"Deanna, I have not married because I have never found another woman to take your mother's place in my heart. That is the reason I will say nothing about you or Mrs. Gibson. I don't want anything to happen to Margaret's daughter. But I have a duty to my country also. Do you understand?"

Strangely enough, she did. She was grateful that he was protecting her so and she told him. But her mind was flying to John and anyone else that would follow looking for her. She prayed wildly that Matt would not try to reach her.

"May I retire, now, Colonel?"

"You may."

She rose and went to the steps. She did not know if she really heard or thought she heard the whispered, "Good night, my dear girl." When she closed the bedroom door behind her and fell on the bed, her whirling brain cried out for Matt to stay away.

Chapter Twenty

Matt lay with his back against a tree. His hat was tilted over his eyes and he was trying to sleep. Deborah was asleep curled in her blanket and Jason, only a few feet from her, gave all outward appearances of being in the same situation as Matt. As Matt slipped from half awake to half sleep, the dreams of Deanna became more real. It was the fuel that kept him going. He had pushed both Jason and Deborah almost beyond endurance, but they had not complained. Instead, they had tolerated his pressure and helped ease his torment as best they could. Now he allowed himself, for the first time in over two weeks, a few consecutive hours of sleep. Mostly the stop was made because he recognized Deborah's tiredness and her refusal to stop until he was ready. Jason, though feigning sleep, watched his brother closely. He had been on the verge of calling a halt to this headlong flight, at the risk of Matt's anger, and getting him to slow down.

The sun dropped from a noon high to hover just over the horizon when Deborah awoke. She lay for a few minutes listening to the quiet sounds of early evening. Then she rose quietly, not wanting to disturb Matt and Jason. Taking a soft handkerchief, she wet it with water from the canteen and wiped her face. Raking her hair with her fingers to relieve some of the tangles, she plaited it and wrapped the braid tightly on top of her head. It was

163

then she had the prickly feeling of eyes looking at her. She turned to see Jason watching her silently.

"How long have you been awake?"

He smiled at her. "Just long enough to enjoy watching you. You're a very lovely woman, Deborah," he added softly.

"Jason," she began.

"I know, you're promised to another man. Has your engagement been announced?"

"Not officially, but it will soon."

"How long have you known him?"

"Ever since we came to America, about five or six years."

"And he just now got around to asking you to marry him?"

Deborah's face flushed a little. "Vern was busy building his plantation up. It has taken a lot of work."

"If you were my woman, nothing would have stopped me from marrying you first. We could have built together."

"Well, I'm not your woman," she snapped, angry at the rush of feeling the suggestion awoke in her.

"No," he sighed, "you're not." He rose from his position and walked to where she sat. He knelt on one knee in front of her and she looked up wordlessly into his eyes. With one finger he traced the line of her jaw to her lips. She sat watching him, afraid of herself, afraid that if she moved it would be toward him.

"Deborah." It was almost a whisper. "I want you. I don't want you just for now or just for a while, I want you for always, and I'll do everything in my power to get you."

She was frozen with shock at the quiet urgency in his

voice. Swiftly, he took advantage of her surprise and lowered his lips to hers. His mouth was firm and demanding. He slid his hand to the back of her head and held her tightly to him when she tried to resist. With his other hand he held hers together in her lap. She was powerless. Slowly his lips parted hers, and a soft sound almost of pain came from her as he devoured what little resistance was left. When he finally lifted his head from hers her head was spinning and her breath was coming in short gasps. There were tears in her eyes.

"I can't, I can't do this to Vern when he is not here. I can't."

He placed both hands on her shoulders and raised her to her feet. She was shaking violently and he knew from the pace of his own desire that if Matt hadn't been there he would have taken her then, despite any protests.

"All right, Deborah, I won't do anything until we get safely back home. Then Vern is going to have a fight on his hands. Do you understand?"

She nodded her head, not trusting her voice.

"Until then, remember this," he said, and before she could protest, he pulled her tightly to him and took her mouth again with his own, moving his hands over her body. She wriggled to free herself, but Jason was a strong heavily muscled man. At his leisure, holding her powerless, he caressed her body until he began to build a fire that matched his. After a few minutes he released her, more for his own good than hers, for he found himself getting lost in her. She gave a low despairing cry and collapsed again on her blanket. It was this sound that woke Matt.

When he rose and came toward them something in the air told him there was something wrong. He looked from one to the other. Then the realization of what was taking place dawned on him. He wished there was something he could say, for to have Deborah and Jason together would have pleased him immensely. Not being able to find any words, he went to gather his things together. It was rapidly becoming dark. He could hear both of them moving about.

"We'd better get started."

They saddled their horses and were on their way within an hour. There had been no exchange of conversation at all. They were on their way almost two hours before Deborah brought her horse to a halt.

"Someone's coming," she whispered. "Look down through the trees."

They watched for a few minutes before they could make out the figure of a man moving stealthily through the trees. He looked as though he knew exactly where he was going and was an expert at not being seen, for they lost sight of him completely after a few seconds.

"Dismount," whispered Matt, "and keep your horses quiet."

They did as he instructed swiftly and quietly, holding their hands over their horses' noses to try and keep them quiet. Matt raised a hand to them then quietly slipped forward. He moved slowly without making a sound. He moved down through the trees and Jason and Deborah lost sight of him. It seemed like hours from the time he left their side, until there was a fleeting glimpse of him again through the trees. Although he watched closely, Matt saw no more sign of the man. His nerves were pulled to the breaking point and perspiration was running down his back. He was kneeling beside a tree with his eyes searching every inch of the area about him when the soft click of a gun hammer froze him.

"Just stay still, Bub," came a soft drawling voice. "Iffen you're who I think you are everything will be all right, iffen you ain't—" he shrugged his shoulders.

Matt stared up at the cool expression on the man's face and knew he would shoot him if he moved.

"Where's your friends?"

"Up on the hill."

"Call 'em down."

Matt just looked at him until, with a dry chuckle, the man nudged him under the chin with the gun. "I said call 'em down here," he repeated softly.

Raising his voice slightly, Matt called to Deborah and Jason, who, with an answering shout, started in his direction. Within a few minutes, they were there, and stopped short at the sight of the man.

"Do you know him, Deborah?" questioned Matt.

"No, I don't think so, but he looks familiar."

The man chuckled again, and, uncocking his gun, slipped it back into the holster on his hip.

"I should, Miss Deborah. I led Miss Deanna up this trail enough times. It's about time I found you. I've been lookin' the last three days."

Suddenly, Deborah's eyes brightened. "William? William Jefferson?"

"Yes, ma'am. One and the same. I've come with a message from Boston."

At these words Matt started to his feet. "A message? From Deanna? How did she know we were here? What's the message?"

"Well, Bub, she didn't exactly send me to you. She sent me to meet whoever was coming up this trail. She described especially you, though, and I already knew her

167

sister. She only had a few minutes but she slipped me a note. It said to warn anybody who's coming up to the Gibson rendezvous was to stay away from that house. It isn't safe. Seems there's a couple officers living there. She can't get out to send any more messages, they're being watched. For some reason, Bub, she especially wanted to stop you."

"Me?"

"Yeah, you're Matt Deverall, right?"

"Yes."

"Well, I was to tell you no matter what not to come near Gibsons. She'll do what she can to get away, but you're not to come."

"William," Matt said. "Deanna is the girl I'm going to marry. What would you do if you were me? Would you leave her to manage for herself while I go back home and wait or would you go in and get her?"

The man smiled. "I'd use my head, Bub. There's a lot of ways into Boston besides Gibsons. I'll lead the way and we'll find you a safe place to stay. Then we'll see what we can do about your lady."

"William," Jason interrupted. "Do you think there would be a place in Boston for Lord Jason Deverall, fresh from England, to see the colonies?"

"Yes, sir," laughed Williams. "Lord Jason Deverall. Is there such an animal?"

"You're looking at him, William. Is there any way we can manage a carriage, William? And I believe some livery for my man here?"

"Yep, I can rassle up just about anything."

"What about me?" asked Deborah.

"Why, Deborah," Jason's eyes glittered wickedly, "you're my tender-loving wife."

Deborah's mouth dropped open and her face turned a bright pink. Slow anger began to fill her eyes when Matt spoke.

"It's a great idea, Jas. We can work it out."

"Y'all come with me. I'll have Lord Jason Deverall and his wife on the road before daylight."

Matt and Williams walked on ahead and Deborah and Jason followed behind.

"If you think you're getting away with anything, Jason, you've got another think coming. I'll play your silly game, but don't you try anything."

Jason stopped and looked at her. Placing his hand over his heart and casting his eyes heavenward with an innocent look, he said, "Deborah, perish the thought. I shall treat you as kindly and tenderly as I would my real wife."

She gritted her teeth and glared at him. True to his word, William had them in a beautiful carriage and dressed like royalty before daylight. They clattered into town and Matt drew the carriage up in front of the Royal Arms Tavern. Stepping down, he lowered the steps and watched with admiration as Lord Jason Deverall stepped down from the carriage with his aristocratic nose in the air, and raised his hand languidly to help his wife.

Chapter Twenty-One

Matt almost choked with laughter when Jason tapped him lightly aside with his walking stick and said haughtily, "See to the carriage, Rob, then go get some supper. I shan't need you until morning."

He lifted Deborah's hand to tuck it into his arm and escorted her into the tavern. Tapping the stick several times against the nearest table, he called for the owner, who came running with a greedy nose sniffing money. Jason looked down his nose at him and said in a rather disdainful voice, "A room, my good man, a clean room. If there is any such thing in this god-forsaken wilderness."

The innkeeper bowing and scraping called over one of the tavern girls. "Take the lady and gentleman to our best room, Mattie. It is a very good room, sir, quite clean."

"Good. And send us up some lunch; I'm positively famished. There is something edible in this establishment, isn't there?"

"Oh, yes sir, yes sir. I shall send you up something right away unless you would like to eat here."

Jason looked positively shocked. "Eat here! My wife eat here, in a common tavern! Really, my good man, you should go back home and learn some manners. This place has caused you to forget how normal people live."

For a moment the landlord's mask slipped and he gave a quick look of suppressed anger, which he covered up

170

immediately, but not soon enough for Jason not to see. "Well," he thought, "William was right. We have come to the right spot."

"Show us to our room, girl," he said.

The young girl was slightly frightened, but scampered ahead of them to show the way.

"Damn English bastards. Maybe I can throw you out personally one of these days," the landlord mumbled to himself at their retreating backs.

After they entered the room and Jason had dismissed the girl with an arrogant wave of his hand, Deborah leaned against the bedpost and almost collapsed with laughter.

"Jason, you were marvelous. I'm sure that everyone you've come into contact with here absolutely hates you."

He sauntered to the bed and sat on the edge with a bright smile and a merry twinkle in his eye.

"I do think I was rather good, wasn't I?"

"Did you see the look on the innkeeper's face when you refused to let me eat in his dining room?" she laughed.

"I'd say the man could have shriveled me to a cinder."

There was another knock on the door and they held their laughter in check until he answered it. The girl had brought back a tray with their lunch on it. When she left, Jason put the tray on the bed between them and began to attack the food with a ravenous appetite.

"Come and join me. The food is really quite good," he said, motioning to the other side of the bed. Hunger gained control of her better judgment and she sat on the bed and began to eat. Soon they were again laughing together and the meal was quite enjoyable.

"Jason, where is Matt and what is he doing?"

"My love," Jason said in his Lord Deverall voice, "my man is circulating among the common people to see if he can get any information."

"Do you think he'll be all right, Jason?" she asked worriedly. "He won't try to see Deanna, will he?"

Now Jason's face became serious. "Don't under-estimate Matt, Deborah. He is a very clever fellow. In fact," the twinkle was back in his eyes, "brother Matt has gotten himself and me out of many scrapes."

"With girls I presume?" she answered coldly.

"Could I hope you were a little jealous, my love?" he asked, narrowing his eyes at her.

"Don't be ridiculous, Jason. What do I care how many silly affairs you've had?"

They were silent for a time while she pushed the food about on her plate.

"Have you had many?" she asked nonchalantly.

"Many what?"

"Affairs?"

His eyes sparkled with undisguised laughter. "Do you really want to hear?"

She dropped her fork back onto the plate and jumped to her feet. With a lift of her chin, she walked to the window and looked out.

"I could care less, Jason Deverall, if you slept with every woman of loose morals in England." She tossed the words back over her shoulder, and kept her head turned away so he could not see the flush of anger on her face nor the confusion in her eyes. The room was quiet and she did not want to turn to see what he was doing for fear of meeting those laughing eyes again! She gave a gasp of surprise as his arms came about her and he pulled her

172

back against him.

His lips were close to her ear and he whispered softly.

"Deborah, my darling, I would lie if I told you I've had no woman before you. But I would not lie if I told you there will never be another after you. I love you, Deborah, and I want you." He turned her to face him. "I want you now."

He was pulling her slowly toward him as he spoke. Although she knew she should fight him, she found instead that she wanted him to kiss her. Deborah could not lie to herself. There was a fire in Jason's arms that she had never found in Vern's. She knew she was lost, and raised her arms slowly to encircle his neck. When his lips finally touched hers, they did not find any resistance. Instead they parted willingly under his, and her body swayed against him. With the soft whispered sound of her name on his lips, he gathered her tightly into his arms. Deborah felt her world spinning and clung tightly to the only stable thing—Jason. They were both lost in the wonder of the moment when an insistent knocking came at the door. Deborah dropped her arms and stepped back startled. Jason gave a hoarsely muttered "Damn" and went to the door. He jerked it open with such fierceness and with such a frustrated angry look on his face that Matt stepped back in surprise.

"Matt," his brother muttered, and stepped back holding the door open. Matt came in and immediately shut the door behind him.

One quick look at both people and Matt realized the situation he had interrupted. He gave a little laugh, which he quickly disguised with a cough. Deborah was fooled but Jason glared at him.

"I've got some news," he said.

"Have you gotten word to Deanna?" Deborah asked quickly.

"No, but William and I have done some circulating, and guess who we just happened to find?"

"Who, Matt? Who?"

"John."

"Marvelous. What did he have to tell you?"

Matt told them the conditions as far as he knew them. John had been warned away from the house by a long-standing signal they had set up for such emergencies. Sarah and Deanna were safe, but unable to move about freely. John did not know the circumstances that held the two women close to the house, but he had warned an over-anxious Matt that it would be dangerous to try anything without getting together and forming a definite plan of escape. Whatever was done would have to include Sarah since she was as much in danger now as Deanna.

"John, William, and the two of us are meeting about ten. Out under the grove of trees just at the north end of town. We have to plan something before then, Jason, so think. We'll try almost anything."

"I'll be there at ten," replied Jason. "Is there anything that has to be done in the meantime?" he added, hopeful that they had found nothing for him to occupy his afternoon.

"Well, it seems you're the only one in our group that can go around buying things without arousing suspicion. We need travelling equipment for Sarah and Deanna. Horses, saddle, etcetera. That's your job. Get them and take them to the stables. John and I will smuggle them out later."

Jason gave an inward groan. This would take him all afternoon, but it had to be done. He looked at Deborah over Matt's shoulder. She blew him a kiss and smiled slowly and promisingly at him. It brought him to his feet.

"I'll see to that right away. Then what, Matt?"

"Then we just lay low until ten, and get together to see what we can come up with."

"Well, since we can't be seen together in town, you go on ahead, Matt. I'll see you tonight."

Matt smiled with sheer wicked enjoyment.

"Oh, I thought I'd stay and talk a while, maybe the two of us could come up with something."

"Get the hell out of here, Matt," Jason muttered.

Matt turned and sauntered slowly toward the door, and once there he turned to Jason.

"Jas, are you sure you . . ."

"Matt," Jason said in a firm voice.

Matt's shoulders were shaking with concealed laughter when he closed the door behind him. He stood still for a minute, then he heard the firm click of the lock.

After he had locked the door, Jason turned back to Deborah, who stood silently watching him. He wanted desperately to recapture the beautiful moment they were sharing, but now he was not sure of her. He could feel a tightening of his muscles, and knew his hands were shaking. He walked to her and stood close looking deeply into her eyes. There was no change of expression on her face and a small tingle of fear began to rise in him. Then she lifted her hands and took his face between them.

"I love you, Jason, I love you," she said as she gently pulled his face to her own and touched her lips to his. The groan of relief he gave was smothered as he gathered her to him and kissed her passionately. Then he lifted her slight form into his arms and carried her to the bed. For this moment, he decided, was theirs, and nothing was going to prevent his having her now. He came to her with a fire that swept her up and held her. Softly caressing her, he felt the first trembling response. His lips followed his hands tracing a path over her soft flesh until she gasped with the pleasure of it. Now he came to her again, this time with the hardness of his body and she reached her arms to accept him. The trembling cry of his name as she rose to meet him swept away all restraints he may have had. He pulled her tightly to him and possessed her fully and deeply.

She lay soft and warm against him afterwards, and he gently touched the path of a teardrop on her face.

"Deborah, I'm sorry if I hurt you. I love you so much, I just couldn't help it."

She dropped her head to his shoulder and circled his body with her arms. Pulling herself more closely to him, he could barely hear the whisper of her voice. "I love you so, Jason. I shall never love or want anyone as I do you. Don't ever leave me. Love me, love me."

He could feel the soft beating of her heart as he pressed her even more closely.

"You are mine, Deborah, and I belong to you. Nothing in this world could ever make me leave you."

With their arms about each other, they lay quiet for some time. He watched the changing shadows of early evening drift through the window as he held her. After a while, his fingers began a soft caress of her back, slipping down the smooth curve of her hip. He thought she was asleep until he felt the gentle pressure of her hands on his back. Lifting himself on one elbow, he looked down into the green sea of her eyes and he knew that words would never have to be spoken as she lifted her mouth again to his.

Chapter Twenty-Two

John sat quietly watching Matt as he paced back and forth. With William, Matt had gone as Jason's representative to buy what was needed. He did not say anything to the two men about Jason's absence. Now it was a quarter past ten and still Jason did not come. Then came the soft calling whistle of the signal. Matt stopped pacing and watched his brother's approach with relief. With a quiet whispered greeting to Matt and William, he slouched down against the tree beside John.

"I'm sorry I'm late," he apologized.

The white flicker of Matt's responding smile flashed in his direction, but he said nothing.

"I'm going to put these horses and all our equipment in a safe place," John said. "When we decide just how we're going to pull this off, we'll be able to get to it easily."

"Good idea, John, do we have everything we need?" William asked.

"Yep, all we got to do now is get a good plan together to get those ladies out of there."

"Well, I for one, don't have any idea how we're going to work this," said John. "Those two are watched so closely I can't even get near enough to give Sarah a signal. Then there's that Captain Webster, he follows Deanna around like a puppy. Word has it he's asked her to marry him."

He was watching Matt as he spoke and could see the firm clenching of his jaw and the rise of color in his face.

"Well, I don't think you have to worry about Deanna, Matt. I've seen her put more than one amorous fellow in his place. She can handle him."

"All the same, I want her out of there."

"I'm worried about the Colonel. He has quite a reputation, too. He's a hard man, and he's all soldier. If he has the slightest idea what those two were doing, I don't think he'd hesitate to throw them in jail—maybe worse."

Matt rose to his feet and paced with impatience.

"There must be some way of getting to them," he said with a slightly desperate edge to his voice.

"If I might interrupt for a minute," drawled Jason. "I've got one little idea I've been playing with ever since this afternoon."

All three men turned and looked at him expectantly. "I wasn't late for the reasons you think, Matt."

The two brothers smiled at one another. "No, I was having a late supper at the tavern. You see I met a few very fine gentlemen, who think the same as Lord Jason Deverall does: that the children in the colonies should be firmly disciplined and brought into line. Then royalty such as us can begin to teach them properly. Oh, we had a very delightful meal, in the process of which I and my lovely wife were invited to a ball. Now if you gentlemen will gather around, I'll tell you what I've come up with and maybe we can work it out."

As the three drew nearer, Jason began to outline his plan. After he had spoken for a few minutes, William and John began to nod their heads. When he had completed

178

his plans even Matt was smiling. John added a few suggestions, and within an hour they had cemented them into a plan that, if it all worked, would have them all free and on their way home in a short time.

"This is going to take some tricky timing, and there's no way to get word to Sarah and Deanna," said William.

"We won't have to. When Deanna sees Deborah, she'll know something's up. She's a quick lady, and she'll follow Deborah's lead. One thing. We have to keep those two girls apart. Even the way you plan to have Deborah dressed, if they stand side by side the game would be over."

"We have to work fast, too. The Colonel is too sharp a man to fool very long. It all has to be done within a half an hour after they reach the party," Jason added. "The ball is a week away. In the meantime, John, why don't you keep trying to find a way to get word to the ladies. It sure would be a help if she had some idea of what was going on."

"I'll keep my eyes open. If there's a way for William or me to get word to them, believe me, we'll do it."

Jason rose to his feet. "Well, I think we all know what we have to do. If all goes well, gentlemen, we'll be on our way home in a week. Now it's late and I think I'll go back to the tavern for a nightcap before bed. I might be able to scrape up more information. Over a drink one can sometimes find out the most remarkable things."

"We'll meet here next Friday night. The party's on Saturday. If anything comes up in the meantime, Jason, have Matt get hold of us."

They agreed, and William and John faded into the night leaving the two brothers alone.

"Jason, what about Deborah?" asked Matt.

179

"What about Deborah, Matt?"

"This isn't just . . ."

"No, Matt, this isn't just," he laughed. "I'm going to marry the girl."

"What about Vern?"

"Do you expect me to give her up because someone else wants her?"

"No, Jas, I certainly know you better than that."

"We'll tell him as soon as we get home. I can sure see your reasons for following Deanna up here. How the good lord could make two of something that beautiful is remarkable."

Matt nodded his head in sincere agreement.

"Well, brother, I think it's time we separated. Where are you staying?"

"I'm sleeping in the loft over the stables."

"Well, there's not much to be done for the next few days except circulate and get as much information as we can. I want Deborah to stay in the room as much as possible. Having her bump into the Colonel or that Captain would upset the applecart. We won't be using the carriage, so that will leave you free to move around."

Matt nodded his head. Waiting until Saturday night with nothing to do was going to be one of the hardest things he had ever done. Jason put his hand on Matt's shoulder. "It will be all right, Matt. We'll get her out of there one way or another."

"I just wish there was a way to get some word to her. I want her to know I'm here. Maybe it would help her just a little."

Jason watched his brother closely and felt a sting of pity. If it had been Deborah in that position he knew how he would have felt.

"I've a fantastic idea, Matt."

"What?"

"What's to stop me from going to visit the Colonel and Captain Webster? It's a wonderful way to get a message to her. We should have thought of that when William and John were here. I've the freedom to go where I choose, so I'm certainly the one to get a message to her."

Matt's eyes lit up with hope. "You'd have to be very careful, Jas. Like John said, the Colonel's no fool."

Jason chuckled, "No, he's no fool. But he might be allowed to think I'm one."

"Thanks, Jas. It would mean a lot to me just to know she knows."

"Sometime in the next two days I'll manage it. Anyway, I want to make sure they bring the ladies to the ball."

The two brothers smiled at each other, then Jason tapped him lightly on the back and left. Matt sat alone for quite some time. To be this near to Deanna and not be able to see or talk to her was agony for him. He knew he would not sleep, so he rose and started for town. Maybe a drink would help ease his troubled mind.

Jason went back to the tavern where he took the steps two at a time. He gave a quick rap on the door. At Deborah's quiet request, he whispered his name and she opened the door for him. She had taken a bath, and the tub of water was still in the center of the floor. Wrapping herself in a sheet, she had been sitting on the bed brushing her hair. When he stepped inside he closed the door and locked it behind him. His eyes told her in no uncertain terms exactly how she looked. He reached for her, but she stepped just out of reach.

"What happened, Jason?"

181

"Later," he said softly, reaching for her again. But still she was too quick and moved away from him.

"Now, Jason. I can't stand the suspense any longer. I've been going crazy."

He realized the anxiety she must have been going through. Sitting on the edge of the bed, he said to her seriously. "Come sit down, Deborah. I'll tell you everything. We've come up with a plan to get Deanna and Sarah out of town. I want to tell you your part in it. It's going to take a lot of courage and nerve on your part to pull it off."

She quickly came to the bed and sat down, curling her feet under her. She had never looked more desirable to him with her beautiful hair cascading over the golden skin on her shoulders. The sheet tucked into the valley between her breasts did more to display her charms then to conceal them. She seemed unmindful of the effect on him as she leaned slightly toward him.

"Tell me, Jason, quickly."

He began to talk, telling her the plan and how they were going to execute it. As he spoke he moved gradually toward her until their shoulders almost touched. She was listening closely to every word he said, and by the time he finished telling her of the plans they had, he was close beside her. He touched a straying curl of hair that hung down over her shoulders. Then he let his fingers drop from the hair and run gently down over the soft curve of her breast. With one deft flip of his fingers, he pulled loose the sheet and let it drop about her.

"Jason," she gasped. "Will you please stop for a minute and finish telling me. I've a million questions."

"And I've got a million answers, and a week to answer them in."

He reached for her again and pulled her warm body over onto his lap. As he caressed her, she laughed.

"I think it's going to be a week to get them answered."

"A week, Lady, this is a question I'm going to be asking you for the next fifty years."

She gave up then trying to take his mind off her. Instead, she cuddled closer and put her arms about his neck. He gave a yelp of surprised pain as she bit the lobe of his ear. He silenced her laughter in the most effective way he knew.

Chapter Twenty-Three

Jason sat in the carriage with his hands folded atop the walking stick. He looked every bit the royal gentleman as he nodded his head to an acquaintance now and then or tipped his hat to one of the town's respectable ladies. The carriage moved slowly through town toward the Gibson house. Matt was driving, and held the reins tightly in his hands to hold back the spirited team. He was enjoying Jason's show almost as much as Jason and took his time bringing them to their destination. When they stopped in front of the Gibson house, Matt stared at it for a few minutes until a quiet sound from Jason brought his attention to his duties. Jumping from the seat, he helped Jason alight and mumbled a few comments under his breath that only Jason could hear that brought a wicked gleam of laughter to his brother's eyes.

He tapped Matt none too gently on the shoulder with his stick.

"Stay close to the carriage, Rob, I don't know how long I'll be."

Matt gazed at the house longingly as he leaned against the carriage waiting. Deanna was only a few steps away and he couldn't go to her. It seemed years since he had held her and the thought created an empty feeling so deep that he was almost ready to accompany Jason to the house on some pretense or other. Jason could see the gleam in his eye and read it well.

"Take it easy, Matt," he said under his breath. "We don't want to jeopardize everything now, do we? I'll get a message to her, one way or another. Trust me, brother."

Matt smiled at him and went about the business of caring for the team while he waited as a good driver should.

Jason strode to the door and rapped with his stick. Sarah opened the door to him and looked at him through chilled, slightly narrowed eyes.

"Yes?"

"My good woman," Jason said majestically, "would you be so kind as to tell Colonel Severn that Lord Jason Deverall is here and requests the pleasure of a moment of his time?"

Sarah did not smile at him, but merely stepped aside to let him enter.

"If you will wait in the study, sir, I'll tell the Colonel you are here. He is a very busy man," she added cooly.

Jason snorted. "No one is too busy to see me. Just tell the Colonel I'm here. Please be quick about it, for I haven't time to dally here all day."

Sarah's cheeks were pink, and Jason happily noted her tightly clenched fingers as she left the room. He would have to remember to apologize to Sarah when he saw her again, which he hoped would be the following night. He waited for several moments before Colonel Severn presented himself.

"Ah, Colonel Severn." Jason rose to his feet rather languidly and extended his hand.

"I've heard so much about you, and since I was riding this way I decided to pop in and meet you."

Colonel Severn was a plain and simple man. He found

himself looking rather coldly at the overdressed, fancy dignitary standing before him. He took the proffered hand, which was slightly limp, and shook it.

"And you, sir?"

"Lord Jason Deverall," Jason said pompously.

"Lord Deverall, I'm very pleased to meet you. Could I offer you a drink, sir?"

Jason sighed, "I do hope you have something better than the Royal Arms has to offer. I swear, I've eaten or drunk nothing decent since I left England."

"Some brandy? I brought it from home when I came."

Jason sniffed and hesitated slightly, as if he wasn't sure the drink would be good enough for him.

"Thank you, sir. I would like some."

Colonel Severn sent for the drinks then turned back to Jason. Motioning toward a chair he asked him if he would like to sit down. Jason looked at the chair as if he weren't quite sure of it either. By this time, Colonel Severn was gritting his teeth and beginning to dislike this obnoxious dandy.

"Is there something I can do for you, Lord Deverall?"

"Why, no, not particularly, Colonel Severn. I'm just jaunting about. Trying to get to know all the better people." He leaned conspiratorily toward the Colonel. "You know these confounded colonials are really a poor lot, aren't they? No refinement whatsoever. How soon are you going to straighten out this little mess so we can bring them a little civilization?"

The cold look cast on him by the Colonel was matched by an even colder voice from the doorway.

"You may keep your civilization to yourself, sir. It would make us all very happy for you to take it and return home on the next ship."

Jason did not have to turn around to see who was talking. It had to be Deanna. He rose slowly and looked at her. "My God!" he thought, "they look exactly alike."

He looked up and down her much as if she were a package he was about to buy, bringing a high tinge of pink to her cheeks and the flash of anger to her eyes.

Colonel Severn rose from his seat.

"Mr. Deverall, may I introduce Deanna Martin. Miss Martin, Lord Jason Deverall."

For a moment, the disdainful look remained on her face. Then Jason could see the sudden light of knowledge in her eyes. He prayed silently she would not give him away.

The look passed as quickly as it had appeared. She dropped him a slight curtsy, and he bowed as though his heart were not in it.

"Good girl," he thought. Now if he could only get close enough to pass her the note he had ready, all would be well.

"You're recently arrived from England, Mr. Deverall?"

"Yes, Miss Martin, within the past month."

"And did you find your journey here pleasant?"

He chuckled to himself. She wanted to know about Matt.

"Quite uneventful. Travelled over with a rather obnoxious gentleman who'd bought a plantation here. Strictly a country farmer type. Uninterested in anything else in the world except his plantation and how happy he and his wife expect to be there. Got rather boring after a while. Man insisted on travelling all the way up with me."

"Who was your insistent planter, Mr. Deverall?" asked the Colonel.

"Had some stupid name, Matthew somebody or other. I really wasn't very interested."

"Are you staying long, Mr. Deverall?"

"Well, I was planning on a longer visit but confound it, madam, there's nothing decent for a gentleman to do here. I'll say my wife is as bored as I. She misses her family very much. I do hope she'll agree to cut our visit short. The only thing that looks the least bit interesting is the ball tomorrow night. You are coming, are you not?"

The Colonel sighed. "I've no choice. It is a function I am forced to attend. I cannot speak for Miss Martin, of course. Do you want to go?"

"I should love to, Colonel Severn, thank you."

"Well, I really must go. My man has been waiting long enough and I've a few more stops to make. I shall look forward to seeing you both at the ball."

Again he extended the limp hand to the Colonel, who shook and dropped it as quickly as possible.

"I'll see you out, sir," said Deanna. The Colonel rose as Jason was leaving, then sat back down in his chair and resumed some work he had been doing previously. As soon as the door closed behind them, Deanna turned to Jason.

"You're Matt's brother?"

He smiled, "Yes, and I'm very very happy to see you, Deanna."

"Is Matt well? Is everything all right?"

"He's right outside."

She made a move toward the door but he grabbed her arm.

"You can't do that, you'll give us all away. Here, take this note. You and Sarah read it well, then destroy it. We're going to get you out of here."

188

"Thank you, Jason. My mother and brother?"

"They're safe at home where you'll be soon."

She rose on tiptoe and kissed his cheek. "Tell Matt I love him."

"I'll save it, and you can tell him tomorrow night."

He bowed over her hand again and opened the door. She stood in the doorway and watched him walk to the carriage. She could see the quick tenseness in Matt's body as Jason told him she was watching from the door. Slowly he glanced in her direction, and she blew him a quick kiss. She caught the flush of his responding smile as he climbed atop the carriage and drove away.

Chapter Twenty-Four

The evening of the ball was a beautiful, warm, moonlit night. The weather suited John and William, but the moonlight had them worried.

"I hope we get some clouds before midnight. Moving around in this bright moonlight is goin' to be dangerous," said John.

"Well, let's get a move on, John," William replied. "Have you got the rope?"

"Yep, I've got everything ready."

The two men were standing together in front of a dilapidated cabin deep in the woods. Now they moved together, and from inside the cabin they brought out six horses. They saddled all six and packed travelling gear and food on their backs. Mounting, they each led two horses toward the town limits. They stopped just outside of town in the same grove of trees where they had all met before. Taking a watch out of his pocket, John looked at it.

"We've got about two hours. By then we should be under the window waiting."

William took his rifle from his saddle and began to examine it thoroughly. Although he hoped he would never have to use it, he was going to be ready for an emergency. John watched him for a few minutes, then with a sigh took his own rifle out and began to check it over.

"You expectin' trouble?"

William leveled his gaze at John.

"I told you that Colonel ain't stupid. If he gets just one small idea in his head, we're done for, and I want to be ready just in case."

John nodded his head and both men resumed the examination of their guns in silence. There was no more conversation between them. Finally John looked again at his watch.

"Well, here we go, it's time."

Both men mounted their horses again and leading them as slowly as possible to the back of the Governor's Palace, they tied them to trees and went as close to the palace as possible, watching the upstairs windows.

Deanna and Sarah were dressing for the ball. Her hands were trembling so badly that for the tenth time she dropped something. "Damn," she muttered to herself.

"Deanna, you've got to calm yourself. As soon as the Colonel sees you, he's going to know something's going on."

"I know," she said in a muffled voice as she slipped her dress over her head. It was a soft blue color and dropped just over the edge of her shoulders. Cut rather low in the front, it showed to advantage the high creamy curve of her breasts. Pulled in tightly at the waist, the gown dropped into a wide full skirt. About her throat she wore a black ribbon with a white rose attached. She had pulled her hair severely up on her head in a round smooth coif. She looked regal. Sarah smiled at her.

"Are you ready?"

Deanna took a deep breath, picked up the white lace shawl and went to the door with Sarah. They came down the stairs together to greet a solemn Colonel Severn and a completely overwhelmed Captain Webster, who offered Deanna his arm with a glowing air of pride.

At the Royal Arms, preparations were quite different. Although the two girls looked alike, tonight there was no resemblance. Deborah was wearing a high ornate powdered wig piled on her head with one soft curl draped over her shoulder. The gown she wore was black, and sewn on the skirt were thousands of tiny pearls. She had made up her green eyes with paint and put a blush of color on her cheeks and lips. High on her cheek she placed a tiny black half-moon beauty mark. In her hand she carried a black lace fan.

"Whatever you do, Deborah, when Colonel Severn or Captain Webster are around use the fan as much as possible. If either sees the resemblance, we're lost."

"Yes, Jason, I will be careful." She spoke so quietly that Jason looked again at her. She was trembling with fear. He went to her and took her in his arms.

"I'll be with you," he whispered. "Don't be afraid, I'll not leave your side until the time comes."

She looked up at him, grateful for his understanding.

"Are you ready, Deborah?"

She lifted her head with determination and nodded. They left the room and started for the palace.

As Matt pulled the carriage to the door, the sound of music drifted out through the open windows. The palace glittered with lights and Matt let his gaze drift to the upper floors, where he saw with relief that most of the upper rooms were dark. After he had helped Jason and Deborah from the carriage, he drove it around to the side where all the rest were together. For a time he drifted from one carriage to another engaging each driver in a short conversation. He worked his way slowly to the side of the palace where, with a quick glance to make sure no one saw him, he slipped into the shadows and around to the back of the house. He could see no one there and for a moment was afraid something had happened to John and William. Then a soft chuckle came from almost beside him and he groaned with relief.

"Get down, boy," came a soft whisper. "We ain't got nothing to do now, but wait."

He nodded and moved beside them into cover where they could comfortably watch the windows without being seen.

Jason and Deborah entered the glittering hall. They stood at the entrance of the ballroom and allowed themselves to be admired for truly they made a magnificent pair. Jason's blazing white ruffled shirt with a silver gray jacket and silvery gray buckles with silver buckled shoes beside Deborah's black gown caused many heads to turn. They continued into the room and presented themselves to Lord Harrison, who was the king's representative. He was quite impressed to have the very wealthy Lord Deverall at his ball.

"Good evening, Lord Deverall, Lady Deverall. I'm very pleased to meet you. Welcome to my home."

"Thank you, Lord Harrison. You don't know how gratifying it is to find some decent social society in this god-forsaken land."

Lord Harrison laughed heartily. "Thank you, Lord Deverall. I do hope you and your Lady enjoy your evening."

"Oh, I firmly intend to, sir. I assure you, I firmly intend to."

They maneuvered their way about the ballroom,

stopping to talk to several people with whom Jason had become acquainted in the last week. He was having a rather hilarious time proving to everyone he saw that he was a pompous spoiled aristocrat when he felt Deborah's hand tighten on his arm. Turning an inquisitive gaze at her, he saw her watching the door. There in the doorway stood Colonel Severn, Captain Webster, Sarah and Deanna.

"Now comes the real test," he murmured to her, taking her elbow as they drifted in their direction. Slowly Deborah raised the fan to cover the lower part of her face. They reached the side of the four who had just entered.

"Good evening, Colonel Severn," laughed Jason. "I would like to introduce you to my wife. Lady Deverall, Colonel Severn, Captain Webster, Miss Martin and Miss Gibson."

"Good evening, Lady Deverall. I'm very pleased to meet you."

Deborah dropped a curtsy and raised her eyes to meet Colonel Severn. For a few seconds, she held her breath. If he was going to recognize her, it would be now. He looked at her for a few minutes, then smiled. He didn't recognize her. Thank God! He didn't recognize her. The relief was almost painful.

Deanna and Sarah were watching her also and as the sisters' eyes met they shared a quick smile between them. Then Captain Webster asked Deanna to dance and she was swept out onto the floor in his arms. Jason also took Deborah to the floor, as he felt they were safer there moving about than anywhere else. Sarah was dancing with Colonel Severn. As the evening wore on, Deborah and Deanna smiled and danced with several men. Each time she was separated from Jason, Deborah was frightened that Colonel Severn would ask her to dance. And then it happened. The soft voice came from her elbow and cut through to her like a knife.

"Lady Deverall, may I have the pleasure of this dance?"

She had to control herself, but the fear was so great she could feel the perspiration trickle down her body. She gathered all her courage and turned to face him, catching a glimpse of Jason's white face as she did.

"I should love to, Colonel," she said softly.

He led her to the floor and took her into his arms. They had made several turns on the floor before he spoke.

"Have we met before, Lady Deverall? I have the feeling that I've seen you someplace before."

She smiled at him. "I think not, Colonel Severn. I should have remembered you if I had met you."

He smiled to acknowledge the compliment, but still had a look of curiosity on his face. When the dance was over, Jason was at her side immediately.

"Jason," she said in just a loud enough voice for the Colonel to hear. "I'm developing a slight headache, I think I shall go up and take one of my powders."

"Of course, my dear. Do return as soon as you can. You take the light from my room when you go away."

She smiled again at Colonel Severn and left their side. Without looking at anyone else she made for the stairs. It took everything she had not to run up them. When she got to the top of the steps, she searched out the right room. Entering the dark room she leaned against the door and gave a sigh of relief. Then she went to the window and opened it quietly. She gave a soft, quiet whistle which was answered immediately. She stood very still, then the figure moved from the shadows and came directly below the window. With a swift toss of his arm, he threw her the end of the rope. She pulled it up. At the end of it was a bundle. She drew it in and laid it on the floor. Moving swiftly, she undid the bundle. Then she began to disrobe. Taking off the white wig, she pulled her hair up into a style matching Deanna's. From the bundle she took a pair of pants and a shirt which she laid out for Deanna. In a few minutes she was an exact double of Deanna in every way. Now she sat and waited quietly. It was only a few minutes before Deanna and Sarah entered the room. The two sisters threw their arms about each other wordlessly. Then Deanna took off her gown and gave it to Deborah. Sarah moved to the window. Tying the end of the rope firmly to the leg of a huge dresser, she gave another signal. Within two minutes, Matt's head appeared above the window sill. Then he was inside. With a low cry, Deanna threw herself into his arms and he held her tightly whispering her name over and over. Although, it was the hardest thing he had ever done, he moved her away from him.

"We've got to hurry."

Taking the end of the rope, he tied it about Deanna's waist. With a quick kiss, he lifted her over the window. Gently he let her down to the ground. When she untied herself, he pulled the rope back up and did the same with Sarah. When she was down, he turned to Deborah. She merely smiled at him and gave him a gentle shove. He kissed her gently on the cheek and slipped over the windowsill, and within seconds was on the ground.

Deborah turned from the window. Now, as Deanna, it was up to her to give them as much time as possible. She went to the door and left the room. Slowly she descended the stairs, to find Captain Webster waiting at the bottom for her.

She was dancing with Captain Webster but she could feel the Colonel's eyes follow her. Since she had come downstairs, he had not taken his eyes from her. Now he moved in their direction. Tapping Captain Webster on the shoulder, he moved toward Deborah and they moved across the floor. "If he would just talk instead of looking at me," she thought in panic. She knew that Jason was watching their every move and felt helpless to come to her aid too soon. The music stopped and she asked the Colonel for some punch. When he had left her side, Jason joined her.

"In another fifteen minutes go back up. I'll signal you when it's time." He gave her a smile of confidence and before the returning Colonel could reach her side, he swept her into his arms and onto the floor. She managed to stay out of the Colonel's way mostly by maneuvering Captain Webster into the garden for a few minutes where she calmly resisted his advances for the final fifteen minutes. When a crestfallen Captain brought her back into the room, she caught Jason's eye. He nodded his head and she excused herself and went up the steps again. Colonel Severn and Captain Webster waited for her at the bottom as they had the last time. The Colonel was determined she would find no way to escape.

Moving quickly Deborah re-entered the same room. Within minutes, she had resumed the clothes and wig of Lady Deverall. As Lady Deverall, she came down the stairs and flashed a bright smile at the two men.

"How are you feeling now, Lady Deverall?" asked the Colonel.

"Ah, I'm afraid the headache is here to stay. If I can find my husband, I'm afraid I shall have to ask him to take me back to the Royal Arms."

"That is too bad, Lady Deverall. I do hope you feel better tomorrow."

"Thank you, Colonel, I believe I shall. Now if you will excuse me, I will search out my husband."

With another quick smile she was gone. Jason was waiting for her and took her arm. "Let's get out of here."

They moved toward the door and were outside in a few minutes. Matt had brought the carriage around in readiness and shortly after they were flying, not back to the Royal Arms, but into the woods at the edge of town. When he pulled the carriage to a halt, William and John came from the trees with Sarah and Deanna. Deanna had already changed to pants and shirt and now Deborah did also. Within a half an hour, the carriage was hidden and the six riders were well on their way toward home.

They were over a week on the way before they slowed their pace. For the first time they made a camp and could afford the luxury of a cooked meal.

Matt and Deanna were engrossed in themselves and making their plans. He tried to explain to her now that he understood how she felt, and from now on her cause was his and they would work together. She smiled with her lips and her eyes gave him the promise of the future.

Jason and Deborah talked of a future also.

"Will you tell Vern when we get back, Deborah, or shall I?"

"I'll tell him, Jason, I owe him that much."

"We'll be married right away?"

"Well, I think it's about time you made an honest woman of me," she laughed.

John and William thoroughly enjoyed the happiness of

the two couples. And William became even happier when Sarah and John began to share the special look relegated to lovers.

In Boston, a bewildered Colonel sat at his desk and pondered what means of escape they could have used. It had amazed him when he found the women gone and he still had not figured out how it happened. Captain Webster came in.

"Did you find any trace, Captain?"

"No, sir, they just seemed to have vanished. I've asked at the Royal Arms for a woman answering Deanna's description, and they said the only woman there that looked like that was Lady Deverall. But that's impossible, sir. She couldn't be in two places at once."

The Colonel gazed at the Captain for a few minutes, then to Captain Webster's amazement, threw his head back and laughed. He laughed until he choked.

"Captain, pack my things. I believe I'm going to take a short trip. There is someone I haven't seen in years and I have to give them long-awaited congratulations."

The Captain went from the room shaking his head as the Colonel's laughter followed him.

Chapter Twenty-Five

The soft fingers of twilight were entangling themselves among the trees. There was a quiet stillness in the air as if the entire world waited for some special event. Clearhaven was quiet. Its windows were as yet unlighted for the evening. Paul Martin sat on his front veranda and gently rolled a cigar between his fingers. He stared dreamily out over the rolling lawn to the river. It had been over a month since his daughter, Deborah, Jason and Matt Deverall had started the trip to Boston to try to find Deanna. He had heard no word, had no sign of anything from them since. The soft clopping of an approaching horse caused him to heave a great sigh. He rose from his chair and walked to the edge of the veranda to greet the man he knew was coming. He watched him dismount and tie his horse then walk slowly to the bottom of the steps and look up at the older man. Mr. Martin smiled.

"Good evening, Vern."

"Good evening, Mr. Martin."

Mr. Martin was about to speak again when another voice came from behind him.

"Good evening, Vern."

Paul Martin turned and extended his hand to the lovely woman in the doorway. Margaret Martin was an exceptionally beautiful woman. Her black hair had no sign of gray, and was pulled back severely into a chignon at the nape of her neck. She had a soft golden glow to her skin. Her figure had not changed since her girlhood. She was still small-waisted with high curving breasts. Her tender smile flashed in her husband's direction and a warm glow of affection came to her blue eyes. She took the hand he extended to her and came to his side. He dropped his arm about her waist and she leaned slightly against him as she smiled at Vernon Markham.

"Has there been any word at all, Mr. Martin?"

"No, Vern, there have been no riders through since they left. If they have gotten to Deanna they would have sent someone to tell us by now."

"Do you think they've run into trouble? Maybe we should go after them."

"No, Vern, Deborah knows the way and all the stopping places. We can't all go running about the countryside looking for each other. We must give them time."

"My, God! . . . Begging your pardon, Mrs. Martin. But they've been gone over a month, sir."

"Consider, Vern, that it takes almost two weeks to get there and two to get back. If they found her it would take some time to get her out. We'll give them another week."

Vern moved his hands in a gesture of anger but said nothing.

Mr. Martin clapped his hand on Vern's shoulder.

"I know how you feel, Vern, believe me. Both my daughters in danger at the same time. I know how you feel. But we've got to give them enough time. One more week, Vern, and you and I will go after them together. Agreed?"

Vern smiled slightly.

"I'm sorry to be so difficult, Mr. Martin. It's just that I'm so worried about Deborah."

"Surely you are, Vern," said Margaret solicitously.

"And you've every right to worry. Paul, how could you have let her go with those two men, alone."

"Margaret! Matt and Jason Deverall will guard Deborah with their lives and Deborah was the only one who knew where and how to lead them. She knew that Matt felt the same about Deanna as Vern does for Deborah. She felt she had to go and I agreed with her. Now we must be patient and wait. We'll give them another week," he said firmly and with finality.

"All right, Mr. Martin," Vern said resignedly. "But if they're not back in a week, with or without help, I'm going after them myself."

He spoke the words slowly and firmly and Mr. Martin knew he meant what he said. Then without another word he turned and mounted his horse. With a light salute, to Mrs. Martin, he wheeled the horse around and left.

Paul Martin and Margaret stood together on the veranda for quite some time without speaking. Then Margaret turned and looked up into her husband's face. There was no doubt or fear in her eyes now, just trust for the man she loved so much.

"Will they be all right, will my daughters be back with me soon?"

He looked down into her blue eyes.

"Margaret, if I doubted for a moment that they would not, I should have been after them before now."

She smiled up at him with a confidence she did not feel. Somehow she had the apprehensive feeling that something was about to happen. He bent his head to hers and kissed her gently.

"Do you know you're as lovely as the day I met you, Margaret? I love you very much. I'll not let anything happen to our girls. Trust me, my love."

She smiled with her eyes and with her lips, but deep down inside the twisting tentacles of fear clutched at her.

They went inside to dinner, which was a solemn affair since the strain of worry hung over the table like a cloud. David, who was a very quiet boy by nature, tried his best to contribute to the conversation. He was a good-looking boy, somewhat resembling his sisters. His black hair was worn a little long and tied back in a queue. He had large hazel eyes and a wide-mouthed smile that lit his face. He was a gangly youth of sixteen, not yet grown into his hands and feet, giving him an awkwardness that caused him much discomfort in the presence of people. It caused him to be quite shy and made it difficult for him to talk to people.

Trying to ease Margaret's worry, for he loved his mother dearly, he offered her the wisdom of his youth.

"Mama, I'm sure Deb and Dee will be all right. They really know how to take care of themselves."

Margaret smiled at her son.

"Of course they will, David. I shouldn't be such a worrywart. Tell me, have you been up to the cabin to see Cat and Deeta lately?"

"Yes, Mama," the boy said excitedly. For any mention of Cat brought the boy's enthusiasm to the surface. "Cat's taking me hunting next week. Papa gave me my own gun and Cat said he'd take me first chance he got."

Margaret cast a look at her husband, who gave a slight shake of his head, warning her as he had done many times in the past few weeks not to baby the boy. She smiled at him again.

"Cat's great, Mama. He knows just everything about hunting and trapping and building things and everything." His hazel eyes glowed with the bright amber light of hero worship.

Both parents were pleased with David's attachment to Cat, and they listened with patience to his admiring chatter. It helped to ease the burden of worry off their own minds.

Soon after the departure of Matt, Deborah and Jason, David had felt a sudden surge of loneliness. The tension of worry had caused both parents to be unknowingly forgetful of the boy. Although he knew they loved him, he still felt slightly lost. This coupled with the painful awkwardness of his age had sent him drifting about the countryside alone. One day while wandering about, he had pulled his horse up in front of Cat's cabin. Cat was away at the time and Deeta had opened the door to him. He had stood awkwardly for a few minutes and tried stammeringly to explain who he was and why he was there, although he really did not know himself. Sensing his embarrassment, a smiling Deeta had invited him in for something cool to drink. When Cat returned, he gave a slightly surprised look but said nothing. David eagerly accepted their invitation to supper, and listened raptly to Cat's description of his day. When it was time to leave, he was reluctant. With quiet understanding, Cat invited the boy to go hunting the next day. From then on, David was literally Cat's shadow. Mr. Martin had come one day to talk to Cat about it, not wanting David to be a nuisance. When Cat had firmly convinced him that he and the boy were friends, the older man was not only satisfied but pleased that Cat would take the time for him.

Mr. Martin laughed. "Are you helping Cat at the

cabin like I told you, son?"

"Oh, yes, sir. I chop wood for Deeta and I helped Cat build the new room on the cabin. I do everything I can, Pa, honest."

Mr. Martin smiled and rested his hand on David's shoulder. It was then with a slightly wrenching feeling he realized that his child son was well on his way to being a man.

"I haven't told you, David, how proud your mother and I are of you."

The boy had flushed with embarrassment but his eyes had glowed with love for his father. The meal was almost finished when the sound of approaching horses could be distantly heard. Margaret raised her hand to her throat in expectant fear. For a few minutes they looked at each other without moving, then almost simultaneously they rose from the table and started toward the door. When they walked out onto the porch, a group of riders could be seen rapidly approaching.

"Please, God," murmured Margaret.

"It's Dee and Deb," shouted David.

"Thank God, thank God," said Mr. Martin in relief.

When the riders finally reached the porch and dismounted there was a shout of joy from David, then everyone was crying and hugging everyone else. Matt and Jason watched smiling as Deborah and Deanna threw themselves into their happy parents' arms. When some of the excitement had subsided, Mr. Martin extended his hand to Matt and Jason.

"I don't know how to thank you for bringing my girls home to us. I've just no words to express my gratitude."

Matt smiled as he shook Mr. Martin's hand. "I don't need any thanks, Mr. Martin. I would like your blessings if Deanna would finally decide to marry me."

Deanna was leaning against Matt and his arm was about her waist. She looked up at him with the glow of love in her eyes.

"You have my blessings, indeed," laughed Mr. Martin, looking delightedly at the two.

Margaret Martin, though, was watching Deborah, who had stood looking at Matt and Deanna until Jason stepped beside her and took her hand in his.

Chapter Twenty-Six

They were seated in front of the fireplace. Deanna sat on the floor leaning against her father's knee. For some time no one had spoken. They had explained everything that had happened from the time Deanna had left until they had helped her escape. Deanna had deliberately left out the name of Colonel Severn. She had planned to tell her mother when they were alone. Now there was an easy comforting silence in the room. A silence of contentment.

David cleared his throat in preparation for the million questions he wanted to ask Matt. With a slight chuckle to himself, Mr. Martin interceded to stop the avalanche of questions before they got started.

"Tomorrow is soon enough for questions, David. I'm sure the men and your sisters are very tired after their long journey. You can ask all your questions then, David."

David looked a little disappointed. But Deborah came to him and with a light laugh kissed him quickly on the cheek.

"We'll answer all your questions tomorrow, David. I for one am exhausted. I feel like I've been sitting in that saddle for years. I need the feel of a soft warm bed for a change."

David smiled at the sister he loved so much. "I'm

sorry, Deb. I didn't realize you were so tired. Sure, we'll talk tomorrow."

Everyone began to stir.

"I guess we'll be heading for Foxmore," said Matt in a tired voice.

"Nonsense," said Margaret. "You'll sleep here tonight. You're much too tired to go any further. You can go to Foxmore after you've had a good breakfast and a night's sleep."

"Thank you, Mr. Martin. I won't argue with you. I'm much too tired and I would be delighted to accept your hospitality."

"Good! I'll have you shown to your rooms."

She went to make the preparations. Sarah had been very quiet, looking occasionally toward John, who was engrossed now in conversation with Mr. Martin.

Deanna went to her side. "Get some rest, Sarah. We'll make plans tomorrow."

Sarah smiled and nodded her head.

When Margaret had taken care of her guests for the night she went back downstairs to make the preparations for tomorrow's breakfast. After informing the servants of the added places for breakfast, she started back upstairs to bed. Deanna stood at the top of the stairs waiting for her.

"Deanna, my child, why aren't you in bed?"

"Mother, may I speak to you privately for just a moment?"

"Of course, dear, but can't it wait until morning?"

"No, I don't want Papa or anyone else to know what I'm going to tell you."

Again, as she had before their arrival, Margaret felt the tight clutch of fear as it knotted her stomach. She nodded her head without speaking and turned to go back downstairs. In the drawing room, they did not light the candles, but sat in front of the still-glowing embers of the fire.

When Deanna started to speak, she kept her voice quiet but looked directly at her mother. By the time she had told her the whole story, Margaret was leaning weakly against the back of her chair. Her face had gone pale and the blue eyes were slightly misted with tears.

"Mark Severn," she said softly.

"Mother, is what he told me true?"

"Yes, Deanna, Mark and I loved each other very much at one time."

"Mother . . . Do you still care . . . a little?"

"Please try to understand, Deanna. I did love Mark. He was a dashing, handsome military hero. I was a very impressionable young girl. It wasn't until after I met your father that I realized what love really was. You cannot forget the first man you ever loved, Deanna. But lives are not built on daydreams. Mark was a beautiful dream, but your father is the reality of my life. He has given me so much. We have shared so much."

"Mother, what if Colonel Severn should follow us here, if you should meet again after all these years. How would you feel then?"

Margaret smiled and rose from her chair. She walked to her daughter's side and knelt in front of her. Taking Deanna's hand in hers, she looked deeply into a young reflection of her own blue eyes.

"I love your father with my whole heart and soul, Deanna, as I love you girls and David. I would have to make Mark understand that everything that ever was between us is over."

"Mother, he still loves you. He told me he never married because you are still first in his heart. He struck me as the kind of man who does not give up easily what he wants. Could he do anything to harm Father?"

Margaret's face turned slightly pale as she caught her lower lip between her teeth. For a few moments she contemplated the idea.

"I don't think so, Deanna. If your father had been clever enough to outwit Governor Rosemond all this time, I'm sure he can handle Mark Severn." She rose now to her feet and went closer to the dying fire as if suddenly chilled.

"Be that as it may, Deanna, we will cross the bridge when we get to it. There is another thing that I must speak to you about."

Deanna looked at her mother questioningly. Margaret turned to face her again. She looked at Deanna for some time before she spoke.

"Deanna, what has happened between Deborah and Jason Deverall?"

The question took Deanna by surprise. They had discussed it before their arrival and decided to say nothing until Deborah had had an opportunity to talk to Vern. Jason had reluctantly agreed, as he had wanted to tell her parents immediately. Deborah had pleaded with him and he had given in to her, but Deanna knew he would not keep silent long.

"They love each other very much, Mama. Deborah wanted to talk to Vern first before anything was said. They want to marry."

"Deanna, do you know how much Vern loves Deborah? The agony he has been going through. He's been here every day for over a month."

"She's going to see him tomorrow, Mama. Vern will have to understand just as Mark Severn will that when two people really love each other they should be together and no one should interfere."

Margaret gave a resigned sigh. There was no way for her to fight this logic, but her heart was filled with pain for Vern.

"It's time you got some rest, Deanna. We'll face tomorrow's problems tomorrow."

Deanna rose from her chair and went to her mother's side. Margaret embraced her and with a gentle kiss murmured. "Good night, Mama, I love you." She left the room.

Margaret Martin sat down beside the remains of the fire and her mind flew back over the years.

"Oh, Mark, why did you have to come now." She put her hands over her face and the hot tears scalded her eyes.

"Oh, Mark, oh Mark," she cried silently.

Deanna climbed the stairs slowly remembering the shocked, frightened look in her mother's eyes when she told her about Colonel Severn.

"Poor Mama," she thought. "She must still love him a little."

She remembered Matt. "No, Mama, you can never forget your first love."

She did not go to her room; instead, she went to Matt's. She turned the knob and found it unlocked. She smiled to herself and stepped inside.

He was sitting up with his back propped against the pillows. He had removed his shirt and she watched the candles send flickering shadows across his body. His eyes met hers across the room.

"If you hadn't come to me soon, I was going to come to you," he said softly.

She smiled. "I had to talk to my mother, Matt. There were some things that had to be said between us."

"They made you cry, Deanna. Do you want to tell me?"

She walked to the bed and looked down at him. Then slowly she removed her clothes. Climbing into the bed, she nestled into the warm embrace of his arms. He held her silently, waiting to see what she wanted to say.

She slowly began talking. She told him everything.

"Your poor mother. What is she going to do, Deanna?"

"I don't know, Matt, but we'll be here to help her every way we can."

"Of course," he said with a smile. He looked down into her eyes. "Do you have any idea how much I love you, Deanna?"

Her lips parted slightly and a soft flush of warmth invaded her body.

"It couldn't compare with what I feel for you, Matt," she said softly. "I love you so," she murmured as his lips found hers. Every kiss was new for them and they lost themselves in each other. He let his hands softly move over her body. He knew every curve of her and he explored each one slowly and thoroughly. He let his lips drift from her mouth to her throat, then his hands followed, eliciting the deep moaning cries of pleasure from her lips. They moved together, keeping perfect time with one another until he held and carried her to the peak of her passion.

"Oh, Matt, Matt," she was almost sobbing with the loveliness of it. "I love you." Afterward he held her close and she laid her head on his chest. After a few minutes he lifted her chin with his fingers and looked deeply into her eyes. She had been crying, and he had felt the hot touch of her tears on his skin.

"What is it, my love?" he asked softly.

"Oh, Matt, I'm so happy. I wish it could stay now, forever. I don't want anything to spoil this."

He smiled at her.

"I am going to keep you happy, Deanna. We have a million tonights ahead of us. Nothing can separate us now."

His lips touched hers again in the gentlest of kisses.

"Stay with me for a while," he whispered. She sighed contentedly and nestled against his chest. In a few minutes she was asleep. He held her in his arms and listened to her quiet breathing. He could feel the soft roundness of her against his body. For a moment he tightened his arms about her. She murmured his name in her sleep and he smiled. After a while he slept, too.

Chapter Twenty-Seven

Deborah sat easily on her horse and held him in check while she gazed down over the green trees to Vern's house. Jason had wanted to come with her while she told Vern the truth but she thought she owed Vern the courtesy of not damaging his pride in front of another.

She had cared a great deal for Vern. He had helped her and her father in a time when they could have turned to no one else. But she knew what she felt for Vern could not compare with the depth of emotion Jason brought to her. She could still feel the tingling warmth of the kiss on her lips as he had held her a moment before she mounted her horse. His strong, muscled arms had held her so tightly they had left her breathless, and his lips had demanded the response they so readily received. She had giggled in wicked delight when he jumped a little as she lightly touched the inside of his lips with her tongue. The devilish light of suppressed laughter appeared in his eyes as he leaned his lips close to her ear.

"I'll carry you up to your bedroom right now in front of everyone if you don't behave," and he laughed at her slightly startled expression.

"You wouldn't."

"Don't tempt me, Lady, I've not got much patience when it comes to staying away from you."

She had given him a light shove and mounted her

horse. Just before she kicked him with her heels, she had leaned down laughing. "I would love it," she whispered. Then kicking the horse sharply, she had moved rapidly away from him. She could still hear his laughter, and it brought a warm glow of expectation of her return.

Now she could feel the sudden nervous pounding of her heart. She was afraid, not of saying what she had to say, but of the pain she knew she would see in Vern's eyes. She remembered, as she paced her horse slowly, the first time Vern had kissed her and told her of his feelings. They had been riding together. She had sensed the strength of his feeling, but he had never said anything. Now as he helped her down from her horse, his big hands about her waist, he had let her down slowly, just barely letting her feet touch the ground. Holding her against him, she could feel the strength in his hard muscular body. Her hands were on his shoulders and she did not remove them. He had lowered his head and taken her mouth gently with his. The kiss was the tenderest, gentlest thing she had ever experienced, and it brought a sudden moistness to her eyes. When he released her, he looked deeply into her green eyes.

"I love you, Deborah."

The strength with which he said the few quiet words left her no doubt of his feelings. But she was unsure of her own. She lifted her arms about his neck and he pulled her body close to his. The next kiss he gave her bore no resemblance to the first one. It took away her breath and left her shaken, as he parted her lips with a demanding force. She could see the desire in his eyes and the slight flush of his face. He was still holding her tightly against him.

"Did you hear me, Deb?"

"Yes, Vern, I heard you."

"I want you to marry me as soon as I get Dartmore ready. I love you, Deb, and I want you more than I have ever wanted anything."

Suddenly she felt unsure of herself. He had said he wanted her, yet he was content to wait until Dartmore was ready. She wanted him to be impractical, just for a moment; to sweep her into his arms and demand she come to him without waiting. She stirred in his arms with a small nagging feeling of guilt. After all he was just thinking of her comfort. The guilty feeling caused her to give a hasty answer.

"Yes, Vern, I'll marry you. As soon as Dartmore is finished."

He had laughed then and held her close in his arms, kissing her thoroughly.

Now, she thought back, she realized the emotion that had made her agree. It was wrong then and she knew it now. It had been so different with Jason. She felt warm all over with the thought of him. Her face was still slightly flushed and her eyes were bright when she pulled her horse to a halt in front of the door. She was about to step down when the door was flung open and Vern came rapidly out. Before she could say anything, his hands were about her waist lifting her from her horse, and she was in his arms. His mouth found hers and he kissed her deeply. Then he pulled her tightly into his arms murmuring her name over and over again.

She had never felt such pain or guilt over anything she had ever done in her life. Gently she released herself from his arms.

"Vern," she said in a strangely choked voice. "Vern, I've got to talk to you. Please?"

There was something in her voice that immediately caught his attention. Holding her by the shoulders he moved her a little away from him, but did not let her go.

"What is it, Deborah? What's wrong?"

He still did not grasp that the wrong was between them.

"I want to talk to you, Vern." It was almost a whisper now. "I have something to tell you, something very important."

He dropped his hands from her shoulders and stepped back from her, but his eyes never left hers. His brows drew together and the corners of his mouth tightened slightly. Their eyes held each others', and she was afraid to drop hers as he tried to read the truth.

"Do you know, Deb, I felt something happening when they told me where you had gone. I had the strangest feeling you would never come back to me. Have you come back to me, Deb?"

"Oh, Vern, I'm sorry. Try to believe me, I care a great deal for you. I wouldn't hurt you for anything in the world." She was crying. Unmindful of the tears, she grasped his arms and held them tightly while she pleaded with her eyes for his understanding.

"You care a great deal for me you said, but you no longer love me, is that it?"

"I don't believe we really loved each other from the start. If we had, do you think we would have patiently waited all this time? No, Vern, if we loved each other we would have married long ago and built Dartmore Hall together. Try to understand, Vern."

"I understand that although you no longer love me or think you no longer love me, I still love you. I've loved you from the beginning and I always shall." His voice dropped and he spoke very quietly.

With a small cry she dropped her hands helplessly.

"Who is it, Deb?" he asked quietly.

"Jason Deverall."

"Do you love him?"

"Yes, Vern, I really love him."

The wince of pain that crossed his face also hurt her. The pain lingered in his eyes long after he smiled at her again.

"Your happiness means a great deal to me, Deb. I wish you the best. When will you marry him?"

"We thought in six months, after Deanna and Matt are married."

"Then you won't be marrying right away?"

"No."

"Then we shall see if Jason Deverall can hold what he has stolen."

"Vern, no one stole me."

"Yes, stole. When you were away from home and caught up with the excitement of the situation. You were away from me, and I didn't have a chance to protect what was mine."

"Vern," she began, but she got no further.

"You can tell him this for me. I love you, and I'll fight in every way I know how to get you back." He spoke hoarsely now with the trembling grip of pent-up anger.

"Tell him to watch, I'll not miss any opportunity. You'll never marry him, Deb. You belong to me, and I'll never let you go."

Suddenly he reached out and pulled her tightly against him. She could feel the pounding beat of his heart as he crushed her body to his. Holding her easily with one arm, he maneuvered the other to her face where he held her chin with one large hand. His face was inches from hers, and slowly he lowered his lips to hers in a crushing kiss. She tried to struggle but was completely powerless to move in his arm. He moved his mouth on hers, forcing her lips apart, probing and demanding until she trembled weakly in his arms. When he finally lifted his head from hers, she sobbed and dropped her head against his chest, unable to move. The tears came freely and she shook with fear. Her mouth felt bruised and her eyes were almost blinded with tears. He held her tightly for another moment, caressing her with his huge gentle hands.

"Vern, please, please," she sobbed. For the first time he seemed to hear her. He released his hold and she almost fell as she moved away from him.

"Don't forget what I said, Deb. Tell him what I said. You were mine, you'll be mine again. One way or another."

It took all the strength she had to get back up on her horse and she could feel his eyes as she wheeled around and left.

She let her horse pick his way home itself while she tried desperately to get herself together. She knew if Jason saw her he would explode with anger, and she also knew that although Jason was a big man, he did not stand a chance against Vern Markham. She arrived at the stable and left her horse with the stable boy. She went straight to her room without seeing anyone. With relief, she closed the door behind her, and threw herself across the bed. She lay for a long time contemplating what Vern had said to her. Vern was not a vicious man, and Deborah decided he was just hurt and angry to say what he did. She decided she would not mention everything he had said to Jason. She was still lying there when a light rap came to the door. It opened slowly and Deanna came in quietly. "Deb, are you asleep?"

"No, Dee, come on in, no leave the candles out, I would rather not have them lit right now."

"Deb, Jason's downstairs. He wants to see you."

"All right, please tell him I'll be down as soon as I change, would you?"

"Of course," said her sister. "Deb, do you want to tell me about it?"

"Not right now. Later maybe, when I get myself collected. Right now I have to face Jason."

Her sister nodded her head in silent understanding and reached out her hand to touch Deborah's arm.

"It will be all right, Deb. You'll see. Jason loves you very much. He'll make you happy."

"I know. Tell him I'll be right down."

After Deanna left she washed her face and changed her clothes and prepared herself to go down to Jason.

Chapter Twenty-Eight

He watched her slowly descend the stairs. He loved to watch the way she moved. When she reached his side she held out her hand to him and he took it, pulling her gently into the curve of his arm.

"How did everything go, Deborah? Did you explain to Vern?"

"Everything is fine now, Jason, Vern understands. I explained that we love each other and plan to marry in six months."

"Did he accept it, Deb?"

"Why do you keep asking, Jason? I told you I explained everything to him."

—She had been standing next to him trying to keep her face slightly averted. Now he turned her to face him and with the tip of his fingers gently touched her cheek, then her lips.

"And what happened to your mouth? It's swollen. Deborah, he didn't hurt you, did he?"

"No, Jason, I hurt him. This was just a small by-product of the pain I inflicted. Please, Jason, let's just forget everything and everyone else. For me, Jason, please?"

He looked at her intently, then smiled his light humorous smile.

"All right, Deb. Everything's forgotten except us.

Come on, let's go tell your parents."

They went into the drawing room and found Margaret Martin alone. It was a strange sight for anyone used to living in that house to see Margaret idle, but she was seated before the fireplace with her hands in her lap contemplating the fire. A faraway look was in her eyes, and a soft gentle smile played about her mouth. She did not hear the two of them until Deborah spoke to her.

"Mama?"

With a small start she turned to face them, and there was a soft glistening hint of unshed tears in her eyes.

"Mama, is something wrong?"

Margaret Martin smiled her bright smile and rose to her feet.

"No, child, nothing's wrong," she laughed. "But if I don't get up and about there will be no supper in this house. Good afternoon, Jason. Is everything well?"

"Everything is just fine, Mrs. Martin. Deborah and I would like to speak to you and your husband for a few minutes if you have the time."

"Well, I've the time, but Paul received some messages this morning and he's been in his study since. I believe something important has happened."

"What, Mother, has something gone wrong?"

"I don't know my dear. Whatever it is, it's gotten your father very upset. I hope he doesn't do anything foolish and give Governor Rosemond a chance to act. He's been waiting patiently to connect your father to this revolution and get control of Clearhaven by confiscating it in the name of the crown."

"Mr. Martin wouldn't do anything foolish enough to give him the opportunity, would he, Mrs. Martin?" asked Jason.

"I hope not, Jason, but my husband feels very deeply about this country," she replied in a worried voice.

"I'll not do anything foolish, my dear," came Paul Martin's voice from the door. "But I will do what needs to be done."

The three turned to look at him. Margaret Martin went to her husband's side and he slipped his arm lightly about her waist. Touching her cheek with a light kiss, he looked at Deborah and Jason.

"Deborah, you look well, today," he smiled. "Jason, how are you?" he extended his hand to Jason who took it firmly in his.

"Mr. Martin, I've something very important to discuss with you and Mrs. Martin, if you can spare a few minutes, sir."

"Yes, of course, my boy, I've some time. What is on your mind, Jason?"

Deborah watched Jason with soft glowing eyes. How she loved this big gentle man. She looked at his hands. They were large and square with a fine sprinkling of hair across the back. She could remember the feel of them against her skin and the memory brought a warm glow to her eyes. Their eyes met for a moment and she responded to his quick smile and the soft glint of laughter that always lurked deep in his eyes. He extended a hand to her and she went to his side.

"Deborah and I would like your permission to marry, sir."

It was the first time in her life Deborah had ever seen her father so surprised. Usually a calm, collected Paul Martin had been able to face any situation with aplomb. But this event had taken him completely unprepared. He looked at Deborah for a long time, his blue eyes holding her gaze. Then he slowly walked to her and placed both his hands on her shoulders.

"What about Vern, daughter?"

"I've been over to talk to Vern this morning, Papa. I tried to explain to him. I love Jason, Papa, I love him very much."

She spoke the words softly and her father could read the truth of them on her face.

He smiled and kissed her gently on the cheek. "Is this what you want, Deborah? Are you sure? I want you to be happy, child."

"Yes, Papa. This is what I want."

He turned to Jason and again stretched out his hand.

"You have my blessing, Jason Deverall. Take good care of my daughter."

"I will, sir," smiled Jason, firmly grasping Mr. Martin's hand again.

Mr. Martin chuckled, and the sound grew until the surprised three watched him in amazement.

"What's so funny, Paul?" questioned his smiling wife.

"I must say these Deverall brothers move quickly when they find what they want. They've only been here a few months and they've taken both our daughters from us." He laughed again and they joined with him. Their happiness sounded through the quiet house.

If the four of them could have seen another situation that was developing, it might not only have stilled their laughter, but caused a great deal of concern.

Vern Markham had watched Deborah ride away until the sound of her horse had faded. There was a black rage boiling in him. He had loved Deborah almost from the day he had met her, and now found that it was an impossible dream to give up. He clenched his fist and the muscle in his jaw quivered with tension.

"I'll not give her up. Jason Deverall. You have a fight on your hands you won't believe. I will not give her up."

He turned toward the stables and a few minutes later had his horse saddled. Pushing the horse, he spent some of his frustrated energy in a mad gallop to town. Stopping at the King's Inn Tavern, he left his horse with a young boy and went inside. Ordering a drink, he sat down at a table before the huge fireplace and glared morosely at everything about him, causing all others in the room to keep their distance from this huge angry man.

He had stayed at the table for almost three hours, ordering one drink after another until he was becoming numb from the effects of the drinks. At the bar he was being watched closely by a tall, handsome, dark-eyed stranger. Although the man watched Vern closely, he made no move to approach him until he was sure he was completely drunk. Instead, he asked quiet subtle questions of the men about Vern. As he continued to watch, Vern's head sagged slightly and he slumped down in his chair. It was only then that the man picked his time to approach him. Pulling up a chair, he set his tankard down heavily on the table, causing Vern to start and look up at him. Although his eyes were barely able to focus, Vern continued to look at the man. "What the hell you want?" he mumbled.

"Good evening, my friend," the man said softly.

"Go away, leave me alone," Vern made a motion as if to stand but could not make it to his feet.

"Sit down, my friend," the man spoke softly again. "You and I have much to talk over."

"Don't want to talk, don't know you, go away."

The man smiled and tilted his chair back slightly. He

225

watched Vern very closely.

"Come sit down. Let me buy one more drink for you. If you want we can drink to your future wife."

It was a blow meant to strike Vern in a vulnerable spot and it succeeded perfectly. The big man sagged back into his chair as if his body were suddenly boneless. Now that he had him in the position he wanted, he leaned both elbows on the table and brought himself closer to Vern. Then in a still quiet voice, he began to speak and after about a half hour of quiet talking, Vern leaned toward him and began to listen. In his drunkenness and his desire for Deborah, Vern said things over his drink he would never have considered saying if he had been sober. The whole story came pouring out. Pointed, decisive questions were asked and answered. Then an offer was made that Vern, after some hesitation, accepted. When the man quietly left his side, Vern continued to drink until his head dropped completely senseless on the table. It took the innkeeper and four other men to carry him upstairs and put him to bed. Because the innkeeper knew and liked Vern so much, he gave him his best room and let him sleep. It was nearly noon the next day when Vern blinked his eyes open, then groaned and shut them again tightly as the room spun around him. His head throbbed painfully and the inside of his mouth was dry and foul-tasting. He didn't want to open his eyes again, but he could feel himself becoming sick. It took him almost an hour to pull himself together enough to get downstairs. The innkeeper was bustling about and greeted him with a smile and Vern winced in pain at the hearty handshake.

"Good day, Mr. Markham," the innkeeper said in a voice which to Vern sounded like a drum.

"Please, Mr. Stoke, my head is about to fall off," he

groaned and dropped into a chair, putting his head in his hands.

Mr. Stoke smiled and without saying anything, brought Vern a drink. Setting it down in front of him with a small chuckle, "Drink this, it might help a little."

Vern took the offered drink wordlessly and drank over half of it before setting it back down.

"Would you please have my horse saddled, Mr. Stoke. If I can stand up, I'm going to try to make it home," he laughed, then winced at the pain it caused. "I guess I'd rather die there."

"Of course, Mr. Markham," Mr. Stoke started to leave the room.

"By the way, Mr. Stoke, you might sum up what I owe you. From the way I feel I must have drunk half your stock."

"You owe me nothing, Mr. Markham. Your bill was paid last night by your friend."

Vern looked at him for several minutes before what he said began to register. Then with a sinking feeling in the pit of his stomach, he asked, "Friend? What friend?"

"Why, the gentleman you were drinking with most of the evening. I thought you were good friends from the way you were talking to each other for so many hours."

Vern dropped his head back into his hands. He couldn't remember a friend; for that matter, he couldn't remember much about last night at all.

"Where is my 'friend' now?"

"I don't know, sir, he left just before you passed out. We carried you upstairs and you slept until now."

"Who was my 'friend'?"

The innkeeper seemed shocked. "Why, I don't know, sir, I've never seen the man before. Don't you know?"

Vern looked at him again and a twisting stab of fear came again to his stomach. The innkeeper, shaking his head, left the room to get Vern's horse. Vern sat still for some time trying to pull together his thoughts. No matter how he tried, he could not remember much about last night. He was still trying to put together the pieces when the innkeeper came back.

"Your horse is ready, sir."

"Well, unsaddle him again, Mr. Stoke," he said softly. "I'm not leaving town until I find my 'friend.'"

Chapter Twenty-Nine

Sarah had made herself as helpful as possible to Margaret and in the passing weeks they had become friends. Margaret was grateful to her for the care she had taken of Deanna in her short stay with her. Although, Sarah did not know the reason, Margaret seemed to be extremely nervous and Sarah tried her best to make things easier around the house. Now she was in the kitchen helping prepare supper. John came into the kitchen quietly and stood watching her for some time. She smiled in his direction and continued her cooking.

"You look right at home here, Sarah," he said.

"The Martins are wonderful people. They make helping them very easy."

"Don't you think you'd be happier in your own kitchen?"

"Of course, but I imagine it will be quite some time before we get back to Boston."

"Well, Sarah," he said softly. "I wasn't exactly thinking of Boston. I was thinking more of right here."

She stopped moving about and walked to him. They stood closely without touching, and she looked into his warm brown eyes.

"Are you asking me to stay here, John?"

"I'm asking you for more than that, Sarah. I want you to do more than just stay here; I want you to stay with me. I want you to marry me, Sarah."

She chuckled lightly. "John, I thought you were a confirmed bachelor."

"Well," he said with a smile, "I thought I was too. After Ann died I thought I never would find anyone I could care that much for."

"And now . . . ?"

"And now I find I care for someone else very much. Will you stay here, Sarah?"

Sarah stood close to John and placed both her hands on his chest. She looked up into his deep honest eyes, and she knew the truth of the feelings he had expressed.

"John," she said softly. Her eyes were serious now and a look of gentle pain crossed her face. "I want you to understand what I'm going to say. I cannot marry you now, no matter how much I care for you, and I do care very much."

He started to speak and she stopped him with a gentle touch of her fingers to his lips.

"Just listen to me for a moment, John. Then maybe you will understand. When my husband and I came to Boston, we were young and newly married. Although my husband was of the highest social class, it was considered that he married well below his station. We lived together for several years with Donald's family who made my life unbearable. In the course of the years, we lived there, I gave birth to two daughters, Caroline and Susan. My husband and his family were determined to keep the girls tied to their English homeland against my wishes. I love my girls very much and we spent the first ten years of their lives together. Then my husband died. Before I could recover from the shock, Donald's family and attorneys had moved to keep me from taking my daughters away from Boston. I found I had some small means left from my husband and I bought my home. Then for the next few years, I tried in every way to get my daughters away. Although we saw each other often, I could not get them away from his family. I refused to leave Boston, much to their distress, unless I could take my girls with me. Now I must go back as soon as possible. If I don't they may send the girls to England before I can stop them."

"You can't go back, Sarah. You've helped spies escape British surveillance. If you go back you would probably be arrested, maybe even shot. I couldn't let you, I wouldn't let you."

"I will go back, John. I will go back soon. I have asked Mr. Martin to give me an escort and some supplies. Within a week I shall be leaving."

"You don't stand a chance alone, Sarah, you know that. After all these years of trying, don't you see you don't have a chance."

"Are you asking me to forget my daughters and take care of my own safety, John?" she asked softly.

"God, no, Sarah! I know you better than that. I'm asking you to let me have a chance first. Maybe there is something I can do."

"I cannot ask you to risk your life for me, John."

"You could ask me for anything, Sarah. I would gladly give it to you."

She smiled again and kissed him gently on the lips. He did not let her away from him but dropped his arms gently about her and held her unspeaking.

"Sarah, give me a month. If I could get your girls here, would you marry me and stay?" He spoke against her hair.

"How could you get them away even if you tried, John? They don't know you and are likely not to go with you."

He chuckled and gave her a slight squeeze.

"You ever hear of kidnapping, Sarah?"

She looked again at him with the slight glimmer of hope in her eyes. At the sight of it, he smiled and kissed her firmly and insistently.

"I'll have your girls out of Boston, Sarah, believe me. I know several men that will help me. We'll kidnap them and explain to them while we're on our way home."

"All right, John, I'm willing to try it your way first. When will you go?"

"Mr. Martin sent for me. There must be something going on. If he wants us to, we'll be leaving soon. I expect to see him when I leave you."

She stirred in his arms, but he would not release her. Instead, he tightened them about her. He lifted her chin with his fingers and kissed her again. This time the kiss was searching, asking for an answer. When he lifted his head, she sighed softly.

"Yes, John, I'll marry you."

"You'll never regret it, Sarah, I'll make you happy, I promise."

They were so engrossed in one another that they did not see Margaret standing in the doorway. Silently Margaret watched them for a few minutes then quietly she slipped back and left the room. She moved slowly away from the kitchen and into the drawing room where she sat down slowly before the fire. She would give Sarah and John some time together before she went back. She was seated before the fire doing something she had caught herself doing quite a bit of lately—daydreaming.

232

Paul Martin stood in the doorway and watched his wife with tiny lines forming between his brows. Since their daughters had come back from Boston, there had been a change in Margaret. Paul loved her very much, and he sensed the nervous tension that had her drawn so tightly. He had not wanted to pressure her in any way; he had wanted her to come to him of her own accord to tell him what was troubling her. Now he watched the lines of sadness form on her beautiful face and he did not know what to say or do to help her.

"Margaret."

"Oh, Paul," she smiled and rising from her chair went to his side and kissed him on the cheek.

"Have you seen John, my dear?"

"Yes, he's in the kitchen with Sarah."

"Could you get him and send him to me, Margaret? It's important I speak to him right away."

"Of course, Paul. What's the matter?"

"Washington has lost New York, they've retreated across New Jersey. I've got to send John to gather men and arms. We need all the help now we can get. I've gathered all the money we own, Margaret. Now is the time that our country needs it."

"I'm proud of you, Paul. You know anything you do I will agree with."

He smiled fondly at her. "I know, Margaret, you have always been with me when I needed you. Won't you let me do the same for you?"

"Me?"

"Margaret, I know and love you very much. Do you think I don't know when something's troubling you? Can't I help?"

"There's nothing wrong with me Paul, it's just a

nervous reaction to the girls coming home and all the preparations for Deanna's wedding. Don't worry about me," she laughed. "I'll go get John."

He watched her leave the room and for the first time in his life he became afraid of something he didn't know or understand.

This time Margaret was humming softly as she came to the kitchen door. The slight flush on Sarah's face told her clearly that she and John had just recently separated.

"John, Paul would like to speak to you in his study."

John gave one last flashing smile at Sarah and left the room. Sarah made some tea and the two women sat at the table to talk.

"Margaret, is there anything more I can do to help you with Deanna's wedding?"

"I think all the preparations have been made, Sarah. You've been a great help to me. It's going to be a beautiful wedding."

"From the glow on Deanna's face lately, I can imagine what a beautiful bride she will make. When do we begin plans for Jason and Deborah?"

"We feel Jason and Deborah should wait at least six months. It will give us enough time to reorganize before we start again." Margaret laughed. "Tell me, Sarah, what is the situation between you and John? Are you happy?"

Sarah knew Margaret was a gentle understanding woman. So she decided to tell her the whole story. She poured Margaret another cup of tea and as she lowered herself into the chair opposite her, she began to talk. The tea sat and chilled as Margaret listened intently to Sarah's story. When she was finished there were tears in Margaret's eyes.

"I'm sure John can get your girls home, although

234

kidnapping them is rather a harsh way of doing it."

"John promised if there is any other way of doing it, he will. But if that is necessary he has my blessings."

"Of course. I know how you must feel."

"I was sure you would understand, Margaret. Now would you do me a very deep favor?"

"Of course, if I can."

"Would you tell me about John's wife. I don't want to hurt him, but I would so like to know."

Margaret looked at the soft kind face of Sarah Gibson and nodded her head.

"John and Ann were very much in love. It was a terrible, terrible thing to happen. They were accidentally killed on the street in town by a drunken, nervous young soldier."

"They?"

"She was carrying John's child when she died."

"Oh, my God."

"For a while, we thought John was never going to recover. In fact, until he started making the trip north for Paul and met you, we were very worried about him. You have done him a great deal of good, my dear."

At that moment, John reappeared in the kitchen.

"Sarah, I'll have to leave. Could I talk to you alone for a few minutes?"

Margaret rose from her seat. "I was just leaving anyway. Where is my husband, John?"

"Still in the study."

"I shall not disturb him. I think I shall lie down a few minutes before supper. Good-bye for now, John."

"Good-bye, Mrs. Martin."

When she had gone, John turned to Sarah.

"I have to leave by dawn. After I do what I'm being

235

sent to do, I'll see to your girls."

Sarah looked at him and realized then just how much she loved him. Walking to his side, she took one of his hands in both of hers and held it to her breast, looking up at him with a soft smile.

"Then let's not waste a minute," she said softly.

He sighed with the release of pent-up tension and took her in his arms. After he had kissed her, they went to her room and closed the door firmly behind them.

Chapter Thirty

Vern had spent most of the day trying to find his so-called friend from the evening before, but to no avail. The innkeeper gave a negative shake of his head to every man who entered the tavern. Finally he realized that whoever his mysterious friend was, he had gotten whatever he came for and was not about to reappear. What worried him was what he might have said to the man in his drunken state. He knew that all the information he was in possession of could cost Deborah and her family a great deal, Clearhaven at the least. Their lives at the most. By the end of the day, he was deeply worried. Slowly he walked his horse toward Clearhaven and an interview with Paul Martin that he dreaded. He knew it was imperative that Paul Martin know what had happened so he could take some means to protect himself and his family.

He arrived at Clearhaven just as the sun was setting and dismounted in front of the house. He was just preparing to walk to the front door when it opened and Deborah and Jason came out. She was laughing at something Jason had said and her green eyes were filled with light happiness. She stopped short and the laughter died on her lips as she saw Vern standing watching them.

Jason had never met Vern before, but he knew from Deborah's reaction who he was facing. He took in Vern's extremely large size, and watched him with careful eyes. Although he thought Vern could have beaten him, probably with one hand, he did not show any emotion except curiosity. He extended his hand to Vern.

"Good evening, Mr. Markham. I'm Jason Deverall."

Vern ignored the hand as Jason thought he would, and looked at him coldly.

"I know who you are, Mr. Deverall. I also know what you are."

"Vern, please," Deborah cried, stepping between the two men and looking up at Vern. "Please. Don't do this, Vern. I shall never forgive you."

He looked into her green eyes. Jason watched the softening of his face as he looked at her.

"He really loves her," he thought.

"All right, Deb," Vern said softly. "But keep in mind what I told you. I've not changed the way I feel and I never shall. I meant what I said." He gave one more cold look at Jason, then passed them and entered the house.

Deborah and Jason exchanged looks. He reached out an arm and encircled her shoulder, pulling her close to him. They walked silently to the stables where they had their horses saddled and rode toward Foxmore to see Matt.

Vern stood inside the door for a few minutes, to get himself together. Then he went in search of Paul Martin. As he started toward the study, his attention was drawn to the stairs to Margaret Martin descending.

"Good evening, Vern," she smiled. "Is there something I can help you with?"

"I'd like to see Mr. Martin for a few minutes if I can, Mrs. Martin. It's very important."

Margaret looked at his tightly drawn face and her heart

caught in her throat.

"What is it, Vern? Please tell me." Her voice had dropped to almost a whisper and the alarm on her face startled Vern.

"I really should see Mr. Martin first," he hesitated.

She went to his side and put her hand on his arm. Looking up into his eyes with a pleading voice she said, "Please tell me first, Vern, please? I have to know."

"All right, Mrs. Martin. Where can we talk?"

Margaret took him into the drawing room where to his amazement she closed and locked the door behind them. Motioning him to a seat she sat opposite him and folded her hands in her lap. As he began to talk, she leaned slightly toward him as if she were afraid to miss a word of what he said. By the time he had explained everything to her, her face had gone gray and her eyes seemed to grow larger and larger.

"Are you all right, Mrs. Martin?" he asked worriedly. He did not realize what the effect of his story was going to have on her.

"I'm fine, Vern," she said quietly. "Please go to the study and tell my husband."

"I'm not sure I should leave you alone. Are you sure you're all right?"

"Yes, of course, I'm fine, Vern" She smiled and patted his arm. "Now go, please, and tell Paul."

He hesitated for a moment then turned and left the room.

She sat frozen in her chair, her face drained of all color. So he had come as Deanna had thought he would. Knowing Mark Severn as she did, she realized that he had planned what he had done, and now possessed the knowledge to destroy her family. It was completely dark

239

in the room before she stood up and left it.

"You have no idea who the man was?" Paul Martin asked again.

"I'm sorry, sir. I did everything to try to find out. It's as if the ground opened up and swallowed him." He raked his hands through his hair and slumped into a chair.

"I'm sorry, Mr. Martin. I've probably ruined everything. I'm really sorry."

"Don't panic, Vern. If he hasn't contacted us or sent the authorities, it must mean he had something definite in mind. There is something he wants from us. Let us wait for a while before we start to move. Knowing Governor Rosemond like I do, if he knew about us he would have been here by now."

Paul Martin sat back in his chair and placed the tips of his fingers together before him.

"No, Vern," he said quietly. "We will be patient and not panic. I've a feeling we will be hearing from your mysterious friend. I just hope we can supply him what he wants to keep his secrets."

Jason and Deborah had ridden over to Foxmore to see Matt, who with Cat's help was working around the clock to have it ready in time for the wedding next week. Deanna had been at home working as hard on the things she would bring with her to her new home.

Hailing them as they rode up, Jason and Deborah were rewarded by the poking of Cat's smiling face out of one of the upstairs windows he was repairing.

"I'm glad someone's come. This man's going to work me until I drop, and without a drop to drink, too," laughed Cat.

"We've brought something to drink," Deborah called up.

240

"Well, I don't know about Matt, but I'll be right down," shouted Cat and his face disappeared from the window. True to his word, he reappeared at the door within a few minutes with a reluctant Matt in tow.

"We'll never get finished in time for the wedding if we keep stopping."

Cat winked at Jason. "And if we send Deanna an exhausted bridegroom, we'll be finished."

Everyone laughed at Matt's embarrassment. They sat on the front porch in the dying light of day and talked happily. Finally Cat rose, stretching his arms over his head.

"Well, I'm going home. Deeta will forget what I look like pretty soon. Good night everyone."

They said good night and watched Cat ride away into the darkness.

Finally Deborah reminded Jason that they must leave also. Clapping his brother on the shoulder, Jason rose and helped Deborah to her horse.

"Oh, by the way, Matt, isn't there another cabin up near Cat's?"

"Yes, why?"

"Oh, I was just wondering. I thought I heard Cat mention them."

Jason mounted his horse and after saying good night, he and Deborah left.

The night was very quiet and Matt sat for a long time on the porch thinking of the week to come, when he would have Deanna here with him. His mind drifted to the dreams he always had of Deanna and their children seated here on the porch with him. With a contented sigh, he finally rose and went inside to bed.

Jason and Deborah rode together for some distance

before she heard the soft sound of his ever-present chuckle on the night air. Pulling her horse to a stop, she waited until he stopped beside her. She looked into his eyes in the moonlight. There it was, the gleaming light of wicked deviltry that was always close to the surface with him. She could not help but smile in return.

"What is so amusing, Jason?"

"Oh, I was just thinking as I watched you ride ahead of me, that the cabin of Matt's is on our way home." He leaned close to her now and touched her mouth lightly with his. "Why don't we stop and look it over for a few minutes," he said softly.

She could feel the warm stirring he always caused in her and merely nodded her head. A bright flash of his smile, and they moved their horses in the direction of the cabin. When they arrived, she was amazed to see the soft glow of light in the cabin. She looked at Jason, whose eyes sparkled with laughter. He stepped down from his horse and went to her side. Lifting his arms he put both hands about her waist, and placing her hands on his shoulders, she let him lift her down. She could feel the hard pull of the muscles along his back as he slid her slowly down the length of his body. Not quite letting her feet touch the ground, he held her against him. Slowly he took her mouth with his, and gently parting her lips with his tongue he kissed her thoroughly. Without saying another word, he lifted her in his arms and carried her to the door. When he pushed it open and stepped inside, kicking it shut with his foot, she received another shock when she looked at the room. A fire had been set and was burning warmly. The cabin had been cleaned until it sparkled. There was not much furniture in it, but spread in front of the fire was a huge black bearskin rug. As she turned surprised eyes to him, his laughter broke loose.

"I've been up here every day for a week. Tonight I had Cat stop and light the fire." Now his eyes became serious as he stood close to her and looked into her eyes.

"Deborah, I can't stand being so near you and yet so far. I thought we could have this evening here alone away from the rest of the world. I love you so. I need you, Deb." His voice dropped to a soft whisper.

He must have mistaken her silence for something else for he moved back from her and regarded her quietly.

"Deb, if you don't want . . ."

"Oh, you fool, Jas," she sighed as she lifted her arms to him. "I'm so glad you did this, I've been wracking my brain to think of some way."

His answering laugh was drowned in her startled gasp as he lifted her high in his arms and spun her about. He carried her to the fireplace where he stood her again on her feet. The kiss he gave her then was so filled with demanding fire that she clung to him dizzily. He was fumbling with the buttons of her blouse and she moved a little away from him. He watched her as she slowly removed her clothes. When she looked up at him again his eyes told her everything she wanted to know. She moved gracefully to the rug and sat down upon it with her legs tucked under her. Still he did not move, but merely stood drinking in her beauty.

"Jas," she whispered softly.

Now he moved swiftly, and within minutes he had thrown off his clothes and was kneeling beside her on the rug. Softly his hands played over her body as he knelt beside her. Cupping her face in his hands he kissed her closed eyes, her cheeks, then his lips found hers and they fell to the rug together. With a groan, he pulled her body

243

close to his. She could feel the hard seeking of his hands over her body and she sighed with pleasure.

"I'm starved for you, Deb," he whispered. "I'll never get enough of you."

Now his insistent mouth travelled over her warm skin, leaving a trail of fiery pleasure behind. Then to Jason's surprise, Deborah sat up. He looked steadily at her for a moment, then smiled as her hands on his chest pushed him back on the rug. He had explored her, knew every inch of her body. Now she too wanted to explore. She kissed him, covering his face and neck with soft gentle touches of her lips, and her hands travelled over his long hard muscular body, down over the soft mat of fur on his chest, and over the curving in his narrow waist to the flat, tautly pulled muscles of his stomach. She let her lips drift in soft kisses over him while her hands found the hard maleness of him. He groaned as he gripped her with his hands and brought her to him. He sighed her name over and over as they moved together. She was lifted with the beauty of their love and carried along on a wave of passion that threatened to overpower her. She clung desperately to him, her rock in this sea of desire. Now they moved in rhythm and she did not even hear the words of love that came from her as they were carried along to the peaks.

They lay together contented for a long time before he spoke.

"Deb, do we have to wait six months to marry?"

She chuckled and turned in his arms to look up into his eyes.

"No, Jas, I don't think we'd better, I can't stay away from you and I'm sure something's bound to happen soon."

Again the sparkle of devilish laughter in his eyes.

"I hope so. Then we'd have to marry right away. Why didn't I think of that before. I could have been working toward it all this time."

Their laughter mingled as he gathered her into his arms.

"We have to go, my lovely."

She nodded, reluctant to leave this beautiful place. They dressed and stood together at the door, looking into the warm, love filled room. With a last gentle kiss, they closed the door and started for home.

Chapter Thirty-One

Matt and Deanna swayed together to the soft strains of the waltz, his arm tightly about her waist he looked into the sky blue of her eyes.

"Do you remember the first time we danced together?"

She smiled up at him.

"Oh, yes, my pirate, I remember. How can I ever forget you stared at me so and I was so nervous."

"I knew who you were, but I simply wanted you to tell me."

He pulled her tightly against him and with his lips against her hair murmured softly, "How much longer do we have to stay here? I want to take you home."

She laughed lightly and squeezed him back. "Not much longer, Matt. We've got to keep all these people who've come to our wedding happy."

"To hell with all these people. Do you have any idea what you're doing to me?"

She pulled slightly away from him and smiled mischievously up into his face. Her eyes turned warm and she parted her lips slightly.

"Matt," she whispered his name softly, then moved back tightly into his arms quickly so no one could see her and raised her mouth and kissed his throat, touching it lightly with the tip of her tongue. She giggled quietly at his reaction, for she could feel the entire length of his body against her. She could feel his shoulders shaking as he laughed softly.

"You're going to pay for that later, Minx," he said huskily as he squeezed her until she could barely breathe.

"Matt, let me go. I'll behave, I promise."

"Well, I'm really not sure I want you to behave, and I definitely don't want to let you go. You feel very good, lady," he laughed.

They were so much in love and caught up with each other that they were oblivious to the affectionate smiles of everyone about them. Cat and Deeta stood by the punch bowl and watched with smiling faces.

"I think those two ought to go home," laughed Cat.

Deeta giggled, "Shhh, Cat. Someone will hear you."

He leaned down close to her ear. "Why don't we go home too, I don't think Matt and Deanna would miss us right now."

Deeta smiled up at him in agreement and they slipped quietly toward the door.

The couple on the ballroom floor was being watched by another couple who looked at them in affectionate envy. Jason looked down at Deborah's face and she read his thoughts well.

"It won't be too long, Jas, I promise."

"It better not be, Deb. Will you come to the cabin tonight?" he asked hopefully.

"I don't know, Jas, if I can get away. For some reason, Mother is very nervous and since Deanna will be gone, she might want me with her."

He nodded in understanding disappointment. "I'm staying there tonight. I'll wait for you just in case." He held out his arms and she slipped into their enclosing circle. He swung her out onto the dance floor.

"Since this is the only way I can keep my arms around you, we're going to do a lot of dancing tonight."

He heard the soft responding sound of her laughter.

Paul and Margaret had moved through the large crowd of people, making their guests welcome and seeing to the drinks and food. Now the hour was getting late and it was time for the young couple to leave. They were saying good-bye to the last of their guests. Margaret kissed her daughter and her new son-in-law and Paul shook his hand and held his daughter close for a few minutes. Then they were gone. Paul stood looking at his wife. "Where were the words," he thought in desperation. "What can I say or do to ease her when I don't know what is wrong." They looked at each other for a few minutes, then Margaret dropped her eyes.

"I shall be up soon, Paul. I've to see to some final arrangements for tomorrow."

"All right, my love," he said softly. "Margaret . . ."

"Yes, Paul?"

"Nothing, I just want you to know how much I love you."

She smiled at him and touched lightly the side of his face with her fingers.

"I know, Paul. I know," she said softly, then she turned and left him.

He could feel a gentle tugging pain but there was nothing he could say or do to stop what was happening. He went slowly up the stairs to bed.

Margaret was coming from the kitchen to go upstairs when one of the servants came to her.

"Mrs. Martin, there's a gentleman to see you, ma'am."

"Me," she said. "Where is he?"

248

"I put him in the study, ma'am. I told him it was late but I thought he might be a guest that got here late. He looks like a gentleman, ma'am. Did I do something wrong, Mrs. Martin?"

"No, no," she said hoarsely, for her heart had begun to pound violently against her ribs and her throat was so constricted she could hardly speak. "Go to bed, Marie, I won't need you any more tonight."

"Yes, ma'am."

When the girl had left, she stood staring at the study door. She knew who stood on the other side, and the fear left her weak and trembling. She lifted her chin determinedly and opened the door. Swinging about, she closed and locked it then she turned to face the man standing by the fireplace.

He stood with his back to her, one hand braced on the mantel and the other on his hip contemplating the now-dying fire.

"Mark," she said softly.

He stiffened slightly at the sound of her voice then turned slowly to look at her. Margaret Martin made a beautiful picture. She had worn a gown of soft rose cut rather low so the soft rising curve of her breasts could be seen. There was the sparkle of diamonds against her golden skin. Her eyes reflected the glow of the fire in the semi-dark room and shone like pools of deep water. He caught his breath slightly at the lovely vision she made.

"Somehow I knew you would still be very beautiful, Margaret," he said quietly.

"What do you want, Mark? Why are you here?"

He gave a light chuckle somewhere deep in his chest and walked toward her. He stood just a few inches from her. So close he could see the tiny pulse throbbing rapidly at her throat. He smiled, for she was reacting as he had wanted her to. He knew then that he still had the power to reawaken the woman in Margaret. She, too, came to the full realization of her weakness and fought blindly to overcome it.

"Did you think I would ever forget you, Margaret? Did you think I would ever really let you go. Do you remember the last time we were together, I told you then I would find you no matter where you went. It has taken me a long time, my dear, but I've found you. This time I'll never let you go. I've hungered for you all these years, Margaret."

"Mark, please!" It was almost a sob. "Please go away and leave me alone. I've made a new life. I . . . I love my husband."

He gave a short harsh laugh. "You and I both know that's a lie, but even if it were true, I couldn't stand to leave you again."

"You did it before," she said violently. "When I needed you the most, when I wanted you the most."

"I was stupid and vain. It took me some time after you left to put the blame where it belonged. I never should have let you go then. But I never make a stupid mistake twice, Margaret."

He reached for her and she knew if he touched her she was lost. Stepping away from him quickly her mind began to work rapidly. She walked to the fireplace then turned to face him again.

"It was you at the Tavern with Vern, wasn't it?"

He laughed. "Yes, it was me. The very young very foolish man told me everything I wanted to know."

"What do you intend to do with your information?"

Before speaking again he walked to the fireplace and

placing one hand on it over her head, he smiled grimly at her.

"Why," he said softly, "I intend to trade it for something I want very badly."

He heard the soft intake of her breath.

"Blackmail."

"Call it whatever you like, Margaret."

She made a move, but this time he was too quick. Dropping his hands, he caught her about the waist and spun her violently into his arms. Now his mouth came crashing down on hers, taking possession. Brutally demanding, his lips parted hers and he tore away the years like a curtain of gauze. She tried to fight him, but he held her arms locked to her sides with the superior strength of his hard arms. He could feel her losing the battle and he forced his advantage. Slowly her mouth softened under his and with a moaning cry she relaxed in his arms. Suddenly his kiss became gentle and she could feel the hard knot of desire build in her as it had in the past. When he lifted his head from hers, she swayed slightly as if she stood on a dizzy height. Now she clung to him to get her whirling world to stop.

"Margaret," he said very softly. "You belong to me. You have always belonged to me."

With a strangled cry she dropped her head on his chest.

"Mark, go away, please go away. If you really love me as you say you do, don't ruin everything I've built. My daughters, my son, my husband. Must you hurt everyone to get what you want?"

"Margaret, tell me the truth. Tell me what I want to hear." He took her by the shoulders and looked deeply into her eyes. "Tell me, tell me. After all this time I have to hear you say it."

"All right," she sobbed. "I never stopped loving you, Mark, never!"

He gave a low inarticulate sound in his throat and pulled her again into his arms. The kiss was not a taking thing this time, but a giving one. She had never felt anything like the sweeping tide of love the kiss told her about. When he lifted his head again, she was molded against him in complete defeat.

"Now, Margaret, you will tell me one other thing I must know."

She looked up at him with the unspoken question in her eyes.

"Deanna and Deborah, they're my daughters, aren't they?"

Chapter Thirty-Two

Margaret stared at Mark and a fiery burning rage began to build in her. It sparked from her eyes so suddenly that he stepped back from her.

"That is something you will never know, Mark. You come back after years of being away and you want to pick up where you left off before you went prancing away on your white horse. No, it was Paul Martin who held my hand as I gave birth to the girls. It was Paul who saw them take their first step, and it was Paul who loved and cared for us over the years. Paul Martin is their father."

"You didn't give me a chance, Margaret."

"How much of a chance did you need, Mark. You were the first man in my life. If you had really loved me, you would have been the last. When I pleaded with you to stay, or take me with you, do you remember what you said?"

He nodded his head. "I remember everything I said to you, Margaret. Don't you think I've had regrets? Don't you think I've lain awake nights wishing I could turn back the clock. I've dreamed of you. Holding you, touching you until it became so real I sometimes thought I was losing my mind. Now I've found you, and you and I both know what exists between us. We have something very special and I don't intend to lose it again. We're like a song, Margaret," he said softly, and now his eyes were holding hers as he gently pulled her again into his arms. "I am the words and you are the music. Without each other we are nothing. Try to combine with any others and it is flat and off-key. Together we sing." The words died to a whisper as he again brought his mouth to hers.

They stood clinging together in the quiet shadows of the half-darkened room. When he finally released her, she was trembling and tears slipped gently unheeded down her cheeks. How could she fight him when he had the power to do this to her? What could she say to protect those she loved?

"Mark," she began.

He waited for her to speak again, watching her intently. "Give me some time, Mark, let me get myself together. Let me think."

"I'll give you a week, Margaret."

She turned away from him with a choking sob, "A week!"

He came behind her and ran the tips of his fingers over her shoulder. "After a week, if you do not tell me your answer, I go to Governor Rosemond with my information. For if I cannot have you, Margaret, Paul Martin will not have you either."

She covered her face with her hands and her body swayed with the pain. If Governor Rosemond was told all this information, Paul Martin would be dead within a week.

"Would you really do this, Mark?"

"There is nothing I would not do, Margaret. I want you to come to me. Meet me anywhere you choose, but I want you."

She looked up at him and realized that he spoke the truth. There was no quarter in his eyes and his mouth was pulled taut and grim.

"All right, Mark, I'll meet you wherever you say."

He recognized the complete surrender and his heart began to pound furiously. He reached for her. She stepped back away and held out her hands as if to ward him off.

"Not here, not in Paul's house. I could not do that."

"Then where will you meet me?" he asked quietly.

"Where are you staying?"

"I've taken a small house on the old Sutter Road. Do you know the place?"

She nodded her head.

"When?" he breathed.

"Tomorrow night." She could hardly get the words out the pain was so severe.

"I'll be waiting, Margaret," he said softly, and with a quiet click of the door he was gone.

Margaret leaned against the door weakly as the full realization of what she had done struck her with blinding force. Slowly she slid to her knees and with wracking sobs, leaned her forehead against the door and cried.

It seemed hours before she had the strength to get up, and she slowly walked up the stairs to her room. Taking off her clothes, she put on her nightgown and got into bed. But elusive sleep was not to come and she was still awake when the soft rays of the sun came silently over the horizon.

As Paul began to stir she closed her eyes and feigned sleep. She could not talk to him this morning. But Paul Martin had slept with Margaret too many years. He could feel the tension in every muscle of her body and he knew she was not asleep. "If only there were some way I could reach her, make her understand that nothing is too big

255

for us to handle together. If I only knew what was hurting her so. Poor Margaret," he thought.

He rose quietly and dressed and when he was gone from the room, Margaret turned her face into the pillow and the fresh hot tears tore her apart. Standing outside the door, Paul heard the soft crying and his heart ached for her, but he knew if he went back in, she would make some excuse for them and brush them away. No, he just had to be patient and wait for her to come to him.

After she heard the outside door slam and knew Paul had finished his breakfast and gone, she rose from the bed. Her body felt heavy and exhausted. She went to her mirror. Her face was very pale and her eyes were red from weeping. She splashed cold water over her face until she felt the skin tingle with the chill. Then, holding a cold cloth over her eyes, she lay back on the bed for a few minutes. When her mirror told her that her face was normal again, she put on her clothes and went downstairs.

Jason and Deborah were already at the table when she arrived and before she could sit down, Sarah also came in. She smiled affectionately at Margaret.

"Good morning, Margaret, did you sleep well? You look a little tired. I can take over the household chores today if you'd rather go back to bed for a while."

Margaret smiled at Sarah. Lately she and Sarah had been more like sisters than friends.

"No, Sarah. It's just a mood. I will feel better today if I'm busy."

Deborah had been watching her mother closely and suddenly realized that since they had gotten home something about her mother had changed. Something was wrong. She wanted to talk to Deanna about it.

"Jason, would you ride over to Deanna's with me this morning?"

"Sure, Deb. There's a few stops I'd like to make too; we'll make a day of it."

Deborah knew he meant the cabin they shared occasionally and hoped her mother did not see the slight trembling of her hands as Jason winked at her across the table.

After Jason and Deborah had gone, Margaret threw herself into her work with the fury of a demon. Even Sarah, who seemed untiring, became exhausted. By supper time, Margaret's high-strung tension was near the breaking point. She had almost decided to wait until Paul came home and go to him. She would tell him everything. Then if he wanted her to leave, she would go. The decision was not even formed in her mind when a rider could be heard approaching. When she was told a messenger wanted to see her, she went out immediately. The man stood before her hat in hand.

"Miz Martin. I've got a message from your husband."

"Yes?"

"He says to tell you he won't be home tonight. Something's come up and he has to stay in town. He'll sleep at the Tavern and see you in the morning."

Margaret thanked him numbly and when the door closed behind him, she suddenly felt defeated.

It seemed even fate was against her. Sarah spoke from behind her.

"Is something wrong, Margaret, has something happened?"

"No, it was just a message from Paul. He won't be home tonight. If you don't mind, Sarah. I think I'll skip supper. I really am very tired. I'm going to bed. Will you

257

see I'm not disturbed?"

"Of course, Margaret. Good night, dear."

Margaret walked slowly up the stairs to her room. Inside she went to the closet and took out her riding habit. Slowly, she dressed, trying not to think of the wrong in what she was about to do. She kept her mind on her family. She loved them and no sacrifice was too great for their protection. When she was ready she extinguished the candles and stood in the dark for a moment. Then she opened the door and looked out. The hall was empty. She left the room swiftly and went to the stairs. She could hear the soft sounds of piano music. "Good. Sarah is at the piano, and from there the door can not be seen." She moved swiftly down the stairs and across the foyer to the door. Slipping out quickly she almost ran across the lawn to the stable. It was empty, and she saddled her horse herself and led him halfway down the lane before mounting. Her destination was over three miles away and she rode at a steady pace. When she arrived at the house, it was very dark. The light flicker of a candle glowed from within. He had heard her horse, for he opened the door immediately. He came to her side as soon as she pulled her horse to a halt. They looked at each other silently for a minute then he lifted his arms to her and she came into them. He brought her down from the horse and stood holding her without talking.

"I'll put your horse away," he said quietly.

She nodded but still did not trust herself to speak. He bent and touched her lips lightly with his and she stood and waited as he led her horse to the back. When he came back, he took her hand and they moved toward the door. At the doorway she hesitated. She could not bring herself to cross it. Without saying anything, he bent and lifted her into his arms. He cradled her that way for a minute, then pushed open the door and stepped inside.

When he stood her on her feet, he did not let go of her. In the semi-dark room she could see the glow in his eyes.

"Margaret, my darling. It has been forever. Come to me, please," he said softly.

Slowly she raised her arms to him and he pulled her very gently against him, savoring the nearness of her. When his lips found hers, they were soft and gentle. Slowly as his arms tightened, his mouth grew more insistent. Now he felt her quiver in his arms and he loosened the flooding tide of his desire. His tongue forced her lips apart and she responded with her own, sending a spark of flame through his whole body. Again he lifted her wordlessly and carried her to another door which he pushed open with his foot. Stepping inside, he stood her down and closed the door behind him. There was a candelabrum burning on the dresser throwing shadows across the large bed in the center of the room. She turned and looked at him, then slowly began to remove her gown. He said nothing until she dropped the last remnants of her clothes on the floor, but rather merely drank in her beauty like a man dying of thirst. "Margaret." Her name came hoarsely from his lips. "Oh, God," he said as he pulled her against the rough fabric of his shirt. Now he kissed her fiercely, and she lifted her arms and brought her body against him while his hands ran down her back and waist and over the soft rounded curves of her hips. He grasped her and pulled her against him. Then with a quick movement, he brought her to the bed. He removed his clothes quickly and dropped lightly down beside her. His eyes took in every curve and valley of her body. Then he dropped his lips to her throat and

259

with a sigh she turned in his arms and pressed his head against her breasts.

"Oh, Mark," she whispered.

It was there again as it had been in the beginning for them. Matching flames that battled each other even as they fought to rise higher and higher. She gave herself to him with an abandon she had forgotten she had possessed. And he accepted her with the gentleness and care of one who truly loves. He said her name over and over as he brought her to him. He could feel the soft caressing of her hands on his back and the velvet feel of her legs as they entwined to hold him.

Now all time was forgotten and he consumed her, lifting and holding her, taking her until she gasped his name aloud. She could feel the rippling of the muscles along his back as he moved into her. They were strong hard muscles and he moved with a fierceness that threatened to tear her apart. She cried out and clung desperately to him as they reached the peak together and held for that long ecstatic moment.

Afterwards, he cradled her in his arms like a child, and kissing away the warm tears gently he lifted her chin to look into her eyes. He smiled a warm smile of love and brushed her mouth with his.

"You see, Margaret, we sing, and it is our song alone. That is why you'll never leave me. We will find a way you and I to be together forever."

"I will not hurt Paul," she said softly.

He did not reply immediately, only pulled her into his arms and gently kissed the top of her head.

"We will find a way," he answered.

Chapter Thirty-Three

John sat on his heels in front of his horse and watched the house for some time without moving. Then he rose and mounted his horse. Wheeling him about he rode rapidly down the hill to where two men waited for him with the extra horses. If all went as he had planned he would be on his way home with Sarah's girls within the hour. He had arrived in Boston two weeks before and had immediately delivered his dispatches. Then after asking a few discreet questions, he found where the Gibsons' girls lived. It was a beautiful home outside the town about six miles, but well guarded. There were servants over-running the place and John had found it impossible to get near. Instead, he had watched closely for comings and goings of the family until he found a repetition in their routines. Every day at tea time the girls were sent in a carriage to the home of an aunt who was a poor relative and so used as an instructress for the girls' musical talents.

For over a week, he had watched them leave. Several times he had followed to see how long they were expected to be gone from home. It was almost three hours from the time they left their homes until the carriage arrived at their front door. John smiled to himself. Give him three hours head start and they would never find them. It took him another week to work out his plans, but today he was

261

ready. As he joined the two men at the bottom of the hill, he spoke quickly and softly.

"The carriage has just left the house. It should come down over the hill in about five minutes."

John and the men melted quietly into the trees on either side of the road. Within minutes, the carriage topped the hill and the driver slowed to begin the descent. John watched and waited quietly and when the slow-moving carriage was almost abreast of them, he spurred his horse with the other men following his lead and converged upon the carriage. The driver, taken completely by surprise, could do nothing but raise his hands when the round barrel of a gun was pointed in his direction.

The girls, however, were another matter. Caroline Gibson could never be accused of being a coward. On the contrary, she was always judged the other way, as having too much courage. She was a beautiful and spirited girl of eighteen. She had soft reddish gold hair that glistened in the sunlight and a smooth creamy complexion that matched it. She had inherited her mother's lovely blue eyes and she had caused quite a stir among Boston males with their flirting glitter. Now, however, they flashed a blazing glow as she struck the first man to approach the carriage. There were bright spots of rage on her cheeks and her body trembled, not with fear, for she did not know the meaning of the word, but with violent anger. She struck the man again and again as he tried to grasp first her then her sister.

"Goddamn, you little she-cat," the man shouted. "Come help me with her, I can't handle her."

"You won't handle me, you two-legged snake," she shouted.

John laughed heartily and went to David's aid. It took the two of them to pull her, scratching and kicking, from the carriage. Her sister was pulled tearfully behind her.

"Don't cry, Susan," she said. "They'll send someone after us right away, and we can have the privilege of watching these animals hang."

"We'll be well on our way to Philadelphia by then," said one of the men for the driver's benefit.

"Shut up, man," said John, hoping he sounded angry enough. Pointing his gun at the driver, he said, "I shall have to ask you to step down, sir. We can't have anyone following us for at least three hours."

Caroline's eyes snapped in his direction when she realized he knew exactly how much time they had. After they had tied up the driver, they pulled the carriage into the trees and left him in it. Taking the girls on the extra horses, they travelled as rapidly as possible.

Caroline did everything in her power, much to John's amusement, to slow them down. She must have been an excellent rider for she tried to control her mount with her knees, since her hands were tied behind her more for their protection than anything else. She glared at John at every opportunity and became even more angry when he seemed to get so much amusement from her.

They had been on the road just under three hours when they came to the hiding place they had chosen. John had wanted to tell the girls the truth as soon as possible, first because he wanted them to change clothes to make it easier for them to travel, and second because he needed their cooperation now to make the trip faster.

When they dismounted, the two others looked toward John.

"You get her down, John. I'm not goin' near her," laughed David.

John went to Caroline's horse and neatly dodged a well-aimed foot. He looked up into the smoldering fire of her eyes.

"Don't you touch me," she snapped.

John finally became exasperated, reached up and grabbed her, jerking her violently from the saddle. He heard her gasping sound, and for the first time since the carriage was stopped, Caroline's face showed fear. She was panting and trying to back away from him.

"Caroline," he said quietly extending his hand to her.

"How did you know my name? What do you want? We have no money. What do you want?" she repeated, and the last sentence came out with a hoarse squeak.

"Caroline, your mother sent me for you."

"Mother! I don't believe you."

Without coming any closer to her, John quietly explained the situation. Slowly the realization came to her that he must be telling the truth, for he knew too much about them to be lying.

Suddenly her face seemed to crumple and tears ran down her cheeks. John reached out his arms and held her until her hysteria passed.

"I'm sorry," she sobbed. "But I never thought I would see Mother again."

"It's all right, Caroline, Susan. I'm sorry I frightened you but I just couldn't ride up to the house and take you. This was the only way I could think of."

She smiled, and when she did her whole face glowed. "I would have given up my soul to see Mother again. John?"

"Yes."

"Would you untie me, please?"

They both began laughing as he reached for the ropes that bound her. After the girls had changed into the riding clothes of Deanna's John had brought along, they rested the horses for a little longer and then they all remounted and started the long trip home.

As they travelled, Caroline questioned John, and slowly the story came out. With a wisdom beyond her years, Caroline put together the pieces of the story John deliberately left out. They had been travelling over a week and Caroline and Susan had come to respect the way John had handled the discomforts of travel for them.

They were seated now around a small fire over which John had roasted a couple of rabbits he had shot. Licking away the last taste of it from her fingers, Susan yawned and stretched her arms.

"I'm going to sleep, Caro. I'm so tired. How much longer do we have to travel, John?"

"Three or four more days should see you safely in your mother's arms," smiled John.

She murmured her thanks and went to her blanket where, with the adaptability of youth, she fell immediately asleep.

Caroline and John sat by the fire alone for some time. The fire burned down into red glowing embers before she spoke.

"John?"

"Yes, Caroline."

"Do you love my mother?"

He gave a little jerk of surprise. He hadn't realized he had been talking so much about Sarah, but now the realization came to him that over the past few days, Sarah had been uppermost in his mind.

"You are a very observant girl for one so young."

She smiled at him. "I'm not so young, John. I'll be nineteen next month. At nineteen, mother already had me."

He chuckled. "Nineteen, that's almost an old lady."

She flushed a little but looked directly at him. "Don't laugh at me. Don't underestimate me and don't change the subject, John."

Now his shoulders shook with the laughter he was trying to suppress for this beautiful child-woman.

"All right, Miss Wise One. I love your mother very much. She wouldn't marry me until she had come back to Boston for you two girls."

"Which you couldn't let her do, right?"

"Right," he shrugged. "Maybe I bit off more than I could chew."

Now they were both laughing together. She reached over and took one of his big calloused hands in one of hers.

"I should be proud to have you for a father."

For a moment, John was speechless with surprise. Then he patted her hands with his free one.

"And I should be more than proud to have a daughter as sweet and beautiful as you. No wonder your mother wanted you here so badly. You must be the sunshine of her life."

"When we get home, we'll be a family again. You, Mama, Susan and me. It will be wonderful."

John felt a tight choking feeling in his throat and he said gruffly, "You'd better get some sleep, young lady. We have to get an early start tomorrow."

She smiled at the pretend harshness of his voice for she had seen the shining glint of moisture in his eyes.

266

Rising, she went to his side and kissed him gently on the cheek.

"Good night, my soon to be Papa," she whispered.

"Good night, Caroline," came out hoarsely from his rapidly closing throat.

For a long time after she was asleep, John stared at the dying fire. The aching desire for Sarah was in every muscle of his body. He thought again of the beautiful child asleep in his care and the urgent desire to get home as rapidly as possible to make his family a whole one again.

Chapter Thirty-Four

Margaret slipped quietly back to the house, leading her horse the last few yards, and unsaddled him herself. She covered the short distance between the stable and the house hurriedly. Then soundlessly opened the door and stepped inside. The house was dark and still. It took only another few minutes and she stood inside the closed door of her bedroom. Quickly removing her clothes, she washed her face and hands, donned her nightgown and climbed into the big bed. She lay still for a long time, trying to find a way to sleep, but the twisting memories of the past and the thoughts of the night kept her sleepless. It was over three hours before she heard a light tap on her door.

"Come in," she called.

Sarah came into the room.

"How are you feeling, Margaret?"

"I'm fine, Sarah, why?"

"You looked unwell at supper last night, would you like to stay in bed? I could bring you some breakfast?"

Margaret smiled. She realized the quality of friendship she had acquired in Sarah, and wondered in a flashing moment if Sarah would understand her situation if she told her. The desire to confide in someone she could trust and ask for advice rose strongly in her.

"Sarah?"

"Yes, Margaret."

She hesitated. "Maybe I will have breakfast here and rest a while longer. If it isn't too much trouble, Sarah."

Sarah smiled warmly at her and turned to the door. "It is definitely no trouble, Margaret. I would be happy to bring you something. I'll be back in a few minutes."

She left and Margaret looked long at the door as it closed behind her, and for some reason unknown to her at the moment hot tears began to slip quietly down her cheeks. Sarah went downstairs to the kitchen where she began to prepare a tray for Margaret. She was moving quietly with her thoughts so absorbed she did not hear the door open quietly.

"I love to watch you in the kitchen, Sarah," came John's soft voice from the doorway. She started and looked quickly toward the sound of his voice.

"John!" she laughed, and crossing the kitchen she threw herself into his arms. He gave a soft murmuring sigh of her name as he buried his face in her hair, holding her tightly. After a few minutes she pushed herself a little away from him.

"John, I can't breathe."

He chuckled, but let her go. Moving to the table, he leaned against it, folding his arms and looking at her.

"Well, John?"

"Well, what, Sarah, love?"

"Oh, John, you can be most exasperating. Did you get to see my girls? Is there any way to get them out of Boston? Oh, John, tell me please, did you get to see them?"

"Oh, that's right," he said snapping his fingers and looking as though he'd forgotten something. "I brought you a little gift from Boston, Sarah."

He moved back to the door and swung it open to reveal Caroline and Susan standing there. Sarah gave an exclamation of delight and with glowing eyes held out her arms into which both girls threw themselves, laughing happily. They were crying, laughing and kissing each other while trying to talk at the same time. John's throaty chuckle could be heard throughout the room as he thoroughly enjoyed the reunion of his soon to be family.

Margaret waited for quite some time, then not being able to sleep, she restlessly rose from the bed and went downstairs. The sounds of happiness reverberating from the kitchen met her ears as she reached the bottom of the steps. She moved in the direction of the kitchen and pushed open the door. The sound and sight of the happiness that greeted her eyes brought a smile to her lips. She watched them for some time before they noticed her presence.

"Oh, Margaret," laughed Sarah happily. "I want you to meet my girls."

"Your daughters, Sarah!" exclaimed Margaret.

"Yes, this is Caroline, my oldest, she's eighteen."

"No, Mama, nineteen," interrupted Caroline, smiling at Margaret and dropping a curtsy. "I'm very pleased to meet you, Mrs. Martin."

"Hello, Caroline."

"And this is my youngest. You are sixteen aren't you, Susan, or have you aged so since I last saw you?"

Susan smiled. "Yes, Mama, I'm sixteen. I'm very pleased to meet you, too, Mrs. Martin."

"Your girls are quite beautiful, Sarah. We must make them welcome. I'll have rooms prepared for you and you can meet the rest of my family at dinner. We'll make it a gala affair."

"They won't be staying too long, Mrs. Martin," John said. "Probably only a few days, or just until Sarah can get her things together. We're going to be married as soon as I can get the minister out here."

"You're not wasting any time, John," laughed Margaret.

"I've wasted enough time," he said, placing an arm about Sarah and reaching for both girls with the other. "It's time I got my family together."

"Very well, John. Can I at least have a small party for them, or are you in too much of a hurry for that?" Margaret's eyes were sparkling with happiness and John responded in kindness.

"A party would be great. A wedding party," he said.

They were talking excitedly when a shouted "Hello" came from the front of the house. Margaret left the kitchen and went out to see who was arriving.

Paul Martin and Vern had just entered the front door. Paul seemed extremely tired and Vern's eyes were solemn. His mouth was pulled into a tight, grim line and he too seemed to be suffering from a lack of sleep.

"What is it, Paul? What's happened?" Her eyes had become full of fear and the tight feeling clutched again at her stomach.

Paul turned to Margaret and replied quietly. "We've gotten several dispatches from many directions, but the tenor of each is the same. A number of things have happened that put an end to any thought we had of not participating actively in this war. The duties we've performed and what we've contributed mean nothing now. We have to commit ourselves now."

Margaret was silent for a few minutes, trying to control her furiously pounding heart. "Tell me all that

271

has happened, Paul."

"Colonel John Stark and his Green Mountain boys have defeated a detachment of Burgoyne's hessians at Bennington, Vermont. Burgoyne has been cut off from supplies from Canada and better still that jackass, Horatio Gates, has been sent in to replace Schuyler. I don't know who's responsible for that great blunder, but I hope we are wise enough to be able to take advantage of it. If we could get to Burgoyne before he can be re-enforced, we have a slim chance of defeating him. Do you realize what that could mean to our cause, Margaret? The possible difference between defeat and victory. We are raising men, Margaret. Our situation is very bad and more men are needed. I shall be taking them to Philadelphia myself. Vern is going and I'm sure Matt and Jason will also when we tell them. If you'll fix my breakfast, Margaret, I'll be on my way to Foxmore to tell Matt and Jason."

"Oh, God," sighed Margaret. "Paul, Matt and Deanna are just married. Surely you cannot expect him to go."

"Margaret," Paul said wearily. "We must do what is necessary to be done . . . all of us." John, Sarah and the girls had followed Margaret out and were watching quietly. John moved to Paul's side.

"What's going on?"

Paul told him as quickly as possible. "General Howe is on his way toward Philadelphia to hunt up Washington's army. Washington is moving up to Chadd's Ford. I think he expects to meet a small force of British there. I would like to be there to help if I can. We're at a place and time, John, when every man, every gun counts. There are impossible odds against us. If we don't hold through this winter well, I fear we will not hold at all."

272

John's face became pale, but he said grimly, "Yes, I guess we all have to do whatever is necessary. You stay here, Paul. I'll go to Foxmore and tell Matt and Jason about our position. You look exhausted. A couple of days rest and you'll feel better. In the meantime, I'll take care of things. It shouldn't take us any more than a couple weeks to get all the local men together."

Paul looked at John. "You know, John, you are always here when you're needed, aren't you?"

He spoke softly but his eyes shone with gratitude for John's understanding.

"All right, you get the men together. We leave here two weeks from today."

"Good," said John with a slight grin. He clapped Paul on the shoulder and turned away. Walking to Sarah, he stood before her and looked deeply into her eyes. She smiled at him and kissed him gently.

"I love you, John. We'll be married before the two weeks are over."

"Thank you, Sarah," he said softly and with a gentle touch of his fingers to her cheek, he was gone.

There was a silence in the room for some time when Paul heaved a sigh and rose to his feet.

"I do believe John is right, I am tired. I think I'll sleep for a while. Will you tell me when John gets back, Margaret?"

"Yes, Paul," she said. Her throat was tight. She suddenly felt a deep sympathy for a man whose vision took him beyond his own life and family to serve others.

While she was watching him leave the room and Sarah was caught up in her thoughts of John, no one noticed the two girls who stood by quietly. Susan, always quiet and shy, stood wide-eyed by Caroline and watched the

273

situation that was unravelling before them. She did not comprehend everything, only the fact that this situation was upsetting her whole world.

Caroline, on the other hand, was a completely different matter. There were not many things that Caroline Gibson could not handle. With her direct honesty and fearless courage, she moved away from no situation. Instead, she met it full on and either conquered it or pushed it aside and moved on. When she had entered the room, her eyes had fallen on Vern, who sat dejectedly on the sofa, his large frame stretched out in exhaustion. She had not taken her eyes from him since. "He is so unhappy," she thought suddenly. "I wonder why?" She had kept her eyes on him, unnoticed by Vern or the others. She had never seen a man as handsome as he, and her heart made a queer fluttering movement in her breast. He had his hands clasped firmly together and she wondered at the size of them. "He could crush me between them like putty," she thought, and a faint stirring went through her body.

Caroline had always prided herself that she formed her own motions in her life stream. She had determinedly promised herself that she would find the things she wanted in life and take them. Now she thought to herself, she had found one of the first things she really wanted . . . Vern Markham.

He stood up and his eyes caught the girls standing alone. He smiled at her, and then his eyes drifted away from hers and he moved to Margaret.

"Mrs. Martin," he said softly. "It will be all right. John and I will watch out for him."

She smiled at him gratefully. "Thank you, Vern. Oh, Vern, these are Sarah's daughters—Caroline and Susan."

Vern smiled again, this time with sincerity, and bowed slightly to the two girls.

Susan dropped a curtsy, but Caroline looked directly into his eyes and smiled warmly, extending her hand to him. In startled reaction, he took it in his oversized hand. Caroline promised herself then, that somehow, some way, she would wipe away the sadness from Vern's eyes and make him smile especially for her.

Chapter Thirty-Five

Deanna curled against Matt's warm sleeping form. She had been awake for a long time, but felt no desire to move and waken Matt. Instead, she curled her arm more tightly about his waist and laid her cheek against his back. She gave a light sigh of contentment and drifted again into a half awake, half dreaming state. She was wakened again when Matt gently lifted her fingers from his chest and kissed them. He turned over and lifted his arm, allowing her to nestle against his side with her head on his shoulder. He dropped his arm about her shoulder and lightly caressed her bare arm.

"Good morning, my love," he whispered.

She smiled to herself. "Good morning."

"What shall we do with this beautiful day, Matt?"

"I'm just as happy to stay right here," he said contentedly. He tightened his arm about her and held her against him. "At least, until I convince myself this is not a dream and you really belong to me now."

She moved to a sitting position and, leaning on one hand, looked down into his eyes. Her blue eyes were soft and warm and a gentle smile was on her face. She was naked and her long, black hair cascaded down over her shoulders. Letting his hands slip down over her shoulders to cup both breasts, he gently moved her toward him and buried his face between them with a murmur of contentment. She pressed his head against her and held him for a few minutes. When he raised his head, she dropped her mouth to his and lowered herself against him. Quickly, he wrapped both arms about her and pulled her down on the pillow, where he again took her lips in a seeking kiss of rising passion. His hands moved familiarly over her and she sighed with pleasure.

At that moment a soft rap came on the door. Matt raised his head, "Damn!"

The insistent rapping came again. Matt muttered under his breath a harsh description of whoever was on the other side of the door, much to Deanna's delight, and wrapping himself in a blanket, he went over and fiercely jerked the door open. The quiet little maid who stood in the doorway was completely intimidated by Matt, and stuttered lamely, trying to explain John's presence downstairs.

A light suppressed giggle from the bed brought a wry grin to Matt's face. With the most charm he could muster wrapped in a blanket, he smiled at the girl and asked her to tell John to wait, he would be right down. When he closed the door, Deanna collapsed into a gale of laughter which dissolved into a shriek as he leapt on the bed and grabbed her up roughly into his arms with a thunderous kiss that left her gasping.

"You stay here," he said firmly. "I'll see what John wants and I'll be right back." Touching the tip of her nose with a light kiss, he left the bed and donned his clothes. Blowing a kiss from the door, he was gone, closing the door behind him. Deanna snuggled back, pulling the covers up to her chin, and sighed happily.

When Matt came down the stairs, John rose from his chair to meet him. "Good morning, John," Matt smiled.

"What brings you here so early in the morning?"

John chuckled. "My watch says ten o'clock. I wouldn't exactly call that early, Matt."

Matt grinned at him. "What's on your mind, John?"

"Sit down, Matt, I've got some things to explain to you. There's been a lot happening, and we need help from you and Jason. By the way, is he up?"

"I don't know. I'll check and have him called if he's not. In the meantime, tell me, John."

"I'd rather explain to you both together if you don't mind, Matt."

Matt looked at him closely, then he sent someone to call Jason. It took several minutes before Jason arrived, looking questioningly from John to Matt.

"What's the matter? Is something wrong?"

"No, well, yes and no," said John. "Sit down you two. I've got something to tell you and something to ask you."

They both sat down slowly, watching John as he began to talk.

Deanna lay waiting for quite some time, then began to wonder why Matt was taking so long. After a few more minutes, she rose, dressed and went down the stairs to find three grim-faced men talking together. She slipped into the room quietly, not letting them know yet that she was there. "If we can be effectual here," John was saying, "we might get France to recognize the independence of the United States. It would mean money and aid, both on land and sea. We need every ounce of help we can muster together."

"And that means," Matt replied, "that Jason and I have to make a commitment."

"Yes."

Matt laughed a short, clipped sound. "It's not the

easiest thing to fight against the country that nurtured you, educated you, and gave you wealth."

"I know, Matt, and believe me, none of us would think any less of you if you decided to stay here."

"Stay here and allow someone else to pay for what I've got? No thank you, John. Whatever price is on what blessings I've got, I'm content to pay. One can't have every good thing in the world like I have and not expect to have to defend it. I'll go with you, and I'm safe in saying you can count on Jason also."

It did not take Deanna long, listening to them talk, to realize the situation. Slowly, as realization dawned on her, her face drained of its color and her body became tense with fear. Still she did not speak, until John, finishing what he had come to tell them, rose to leave. Then for the first time, they saw Deanna standing there.

"Deanna," said John, looking at her with sympathy. "I'm sorry this had to happen now."

She tried to smile at him, but could not quite accomplish it.

Without saying any more, John passed her and left the house. Jason came to her and patted her gently on the shoulder, then he also left. Matt and Deanna looked at each other without speaking for what seemed interminable minutes.

"Deanna?" Matt questioned softly. Then he held out his arms to her. With a soft sobbing sound, she threw herself in them and he held her. "You heard everything?"

"Enough to know what's happening; enough to be afraid."

"You know I have to go, Deanna. I'm afraid you and all your family's love for our country has rubbed off on me," he laughed. "My little patriot," he said softly. "The time has come when we have to stand up for our beliefs. I love you beyond all reason and I want to build a good life here with you and raise a family. If I have to fight for it I will."

Now Deanna lifted her face from his chest and looked at him. Along with the fear of heartbreak in her eyes, was the bright glimmer of pride in him. "I love you, Matt."

Jason, too, felt the shock work its way through him as the words John had quietly spoken came through to him. He wanted more than anything to see Deborah, to hold her, to convince her family to let them marry immediately. He went directly to the stable where he waited impatiently for his horse to be saddled. Then a thought came to him and he chuckled to himself. Instead of pointing his horse toward Clearhaven, he guided it toward what he now considered their cabin. Within half an hour, it came in sight and he smiled again to himself. He was right, he knew her so well. She was there, waiting. He dismounted and went to the door and pushed it open. She stood in the center of the room. He walked slowly to her and gathered her into his arms without speaking.

"Oh, Jason," she whispered against his chest. "I'm frightened."

"I know, love," he said. His lips brushed her hair as he drew her even tighter against him. "I guess I am too, a little."

She looked up, her eyes sparkling with unshed tears. "What's going to happen to us, Jason?"

Jason's face was calm, and he laughed lightly. "We are going to be married just as soon as I get back from this, and we're going to have children and live happily ever after just like Prince Charming and his princess."

"Tell me, Jason," she said. "Tell me of tomorrow and all the other tomorrows we will share. Tell me that you love me," her voice died to a soft whisper. "Show me you love me."

His lips caught hers in a blinding, searing kiss that drove every other thought from her mind but Jason's hungry love.

Within the next two weeks, Clearhaven was a beehive of activity. Paul made use of every expendable piece of equipment all three plantations had to offer. He left most of the equipment-gathering to Cat, who was extremely efficient along these lines. Cat, to Deeta's silent distress, was expecting to go along with them, but succumbed to Paul's logic that someone was just as desperately needed at home to maintain a source of supply and care for those that were left behind.

"Cat, who else can I trust to get the things I need to me intact and quickly? You've got to stay here and run both Foxmore and Clearhaven. Not only that, but you've got to keep an eye out for the welfare of Vern's place too. No, Cat, you're too valuable here for us to drag you away."

"But, Mr. Martin," Cat began. "I feel that I should be helping in the fight too."

"What better way than to keep supplies flowing. I have a feeling that you will be the difference between life and death for us this winter."

"All right, I'll do the best I can," Cat replied with resignation. Although she had not said one word against his going, Cat could feel Deeta's relief when he agreed to stay at home.

With Vern and John helping Paul to gather men from all over the area, Vern was almost inexhaustible and

Caroline took advantage of every moment to be near him by offering to keep records of men and equipment for him. They travelled the area together compiling lists of men and equipment that were available. Caroline urged Vern to talk as much as possible, making herself available as a listener. They discussed Vern's feelings toward everything . . . everything except Deborah. He skirted the subject agilely, but she could see the frustration and anger in his eyes when the unwelcome thoughts did overcome him.

Although Vern smiled and was friendly toward her, he showed no sign that the situation would ever be any different. Caroline had surreptitiously asked questions of everyone until, without their knowing it, she had accumulated the whole story of Vern and Deborah. Now she understood the reason for Vern's unhappiness and was more determined than ever to change it. As they walked, talked, rode and planned together over the days, she fell more and more in love with him. At night her dreams left her tossing restlessly on her lonely bed. There were now only four days until they left. John and Sarah were to marry tomorrow. She determinedly decided that no matter what the consequences, she was going to tell Vern how she felt about him.

The day of the wedding dawned bright and clear. There had not been many preparations made as John and Sarah had decided they wanted only their close friends and family there. Sarah was beautiful in a dress of soft blue holding a bouquet of wildflowers that the girls had picked for her. John showed no sign of nervousness, and his eyes had a soft warm glow for Sarah alone. The ceremony was short, and when John finally took her into his arms to kiss her everyone clapped and shouted loudly.

There was a small dinner where everyone tried valiantly to pretend that this happiness was going to last forever.

When evening came and the fiddler picked up his bow to start the music, all their friends had arrived and Sarah and John led off the dancing, wrapped happily in each other's arms.

Caroline watched Vern as he moved restlessly about the room. Often his eyes went to Deborah and Jason, who danced together completely engrossed in one another. As she watched, she could see the touch of pain whisper across his face, and it caused her pain to watch. She had to fight the desire to go to him and take his face between her hands and kiss away the pain. Instead, she went to him and, smiling up into his face, asked him if he would dance with her. When he took her in his arms she felt the familiar throbbing of her heart and the flush of heat that engulfed her.

"You are an unconventional young lady, aren't you, Caroline?" he laughed. "Do you always go after what you want?"

"Of course, do you know any better way of getting it?" she asked.

He threw his head back laughing. It was the first time she had seen him laugh so heartily and it made her smile.

"What do you want?" he asked, now his eyes were smiling down into hers.

"Let me keep them that way," she thought. "Let him understand I want to make him happy."

"Vern?"

"Yes, Caroline?"

"Would you come outside with me? There is something I must tell you."

"Can't you tell me here? Is it that serious?" His

eyes sparkled.

"It is to me, Vern," she said quietly.

Somehow he began to realize she was very serious and so danced her in the direction of the door. When they were outside, he dropped his arms and looked at her.

"What is it, Caroline? What has made you so serious suddenly?"

Her eyes grew wide and luminous, and they held his attention as she stepped closer. The soft scent of her perfume rose to him. He could not help the reaction of his body, but held it in check while he watched her. Now she stood very close to him, her body almost touching his.

"Do you still love Deborah, Vern?" she asked softly.

His face froze suddenly and he looked as though he had been struck violently. She reached out and grasped both his arms and could feel the hard tenseness of his muscles.

"Please don't be angry with me, Vern. I must know. You see I love you. With my whole heart and soul, I love you and I want you."

Still he had not spoken, but looked at her with an unreadable expression in his eyes.

"Yes," he said softly. "I still love her."

"You know that she is going to marry Jason?"

"Yes, I know."

"Vern," she sobbed. The tears were falling unheeded down her face. She reached for his hands and put them about her. Moving tightly against him, she put her arms about his neck.

"Hold me, Vern. Feel me in your arms. I am a woman, a woman who loves you, a woman who wants you. I would do anything in my power to make you happy. Let me help you forget what you cannot have."

Slowly she drew his head down to hers and put her lips against his, parting hers and touching his lips lightly with her tongue. Vern was a very strong, healthy man, and he felt the desire rise wildly in him. With a soft groan, he gathered her up in his arms and walked toward the stable. Inside, he moved quickly, crushing her to him until she cried out. His hands moved swiftly over her, and he found her willing, in his arms.

"Vern, Vern," she sobbed. "Love me."

When he had removed her clothes and his, he dropped with her to the fresh hay. Taking her mouth in his, he parted her lips with an insistent pressure. His mouth moved over her body with light touches of his tongue, leaving a hot burning fire of delight in its wake. She caressed him with her hands, enjoying the feel of his hard muscled frame. When her hands finally found his maleness, she gasped in shock. He was so huge, he would tear her apart. He seemed to sense her fear, for suddenly he became gentle. Using his hands expertly until he knew she was ready for him, he entered her slowly and gently. She gave a sharp cry and he covered her mouth with his. Her body lifted to him now, and he took her completely. She could feel the hard flame of him deep inside her and she gave herself to him with complete abandon and a flame of passion to match his.

She was crying very softly and he held her gently.

"Caro, I'm sorry. I'm so damn sorry. I didn't mean to hurt you."

He kissed away the tears and looked at her.

"Oh, Vern, the only way you could possibly hurt me is to tell me you don't care. I know what happened was my doing, but I want it to mean something to you."

He sat up and for several minutes, did not say

anything. Her heart began to beat furiously with fear.

"Caro, try to understand. It meant a lot to me. Maybe it's you who can help me get over this." He turned to her and smiled. "We'll try, we'll try, Caro," he whispered.

With a happy laugh she threw herself into his arms and they lay together contented for the moment, not thinking about tomorrow.

Chapter Thirty-Six

Burgoyne was now in critical condition. He had no help coming from any direction and his supplies from Canada had been cut off. He fought an indecisive battle at Bemis Heights, and suffered a defeat near Saratoga, where Arnold fiercely attacked him. The poor hessians were greatly alarmed and refused to fight anymore. Burgoyne's army had dwindled to six thousand. He surrendered, Oct. 17, 1777 to Gates, who obtained an honor he didn't deserve. As a result, France did recognize the independence of the United States, loaned some money, and promised a great deal of aid on land and sea, very little of which was really performed. It was a great advantage to the Colonies because it meant England had to fight France once more, who was then joined by Spain and later Holland.

At Clearhaven, the day for leaving inevitably came. It was a subdued group of women who watched as the final preparations began. Horses were saddled and brought to the front of the house at Clearhaven. When there was nothing left to do but say good-bye, this was done as quickly as possible, for the pain of extending it had grown too severe. Every one of the women had sworn to herself that she would not cry, but instead to try her best to supply the necessary strength her man needed. Arms enfolded loved ones, deep and lasting kisses were exchanged. Then, suddenly, they were gone.

The sudden silence hung in the air like molten lead, each woman wrapped in the memories of her private good-bye. Margaret was the first to shake herself free of this numbing lethargy.

"There are things that must be done," she said quietly. "We have sadly neglected our homes the last few days. Now we must get back to our duties. Deanna, you will stay here tonight, won't you?"

"Of course, Mother. I don't think I could face going home alone right now, anyway."

"Why don't you just stay with us, Deanna, until Matt gets home?"

"No, Mother. I'll be all right. Cat has promised to come every day. I want Foxmore to be warm and waiting when Matt returns."

"All right, my dear," she said, smiling in understanding. "Come let's get some lunch and get started."

She went inside and Deanna followed her. Within a few minutes, Sarah also went in. For some time, Caroline and Deborah sat in silence. Then Deborah turned to Caroline.

"Caroline, I want you to know how happy I am about you and Vern. He is a wonderful man, and he deserves someone as strong and beautiful as you."

Caroline smiled sadly. "I don't know if I can make him forget you, Deborah."

Deborah started to speak, but Caroline interrupted. "I know that he still loves you. But I want you to know I'm going to do everything in my power to wipe you out of his heart."

The two women looked at each other with complete understanding. Then they laughed together, and joining arms walked into the house.

It was almost a three-week journey to Philadelphia, and Paul recruited several more men along the way. His men bore no uniforms, and each man had to supply his own food and equipment. They joined Washington's rag-tag army. It was reaching well into late fall, and as they watched the faces of the men who had fought under Washington at Trenton and Princeton, they were stirred by the determination of this hastily gathered, ill-equipped army. When they arrived, the main body of the army was in retreat from the severe loss at Philadelphia. One would suppose that General Howe would naturally want to hunt up Washington's army and defeat it. Instead, he captured Philadelphia, and at the same time, held New York. When Washington arrived at Chadds Ford, he met the British and for a time prevented their crossing. But a detachment of the latter crossed farther up the stream and outflanked Washington, who was compelled to retreat. Washington retreated and Howe entered Philadelphia. Washington attacked him in the suburbs of the city at Germantown on October 4th, 1777, but owing to a fog and tactical mistakes, he was defeated and retired to Valley Forge on the Schuylkill River for winter quarters.

Howe spent the winter in Philadelphia, but accomplished absolutely nothing in a military way. Many of the Philadelphians, especially the Quakers, were opposed to war anyway, and Howe divided his forces without accomplishing anything.

"I thought we were to meet in Philadelphia, Paul?" questioned John.

"Philadelphia has fallen to the British. We're all in

retreat now. I feel so inadequate, bringing this handful of men and these meager supplies to a man who needs so much now, deserves so much more."

"Where are we headed?" asked Matt.

For quite some time, Paul did not speak. His eyes looked into some uncertain future. There were tight, drawn lines about his mouth and the first hint of the defeat of a dream was engulfing him.

"I don't know, I don't know," he said almost in a whisper. "I know we cannot, dare not, stop here. We must go on, we must not be defeated now or we may never stand on our feet again. We will join the main body of the army, and I shall ride ahead to General Washington and tell him of my . . . contribution." He gave a mirthless chuckle and moved his horse away from them.

It was several hours before they saw Paul again. The army had finally slowed to a grinding halt, and preparations for encampment had begun. Makeshift tents and lean-tos were erected—anything in which a man could take shelter for the night. Matt, Jason, John and Vern had erected a small tent and made a fire over which they had brewed a pot of coffee. No one spoke much, for each man was unsure of their future and wondering about the ones they had left behind. Suddenly Matt began to chuckle.

"What's so funny, Matt?" questioned his brother, whose sense of humor always lay just beneath the surface of all other emotions.

"Look at us, Jas. Lord Jason Deverall and his brother, Matthew, cream of London society, wealthy members of English Royalty. Squatting in front of a fire, making ready to sleep in a tent, following a man of whom we know nothing, for a cause about which we know even less. Preparing to fight for a country to which we've belonged for only a year, and against a country which we've belonged to for a lifetime. Doesn't it strike you as rather ridiculous?"

"Well, if you think of it that way, Matt, it does. But lately I've been thinking of the situation from another point of view. It's not just Deborah or Foxmore, it's . . . Well, it's a way of life they're fighting for that I've come to believe in. A man should not be a chattel to another. I never knew the real situation between our countries until I came here. I like these people and their ideals. I've read the new document they've written up, their 'Declaration of Independence.' It's a wonderful thing and a great philosophy to build a country and to live by . . . It was hard for me at first, as I expect it was for you, since we've never had to worry about a little unimportant thing like freedom. Now, I guess I sort of think of this country and Deborah along the same lines. I have to love one to love the other."

Matt nodded his head and smiled at his brother again.

"I think you and I have been taken in by a couple of beautiful patriots."

Jason laughed heartily. "I can't think of a better way to be taken in, or a better cause to be taken in with. I, for one, have only one regret so far, and that's not being able to marry Deborah before we left. A situation I intend to remedy as soon as possible."

They talked and laughed together late into the night, then rolled themselves contentedly into their blankets to sleep. It was the last of laughter and contentment they would know for quite some time.

The large, ebony giant of war, who had taken a short nap, now stretched its sinuous muscles and awoke. His

291

yawn was the roar of muskets, and the stretching tentacles of his muscular arms reached out and grasped Washington's army and shook it violently. Shook it, then dropped it so heavily that men were stunned by the force. The faces of men, who smiled yesterday, were filled with pain and misery today. Some of the faces disappeared and were replaced by blank-eyed hard men who had seen the giant at work before. The men, such as Paul's, who were not hardened yet to battle, were initiated quickly as the giant tempered his new-found ore into blades of steel. Blades that struck and were either broken or discarded, or that became sharpened and blazed with brilliant fire.

Paul moved through the ranks of his men, who had been drawn back exhausted and given a few hours in which to rest. He had known every man who had come with him, and was mentally putting names to the missing faces. Beside each campfire he stopped and spoke softly to the men gathered there, encouraging and instilling confidence in a cause in which his faith never faltered. He smiled and laughed with some; talked quietly with others, always suiting his words to the situation. His men loved him.

Jason and John sat in front of their tent, where they nursed a small fire and held cups of hot coffee to their cold lips. It was late October and a sudden, cold blast of northern air had descended upon them. The two men sat silently, watching Paul's progress from fire to fire. Jason spoke first, looking at John with eyes more serious than at any time in his life.

"He's a remarkable man, John. I don't think anyone else could have kept this group going like he does." John nodded and turned his attention to Jason. He had changed so much in the past six weeks that it continually amazed John. The sparkling laughter was gone, the eyes no longer glittered with suppressed humor. Instead, they shone with a fierce, cold light that startled John and caused a nagging worry. He would have chosen to keep Jason as he was; not as he was slowly becoming.

Paul stopped by their fire and knelt, extending his hands to the warmth. "Jason, John, how are you?"

"Fine, Paul. How are things going?"

Paul shrugged and gave a short mirthless laugh.

"For an army short on men, short on provisions, and short on time, I guess we're doing all right. Where's Matt and Vern?"

"They're both asleep. Matt's so tired, he can hardly move. And Vern, as usual, had been doing the work of six men," replied Jason.

"Would you like some coffee, Paul?" asked John. John extended the cup to him and they sat quietly for several moments without speaking.

"Paul, why aren't you sleeping? You need some rest," said John.

"Ah, John. This is my rest. I had to get away from looking at men as so many marks on a map, and get here to look at them as men, my men. After a while, it gets so impersonal that you forget men are dying each time you rearrange those little markers."

"How do things stand?" asked Jason.

Paul gave a dry chuckle. "We lose more battles than we win, and still we progress. Can you understand that, Jason?"

Jason nodded his head and remained silent.

"We're going to have a bad time this winter. We're short on provisions and equipment. It will be hard to keep these men together. I've sent a messenger home to tell Cat to load everything Clearhaven, Foxmore and Dartmore have in the way of provisions, and bring them here. It won't be much for this many, but it will help some. We can't give up now, we can't.'' His voice died to a whisper and he gazed into the fire unseeing.

The two men exchanged glances but remained silent, watching Paul. In a few seconds, Paul shook himself from his lethargy and laughed.

"I'd better move, I'm expecting those wagons any time. I want to be there to make sure things get to where they belong.''

He rose slowly and stiffly, and with a slight wave moved away from the two men. They watched him until he disappeared from view.

"I'm worried about him. He gives so much of himself, there won't be anything left when this is done. I wish he could get home for a while.''

John spoke quietly and Jason nodded in agreement. The desire to get back home to the sane world with Deborah in it welled up in him. It brought a trembling in his body and moisture to his eyes. He rose and stretched, afraid John would see his fear and not understand.

"I think I'll get some sleep, John.'' He touched the other man gently on the shoulder and stepped inside the tent. Without removing his boots, he rolled in his blanket and lost himself in the only way possible . . . dreams.

John sat for a long time contemplating the fire, watching a parade of pictures flow past his eyes . . . Sarah, Caro, Susan. The last four days he had spent at home had been a beautiful miracle for him. He had acquired a complete family in every sense of the word. Now, he realized he had to do what he was doing to protect and secure what he had found. He was so lost in his reverie that he did not notice the young man at his side until he spoke for the second time.

"John . . . John."

He shook away the dreams and looked up at the boy.

"Jason's wanted down at General Washington's quarters."

"Jason? Why? What's going on?"

"I don't know, a bunch of wagons came in and all of a sudden, Mr. Martin comes out and yells for me to go get Jason. So here I am. You better get him up, pronto. He's wanted right now."

John nodded and moved into the tent quickly. He knelt by Jason and shook him.

"Jason, Jason."

"John, for God's sake, it can't be morning already. I feel like I just went to sleep."

He sat up and looked around. "If it's not, man, you better be waking me up for a good reason."

"You're wanted in General Washington's quarters."

"Me? Why?"

"I don't know, but they want you now. You better get up, get yourself together and get down there."

Jason unrolled his weary body from the inviting warmth of the blanket and rose to his feet with a groan as every muscle he owned protested. He lifted the blanket from the floor and wrapped it about him and started for the General's tent.

When he arrived, there was a large cluster of wagons sitting in front. He heard a shout and before he could see what was going on, Cat was there thumping him on the back and laughing. Paul Martin was standing in front of the tent, and for the first time in weeks, Jason saw a smile on his face. He pulled himself away and went to Paul.

"Did you send for me, Paul?"

"Yes, Jason. It seem Cat brought you a gift from home." His eyes sparkled with delight at Jason's blank look. He looked from Paul to Cat, stunned by their happy laughter.

"It's in the tent, Jason. Go on in. General Washington has gone for a while."

Still he stood looking questioningly from one to the other until Paul gave him a shove, and he lifted the tent flap and went inside. The tent was almost dark. The remains of a candle sputtered on the table. A young man stood with his back to Jason, studying the maps on the wall. A prickling sensation moved up his spine, and a hard knot formed in his stomach. He knew this boy well, very well. He was completely paralyzed when the boy turned away from the maps and removed his hat. Deborah smiled up into Jason's face and spoke his name softly.

Chapter Thirty-Seven

He didn't know whether he spoke her name or not, or whether he simply reached for her. He only knew that suddenly she was there in his arms. He held her so fiercely that she gasped for breath, then he kissed her over and over as if he wanted to devour her completely.

"Jason, Jason," she sighed.

It was a long while before he realized where they were. Then he took her by the shoulders and held her away from him.

"What the hell are you doing here, Deb? Do you want to get killed. I'll string Cat up for this."

"Don't blame Cat, Jas. He didn't even know I was on one of the wagons until we were too far to turn back."

"Why, Deb? It isn't that I don't want you, I've dreamed of nothing else since we left, but this is too dangerous a place for you."

She smiled at him and tilted her head to the side looking from under her long lashes. "I had to come, Jas. It was very important. Tell me, Jas, do they have a chaplain here in camp?"

He nodded his head looking at her with a million unspoken questions in his eyes.

"Then," she said softly, "I think you'd better call him and have him marry us right away. I wouldn't want your son to be born without your name."

He stood frozen, staring at her, then his face broke into a smile and he looked at her with such a surge of love in his expression that it brought tears to her eyes. Then slowly and tenderly he gathered her to him and held her. She realized he was trembling and pulled herself away and looked up into his eyes. They were filled with tears. His lips found hers now and it was such a tender kiss that she melted against him and gave herself to the joy it brought. When he finally released her and found his voice, he asked, "When, Deb?" his voice cracking hoarsely.

"In May. I just couldn't wait to tell you, Jas. I wanted you to know."

"Oh, Deb, I love you so much, I'm sorry it has to be this way. I feel like I'm cheating you."

"Jas, you're not cheating me. You see it really doesn't matter how we get married, it only matters that I'm near you even if it's just for tonight."

He held her tear-stained face between his hands and looked deeply into her eyes, and saw the truth of her love for him coming from the depths of her soul.

"My child," he murmured, touching her face with feather-soft kisses until she almost cried out with the pain of happiness.

She moved away from him for a minute. "Don't you think we'd better get things going, Jas, or else I'll have to leave before I get a chance to really show you how much I love you."

"Oh, yes," he said quickly and she laughed as he beat a hasty retreat to the doorway. He stuck his head out and was surprised to find Paul and John with Matt, Vern and the chaplain they had sent for waiting outside.

They laughed unanimously at his startled look. "Cat

told us who was here, and we just took it on ourselves to invite the chaplain," Matt said with a mischievous grin. "Of course, if you don't need him, I'm sure he has things to do."

"Reverend Mitchell, could you perform a wedding here, sir?" asked Jason as he stepped out of the tent. "I'm sure we have enough witnesses."

Rev. Mitchell smiled and assured Jason it would be his pleasure to perform the ceremony. They all entered the tent, and Jason pulled Paul aside.

"Shouldn't we go somewhere else? I'm sure the general needs his tent."

Paul smiled at Jason and whispered quietly.

"Don't be a fool, Jas. Why do you think he isn't here? He's turned it over to you and Deb for the night. Oh, by the way, he said to tell you and your new bride congratulations and that you two are probably doing more for the moral of these men than anything else could do."

Jason smiled with relief and went to Deborah's side, and slipping an arm about her waist pulled her against him with a light smile.

The ceremony was short, and within a few minutes, Jason found himself being clapped on the back and heartily congratulated by all present. Matt turned to Deborah and kissed her gently on the cheek.

"Welcome to the family, sister," he said softly.

Deborah's eyes filled again with tears for she knew that when Matt looked at her he was seeing Deanna.

"Thank you, Matt."

When the men started to leave, Cat reached beneath his coat and pulled out a bottle, setting it on the table he smiled at Jason and Deborah.

"Carried that all the way up here without nippin' at it just for this occasion. Good luck you two." He smiled and left the tent. Outside he found that all the men had gone except Matt.

"Come to our tent, Cat," he said. "You can spend the night with us."

Cat cast a quick look in Matt's direction then put out a hand to stop him. He winked an eye and held up a finger. With a grin, he pulled another bottle out of his coat.

"What do you say we tie one on, Matt?"

Matt chuckled, then threw his arms about Cat's shoulder and laughing together they proceeded to Matt's tent where within three hours Cat was lowering a completely unconscious Matt to his blankets and covering him with a sad expression in his eyes that he would have never let anyone else see. Then he lowered himself to his blankets, rolled them about him and slept.

It was hours later when Deborah woke, suddenly feeling cold. She opened her eyes to find Jason leaning on one arm looking down at her. He had pulled away the blankets and placed his hand flat on her belly. It was the touch of his hand that wakened her. Their eyes caught and he smiled.

"I wish I could be home with you to feel him grow, Deb," he said softly. "But I promise if there is any way possible, I'll be home in May. I'll be with you when he's born. I promise."

She gave a small gentle sigh and lifted her arms about his neck, pulling his head down to hers. She felt his mouth tender on hers, not demanding or forceful but giving her all the love in his heart. His hands moved over her with soft feather-like touches that caused her to burn with the fire he always roused in her. She moved her body against the warmth of his. She could feel the tight hardness of his body demanding hers, but still he was slow and gentle. He wanted her to know now and for all time that his love was a giving thing not a taking one and that she was part of him, heart, soul and body. He lifted her gently to him and entered her slowly, savoring the burning heat of their passion, holding it off as long as possible to enjoy the bittersweet feel of it burst through him like liquid fire. He could hear the soft words of love she whispered as her body rose to meet him, and still he held it away moving gently, slowly until neither of them could stand it any longer.

She sobbed his name and her hands caressed the long hard muscles of his body as she pulled him tightly against her. They moved together. He enclosed her and held her to him as they reached a degree of passion they never had felt before. He could feel the throbbing beat of her heart as he held her tightly. It matched the pounding thunder of his own.

"Deb, oh Deb, Deb . . ."

They reached a sudden explosion so deep and so brilliant that it blinded them and left them clinging to one another.

Now he held her curled against him and for a time she slept again. He did not sleep, for he wanted every memory he could gather to hold him through the days to come without her. He was still awake when dawn slipped quietly in and touched him with the icy fingers of reality.

"Deborah," he said softly, kissing her gently.

"Wake up, Deb, it's morning."

"No," she said without opening her eyes. She moved tighter against him and buried her face in his shoulder. "Make it go away, Jas. I don't want to see it."

301

"Deb, please. Let's not make this any harder than it is. Believe me, I don't want to let you go, but we have to."

"I know, I'm sorry, Jas. I didn't mean to act like this. It's just that I can hardly bear to leave you."

"We'll be together soon," he smiled. "May's not so far away, and remember I promised. You take good care of my son until I get home."

There were tears in her eyes which she gulped back determinedly and she nodded her head, not trusting herself to speak.

"We'd better get dressed. We've taken advantage of the General's hospitality. I'm sure he needs his quarters back to run the war."

The old Jason had returned, the sparkle of suppressed humor lit his eyes and he reached for the untouched bottle Cat had left on the table. They had no desire for any intoxication except their own. He handed her the bottle.

"Take this home and keep it handy. We'll need it to celebrate when the baby comes," he laughed.

They rose and dressed without talking again. They were dressed and ready to leave when someone rapped gently on the pole in front of the tent.

"It's probably Cat coming for you," said Jason. "Come on in, Cat."

The flap was pulled back and when he looked to see who it was he gasped with shocked surprise and almost leapt to his feet.

"General Washington, sir," he said stiffly.

Deborah turned surprised eyes on him also. He stepped closer to Deborah and smiled at her.

"I've come to see firsthand the beautiful young lady who has destroyed all protocol and come to a battlefield

302

to marry her man." His eyes were friendly and watched Deborah's startled blush with amusement.

"Congratulations, my dear child. You and your husband are the heart and reason of our cause, and I wish you the very best."

"Thank you, sir," whispered Deborah. "I thank you also for the use of your tent. I hope you had a comfortable night."

He chuckled, "Quite, quite, my dear. Now if I may have my tent back I must be about the business of winning this war so I can send this young man back to you. I wouldn't want you to have to come after him again."

Deborah giggled nervously in response. Jason extended his hand to her and they left the tent to be greeted by a huge crowd of men who gave a rousing cheer for Deborah.

There were tears again, this time in everyone's eyes, as he lifted her to the wagon. She bent down to him and kissed him again, bringing another happy shout from the watchers. Jason watched the wagon until it was out of sight. Already he could feel the emptiness the lack of her presence always brought. Matt stood beside him, and when he finally realized he was there, they exchanged silent looks of understanding and headed back to their own tent.

Chapter Thirty-Eight

Margaret swore silently to herself as she burnt her fingers for the tenth time on the oven trying to remove the bread. Sarah gave a chuckle and went to help her.

"Margaret, you can't do everything yourself. For the past six months you've taken on every job around here. It really doesn't work, dear."

"What doesn't, Sarah?"

"Trying to make yourself so exhausted you sleep. I've tried it. Thoughts and dreams just don't go away. Margaret . . ."

"Yes, Sarah."

"Let me help you," she said softly. "I know something is desperately bothering you. I've seen you ride out at night. What is it, Margaret? Can't you tell me? Let me do as much as you've done for me and my girls."

Margaret looked at her for a long time as though deciding what to say. For one heart-breaking moment she wanted so desperately to tell someone of her anguish.

"I'm just edgy now, Sarah. I'll be all right, really." She patted her hand ignoring the look of sympathetic understanding on Sarah's face. Sarah watched her leave the small out-kitchen and start across the yard to the main house. She felt a heaviness in her and shook her head sadly as she turned back to her work.

Margaret crossed the yard quickly, loosening the ties

of her apron as she walked. When she stepped inside the main house she dropped the apron on the chair and started upstairs. She wanted to take a bath, but most of all she wanted to be alone for a while. It seemed that was all she ever wanted anymore.

She had taken a few steps up the stairs when a knocking sounded on the front door. She moved slowly to the door and opened it. A young man stood before her removing his hat politely.

"Mrs. Martin?"

"Yes."

"I'm supposed to deliver this note into your hands and no one else's, ma'am. Are you Mrs. Martin?"

"Yes, I am Mrs. Martin." She smiled and accepted the folded piece of paper he handed her. Then he bowed slightly and with a quick smile, he left. She stood looking at the note, knowing what it contained. Slipping it into the pocket of her dress, she again climbed the stairs to her room. She closed and locked the door behind her before she removed the note and slowly opened it.

Margaret,
    I must see you, it is very important. Meet me at the house tonight. Please come, my dear. Much depends upon it.

All my love,
Mark.

She crumpled the note into a small ball in her fist and shoved it back into her pocket. It was several minutes before she moved, then slowly she began to remove her clothes. She wrapped herself in a robe and sent for water for a bath. When it came she sat in the warm water laying her head back against the tub and allowing the heat to penetrate and relieve the tired aching of her body. Without even realizing it, she had begun to cry, soft sobs that wracked her body and caused an aching that nothing could relieve. Moments later she rose from the tub and began to dress for supper. After the meal, she would make her excuses and again she would go to meet Mark.

No one except Sarah recognized the change in Margaret, and the girls chattered happily about Deborah's expected child. Deborah had blossomed beautifully, her eyes held a sparkle and her skin was soft and glowing. She laughingly displayed the size to which she had grown and claimed she had to be carrying at least twins from the way they kicked.

By the time the meal was over, Margaret's nerves were screaming, and her face had paled, making her eyes seem enormous. Sarah watched her worriedly and was not a little surprised when she claimed a headache and made an excuse to go to bed early. After she left the table, Sarah also made an excuse and went rapidly up to her room, where she swiftly changed into riding clothes. Quietly, she slipped out to the stables where earlier she had saddled her horse and kept him ready. She had only to wait a few minutes before Margaret appeared, saddled her horse and left. Waiting as long as she dared, Sarah followed, staying off the road and just keeping Margaret in sight. When Margaret dismounted in front of a house, she pulled her horse as close as possible without being seen and watched as the door opened and a man stepped out on the porch. The two on the porch flowed together, and he held her in his arms for some time. Then, very gently, he lifted her and carried her inside, kicking the door shut behind them.

Sarah sat stunned, for she had immediately recognized the man on the porch as her uninvited guest in Boston, Colonel Mark Severn. After a while she turned her horse and headed home.

"Please, put me down, Mark. We've got to talk."

"We waste so much time talking, Margaret. I love you. Why do we always begin a battle of words first?"

"You said it was important, that you had something to tell me. What is it, Mark?"

He sighed but stood her gently on her feet, not taking his arms from around her. Then he lifted her chin and looked deeply at her.

"I'm leaving, Margaret," he said softly.

She gave a start as a sudden unreasonable jolt of fear went through her.

"When, Mark? Why? Where?"

"Well," he laughed. "I would tell you, my love, but I really believe you would inform on me and I just can't afford that to happen. I'll tell you when—tomorrow morning—and I'll tell you why—because we're fighting this damnable unwinnable war—but I cannot tell you where."

He pulled her tighter against him, holding her cheek against his chest, and she could hear the steady pounding of his heart.

"Listen to me, my darling. Listen well. I will be leaving in the morning and I will never come back here. I have made it impossible for Governor Rosemond to cause you any more trouble with a little well-placed blackmail. Margaret, I love you more than my own life, and I will not stay and make you any more unhappy than I already have. After we lose this war, and we will lose it, my dear, as we have not the spirit and determination you have, I shall resign my commission in the army and go home. I want you to know that if you ever need me, you have only to write. I shall give you the address before I leave. I shall come if you send for me. Do you understand, my love?"

She nodded her head, unable to speak.

"Then love me tonight, Margaret. Give me the dreams on which I shall have to feed the rest of my life." He lowered his mouth to hers. "Love me tonight, Margaret." With a small groaning sigh she gave herself to him.

It was just a short time before dawn when Margaret slipped back into her room. She quietly closed the door and began to undress when the sense of someone's presence struck her. She reached over and lit the lamp and turned to face Sarah who sat quietly watching her.

"Now, Margaret, my dear, can you tell me what Colonel Mark Severn is doing here and what the two of you are doing together? Margaret, I simply want to help you. Please tell me."

"You followed me."

"Yes, I saw you meet Colonel Severn. I just can't think wrong of you Margaret, I love you as a sister."

"Oh, Sarah," she sobbed throwing herself to her knees. She lay her head on Sarah's lap and cried. After a while she began to talk and soon Sarah understood. With tear-filled eyes, she looked at Margaret.

"Your secret is safe with me, Margaret. If you need me, I'm your friend. Remember that. Now try to get some sleep. If he is gone maybe you can forget again and when Paul comes back you can pick up the pieces of your life and start over."

Margaret understood and got into bed. Sarah turned off the lamp and with a softly whispered "Good night" left the room.

Margaret lay awake. "Oh, Sarah, how can I ever forget the one I love more than anything else in the world?"

Sarah went downstairs and began early preparations for breakfast. By the time most of the household was stirring, everything was completed. A surprised set of servants came into the kitchen only to find their morning work finished for them. While they finished last-minute touches and went to awaken the rest of the household, Sarah went to her room. After she had closed the door behind her, she locked it. Then she removed from her pocket a small slip of paper which she placed between the pages of the Bible that sat on her night table. The paper contained the address Mark had given to Margaret. Sarah knew that Margaret would never send for Mark no matter how bad things were, but she promised herself that when Paul came back, if things did not work out, she would write. She felt deeply, after knowing Margaret's full story, that she deserved some happiness and she also had the deep conviction that her happiness lay with Mark Severn and not with Paul Martin. She put the address aside for now, but she knew without a doubt she would use it if she felt it was necessary.

After she had washed and changed from her riding clothes, she went down to join the rest of the family at breakfast. She made some excuses for Margaret's absence, and went on eating, quietly listening to the easy conversation.

"I'm going into town today, Deb," said Deanna. "Can I get you anything?"

"Oh, how I wish I could ride with you, Dee. It seems so long since I've ridden."

"I could just see you, Deb," her sister laughed. "I don't really think we can find any riding clothes to fit you

309

and definitely not a horse to carry you."

Deborah giggled happily, placing her hands on her rounded belly. "It's the end of March, now. If I keep on growing like this, I'll have an elephant in May." Her face sobered. "Only two months. I hope Jason can come home," she added softly.

"Well," Deanna said quickly. "I'm off. I'll see you all about three, and I'll bring you back some of that candy you like so well, Deb."

She flashed them a quick happy smile, and with a light wave left the house and walked rapidly to the stable. After her horse was saddled, she mounted and for a while she gave him his head, letting him run off his excess energy. Then at a slower steady pace, she covered the distance to town. When she arrived in town, there seemed to be considerable confusion, and addressing the first person she saw, she asked what was happening.

He spat on the ground and glared in the direction of the activities. "Damn British bastards are finally leaving," he said. "And good riddance, too."

He moved away from her, and easing her horse slowly forward, she could see the formation of British soldiers, and then her attention was riveted on the officer standing on the porch making preparations to leave. Colonel Mark Severn! Suddenly all the pieces seemed to fall into place. She eased her horse forward again and was almost beside the porch when he suddenly looked in her direction. Their eyes met and he held hers for a long time before he smiled slowly and inclined his head in a slight bow.

"I must talk to you," she mouthed the words, knowing he could not hear her over the crowd. He nodded slightly and pointed to a store on the opposite side of the street.

310

She waited for him, watching him move through the crowd.

"He is a very handsome man," she thought.

He reached her side and smiled down at her.

"So we meet again," he laughed. "And which one are you today, Lady Deverall or Deanna Gibson?"

"Neither," she smiled. "I'm Deanna Deverall, Lord Deverall's sister-in-law."

"Some day you must explain to me the details of your escape. I must admit it was well done, my dear."

"How long have you been here, Colonel Severn?"

He watched her closely now. "Since you got back. I followed very closely, but you managed to stay a couple of days ahead of me all the way."

"I have one more question, Colonel."

"Let me tell you without asking. Yes, I've seen your mother. Yes, I love her as much as I ever did, and no, I will never come back to cause her any problems. Does that answer all your questions?"

"I'm sorry," she said softly. "I know how you must feel."

"No, my child, you do not know, for I am leaving more than just the woman I love. Someday maybe I can tell you. For now, God bless you and good-bye."

He leaned forward and brushed her cheek lightly with a kiss, then with a quick smile and a salute he was gone. As she watched him walk away a growing sense of loss filled her and for some unknown reason, she found her face wet with tears.

Chapter Thirty-Nine

Washington's army stirred after the long, disastrous winter at Valley Forge. The winter at Valley Forge was one of the darkest periods of the war. Through the impotence of Congress, the rascality of contractors, and the lack of systems, the army was often without food or clothing. Men went barefoot in the snow, and many froze to death or starved. During this winter, there was a plot called the Conway Cabal to supplant Washington. It was discovered, and failed, and the small army of patriots was grateful. Its authors were never punished. The only ray of light in this dark hour, was the arrival in the colonies of an accomplished German officer, Baron von Steuben, who, by the greatest expenditure of energy, drilled the troops until they began to become effective.

Jason began to feel desperation rise as the sluggish army began to stir. March came and passed. April brought drenching rain. Even in the severest of weather, Baron von Steuben drilled and drilled until the men were nearly exhausted, but Jason and Matt agreed, they were slowly beginning to turn into a reasonably disciplined army.

With a grimness Matt never knew Jason possessed, Jason became determined that no matter what, even if he had to be labelled a deserter, he was going to be home in May. They were eating a cold, unappetizing supper by a half-dead fire when a message was brought that Paul would like to see them. Jason weaved wearily as he rose to his feet and extended a hand to help Matt. There was a tiredness in him that went beyond anything he had ever felt before. He was dirty, unshaven, and his clothes were rags compared to his usually fastidious dress. His greatest desire was to lay his head against Deborah's breast and sleep forever.

Matt and Jason moved with slow plodding footsteps toward Paul's tent. When they went inside, they found both John and Paul together, sharing a drink. They were a little surprised at the enthusiasm of their greetings.

"Paul," Jason questioned, "is something going on? You look extraordinarily happy for a man in our—rather uncomfortable position."

"Well, I'm not happy about our position, but I sure am happy about yours and Matt's."

"Mine?"

"General Washington has listened finally to my rather insistent pleas for a favor."

"A favor?"

Paul smiled. "You and Matt have been given time to go home . . . at least until the end of May. I think that will be long enough for what you need."

For a moment Jason stood in stunned, disbelieving silence. Then the words finally reached him. He gave a half-choking sound between a cry and a laugh as he grasped Paul's hand and shook it with considerable enthusiasm. Jason could not really speak, so Matt said the words of gratitude for him.

"Paul, we'll never forget this."

Paul grinned. "I never thought you would. It's my sly way of keeping you and your brother's attention." Then

313

his smile faded as he held up a hand to stop their words.

"You both understand you must be back here before the fifteenth of June. There's something coming up and we'll need every man and every gun we can get."

"We not only understand," Jason replied, "we give our word that when the time comes, you get whatever you need that we're capable of giving. You've just given me the greatest gift of my life. The chance to be there when my child enters this topsy-turvy world. I'll be grateful for the rest of my life."

"You and Matt had best get going. The longer you stand here talking to me, the less time you have to spend with my daughter and my first grandson."

"Paul?" Matt asked. "Why don't you come with us for a few days? You've worked like a madman here, you need the rest."

"No, not now, Matt. If we win the freedom we're all fighting so hard for, I'll have all the time in the world to handle my grandson on my knees. Now you get going, both of you, before something comes up and your leave is cancelled."

Matt and Jason again shook hands with Paul and John and then left to make preparations for the journey home.

Paul sat down tiredly and slowly poured himself another drink. His eyes seemed to be focused on some faraway vision that only he could see.

"Paul?" John questioned.

Paul gave a half-startled laugh as though he was being drawn back reluctantly from some dream world where he was at peace.

"Yes, John?"

"Something wrong?"

"No," he laughed again, but the laugh was hollow and

314

haunted. "I'm just wondering how this will all end. Are we right, John? Will we be here to see our grandchildren, to give them the kind of life we want them to have?"

"Don't have reservations, Paul. What we are doing is not only the right thing, it is the only choice that we could take with honor, and I'm sure that if you looked closely you would see that Matt and Jason feel as strongly as we do. They've become the strongest patriots we have. A man's loyalties and patriotism are where his heart is, and both those boys have firmly buried their hearts here in this country."

Paul could not put into words the feeling of dread that had overcome him, mostly because he did not understand the strange feeling of lethargy that held him.

"You're right, John. Come on, let's have one last drink and then get over to Baron von Steuben's quarters. I'm sure," he said dryly, "he'll have some work ready for us when we arrive."

Matt and Jason made hasty preparations for the trip home. Using one of the wagons Cat had left after bringing supplies and one old, rather decrepit horse, they began the tedious trip to Clearhaven.

At Clearhaven, the last days of April brought a light feather touch of spring to the air. Deborah stood on the front porch of Clearhaven so that her view of the front lane was unobstructed. Every day, she would take a few minutes to stand so, always keeping the lane in view. She was quite heavy now with child. She laid her hand gently on her belly as the baby, as if in response to her thoughts, moved and caused her to smile at its sturdy thrusts. As the days grew closer to her time, she was filled with an anxiety for Jason's presence. How desperately she wanted him, wanted the feel of his strong hand

315

holding hers.

They had heard rumors of many small battles and of the agony of Valley Forge. But no definite reports had been sent. They all prayed daily, prayed . . . and waited.

She sighed and was about to go back into the house when her mother came out.

"Don't bother to come in, Deborah. Just sit out here and relax. Everything is finished. In fact, Sarah and I were just coming out to join you."

Deborah sat down in a small rocker and sighed contentedly, then she rose again immediately at the sound of an approaching horse. They all watched the lane expectantly and soon one rider came into view.

"It's Deanna," Margaret said.

Deanna dismounted, tied her horse and climbed the steps, seating herself on the top step and leaning against the pillar.

"Is there any news, Deanna?" Deborah asked hopefully.

Deanna gave a negative shake of her head and reached out to gently pat Deborah's hand.

"I've been in town all day. There's been no word."

Sarah sat down beside the two girls, but Margaret stood watching the deserted road. A quiet feeling, a feeling of stillness overtook her. For a moment she had a terrible feeling of loneliness as though she were away from everything and desperately alone.

"Paul," she murmured.

"What, Mother?" asked Deborah.

"Nothing, I was just thinking aloud," she smiled. Turning away from the road, she looked at the women seated around her. Everyone felt the same gripping fear, and each of them held herself under control for the benefit of those about her. It was a chain that supported them all and Margaret knew she could not break it.

"I think I shall go up and change and take the buggy and go back to town for a while and visit Mrs. Slone. She's waiting word from her boy."

She went inside and closed the door behind her.

"I'd better go home," said Deanna. "I've got to take a bath. I've been on this horse so long I smell like him."

She waved good-bye to Sarah and Deborah. They watched until her horse was out of sight, then Sarah turned to Deborah.

"Deborah, why don't you go and lie down for a while. I know you haven't been sleeping well. I've heard you up at all hours. That's not good for the baby, you know."

"Maybe I will just for a while, Sarah. I really seem to tire easily."

She lifted her swollen body slowly from the chair and went inside the house. Climbing the stairs slowly, she went to her room and lay down across the bed without removing any of her clothes. She wanted to be ready if any news came. With thoughts of Jason in her mind, she drifted off into a dream-filled sleep.

Sarah was alone in deep contemplation about the changes the war had made in the people she loved so dearly. Caroline, the lovely daughter who loved a man who dreamed of another; Margaret, torn between two men she loved who stood as mortal enemies; Deanna and Deborah, who had sacrificed so much for the freedom they held so dear. John, her John, whom she loved with every fiber of her being. She began to wonder if the cause of freedom was worth the lives of the people who sacrificed so much for it. She shook her head with a deep sigh and stood to go into the house when a soft sound caught her attention. It seemed to come from a long way. The rattle of horse harnesses, the plodding sound of a horse's hooves. Her heart leapt into her breast, and she shaded her eyes with her hand to look down the road. She could see nothing. Then in the distance, a wagon!

"Oh, God," she whispered, clutching her hand at her breast to control the furious beating of her heart. Closer it came, then it turned into the lane leading to Clearhaven.

With a choking sound in her throat, she came down the steps and started down the lane walking slowly, trying to see who sat on the wagon. "There were two, only two!" she thought in anguish. "Which two?"

As they drew closer, she could finally make out Jason and Matt. She looked at the two of them, red-eyed and dirty, completely exhausted. They were thin and ragged, but smiling nonetheless.

"Jason . . . Matt, it's so good to have you home. Where . . . where are John and Paul . . . and Vern?"

Jason had not spoken at all, but seemed to be moving in a daze. When they stopped the wagon in front of the house, he sat still, looking at it for a few minutes as if he could not believe they were really home. Then he moved with the slow, jerky movements of a man on the brink of collapse.

"Sarah," his voice was a hoarse croak. "Where is Deborah?"

"She's upstairs, lying down, Jason. Shall I go get her?"

"No," came the rasping sound again and before she could speak, he climbed the steps and entered the house.

He climbed the stairs barely making one step at a time until he came to Deborah's door. He opened it quietly and went in. He could see her curled on the bed asleep,

318

and walked to her side. Kneeling down by the bed, he took one of her hands in his and spoke her name softly. She opened her eyes and he immersed himself in the sea-green pools. She sat up quickly on the bed and he rose slowly, sitting on the edge of it. Very gently, he pulled her over into his arms.

"Jason," she cried, the sobs choking in her throat.

"My love," he whispered. She began to cry, and wrapped her arms about his neck.

"Oh, Deb . . . Deb . . ." His big body trembled, and she looked closely at him. He was shaken with exhaustion. She pulled his head down and held it close to hers while she whispered gently to him, cradling him in her arms and comforting him as she would a hurt child. Her eyes were blinded now with tears, for she could feel the pain that was being washed up in him.

Slowly she eased him down onto the bed beside her and she lay by him and stroked his face with her hands until she felt the stiff muscles relax and his eyes closed in sleep.

She moved gently from the bed and stood looking at him.

"Oh, Jason, my darling," her mind cried out to her. She removed his boots and pulled a blanket over him then she lay back down beside him and held his head against her breast, listening and being grateful for the steady beating of his heart.

"Is Deanna here, Sarah?" Matt questioned.

"Oh, Matt, she left here only a few minutes ago to go home. You're too exhausted, Matt. Let me send someone for her."

"No, Sarah. I want to go home, and it might as well be

now. I'll be all right, just as soon as I get there."

He lifted the reins and urged the horse forward. Sarah watched as the wagon moved slowly toward Foxmore.

Deanna had prepared herself a warm bath. Luxuriating in it, she lay back with her eyes closed and gave free rein to her fondest memories. The days she had spent here with Matt. She did not hear the approaching wagon, and in her half-asleep state, she did not hear the footsteps that stopped outside her door. Matt pushed the door open slowly and stood drinking in the lovely scene before him that he had remembered so well in his dreams.

"Deanna, my dreams didn't lie. You are the most beautiful woman in the world."

Deanna sat upright, her eyes widening in surprise.

"Matt," she whispered. He walked to the tub and reached down. Taking both her hands, he pulled her up and into his arms, murmuring her name as his mouth sought and found hers. He held her so fiercely against him and kissed her over and over as though he were afraid if he let her go, she would disappear.

"Let me look at you," she said anxiously as she held him away from her. "Oh, Matt, you look so terrible, you're so thin. Let me get you some food and clean clothes."

"The clean clothes can wait, and there is only one food I need for survival now. You, my love . . . just you."

He pulled her back into his arms and held her, rocking her gently and enjoying the warm clean smell. Their eyes held as he loosened his hold long enough to bend and lift her into his arms. The urgent need for her was such a burning demand that he could no longer deny it. As he laid her on the bed, she reached for him and drew him down against her. With a sigh of utter pleasure, he threw

320

aside the clothes he was wearing and with slow movements, he eased himself within her. There was no wildly passionate taking, but a tender, gentle blending. He wanted to stay within her forever, to lie in the warm safety of her loveliness. She felt his need and closed her eyes and rocked him gently until she felt his release and the trembling relaxation of that tensely muscled frame.

"I'm sorry, Deanna," he said against her throat. "I couldn't help it. I've dreamed of you so, held you so in my dreams so often I guess I just couldn't control my need for you any longer."

"Shhh, Matt, my love," she whispered. "It's all right. As long as I have you here, to hold you, to feel you. It's enough for now. Rest, now, my darling . . . rest."

He lay his head against her breasts and she held him against her as she caressed and soothed him as one would an injured child. Soon she felt him relax, and with a half-smile about her lips, she held him close and felt the contentment and peace she had yearned for for so many months.

Jason slept a full forty-eight hours, and when he awoke, he was ravenously hungry. Deborah came smiling into the room followed by a young boy carrying a tub and two others each with two pails of hot water. They set the tub on the floor, filled it quickly and left.

"No, sir, if you can get out of that bed, it's time for a hot bath. You really don't smell too good, you know," she laughed.

The first movements he made brought a groan as every muscle in his body complained painfully. Finally, with anguish, he rose from the bed and wrapped a blanket about him. He went to Deborah's side and put an arm

321

about her.

"You seem to have grown some since the last time I saw you, Lady. Has my son been behaving?"

"The son is like the father, eternally kicking and causing mischief and keeping me up late at night with cravings for the most unbelievable things. I swear, if I had to carry him one more month, I couldn't move at all."

Jason smiled at her and laid his hand on her belly, just in time to get a resounding kick from the child within. He chuckled, and the sparkle of laughter in his eyes made her catch her breath.

"Jason," she said quietly.

"I know, Deb, I know. I'm so happy to be back here that it hurts. If I haven't told you before, I love you. I'm going to spend the next hundred years telling you just how much." He kissed her again lightly, then dropped the blanket and stepped into the tub. The groan this time was one of pleasure as he closed his eyes and sank back into the water. Deborah knelt beside the tub and began to lather her hands with soap and rub them over his body. "How thin he is," she thought. "I must take care that he doesn't become ill." She wondered just when Jason had his last decent meal. She rubbed and soaped his body until the water began to chill, then she forced him from the tub and back into the bed she had prepared. Then she sent for the tray of food and sat on the edge of the bed and watched him eat. Soon they were laughing and talking together, leaving the rest of the world outside their door.

The next three weeks were spent in an atmosphere of laughter and love.

Deborah was brought to bed in labor three weeks after they arrived home. She had been asleep, curled against

Jason's warmth, when the first low ache began. For a long time, she lay still knowing what was happening and trying to fight her fear. Finally a pain struck that caused a gasp to escape her and brought Jason awake.

"Deb?"

"The baby, Jas, I think your son has decided he wants to see his father. Would you call Mother and Sarah, please?"

He rose immediately and went for Sarah and Margaret, then he returned to their room and with a face filled with worry, sat on the bed and held her hand.

As the pains came quicker, Sarah and Margaret tried to get him to leave. He refused quietly at first then more firmly when they insisted. He held her hand when the worst of the pain struck and she cried out his name and squeezed his fingers. Beads of perspiration coated his forehead as he watched with fear-filled eyes as Deborah fought to give birth to their baby. Off and on, she would open her eyes between pains and she would smile to see him still there. At those times, he would wipe her forehead with a cloth and talk softly to her. Then as the pain struck again, he would grasp her hand in his and hold tightly.

Their son was born twelve hours later and Jason was the first to hold him. He carried him to the bed and sat down, lifting one of Deborah's hands to his lips. She smiled wearily at him and held up her arms. He put the baby in them then smiled at her.

"Thank you, Deb. He's beautiful. Thank you for my son."

"What shall we name him, Jason?"

"Well, Deb. If it's all right with you, I'd like to name him Paul Matthew," he said softly. She swallowed the tears of pride in her husband and nodded silently.

Jason lifted the baby in his arms and said very softly.

"Welcome to the world, Paul Matthew Deverall."

Time slipped away rapidly . . . too rapidly. Days rolled into weeks. Before they were too prepared to think about it, the time had narrowed down to just a few hours.

The morning they were to leave, Matt awoke to find himself alone in his bed. He looked about the room. There was no sign of Deanna. He rose from the bed and was sitting on the edge when the door opened. Half light of early dawn lightened the room.

"Matt, what are you doing up so early. Get back into bed. You have hours yet and you should get all the rest you can."

"Is that an invitation, love?" he grinned. "If it is, I would be only too happy to accept."

She laughed and walked to him and placed both hands on his shoulders. Slowly, she bent down and kissed him gently. She stood before him, and their eyes held for that long breathless moment.

"Oh, Matt, I hate your leaving me again. Please, guard yourself well. I could not bear it if anything happened to you. It would be my fault."

"Now, that's a ridiculous thing to say. How could it possibly be your fault."

"I got you into all this mess. You would have gone on with your past life quite happily if it hadn't been for me."

"Oh, Deanna, you foolish woman. You have filled an empty life with more love, more purpose, more commitment than I ever experienced before. Yes, without you, life would be different. It would be long days and nights of nothingness, without life and without love. Through you I've found a place to put all my thoughts and my dreams. Whatever I have to give in return, I consider well worth it."

He lay back on the bed pulling her with him, and she sighed contentedly as the familiar touch of his hands brought the glowing embers of her desire to full flame. Their love was a gentle thing now, so gentle it made her weep. He caressed her, closing his eyes and moving his hands over her as though he wanted to memorize everything about her. He came to her then, pouring out all his pain and loneliness and she absorbed it, leaving him whole again. They lay together for a long time without speaking, watching the dawn brighten into a new day. There was no need for words. They had molded into one as surely as though they were forged together.

Cat helped Jason and Matt load supplies on the wagon. Supplies that were sorely needed after the disastrous winter of Valley Forge. Reluctant farewells were said and the women stood in silence and watched until the wagon was out of sight.

They made what speed they could with the heavily laden wagon, and arrived in camp on the sixteenth of June. The supplies were welcomed by Paul and John, who distributed them as best they could.

Howe was now succeeded by Sir Henry Clinton, who evacuated Philadelphia. Washington started after him and overtook him at Monmouth, New Jersey, where they fought a long and bloody battle on June twenty-eighth. The British retreated to New York, losing men and munitions along the way. Munitions that were a welcome addition to Washington's ill-equipped army. George Washington wrote in his diary that year that "scarce any state in the Union has, at this hour, an eighth part of its

325

quota in the field and little prospect I can see of ever getting more than half." He added that, "instead of having the prospect of a glorious offensive campaign before us, we have a bewildered and gloomy defensive one." Then came the amazing news that King Louis XVI of France was commiting the greater part of his fleet to the American Revolution.

Washington was elated at the news. If the French fleet could hold at bay the English ships, Washington was determined to meet the British at Yorktown. The activity and purpose was necessary to keep the army together. A destination, a reason, a goal to activate men's minds and loyalties. The destination: Yorktown, Virginia. The reason: the arrival of Cornwallis was to take over Arnold's command of the British forces. The goal: victory of any kind to lift the morale of men almost defeated.

Paul Martin used every means at his command and all the personal strength he owned. He pulled together the men under him by sheer force of will and had them ready. They were exhausted, hungry, poorly dressed and ill-equipped. But he had whipped their spirits again as he always could and like Matt, Jason, Vern and John, they were ready to follow him into hell, if necessary.

They had been molded well by the awakened giant of war as he lifted them from his furnace, bright shining blades of the hardest steel. Unsheathed now, they were swung in the mighty arm of the god of war to meet the bright glowing flame of the British army.

The last great act in the drama for independence was about to begin, and the players in the great drama were more than foes in universal beliefs, but foes also in a drama of their personal lives.

On the bluffs above the York River, General Washington's American troops along with those of the French were to fight a great battle in their revolution. With these troops was Paul Martin. In opposition was General Cornwallis and 75,000 of the finest British troops. In this company was another man who prepared for battle, Colonel Mark Severn. Cornwallis took possession of Yorktown, which was really of no possible use to him. He and Lafayette had been playing hide-and-seek with each other for quite some time, and after his last contact with Lafayette and under what he assumed were orders, he fortified Yorktown.

"We are trapped here if the French fleet can hold our ships at bay," argued Colonel Severn.

"Colonel Severn," Cornwallis replied arrogantly, "need I remind you, sir, we are under orders? We shall hold this position until relief comes. We expect the fleet and relief troops soon."

"But . . ."

"Colonel Severn, we will hold here," Cornwallis said in cold, clipped words.

Mark looked at him and knew that the way he had felt about this conflict for quite some time was about to be proven true. When Washington heard about Cornwallis' position, he feigned as if about to attack New York, but quickly moved south and besieged Cornwallis. For the first time in the war, the military odds were against the British and escape was impossible.

It was fall, the year was 1781. Cornwallis had gathered his forces here to take advantage of the good seaport and harbor. The wisdom of this move was, at that moment, doubted by only one man—Mark Severn. Cornwallis expected relief troops to land from the sea and with them he would crush George Washington and his revolution for all time. But on September fifth a British fleet trying to gain entrance to the Chesapeake Bay was met by the twenty-four French fleet ships, under the command of Admiral DeGrasse. The battle that followed resulted in a strategic victory for the French allies and dashed any hopes Cornwallis may have had for relief from the sea.

In early October the siege of Yorktown began in earnest. George Washington's army, with support of French soldiers, moved their forces within firing range of the British.

It was the tenth day of the battle. The fighting was fierce and bloody. Charge after charge was made on the lines of the British. The small army of Washington's fought so fiercely that Cornwallis had to remove his quarters to two tiny cave-like rooms where he lived and guided the battle in its last days.

Seventeen days passed. Long bloody days in which the losses on both sides were extremely heavy and the final day fate reached out to touch and change the lives of the Martins and the Deveralls. Matt had been close to Paul when the final charge had started. He was within three feet of Paul when the first ball struck. He saw Paul stumble and go down on his knees, then another ball struck and Paul collapsed in a heap. Matt ran to his side and knelt beside him to turn him over. He was still staring in disbelief when a blinding searing pain made him cry out, then a soft smoky cloud of blackness appeared and he tumbled into it. He dropped heavily across the body of Paul Martin and lay still.

After seventeen days of heavy fighting, and more than six long years of war, the American army of shopkeepers and farmers defeated Cornwallis and seventy-five hundred of Britain's finest troops.

Two days later, on October nineteenth, 1781, the defeated British army, marching to the popular children's tune of the day, "The world turned upside down," laid down their arms. Cornwallis and several of his officers, among them Mark Severn, surrendered and left American territory. The surrender at Yorktown signified an end to British rule and the bright new beginning for a proud nation.

Chapter Forty

The battle was over, and a decisive victory had been won, but the cost was almost unbearably high. Men searched the battlefields for dead and wounded . . . for friend and relative. Vern and Jason had found each other, and now moved wearily among the casualties. It was Jason who first spotted Matt and Paul. An agonized cry came from him as they ran to them with their last remaining strength.

"Matt, Matt!" cried his brother. "Oh, God, not Matt. Please?" he prayed silently as he ran. When he reached his brother's side, he dropped heavily to his knees and through a haze of tears, gently lifted him from Paul. Vern dropped close beside him and helped turn Matt over.

"Paul's dead," said Vern softly, and he reached out his hand and laid it for a moment on Paul's chest.

Jason was groaning his brother's name over and over as he laid him gently on his back.

"He's alive, Jason. He's alive," said Vern.

"How bad is he?" gasped Jason.

"I don't know. He's been hit in the back and it came out through his side. I don't know how much damage it's done. We've got to get him back to the doctor. Give me your blanket."

As quickly as his bone-weary body would move, Jason took his blanket, and together they wrapped Matt tightly in it. Jason moved to pick him up and almost cried out at the violence of his body's reaction. Vern put his hand on Jason's shoulder.

"Let me carry him, Jas," he said quietly. Without any seeming effort, Vern lifted Matt's body in his arms and with Jason carrying the equipment, they moved as rapidly as possible in the direction of the medical tent. When they arrived, they were stopped by a huge soldier who stood outside the medical tent.

"You can't go in there," he said firmly.

"This man's hurt badly, he's dying. I've got to get him in to the doctor," said Vern.

"Man," the soldier said more gently now, "don't you think they all feel the same." He pointed at a huge group of men gathered under a grove of trees. The pain of the wounded men could almost be felt.

"The doctors are working as fast as they can. You'll just have to wait your turn."

Jason looked at Vern, who shook his head negatively.

"Matt won't make it that long, Jas."

Grimly Jason set his teeth and lifting his gun, put the barrel of it against the soldier's throat with one swift movement.

"You step aside or I'll blow a hole in you they'll never be able to repair," he said.

The soldier gulped and turned slightly pale, then he stepped aside and Vern carried Matt inside. They both stopped short, and a wave of nausea engulfed them. The mass of groaning, pain-filled humanity lay worked on by several blood-smeared doctors with blank agonized faces was so overwhelming that Jason almost became sick. Vern's face also had turned slightly green and he shook through every nerve he owned. A young boy's body was being lifted off a table minus a leg and the doctor turned and shouted at Vern.

"Hurry up! Over here. Lay him on the table."

The coldness of the man's voice stopped Vern for a second. He felt the deep urge to take Matt and leave the tent for the bitter fear deep in him told him Matt would never survive this tent of subdued violence. Instead, he moved forward and laid Matt on the blood-smeared table and unwrapped the blanket. With deft fingers, the doctor cut away the cloth from around the wound. He stood and looked closely at it for a few minutes. Then turned to Vern.

"Roll him on his side and hold him," he said impersonally.

When Vern turned Matt toward him, Jason came to his side.

"I'll hold him, Vern," he said grimly. He grasped Matt in his arms tightly while the doctor probed and examined the wound. Although Matt was unconscious, his body reacted to the pain of the examination. He moaned softly and mumbled something incoherent. The doctor worked swiftly to clean and repair as best he could. Within a few minutes, he looked up at Jason with a sad expression.

"I've done all I can do. All you can do now is take him home and pray. He's lost a lot of blood." Jason caught his lower lip in his teeth as he again wrapped Matt gently in the blanket. For a few minutes, he held his brother tightly against him. There were unfelt tears running quietly down his face.

"If I could only give him mine, I would," he thought, holding him. "Come, Matt, live! We've got to go home."

Vern came to the other side of the table and together they gently lifted him and carried him out.

332

It was several hours later before Matt began to stir. Then he moaned and blinked his eyes. They were glassy, and to add to Vern's fears were filled with the bright shine of fever. He put his hand on Matt's head. It was blazing hot. For the second time that day, Vern felt the fear that Matt would not make it. He looked over at Jason, who had almost collapsed in an exhausted sleep. He didn't know what else to do and the knowledge of this made him more frightened than he had ever been in his life before. He sat and watched the two men for a long time. The bitter resentment he had felt against Jason had been washed away in the blood and fire of the battle. Now, a new thought spun about in his exhausted brain. A pair of soft eyes laughed up at him in his dreams and he could feel the softness of her golden hair against his cheek. "Caro, Caro, I've been so blind and stupid," he thought. "I almost overlooked the beauty of what I could have for a false dream that was never mine."

Matt's moaning and mumbling brought his attention back to their situation. He had to do something to help Matt but he was completely lost as to what. He moved over to Matt's side and checked the bandages about his body. There was no fresh blood, so the wound had not reopened. It was the fever that was the problem. He took all the blankets they had between them and wrapped Matt tightly. Then with his handkerchief, he continually wet it with water from his canteen and laid it on Matt's hot face. It was inadequate and he knew it, but he didn't know what else to do.

Matt began to groan in pain and he called out to Deanna over and over, talking to her, telling her of his plans, his love, sharing again the time they were together. The pain of listening was almost as hard on Vern.

Jason came awake with a start after just a couple hours of sleep. He moved quickly to Vern's side where he looked at Matt, and the fear twisted in him like a knife. Matt was dying, and he knew it, and was powerless to do anything about it. He sat and listened to the wanderings of Matt's mind until he wanted to cry aloud.

It was almost dark, and Vern lit a small fire. There was nothing to eat, but that was a situation to which they had become accustomed. They did not speak, for neither of them had the words to comfort the other. There was the sound of footsteps approaching and then into the light of the fire came John.

He looked toward the man wrapped in the blanket and at first did not know who it was.

"Who is it?" he asked.

"Matt," said Vern.

"How bad?"

"I don't think he's going to make it. I don't know what else to do for him. Do you know Paul's dead?"

John gave a silent nod of his head. "I helped bury him," he said softly.

"Now let me look at Matt."

He knelt at Matt's side and with the gentlest hands Vern had ever seen, he unwrapped the bandages.

"Build up the fire, Jason. Vern give me your knife. Pour out some water in something and set it to boil, quick! We've got to move fast."

Vern felt a quick relief and admiration for John, who always seemed to know what to do in any situation. They set about doing what he ordered and watched, strong faced, as John worked quickly and gently. After almost an hour, John pulled the blanket over Matt again.

"Well, we have to wait now, and I guess all we can do

is pray."

Jason watched John as he leaned wearily back against the tree and closed his eyes. Paul had said John was always there when he was needed and he was right.

"John?" he said softly.

"Yes, Jas."

"Thank you."

John opened his eyes and smiled at him. Then he closed them again.

Jason went to his brother's side and lifting his hand in his, held it and continued to watch. Matt's fever continued to rage and Jason became desperate.

"We've got to get him home. John, we've got to get him to a doctor."

"You're right, Jas. I'll do my best to round up some kind of transportation."

Although he tried his best, there were no wagons to be found and for the first time, John, too, became frightened that Matt was going to die. They could not move him. Every day they cleaned his wound and worked feverishly to save him, but the heavy hand of dread held them and they slowly began to admit that their ministrations were useless and that daily Matt was growing weaker and weaker.

They were seated about the campfire late at night, none of them able to sleep, listening to Matt's incoherent babbling as his fever blazed higher and higher. None had the ability or the words to comfort the others. Vern had lived with and fought with Jason for months. Now he began to realize what Jason and Deborah shared. He knew also what he had almost lost. He vowed to himself that if they all got home safely, he was going to tell Deborah. Then he was going to the woman he knew now really loved him and if she would still have him, he was going to marry her immediately. Vern looked up from the fire and saw Jason's eyes intent on him. For the first time since their acquaintance, Vern allowed his eyes to soften to friendliness. Jason's quick smile told him that no words were necessary.

The three of them were so engrossed in their own private thoughts that none of them heard the creak of wagon wheels. A quiet voice from outside the range of the light of their fire aroused all three.

"Can a friend share supper with you?"

"Cat!" Jason cried.

Cat stepped into the light and looked around at their faces. His smile faded as he searched for one face in particular.

"Where's Matt?" he questioned.

"He's in the tent, Cat," Jason replied. "He's been hurt bad. We had no way to get him home."

Cat went into the tent. When he reappeared his eyes were clouded and his face grim.

"I have a wagon. I was looking for you with supplies. I didn't know the war was over until today . . . Jason, we've got to hurry. Matt's dying."

They put out the fire and gathered their few remaining belongings together. Cat wrapped Matt in a blanket and gently lifted him to a bed they had made in the back of the wagon. They began the journey home without taking time to rest, each of them aware that every second counted if they wanted Matt alive.

They arrived at Clearhaven first hoping that everyone had gathered there. They were right. As though some hidden hand had reached out and touched her, Deanna had risen early and ridden over from Foxmore to see her mother and Deborah and the baby. Some silent urging drew her there. She could not have put a name to it if someone had asked, she only knew it was the place she needed to be. Before the wagon could even come to a complete stop, the door was thrown open and Deborah was in Jason's arms. Deanna stood frozen in the doorway.

Vern, Jason, John, Cat, everyone was there except her father and Matt.

"Matt?" she questioned, her eyes wide with fear.

"He's in the wagon, Deanna," Jason said gently. "He's been hurt bad, we have to get him a doctor."

Deanna ran to the wagon side. Tears fell unheeded as she looked down on Matt's unconscious form. Vern and Cat lifted him from the wagon and carried him upstairs and laid him on the bed.

"I'll go for the doctor," Cat said as he turned to Deanna. "I'll get him here as fast as possible. Don't worry, Deanna. Matt's strong. With your prayers, he'll make it."

"Hurry, Cat," she whispered. "Please hurry."

Margaret had stood quietly, her eyes and John's meeting over the heads of the others. When Matt had been carried upstairs and Cat had gone for the doctor, John went to Margaret.

"Margaret."

"I know," she said softly. "I think I've known for some time. Come in, John and tell me."

He followed behind her, amazed at her calmness, not knowing it was the heavy burden of guilt that was close to destroying her. She sat down in a chair and motioned John to another.

He slowly eased himself into a chair watching Margaret, then he began to talk and she sat quietly listening with her hands folded still in her lap. They sat talking for a long time, two strong people sharing their strength for the benefit of those they loved. After a while, the sound of an approaching horse told them of the doctor's arrival. When he came running up the steps and into the house, Margaret directed him to Matt's room. John continued to tell Margaret about the last three weeks when the three of them had gone almost completely without sleep and very little food in an all-out effort to get him home. When he finished speaking, Margaret said nothing, merely rose still dry-eyed and went quietly upstairs to stay with Deanna.

As Deanna stood beside the bed, looking down at Matt, the tears came. She sat on the bed and held his hand and looked at his face. He was thin and pale. Slowly she bent forward and touched his lips with hers. He moaned softly and mumbled her name. It was then that she dropped her head beside his on the pillow and gave in to the heart-breaking tears that almost tore her apart. She remained so until she heard the knock on the door.

"It's Doctor Carter, Deanna. Please let me come in, now."

Deanna lifted her head from the pillow, then nodding slightly she rose and opened the door. The doctor stood outside the door with Margaret.

"Dr. Carter," Deanna said quietly touching him gently on the arm. "Help him, please?" Her voice died to a whisper.

The doctor was hard put to cover up the choking in his own throat as he nodded and patted her consolingly.

"I'll do my best, child, I'll do my best." He went in and closed the door behind him.

Margaret put her arm about her daughter's shoulder

and held her, trying to make her pain easier, not letting her know of the pain in her own heart that was almost destroying her.

It was over an hour before the doctor came back out of the room. Deanna was there waiting.

"Doctor Carter?"

"Deanna, my dear. I have done as much as it is possible for me to do. He is weak, but he is fighting. There is nothing to do now but wait and pray. If the fever breaks by morning, he stands a very good chance of survival. That is all I can tell you, child."

"Thank you, Doctor Carter."

He nodded, smiled at her and left. She went back into the room. Matt was lying very still on the bed. The bandages that bound his body were fresh and white, and his arms lay still at his side, giving her the feeling that he was helpless and needed her strength. She sat down again on the bed, gently and lifted his hand and held it and began to speak softly to him, although she knew he couldn't hear.

"Matt, I love you so. You cannot, you must not die. Please, my darling, how can I go on if you leave me now? I want you so, Matt, I want to bear your children, I want to hear you laugh, I want to make love to you. Matt, come back from wherever you are, come back to me, Matt, come back to me." She sat through the hours speaking softly to him. Reliving their hours together, talking, talking as if she could pull him back from the jaws of death.

At some time Margaret came in and tried to get her to leave and get some rest. She shook her head without taking her eyes from Matt. Dawn came, and still the burning fire in his body raged. Quiet, gentle tears were

339

falling from her eyes, and fear began to squeeze its tight fist around her heart. She rose from the bed and went to the window, and pushing it open she watched the first streaks of dawn light the sky. She wrapped her arms about herself as if to contain the grief she held and laid her head against the window and closed her eyes to feel the soft fresh morning breeze.

"Deanna." It was the softest whisper.

She had been listening to him moan and call her name all night, and it was several minutes before she realized that the sound of his voice was different. Her throat grew tight and she turned fearfully and looked at him.

He was looking at her, and their eyes met and held. His eyes were clear and bright and filled with love. She moved again to his side and bent to brush his lips with hers.

"Welcome home, my love, oh, my darling, welcome back."

Caroline had remained in her bedroom after she had looked down from her window and watched their arrival. She was afraid. Afraid to go down those stairs and look into Vern's eyes. For the first time in her life, Caroline felt despair, and she could barely contain it. She listened as they carried Matt to his room. Slowly she sank to the edge of the bed and covered her face with her hands, allowing the silent, hot tears to fall. The door moved slowly open and Vern stood in the doorway and looked at her dejected figure.

"Is this a way for a woman to greet her future husband when he has been fighting a war for her? It really won't do, ma'am. If we're going to have a good marriage you'll have to be more demonstrative than this."

Slowly her hands fell, she looked up at him in disbelief. Rising from the bed, she went to him. Tentatively, she reached out and touched him.

"I remembered all this time," he said softly. "A beauty who seduced me rather shamelessly. I'm looking for her . . . I don't want to lose her."

"Oh, Vern," she sighed. Slowly his arms came about her and he held her against him, and for the first time a feeling of peace and contentment overcame him for he knew he was home.

After Cat had gone for the doctor, he went to his cabin where Deeta greeted him with enough enthusiasm to last a lifetime.

Time slipped away, days moved into weeks. Life picked up a tempo and moved everyone along in a glow of happiness, everyone except Margaret. Sarah had been watching Margaret since word had come of Paul's death. Outwardly, she seemed to be accepting it, but Sarah knew that inside she was punishing herself for some sense of guilt.

She worked feverishly for everyone's comfort, and late at night, Sarah could hear her moving about the house in restless torment. Occasionally, she would watch from the window and see her ride out after she thought everyone else was asleep. After several weeks of watching, she could stand it no longer and approached Margaret one evening after everyone had gone to bed.

"Margaret, may I talk to you for a moment?"

"Of course, Sarah. Is something wrong?"

"I don't know. I want you to tell me. What's wrong? Why are you pushing yourself?"

"Oh, Sarah, I cheated him so. I gave him nothing in

341

return for all he gave me. Now there is no way to repay him for all he gave me."

"And so you blame yourself for his death? Nonsense, Margaret," Sarah said harshly. "Paul Martin devoted himself to his cause as selflessly as humanly possible. All the love from you that you had to give could not have changed things one bit. You gave him years of love and contentment. You gave him children, you gave him a happy home. You gave him all you had to give and he knew and loved you with all his heart. But he's gone, Margaret. I know how you feel, but you are still alive and you have a long life yet to live. You have a family who loves you. You cannot live in the past, Margaret. You must put old memories where they belong."

"I don't know what to do, Sarah," she said softly. "I cannot seem to find myself. I feel lost and alone."

"I know what you must do."

"What?"

"Send for Mark."

"No!"

"Why?"

"I don't deserve another man's love. Maybe if it hadn't been for Mark, I would have been free to give Paul what he needed. Maybe he would still be here."

"Oh, Margaret, that is a terrible way to think. You deserve all the love and happiness you can get."

Margaret shook her head negatively, and rose to her feet.

"I don't want to talk about it anymore, Sarah," she said softly. "Leave things be, just leave things be."

She left the room and Sarah watched her sadly. She was standing quietly watching the doorway through which Margaret had gone when her thoughts were interrupted by a loud shout from the porch. The door burst open and John rushed in. He grasped her up in his arms and whirled her around until she became dizzy.

"Good heavens, John. Put me down." She laughed. "Whatever has happened?"

"The peace treaty is signed, Sarah," he said, happily shouting it again. "Officially the war is over."

Pandemonium broke loose and everyone gathered together to share the happiness the news brought. Even Margaret laughed and cried with them while inside her heart seemed to freeze into a solidity in protection from the future.

They planned a celebration, laughter and gaiety prevailed and the party was quite a success. All their neighbors and friends came and it lasted into the wee hours of the morning.

After the last guest had gone and her family had retired for the short balance of the night, Margaret sat before the bright remains of the fire. She was contented now, and although she was not happy, she felt that she could bear the balance of her life. With a deep sigh she rose from her chair and walked slowly upstairs to bed.

In her own room Sarah sat by the window in deep thought. John was sound asleep and the room was quiet. She sat for a long time, then she rose slowly and went to the desk. Lighting the lamp, she pulled a sheet of paper from the drawer and began to write.

"Dear Mark . . ."

Chapter Forty-One

The ship's white sails billowed out, filled with a stiff early-morning breeze. Mark Severn stood at the rail and watched the shores of America fade into a thin line on the horizon. He wondered just what Margaret was doing at that moment. "Now that this bloody war is over," he thought, her husband would come home to her. He allowed his mind to dwell agonizingly on their reunion. Angrily, he thrust the picture from his mind. He knew that he alone was guilty of his loss. If he had never left her in the beginning, she would be his now, not only Margaret, but . . . he would not allow himself to think about it any longer. If he did he knew it would drive him mad.

He went below deck to the cabin he shared with three of his friends. They were playing a game of cards and joyfully invited him to join them. He refused, and poured himself a drink. He propped a pillow behind him and lay back on his bunk and slowly sipped his drink.

One of the men who sat at the table in the card game watched Mark surreptitiously under furrowed brows. Mark, he thought, had not been himself for quite some time. He wondered just what it was that preyed so heavily on his friend's mind. Jeremy Mackenzie had been a companion and friend of Mark's from the time they were boys. They had taken their education together, gone to

344

the military academy together, gotten drunk together, and confided their secrets to each other for as long as Jeremy could remember.

He had stood by Mark in some of his escapades, both romantic and otherwise. It was Jeremy who helped Mark regain his equilibrium when he finally discovered that he had lost his beloved Margaret to another man. Now Jeremy began to wonder if Mark had really regained his footing. Having to fight a war against a country to which a woman he had loved had gone with her husband was enough to unnerve him, and Jeremy felt that somehow the two things had something in common. Mark had never told Jeremy where he was going all the nights he had disappeared, and because he seemed so happy Jeremy had not questioned him. It was only now, when they were leaving, that he put two and two together and came up with the obvious answer . . . Margaret.

Throwing all caution aside, Jeremy decided that at the first opportunity for some privacy, he was going to ask Mark. But the opportunity did not come until several days later when he came below deck to find Mark alone in their cabin. He closed the door behind him and smiled.

"We're only two days from home. It will be good to see the white cliffs again."

"Yes . . . home," Mark answered. "What are you going to do after we arrive, Jeremy? Are you planning on staying in the military?"

"No, I think not. I think it's time I plan on staying home for a while. I want Louise to remember that I'm still the father of her children. I shouldn't want the old girl dashing about looking for someone to fill my shoes."

He watched the shadow cross Mark's face and knew his instincts had been right from the beginning. He had always known why Mark had never married. There had been no woman who had filled Mark's mind and heart as Margaret had.

His face grew serious. "What is it, old chum? What's been eating at you for the past few months?"

Denial was on Mark's lips, but when his eyes met Jeremy's he knew there was no use. Jeremy knew him as few others did. He alone knew about Margaret. "I've seen her, Jeremy," he said quietly.

"I kind of suspected you had. Do you want to tell me what happened?"

"I spent the last few days with her, but she refused to leave him, to hurt him. There was nothing more I could do. I left her in peace as I probably should have done from the start."

"Can you do it now?"

"I don't know, but I have to try. If only it weren't for . . ."

"For what?"

"She has two beautiful daughters, Jeremy. Twins."

"That's not really a very unusual thing for a married woman, Mark."

"They're mine, Jeremy . . . mine."

"You know that for sure, Mark?"

"Yes . . . I know for sure."

"My God, man, I'm sorry. What are you going to do?"

"What can I do. Stay away and let her have some happiness. But Lord, it's hard. They're so beautiful, Jeremy, so very lovely, and how I long to hear them call me Father. What I would give if she were free. I'd spend the rest of my life trying to make up for all the pain I have caused her."

"But she isn't free," Jeremy reminded gently.

"No . . . no, she isn't free, and I'll never be free either."

"You've got to make a life for yourself, too, Mark. You have an obligation. You're the last of the Severns. There's a title and a great deal of money. Whether you like it or not, you have things you have to do also."

"I'm almost forty, Jeremy, a little old to be siring sons."

"Be damned, Mark, you're in the prime of your life. Look around, Mark. Find a good woman and settle down. It may not be the great love you and Margaret had, but sometimes you have to settle for second best in life. It's better than nothing at all."

"Is that fair to another woman? I would always be looking at her and thinking about Margaret. No, I think it's better this way. I'll find something to fill my time, but I don't want another woman to fill my life."

Jeremy opened his mouth to argue.

"Forget it, Jeremy. That's the way it is, that's the way I prefer it. Be a good friend as you've always been and leave it die here."

There was no argument that Jeremy could use against that. He nodded and let the subject drop.

Mark and Jeremy retrieved their luggage at the dock, hired a carriage and proceeded to Mark's home, where Jeremy had been invited to stay for a few weeks.

Severn Hall was a majestic home. It was a large tract of land approximately 30,000 acres that had been deeded to the Severns over a hundred years before.

The "H" shaped house had many large rooms. Four balancing dependencies contained the kitchen, school-room, office and stores building. Boxwood outlined the flowerbeds in the garden, and oyster shell paths offered pleasant strolls beneath crape myrtles and dogwoods. The fire crackled in the fireplace, which was large enough to roast an ox. There was a magnificently carved staircase that led to the upper floor.

Mark and Jeremy stood in the entranceway and looked about the huge, beautiful, empty home. Outside of servants, Mark would live here alone. The thought, for one wild moment, almost overwhelmed him and he felt the urgent desire to run as far and as fast as he could. But he knew that not only could one not run away from memories . . . but there was no place and no one to run to.

"Jeremy, let's leave our unpacking until later and go down to the tavern and have a drink and some supper."

"Good idea."

At the tavern, Mark was greeted by friends. They ordered their food, but Jeremy noticed that Mark reached more often for his glass than for his fork. By the time they were ready to return home, Mark was exceedingly drunk, and Jeremy was not in much better condition. They made their way unsteadily to the door of Severn Hall, but Mark stood still and looked at the closed door.

"I can't do it, Jeremy," he said in a slurred voice. "I can't live alone in this great stone monstrosity."

"Mark, come to Scotland with me. Stay for a few weeks, at least, until you get yourself together. Louise would be only too glad to have you."

"Let's go tonight, now," Mark said as he leaned against the door for support.

"Good," Jeremy agreed. "We'll send for our clothes. C'mon let's get the coach. You wake up the coachman and we'll be on our way. Won't Louise be surprised to see the both of us," he laughed.

348

Both of them were entirely too drunk to worry about their disgruntled coachman as they urged him from his bed. In an hour, they were aboard the coach and on their way down the rutted roads toward Scotland. A few minutes after their departure, both were passed out on the seats of the coach while the coachman cursed them both and all their ancestors.

The sudden jolt of the coach brought Mark awake in the early light of dawn. For a few minutes he could not place either where he was or why he was there. He looked across at a sleeping Jeremy and slowly the pieces of last night's drunken spree cleared in his mind.

"What the hell did it matter where they were or where they were going as long as it wasn't back to that dark lonely house," he thought. He leaned back on the seat and closed his eyes against the throbbing headache. "Maybe a few weeks with Jeremy and his lovely wife Louise would help him get himself under some control. Grimly, he decided that he would straighten out his mind and try to head himself in some constructive direction for the future. He could not continue as he was; his pride wouldn't allow it. Given enough time, he would get himself under control. Some way, somehow, he would learn to live without her.

The journey to Jeremy's home took them over five days. Along the route they stopped only to eat, sleep short hours, and rest the horses. Louise greeted her husband with happy tears and called together the children, two of which were already married and the youngest of which was a lovely girl of sixteen. They made Mark welcome, and for the following two weeks filled him with delightful meals, good company and the very best medicine he needed—the understanding of kind-hearted friends. Jeremy was very pleased to see Mark laugh unrestrainedly and grow calmer. They were seated in front of the fireplace early one evening sipping brandy and making small talk when the sound of an approaching carriage could be heard. With a small half-smile on her lips, Louise rose and left the room. Jeremy, who knew his wife extremely well, knew immediately that some planned thing was unfolding before him. He laughed to himself and realized he was very curious what his mischievous wife had planned, and better still, just who she had planned it for. Both his questions were answered almost immediately when Louise returned, accompanied by three people, two women and a man. Both Mark and Jeremy rose to their feet.

"Jeremy, dear, I would like you to meet two new neighbors of ours. They moved into Dunker Hall just a few weeks after you left," she gestured to the man first. "This is Lord Jeffery Chapin and his wife Lady Ellen Chapin and this," she said with her eyes sparkling, "is Ellen's sister, Alicia."

Introductions were acknowledged and the three were urged to sit and join them. Mark's eyes caught Louise's above their heads and she winked brazenly at him, causing him to chuckle to himself. There was no sign from him that he knew exactly what Louise was up to.

Alicia Charters was a very lovely woman, Mark had to admit. She was slender, and he guessed her age to be somewhere around thirty. Her golden hair was coiled atop her head and she smiled easily at him with cool blue eyes.

"Good evening," she said softly.

"Good evening, Miss?"

"Mrs," she replied. "I'm a widow, Colonel Severn."

"Colonel no longer, Mrs. Charters. I've finished with the army. I'm home for good."

"You were involved in that . . ."

"Revolution," he supplied with an amused smile. "Yes, I was."

"My husband was killed there, over a year-and-a-half ago."

"I'm sorry."

"Thank you. I'm sorry if I sound a little bitter."

"That's understandable," Louise replied. "To be made a widow so young is really a disastrous thing."

"Shall we talk of something else," Alicia said.

They spent a quiet evening together and Mark soon discovered that the Chapins and Alicia had been invited to stay the weekend. Louise planned the weekend carefully so that she could throw Mark and Alicia together alone as often as possible. A fox hunt was arranged for the following morning. Louise knew Mark and Alicia were both excellent riders and she prayed that this was the beginning for two people who, in her estimation, had much in common.

Alicia came from a wealthy and prestigious family and had the education and ability to become the wife of a lord. That Alicia was physically attracted to Mark was obvious. Alicia and Louise had been friends too long for Louise not to see the obvious signs.

After the fox hunt a ball was held, at which Mark enjoyed himself thoroughly. He danced often with Alicia, sending Louise's hopes spiraling. Mentally she was already making preparations for a wedding that she would insist on being held in her home. She stood by Jeremy's side and watched Mark and Alicia circle the floor again intent on whatever they were talking about.

She had her secret hopes that it was something romantic. Jeremy watched her, amused at her efforts, but with the deep premonition that they would come to no avail. He too would have liked to see Mark settled and happy, but was forced in all honesty to believe it was an impossibility. Mark had not been able to release Margaret from his heart for the first nineteen years of their separation and Jeremy felt it was just as impossible for the next nineteen. Louise hummed lightly to herself and Jeremy chuckled drawing her attention.

"What is so funny, Jeremy?"

"You, my dear," he said fondly.

"Oh," she laughed. "And what is so amusing about me?"

"Your eternal efforts to see that every man and woman in your immediate vicinity is married."

"Just what about that makes you so happy?"

Jeremy slipped his arm about Louise's waist. "Because it tells me, love," he said affectionately, "that you consider it a happy state and I am not only flattered, I'm grateful that you feel so."

Louise's eyes warmed as she smiled up at her husband of twenty years. "You've made me very happy, Jeremy. I wish every woman were as lucky as I."

"Well," he smiled and motioned toward Mark and Alicia. "Maybe you'll be a success this time. From all outward appearances, Mark seems to find Alicia attractive. Maybe your matchmaking will fill that empty void he has carried with him all these years."

"Oh, Jeremy," Louise said, her eyes turning serious. "I know that Mark will never love anyone else as he did Margaret, but I would like him to have someone to make the rest of his life bearable and maybe give him the children he has always wanted. Alicia is a gentle and beautiful woman. She also is not a fool. She would never marry him if she didn't love him, and if she does marry him she will do everything in her power to make him happy. I just hope Mark is not foolish enough to pass up what he can have for a dream that can never be."

Jeremy nodded, his eyes following the two dancers about the floor. "I hope so too, love," he said softly. "I hope so too."

Alicia smiled up at Mark, enjoying the feel of his strong arm about her and the warmth of his smile as they swirled about the floor.

"Are you planning on staying in Scotland long, Mark?"

"I really hadn't made definite plans for the distant future, Alicia. For now, today is enough for me."

"But," she said softly, "what can one expect from the future when one does not plan it, guide it or look forward to it?"

"Why expect? Why not let whatever comes, come?"

Alicia looked at Mark in silence for a few moments. She felt the strong emotional current that flowed in him, but could not, for the moment, understand. There was a silent pain that lurked deep in his eyes and she found herself wanting to comfort him in some way, to reach out and ease whatever black memory hurt him so.

"Can you, or any other person, live a happy life like that, Mark, just waiting, allowing things to happen at random?"

"What makes you think everyone is entitled to a happy life? For some there is more or less just existence, the ability to handle only the todays and leave the tomorrows for the young to seek."

"Young?" she questioned. "Mark you are far from an old man. There is a long life to be lived. Why just accept whatever it has to offer when you have every means to mold it in what you want it to be."

"Maybe," he said firmly, pulling her closer to put a stop to her words. They were words he did not want to hear at the moment. Alicia was a little upset when Mark did not ask her to dance again for the balance of the evening. Then she realized the obvious. She had somehow touched on a wound too recent, too painful for him to explore. She vowed to be more careful in the future. "If," she thought, "there is a future."

The weekend was over, and Alicia accompanied her sister and brother-in-law home. Their estate bordered on Jeremy's, but was still over two days' coach ride away. Jeremy valued his privacy and yet he was the first to welcome guests. He had been subjected as a child to perpetual travel. He was an only child born of wealthy parents who had the obsession that Jeremy would be happy if he saw and did everything the world had to offer. Instead of giving Jeremy the hunger to learn that his parents expected, it gave him a hunger for a solid, permanent peaceful home of his own.

Although they pushed him in the direction of the wealthy connoisseur, Jeremy chose to go to a military academy at eighteen. Neither of his parents understood what he wanted. Every girl of marriageable age had been literally pushed into his arms by parents like his who were secure in their beliefs that wealth should marry wealth. To their distress, at twenty-two he fell in love and married the daughter of his instructor at the academy. Louise was not the beautiful debutante they wanted for their son, but she held all the qualities Jeremy had always looked for in a wife. She was shy, even-tempered and of extremely quick intelligence. Not only did he love her physically, which he did thoroughly, but he admired the fine quality of her mind. They could talk, as friends, which was something almost unheard of in that day. She understood Jeremy thoroughly and was always a willing listener. But the most cherished gift Jeremy felt she had given him were his children. There were five of them, each loved in their own separate ways. The oldest, son Randolph, resembled his father in every way possible. The second son, Gordon, was a pleasant combination of the two parents. The next two, Gregory and Jeffery, were twins, both fair and blue-eyed like their mother. The youngest, Jeananne, was a slender, delicate girl with her father's red-gold hair, green eyes and a fiery temperament. Jeremy loved her to distraction. Next to Louise, she was the dearest woman in his life.

The meeting of Jeremy and Mark came about when Jeremy and his family were visiting Mark's parents at Severn Hall. As completely unalike as they were, they immediately became good friends. Mark's father often said they were the two opposite sides of the same coin. Their friendship spanned the years and they both decided to join the military at the same time.

Mark was grateful for Jeremy's questionless understanding. As the days at Jeremy's home passed by he realized he might not have gotten through without a place of sanctuary. Just as he knew he had to begin somewhere to plan the balance of his life, yet he tried his best to consciously ignore it.

Mark, over the next month, visited Alicia often, but now his guarded conversation kept her at arm's length. He knew that Alicia was falling in love with him and he cursed himself for the lethargy of mind that kept him from leaving. He recognized it as fear—fear of facing life without Margaret in a silent Severn Hall, yet knowing he would ask no other woman to reside there.

He and Jeremy were seated at the chess board after a long and leisurely dinner. The room was silent as they sipped their brandy and contemplated the next strategic moves. At that very moment they heard the arrival of a carriage and muffled voices from the front entrance hall. After a few minutes, Louise came to the doorway accompanied by a stranger to Mark.

"Jeremy, Sir Francis would like to speak to you for a moment." She stepped aside and ushered in Sir Francis Braham. Both Mark and Jeremy rose to their feet, but Jeremy walked toward the newcomer with outstretched hand and a broad smile.

"Sir Francis, how good it is to see you. Do come in, I'm delighted you are here." He shook hands enthusiastically with the older man, then guided him toward Mark.

"Come in and meet my oldest and dearest friend, Mark. Sir Francis, this is Mark Severn, recently retired Colonel of his majesty's army. Mark, this is Sir Francis Braham, one of the greatest representatives Parliament has ever had."

"Retired now, my boy," Sir Francis chuckled as he extended his hand to Mark. "Pleased to meet you, sir. I've heard innumerable stories about you."

Mark cast a pretend look of anger at Jeremy. "All good I hope, sir?"

"Quite, quite."

"Come, join us for some brandy," Jeremy said. He poured a brandy for Sir Francis, who walked across the room and stood in front of the fireplace.

Sir Francis was a man of short stature. He was florid of face and had white hair and a thick white moustache. He also had calm and appraising blue eyes that were watching Mark closely.

"How is everything in London, Sir Francis?" Jeremy questioned.

"Well, the results of the war, although epoch-making in the long term as bringing into existence the republic of the United Colonies, are in short term less significant."

"How, sir?"

"They have been misjudged by our contemporaries. Many other countries think we are permanently weakened. There is some political confusion and some people think to eat of the corpse. There are forces that are trying to reduce the king's power."

"I will admit, sir," Mark said, "that the revolution was fought inexpertly by us. We fought half-heartedly in the expectation the colonies would submit. They also had some unexpected help from France."

"You are an observant man. I expect," he said softly, "that within the next two years, we will be isolated. Some neutrals are determined to form an armed neutrality of the north. If they do, we stand alone. Outwest Indies are at the mercy of the French and the Irish are again uprising."

"Sir Francis," Jeremy said gently. "You have not journeyed here just to tell us this. Since we have been so recently involved, we know just how the situation stands."

"Quite right again, m'boy," he said softly. He was speaking to Jeremy, but his eyes held Mark's, who had sat back in his chair with a slight expectant smile on his face. "I need some help, quickly, and secretly."

"Just what kind of help do you need?" Jeremy asked.

"I need a . . . forceful messenger. One who can not only carry the messages of assurance I send but have the courage to support them among some of England's greatest enemies. I was thinking of asking you, Jeremy, but I fear for my life, lest Louise should find me out. No . . ." he chuckled and Mark's smile broadened, "I do believe I have found my man."

"Where, Sir Francis?" Mark questioned gently.

"Several places, with names so obscure you will never recognize them."

"For how long?"

"I imagine a little over a year."

"Mark! For God's sake, at least give it some thought," Jeremy said quickly for he too had seen the gleam in Mark's eye and this smile on his lips.

"I already have, Jeremy. It is the best thing for me right now. Maybe by the time I come back, Severn Hall will not be such an obstacle."

Jeremy sighed. He knew there was nothing he could say that would be effective in stopping Mark from doing whatever he wanted.

"Come to see me in London in three weeks. All will be prepared. You can leave within the month."

"Agreed," Mark replied.

Jeremy sighed and threw up his hands in despair, which brought a mild chuckle from Mark. The conversation went on to other things and after another hour or so, Sir Francis rose to leave and was escorted to the door by both Jeremy and Mark. After Jeremy had closed the door, he turned to Mark.

"Now, Jeremy," Mark laughed. "Before you get excited, something like this is the best thing for me. To be active and away from Severn Hall for a while longer. It was a very opportune meeting."

"Damnit, Mark. You can't run for the rest of your life. You have to stop, turn around, and face it."

"I know that, Jeremy, old friend," Mark said gently. "But give me a little more time."

"What about Alicia?"

"It is not meant to be."

"She loves you."

"I know."

"What are you going to do about it?"

"The wisest thing I can do . . . leave."

"What do you think you're going to find out there."

"That's just it, Jeremy. I'm not looking for anything. I need time. Maybe when this trip is over, I'll come back able to face Severn Hall and all the other responsibilities. Leave it be, Jeremy. I've made up my mind and I won't argue about it with you. I'll be back in a year."

Jeremy sighed. "All right, Mark, no more arguments. I just want you to quit chasing a dream and take what you can so easily have."

"We'll see what the year brings."

"Louise is planning a garden party in a couple of days. I'm sure Alicia will be here. Will you tell her then?"

"No, I'm riding over tomorrow morning. The best thing, when you have something difficult to do, is to do it as quickly and painlessly as possible."

"I guess you're right."

"Where is Louise now? I would like to speak to her."

"She is in the garden, I believe."

Mark left a silent Jeremy and went in search of Louise. He found her in her garden overseeing preparations for the party.

"Louise, may I walk with you a while? I would like to talk to you."

"Mark," she laughed, as she tucked her hand under his arm. "You are so serious. Are you going to be angry with me?"

He laughed also. "You know it's downright impossible to be angry with you. But there is something I want you to understand."

She stopped walking and turned to face him, her smile faded and her eyes became filled with tenderness.

"I do understand. Mark, you are Jeremy's dearest friend and I hope mine also. I cannot bear to see you hurt, no more than I can bear to see you spend the rest of your life lonely. You cannot do anything to change the past, Mark, but you can control your future. Jeremy has told me that you met Margaret in America." She watched his eyes darken at the mention of her name.

"I know how much you love her, Mark, but it is an impossible love. I know that, and in all honesty, so do you. It hurts me to think of you being unhappy. Reach out and let someone try, Mark. Sometimes second best turns out to be the best thing after all."

He bent down and gently kissed both her cheeks and tears filled her eyes as she saw without doubt none of her words had touched him.

"Don't mother me, Louise. I don't know if I can make you understand, but try. There is no other woman for me. I have loved Margaret for nineteen years and I shall go on loving her until the day I die. Do you see how very unfair that would be to Alicia or to any other woman?"

"Oh, Mark," she said gently.

"And don't pity me. I have shared a love only few have ever known and I carry enough sweet memories to

360

sustain me for the balance of my life."

He smiled again and touching her chin lifted her face to him and kissed her lightly. "I'm going over to Alicia's in the morning."

"You won't reconsider?"

"No, my dear. I won't reconsider."

"All right, Mark. Whatever you wish. But, if you ever change your mind, you will come back to us, won't you?"

He nodded, then bowed slightly and walked away from her.

Mark slowly rode to Alicia's, trying to form the words in his mind that would be the gentlest. He arrived at Dunker Hall to find most of the windows darkened. He knocked several times before the door was opened and he was completely taken by surprise to find it opened by Alicia herself. Her eyes widened in surprise and pleasure.

"Mark?"

"I'm sorry to call in such an unseemly fashion, Alicia, but it is imperative that I talk to you. Could I come in for just a few minutes?"

"Of course," she stepped aside and held the door open. Closing it after him, she turned and led the way into the study where she had been reading.

"Can I get you something to drink?"

"Yes, a little brandy would be fine, thank you."

Now that Mark was in her presence, he found it was definitely not going to be easy to say what he had to say.

"Please," she said softly. "Sit down, Mark."

That was the first moment he realized he was still standing in silence. He sat and watched her pour him a glass of brandy. Then she sat opposite him and waited silently for a few moments while he sipped his drink.

"Are you alone, here?" he queried.

"Only for a few hours," she laughed. "The servants have a night out and my sister and Jeffery have been invited to the theatre and a late dinner at the Morrison's."

"And you?"

"I . . . I felt like being alone for a while."

"I see." He sipped his brandy meditatively.

"What is it, Mark?"

"What?"

"What you came to talk to me so urgently about?"

Mark stood up and walked to the fireplace. He watched the flames lick about the logs with red and blue tongues, then he said softly, "I'm leaving, Alicia."

There was a poignant silence behind him then her soft voice said, "When?"

"Tomorrow." Without turning about he began to explain just why he was going. She remained silent until he finished. He heard her rise and walk to his side. He turned his head and looked at her. Although there was a suspicious moisture in her eyes and a tremulous smile on her lips, she had herself under control.

"You've told me all the reasons you had built, Mark. Now, will you tell me the real reason you are going. It is because I have been so foolish as to let you know I've fallen in love with you."

"Don't, Alicia. Don't make this any harder for either of us."

"Tell me about her, Mark, about Margaret, the ghost I cannot exorcise. What is she like? I must know."

"Stop it, Alicia."

"Oh, God, you make me furious, Mark. When will you realize that you cannot have what you want? Why will you run away from the fact that given enough time, I

362

might be able to make you happy . . . someday even make you forget?"

Mark's iron control over his emotions was breached by this. He turned toward her and took her by the shoulders and gave her a shake.

"Do you want to be married to a man who will hold you like this," he said and drew her tight against him, "kiss you like this," he said and his hard, demanding lips took possession of hers, "and make love to you while he thinks of another woman?"

She was visibly trembling, but her eyes defiantly held his.

"If that man is you, Mark, yes . . . yes, I want the chance to help erase the memories that hurt you . . . Yes, I want to have you hold me, kiss me, make love to me if it brings me closer to the day when I can erase her from your heart forever."

"Alicia," he said softly, his hands still holding her shoulders, "I don't want to hurt you, and hurt is all you can ever get if you love me. Don't, for the love of God."

Alicia stepped closer to Mark. The tears fell unheeded now as she slid her arms about his waist. "Ask the sun not to rise, Mark, ask the wind not to blow, but please don't ask me not to love you. Mark, you've told me they expect you in London in two weeks. Give me those two weeks. Let me share your love for that long. If you must go, then I will ask for no more."

"It's unfair to you, Alicia."

"No, for I would rather have those two weeks and their memories than to have never shared your life at all."

She could see the hesitant anguished look in his eyes and pressed against him. She felt his strong arms tighten about her. With a half laugh, half sob she raised her lips to his.

"Maybe," he thought desperately, "maybe Alicia can wash the memories of Margaret away." But with that thought was the deep doubt of that possibility.

Slowly his demanding lips parted hers and his hands found and loosened the pins from her hair. He heard her soft sigh of pleasure as his hands searched her body. His lips found and tasted the sweet taste of her as they moved from her lips to her throat and on until they found the valley between her soft rounded breasts. The clothes she wore were loosened expertly and her gasp of pleasure intensified as his warm hands caressed her. He lifted her and in a few quick strides carried her to the couch. Alicia's body lay in ivory beauty against the dark fabric of the couch. His clothes discarded, Mark knelt beside her. Lifting her arms in willing surrender, Alicia felt his hard lean body come against hers. Mark sought, in the depths of her, that blazing glow of intense desire he had felt in Margaret. He sought in vain, for even as he entered her, as he heard her murmur words of love, as he felt her reaching for him with every fiber of her being, he knew it was no use. Though his body enjoyed hers, his heart and mind were left wondering in a depth of black seeking for which he knew only one other human carried the light that could brighten it. Her body, trembling and moist in his arms after a shattering climax, made him realize that it was impossible for him to hurt her again as he knew she would be hurt when she read his face. Slowly he lifted his eyes to hers and watched the silent tears form in her eyes. Without a word, he rose and picked up his discarded clothes and began to dress. His back to her, he could hear her muffled crying. He cursed to himself for his inability to ease the pain she felt, the pain he knew so very well. He turned to look at her. Alicia was a very beautiful woman. Her golden hair tangled by his hands framed her tear-stained face. Her body, slender and pale, was exquisitely lovely. "I'm sorry, Alicia," he said miserably. "I did not want this to happen. I did not want to hurt you. Can you forgive me?"

She rose from the couch and went to him. Without clinging to him she gently laid her head against his chest. Slowly his arms came about her and he rocked her silently against him until he could feel she was slowly regaining control of herself. She looked up into his eyes and for the first time a gentle smile was on her lips.

"I envy her, Mark. I only wish I could give you what you need. I'm not sorry for what we've shared and if I thought for one minute it was enough to hold you here, I would do so. But I know it is not. Will you remember that I love you, Mark, and that if you want to return here when your year is over, please come to me? I shall wait that long in the hope that you will discover that we could share a happy life together."

There was nothing more that he could say. Alicia took her clothes and left the room. He heard the quiet retreat of her footsteps as she climbed the stairs and the soft click of her bedroom door. He left and rode slowly back to Jeremy's. The next morning he informed them of his plans to leave for London immediately. Neither Jeremy nor Louise was surprised.

"What are the definite plans, Mark?" Jeremy questioned.

"London, first, then I imagine several ports. I should be back by the same time next year."

"And Alicia?" he said gently.

"Alicia knows I'm going. Leave it at that, Jeremy.

365

Someday, I may be back, but for Alicia and me there is no future."

Jeremy and Louise walked with him to his carriage the next morning and said a fond and quiet farewell. They watched as the carriage rolled down the drive and out of sight.

At that moment, Mark's secretary, who had been taking care of Severn Hall in Mark's absence, held a white envelope in his hand which he looked at in obvious annoyance. The letter had been lying on the table almost from the day after Mark had departed. Now his secretary made up his mind. He would send it along to Jeremy's home, for it was the kind of personal mail he never opened. The handwriting was obviously female, but the address from which it came was the only thing that surprised him. Now, he made up his mind and decided that when the post arrived next week, he would see it on its way.

The fateful letter left Severn Hall the next day. It arrived at Jeremy's home over a week and a half later. At first, Jeremy looked at it in surprise, then the return address came to him and his heart jumped. "Could it be possible?" He looked at Louise, who was as worried as he, then with grim determination and a mumbled apology to an absent Mark, he tore open the letter and read.

Dear Mark,

I do not know if what I am about to do is right or wrong. God must be my judge. I only know that it breaks my heart to see someone I love as dearly as I do Margaret suffer so. I am writing to you, not because Margaret will not, but because Margaret is overcome with some kind of guilt. You see, I know

366

of your love, and I know that you left this country reluctantly and still deeply in love with her. During the last few weeks of the war, Paul Martin was killed in battle, and since that day, Margaret has been punishing herself with guilt. For some reason, she believes that Paul's death was punishment for loving you, and she does love you, Mark. I know. I watch her day by day, night after night. She is silent. She smiles seldom, she works too hard and she allows this agony to continue because she feels it is something she deserves.

I don't know what is in your heart now, Mark, but I feel I had to tell you what the situation was. If you still feel the same, if your love for Margaret is still strong, then come, come and tell her. Come and with the grace of God, you can give Margaret a whole full life again.

I am not telling Margaret that I have written to you. It is best that way. Then if your feelings have changed and you decide not to come, then Margaret will not be hurt again.

There is nothing more I can say, Mark. I have told you what the situation is here. The choice is yours.

God Bless you,
Sarah McMahon

Jeremy sank into a chair with a groan. "Of all the times for the post to move with rapidity. Couldn't it possibly have come just a few days sooner," he thought.

As if to echo his thoughts, Louise said, "Jeremy, go to London as rapidly as you can. Maybe you might be able to catch Mark before he leaves. Try, Jeremy."

Jeremy left that day, travelling as rapidly as the coach could go. He arrived in London and went immediately to the home of Sir Francis Braham. When Jeremy was shown into Sir Francis' library, he was greeted warmly.

"Jeremy, my boy! What a pleasant surprise."

"Sir Francis. It is imperative that I see Mark Severn before he leaves. It is of the utmost urgency. Where can I find him?"

"Oh, Jeremy, that is impossible. Our plans were organized earlier than expected. I'm afraid Mark left on the morning tide for the colonies."

Jeremy sat down slowly. "Sir Francis, I must explain something to you, then I must ask for your help. You must tell me just how and where I can reach Mark, for I swear to you, his life, his heart, his future depends upon it."

Chapter Forty-Two

Christmas 1782 at Clearhaven was being looked forward to with a great deal of excitement. Preparations had begun weeks before. Margaret had supervised the decorating of the house and there was an abundance of holly, mistletoe and glowing candlelight. Matt and Jason had cut a huge well-shaped pine tree and the family enthusiastically had gathered together to spend a merry evening and to decorate it.

Margaret had planned a huge Christmas ball to be held the week before Christmas. It was two days before and hectic preparations were being made for the food and lodgings of the many guests who had been invited from long distances. Every servant moved quickly and smoothly under Margaret's guidance. In her quiet gentle way, she kept herself and everything about her under control. But Sarah watched her with eyes that were dark and saddened.

Vern and Caroline had a small wedding on the first of December and were back from their short honeymoon in time to join in and help prepare for the festivities. It had been weeks since Sarah had written to Mark. Now she had given up hope that he would come. She had resigned herself to the fact that he had chosen not to return. She was determined to help Margaret in any way she could. What was upsetting her now was the fact that since they were married, she had never kept a secret from John . . . until now. It was difficult for her not to tell him, and she wondered how he would react to her interfering in Margaret's life.

It was late in the evening. The ball would be in two days, and Sarah was working over the gowns she was sewing for Susan. Everyone else was abed and she knew that John only sat and smoked his pipe because, as he had told her many times, he did not like the emptiness of their bed when she was not there.

Her mind tossed the thoughts of Margaret and Mark about. She did not notice the intent look in John's eyes as he watched her hands flutter nervously with her sewing. He gave a low, throaty chuckle and she looked up at him inquiringly.

"When you got a problem, Sarah, you always try workin' it off. Why don't you try talkin' it off?"

She laid her sewing down and looked at him. This man, to whom she had been married for such a short time, knew every thought in her head. Their eyes caught and held, and he smiled and patted the seat next to him. She rose and crossed the room and sat down beside him. He put his arm about her shoulders and drew her against him. She laid her head on his shoulder. They sat quietly for a few minutes while she desperately searched her mind for the words to tell him just what she had done.

"What is it, Sarah?" he asked gently. "You're upset about somethin' and it certainly can't be a problem so big we both can't handle it."

"John, I'm afraid I've taken it on myself to do something I shouldn't have. Now I wish I had talked to you about it first."

"Why not talk to me about it now, maybe I can help."

She sighed, remained quiet for a few minutes, then she began. She told him first about how she had discovered the affair between Mark and Margaret.

"I'm not faulting her, John. Now that I know the whole story, I don't blame Margaret. She loves him very much. She swore she would never see Mark again and I believe if Paul had returned Margaret would have kept her word. But what she is doing now, John, is wrong. Paul is dead. Margaret is not to blame, either for that or for loving Mark. But she refused to send for him."

"So?"

"So, I wrote to him. I told him about Paul's death, about how miserable Margaret is and . . . and I asked him to come. Was I wrong to interfere, John?"

John kissed the top of her head and drew her even tighter against him.

"Sarah, I guess no one knew Paul Martin better than I, or loved and respected him more. I know, in my heart, the last thing he would have wanted would be for Margaret to sacrifice herself to his memory. He did what he believed with all his heart was right. She had no responsibility for what he did, for with or without Margaret, Paul would have done the same. She shouldn't be allowed to feel quilty. In my opinion, Sarah, you did the right thing. I only hope he comes. And if he comes can convince Margaret of how he feels and what is best for the both of them. She's got to put Paul to rest."

Sarah closed her eyes. "John, it's been so long. Too long. Mark has had plenty of time to have received my letter and gotten here. I'm afraid, I'm afraid he's not coming at all."

"Sarah, if Mark loves her as he said he does, and if he has received your letter, I'm sure he'll come. Many

371

things could have happened to have slowed him down. You know how undependable mail can be. In fact it might be a good idea to send another letter in case the first has been lost. I've known mail to reach its destination months after it was sent. Then consider the time it would take him to make arrangements and to book passage, and the weeks it takes to get here. The journey just from Boston to here takes considerable time. All in all, you will have to agree it really has not been enough time for him to get here, putting aside any minor difficulties he might have run across on the journey. Have faith, little matchmaker. It will all work out for the best."

Sarah reached out and slid her arms about John's waist and gave him a fierce hug. "Oh, John, Paul was always right about you."

"About what, love?"

"You're always there when you're needed."

He chuckled and this time he pulled her into his arms and kissed her thoroughly and leisurely. "Then, why don't you show me just how much you appreciate my finer points, my darling."

She laughed as he stood up and pulled her again into his arms. Arms about one another, they slowly climbed the stairs to their own small sanctuary.

Matt and Deanna arrived the next morning to help with the finishing touches for the ball. Jason and Deborah arrived a few hours later with young Paul. The family was complete when Cat arrived with Deeta.

The morning of the ball was very cold and Margaret had the huge fireplace burning brightly. They spent an entertaining afternoon playing with young Paul on the thick fur rug in front of the fireplace. The child was just walking and beginning to mimic sounds he'd been hearing. Trying energetically to talk, he was, it was obvious, not only the bright spot in his parents' life but the center around which Margaret's world revolved. She devoted most of her energies now to David and young Paul. David had turned into a tall, strong and very handsome young man. It was also obvious that there was a delightful case of puppy love developing between him and Sarah's daughter Susan. They found each other's company quite satisfactory.

Sarah was very worried now not only how Margaret would accept Mark's coming, but that if he came, how David might accept the presence of a new man in his adored mother's life.

"John, what do you think we should do?"

"I'm not too sure. I would say that Cat knows him probably better than anyone else. We should talk to him."

At the first opportunity, John took Cat aside and told him what the situation was and asked Cat what he thought they should do about it.

"If you agree, I'll handle it," Cat suggested.

"I not only agree, I'm very relieved that you'll do it. I don't exactly know what to say to the boy and I know he has a great deal of admiration for you, Cat. So, it's up to you."

Cat found David alone putting several gaily wrapped packages under the tree. David had grown quite tall, almost six feet, and his slender frame had begun to fill out and take on the heavily muscled look of manhood. He was still a rather shy boy, but quick to smile. He bore a striking resemblance to his sisters, with his gleaming black hair, and sported a full black moustache of which he was inordinately proud. David looked at the world

373

through Paul Martin's honest, gentle amber eyes.

"Got a package under there for me?" Cat questioned.

David grinned. "Of course, one for you and Deeta also, and I want you to know I'm quite proud of the fact that I made them myself. I hope Deeta likes hers."

Cat chuckled. "Deeta would like anything you made her, David. You're a favored person in her life. Sometimes, I'm a little jealous. I think she worries more about you than she does about me."

"Oh, Cat, now that's not true. You know Deeta adores you. Why . . ." he stopped as he caught the gleam of humor in Cat's eyes and grinned.

"What have you gotten for your mother?"

"Well, first, I bought that white lace shawl she wanted so badly, then I thought . . . maybe I should have bought that string of pearls she admired so at Gilbert's the last time we were there. What do you think, Cat. Which would she like the best?"

"David, I'd like to talk to you about that. Let's go into the library. I have something to tell you." David looked closely at Cat and realized he was unusually serious.

"All right, Cat. Is something wrong with Mother? She's not ill or anything, is she?" he asked worriedly.

"No, David, your mother is fine. There's just a little problem that I'd like you to understand before it's thrust into your lap."

They went into the library and Cat closed and locked the door behind them. He went to a small table and poured a small glass of brandy both for himself and for David.

"David," he said as he handed him the glass. "You know since your father is gone, your mother is rather lonely."

"Lonely. She's got me, Deb and Dee and little Paul. There's certainly enough family to keep her from being lonely."

"You're a man, David. You know that's not enough for a man or for a woman. Your mother needs someone to share the rest of her life with."

"Are you trying to tell me there's a man in her life. That's impossible."

"Why?" questioned Cat.

"Why? There's been no one calling on her. No one coming to see her. I would know."

"David, sit down. There's a little story from the past I think you should know."

David sat, and the drink was left untouched as Cat began the story. David was very still until Cat finished. Then he stood up and walked to the window and looked out with unseeing eyes. Cat knew his mind was going back to his father and the love his parents had shared with him. Cat had helped David through a lot of problems in the last few years. He felt he knew David's character better than anyone. He watched David in silence and saw a boy slowly turn into a man.

"She loves him, this . . . Colonel Severn?"

"Yes, David. She has loved him for many many years."

"That's kind of hard to take, knowing how my parents were."

"She devoted her life to your father. She made him happy, David. Don't you think she deserves some happiness, too?"

David sighed. "Of course she does. I love her too, Cat, and if he can make her happy there will be no interference from me."

375

"Your mother has no way of knowing that Sarah wrote to him. We . . . we don't even know if he is coming. But if he does, well, we wanted you and the girls to know about it first."

"Thanks. If all you say is true, Cat, he would be a fool not to come."

"Crossing the ocean in December is an extremely dangerous thing. He might wait until spring."

"If I loved a woman, I certainly wouldn't let something like that stop me."

"Neither would I. That's why I'm almost sure he'll be here one day soon. Sarah is explaining to your sisters now, but I think Deanna's known for a long time, and I expect no trouble there."

Cat was right. Both girls were enthusiastically happy and prayed that Mark would come.

Deanna put the finishing touches to her hair and looked at herself in the mirror. The dress she wore was a deep blue and highlighted her wide blue eyes. A thin strand of pearls about her neck and small pearl drops on her ears completed her preparations. She turned from the mirror to find Matt seated in a comfortable chair, intently watching her. She smiled as she watched him rise from the chair and walk to her. He slid his arms about her and held her gently against him.

"You are lovely," he whispered against her hair. "And I'm so very grateful that I found you."

She lifted her lips for his kiss and held him to her, enjoying the strength of his arms about her and the feel of his lips on hers.

"And what would milady like for Christmas?" he smiled down at her.

"Something only you could give me, Matt."

"And that is?"

"I'm envious."

"You! Envious of what?"

"Deb and Jason."

"Now, why would you be envious of Deb? She certainly doesn't have anything you don't have."

"Oh, but she does, Matt."

"I don't understand."

"Paul Matthew."

Matt remained silent for a few minutes, his eyes grew gentle as he tightened his arms about her.

"I want your child, Matt . . . our child."

"I assure you, ma'am, it will be my pleasure. That is one request that I would be only too happy to give. When do you suggest we start? Now?"

She laughed. "It might be better if we waited until after the ball. It might cause a little confusion if we said we couldn't come down because we were too busy making a baby."

"Well," he said seriously. "You won't forget to remind me later? In all this celebrating, I might just forget." He laughed again. "But I seriously doubt it. Come along woman. Let's get this party started. The sooner it's started, the sooner it will be over." They laughed together as they left the room to join the family.

Deborah and Jason stood over the crib and watched Paul sleep.

"Oh, Jason, I'm so happy tonight. God has blessed me with everything a woman could want. A wonderful family, a husband whom I love to distraction and a child so beautiful. The only thing we need to complete everything is for Mark Severn to come. Do you really think he will?"

"I don't know, Deb. I know that if I were he, nothing in the world would keep me away."

"No one has told Mother?"

"No," he laughed. "It's the best-kept secret in the world. I honestly never have thought I'd see the day three women could keep a secret for so long."

"We had best go down."

"One last kiss before we go. I might not have another chance to kiss you all evening."

He kissed her then, leisurely, capturing her mouth with his until he felt her tremble in his arms and tighten her arms about his neck. He smiled in satisfaction as he looked down into her sea green eyes.

"Keep that thought in mind till later, love," he said softly.

She nodded with a smile and after kissing their son good night they went down to join the already gathering family.

Clearhaven glittered with lights, music and laughter. Margaret moved among her guests as regal as a queen. She was wearing a red velvet gown daringly cut to reveal her soft golden shoulders and the round creamy rise of her breasts. Her midnight hair had been drawn high on her head in a smooth coil surrounded with a tiara of glittering diamonds. A thin chain strung with tiny diamonds glittered at her throat. She was stunningly beautiful. Couples whirled about the floor in a gay waltz. Margaret smiled as she watched her family. Matt and Deanna, Jason and Deborah, Vern and Caroline . . . their eyes sparkling and smiles bright. If for a moment she felt the frightening tinge of loneliness, she brushed it aside. Margaret moved among her guests making them welcome and comfortable. She smiled brightly with a smile that extended no farther than her lips, and deceived everyone except her family, who watched her with worried eyes.

"Margaret," Sarah said, "I've taken the liberty of inviting the new Governor and his family. I hope it is all right with you. I met Governor Monroe's wife in town. They are so new here and so worried about meeting everyone. It's quite difficult for them. He's a planter from upriver and was pressed into service by the Congress to help in the transition period. I thought we might be able to make it a little easier for them."

"Sarah," Margaret laughed, "of course it's all right. If there's anything we can do to help we must assure them they need only ask. How many have been invited?"

"Well, there is the Governor, Crayton Monroe, his wife Jennifer, their son Brandon and Mrs. Monroe's brother Lucas Olivier, who is visiting them at the moment."

"Four, that is no inconvenience. Four will hardly ruffle Mrs. Tucker. Her kitchen is getting well used to producing food at a moment's notice. With all our family together, it's getting to be somewhat of a habit. I'll go and tell her now so she can prepare."

Sarah watched Margaret make her way to the kitchen. "Nothing," she thought, "ruffled Margaret. She always seemed to be prepared for anything." Maybe that was what disturbed Sarah so. Margaret had enclosed herself in an icy world where nothing could touch her or hurt her again, and Sarah wished desperately that something or someone could come along and destroy this barrier.

"Oh, Mark, Mark, where are you? Why don't you come?" she whispered to herself. She felt a comforting hand gently touch her waist and knew without looking John was near. She smiled to herself.

"A penny for your thoughts," John chuckled. "You seem so far away."

"Not really. I was just telling Margaret about our invitation to the Governor. She will make them welcome."

"Did you expect anything else? Margaret Martin is always the gracious lady."

"I hope she'll still be gracious when she meets Lucas Olivier."

"Why, Sarah!" John laughed. "Are you matchmaking?"

"Not exactly, John," she replied. "But he is an attractive man. I can't see how a man as handsome and eligible as he has remained unmarried all this time."

"Maybe he's been looking for something he hasn't found, and won't settle for less."

"Have you met him, John?"

"Yes, a few nights ago."

"What do you think of him?"

"I like him. He seems to be a strong, forceful person who knows what he wants. He has a good reputation as a planter. I guess he's taken over the operation of his brother-in-law's place until he finishes up his term of Governor, doing a good job of it too I hear."

Their attention was again drawn to the door as Margaret reappeared. She made her way toward them stopping occasionally to chat with people along the way.

"Sarah, John, why aren't you two dancing? With such music I should think you could hardly keep yourselves from doing so."

"Ha!" John laughed. "I've just taken the first opportunity to get my wife safely out of reach of all the lecherous gentlemen around."

"Lecherous!" Sarah responded quickly with the shining laughter in her eyes. "Who has been dancing with all the pretty girls in the room, John McMahon. I'm not sure just who the lecherous gentlemen are in this room."

John gave her an evil look with one eye closed that set them both to laughing.

"Come," he said in a deep mysterious voice. "Let me take you for a walk in the garden little one."

Sarah laughed. "And just what are your intentions, sir?"

"Disreputable, madam, I assure you. Quite disreputable." He tucked Sarah's arm in his and drew her with him toward the huge open doors to the veranda. Margaret watched them enjoying the warmth of their obvious love for each other. Before they reached the door, Sarah's attention was again drawn to the entrance to the ballroom. Four people stood there quietly. "John, the Monroes are here. I shall go and introduce them to Margaret."

"All right, but don't be long. I don't aim to share you even with the Monroes. And especially," he motioned toward them, "that good-looking blond giant of a brother she's got."

She moved away to the sound of John's laughter. At a silent look Margaret joined her.

"Good evening, Governor Monroe and Mrs. Monroe," Sarah said. "I would like to introduce you to your hostess, Margaret Martin."

"It is a great pleasure to meet you, Mrs. Martin," Crayton Monroe said, his voice deep and warm. Margaret smiled and extended her hands both to Crayton and his wife, Jennifer, who took it with a deep sigh of relief.

"Thank you, Governor Monroe and welcome to my home."

"This is my son, Brandon," he replied. Brandon stepped forward and bowed formally. In Margaret's estimation, he was almost the same age as David. His manner, though outwardly shy, did not conceal the bright intelligent eyes that contained the same glow of devilment she had seen so often in David's. "And this," he motioned to the tall man who stood beside him, "is my brother-in-law, Lucas Olivier."

Margaret's eyes were drawn to the giant of a man that stood at Crayton's shoulder. He stood six foot-four inches, and his shoulders were immense and seemed to desire to thrust from the jacket he wore. Though tall, he was slender of waist and hip. His dark blond streaked with shades of pale blond hair was thick and just a shade longer than the style of the day. He had a moustache to match. His eyes were a deep shade of green with gold brown flecks. They smiled at Margaret with a glow of admiration.

"Good evening, Mrs. Martin." His voice sounded like velvet over steel. "I would like to thank you also for the invitation. I would certainly not want to return home without having the pleasure of meeting someone as lovely as you."

"Thank you, Mr. Olivier, you're very gallant."

"I beg to differ with you, madam," he grinned. "Olivier's truth is not gallantry."

His smile lightened his rough-hewn face as though someone had turned a light on behind it. She guessed his age at somewhere near forty, and, as Sarah had, wondered why a man as attractive as he had not found a woman, or women, to share his life with. Margaret withdrew the hand he had continued to hold.

"Welcome to our home. Won't you please come and meet the rest of my family. I hope we can make your Christmas enjoyable. I'm sure being away from home on holidays can be depressing. Come and share our Christmas with us, as part of our family."

"How very kind of you," Jennifer said. "We sincerely appreciate your kindness."

Margaret escorted them about, introducing them to her family, aware that Lucas' eyes had not left her for a moment. The look in his eyes held questions, questions she did not want to hear and questions to which she had no answers.

It was over an hour later when Margaret became aware of another fact. Brandon and Susan were whirling about the dance floor, oblivious to the broiling emotional state in which David found himself. He never would admit to anyone his possessive feelings toward Susan. She had been a friend to him and he to her when she suddenly found herself transplanted into a strange home with strange people. He found he could talk to her about things that he could never reveal to anyone else, and she had confided in him as a young girl would a big brother. Not once did David mention to her that his feelings ran deeper than friendship, for he thought he had a lot of time and he did not want to rush her. Now as he watched Susan laugh at something Brandon was saying, he felt the distinct urge toward murder. He tried his best to ignore them and fooled everyone . . . except Margaret, who knew her son so well. She knew him well enough to know that he was now a man and that his pride would be damaged if she tried to interfere. She made her decision then and turned her eyes away from her son's angry face.

"Very wise decision," came a gentle voice from beside her. She looked up to see Lucas smiling down on her. "He'd never forgive you if you treated him like a child."

"How . . ."

"How did I know?" he chuckled. "Your eyes are lovely, but they reflect your thoughts like mirrors. In fact right now you are thinking 'What's this impertinent stranger talking to me like this for?'"

"I'm not."

"You're not? Really?"

"Well . . . maybe something along that line." She laughed with him.

"Since I've disgraced myself thoroughly as a guest may I throw myself on the mercy of my hostess and ask her to dance with me?"

There was no graceful way Margaret could refuse so she took his arm and he led her to the floor. She felt the hard muscled strength of the arm that slid about her waist, yet he held her gently as though she were fragile. She was surprised at the ease of one as large as he, and looked up at him. She flushed when she realized that again he had read her thought.

"Dancing with someone as beautiful and graceful as you would make anyone look good."

"Thank you," she said softly, but her eyes fled his piercing gaze.

"Are you staying with your sister for long, Mr. Olivier?"

"Can't we be friends enough to be on a first-name basis, Margaret. My name is Lucas."

"Of course, Lucas, but you didn't answer my questions?"

384

"Am I staying for long? Well, the planting season doesn't begin again until spring, so the plantation can run quite well under the fine care of our overseer. I think I will stay for at least three months. Does that answer your question?"

"Yes."

"Now, may I ask you one?"

"Yes."

"Can I see you again?"

"Lucas . . . I . . ."

"Are you afraid of me?"

"Of course not!" she replied indignantly.

"Then why not humor a stranger and show me about the area. I don't have to ask you if you ride. I would bet my life you do and excellently as well."

"Yes, I ride."

"Then will you go riding with me tomorrow and show me about?"

"Not tomorrow . . . I . . . I have other plans."

"The day after?"

"All right, day after tomorrow. It will have to be early for there is much work to be done around here that I must see to."

"It must be quite difficult for you without a man to help you run the place."

He watched in fascination at the fire that kindled in her eyes.

"I manage to run this place as well as Paul ever did, or as well as any man could do. If you think I'm helpless because I'm a woman, you are wrong, Lucas. My son works hard and I have all the men to depend on in an emergency that I need. Matt, Jason, John, Cat. They are all there in case I need them, but until now, I've been

385

quite capable."

"I apologize. I didn't mean to upset you, and I didn't mean that the way it sounded. I only meant that you must miss your husband and that it must be a lonely job trying to hold a family together alone."

Margaret had thought she was beginning to succeed in burying the guilt she felt, but now it reared its monstrous head again. Mark stepped into her mind and heart as he always could and she felt the piercing pain of deep loneliness. For a moment she was dizzy with the blinding flash of her longing. Her face paled and for an instant, Lucas thought she was going to faint.

"My God," he thought. "What terrible thing did I stumble upon in my stupidity that hurt her so deeply?" He was about to ask her if he could help her to a place where she would lie down for a moment when he watched her gather her strength. She inhaled deeply and drew herself away from him. At the same time he saw her eyes become shuttered against him. She retreated to a place he could not reach. It aroused in Lucas an emotion he had not felt for a long time and did not welcome. In the flash of a moment he realized that he wanted this woman, completely and desperately. It was a feeling he had promised himself many years ago he would never succumb to again.

Margaret managed to stay a room's-length away from him for the balance of the evening. Lucas was not the only one who was aware of it. Cat and John stood together at the edge of the ballroom, both understanding what was happening yet knowing there was nothing they could do about it. Sarah also watched, but she promised herself that she was going to talk to Margaret. If need be, she would tell her that she had written to Mark months ago and the letter remained unanswered. She wondered if she would have the ability to hurt Margaret so, but the answer came before the thought was ended. No! No she could not, but if she arranged things, maybe Lucas Olivier would be able to reach Margaret. She would do anything to make Margaret happy again, to make her smile again.

To Margaret, the disastrous ball seemed to last for hour after miserable hour. Hours she smiled and smiled until she felt her face was frozen. Conversation she could not remember flowed about her. She danced with others while keeping one eye on Lucas. She could not bear his ability to look into her for another minute, for she could not even bear to look into herself.

Finally it ended and she found herself at the door bidding her guests good night. Lucas had stood aside until his sister and brother-in-law had gone to their carriage, then he went to Margaret.

"Good night, Lucas."

"Good night, Margaret. Don't forget we have a riding engagement day after tomorrow. You aren't going back on your word, are you?"

He knew he had said the words as a challenge, just as he knew her pride would not let her refuse.

"I do not give my word lightly, Lucas. I remember. Early, just at sunup. I have a lovely view I think will make it all worthwhile." Her face was controlled, the smile pleasant but cool, the eyes fathomless.

"It would be worthwhile in a dense fog," he laughed. "I'll be here early. I'm usually an early riser anyway. I'm not the type of man to waste a valuable moment."

"I can tell that, Lucas, but don't expect too much. That way you will not be disappointed." She extended her hand to him as she had to all her friends. He engulfed it in his huge one and carried it slowly to his lips, then he turned it over and lightly touched her wrist where the pulse beat frantically with his lips.

"Good night, Margaret," he said softly, then in a moment he was gone and the door clicked quietly behind him. Margaret closed her eyes, for Lucas had done the one thing he should not have. The gentleness of the kiss had flung open the doors of her memory and as she turned and slowly walked up the stairs to her room, she knew in complete finality there was no room in her life for Lucas Olivier, for her heart beat with one resounding sound. Mark . . . Mark . . . Mark.

Chapter Forty-Three

Brandon Monroe sang, off-key and loud, as he dressed early the next morning after the ball. He was happier than he'd been since he finished school and came home. He discovered soon after his arrival that his father had accepted Congress' request that he take the post of Governor of Virginia during its transition period until a permanent governor could be elected. It was a disappointment to him, for Brandon was, he thought, in the best years of his life and their moving would curtail his activities among his group of friends—not to mention the girls he knew. Thinking of the girls in his past brought his attention to the reason for his ebullience this morning. "Susan . . . Susan with the pretty auburn hair . . . Susan with the shy, dimpled smile . . . Susan with the bright laugh and honest gaze . . . Susan . . . Susan . . . Susan."

He'd never felt this way about any girl in his life before. Not that his life at twenty-five had been such an expansive one, but he had his share of girls. They had been easy for him from boyhood. His easy charm, sense of humor, and blond good looks had drawn them like magnets. People had told him so often that he resembled very much his Uncle Lucas when he was younger. Brandon was pleased with this for there was no one in the world he would rather be like than his Uncle Lucas.

His admiration for Lucas hovered near hero worship. He'd tried to pattern himself after Lucas the best he could. He remembered many things he'd learned from Lucas. Some pleasant and some not so pleasant. The only time Lucas had ever corrected him had been a firm and violent lesson that he had never even told his father about. He had been eighteen, and prepared for college. He was proud of himself, and, he admitted now, extremely conceited. He was a tall, well-built boy, heavily muscled. In a feat of showing off his prowess in front of a girl, he had taken advantage of a boy quite a bit lighter and somewhat younger than himself. It had made him feel very strong and powerful when he had beaten the boy, at least until Lucas had found out about it the next day. He would never forget Lucas' quiet appearance at his door the morning after.

"Good morning, Brandon. Feel well this morning?"

"Yes, sir. I feel great."

"Good. Care to go for a ride with me?"

"Sure, Uncle Lucas. Wait, I'll be dressed in a few minutes."

"Take your time, I'll wait."

Brandon had dressed quickly and they walked to the stables together. Their horses saddled, they rode for over an hour until they came to a nice quiet glade surrounded by trees. There, Lucas reined in and dismounted. He loosened his horse's saddle and let him graze, and Brandon did the same. Then he stood facing Brandon, and Brandon was surprised by the quiet cold look in his eyes. Slowly, Lucas began to unbutton the jacket he wore and roll up the sleeves of his white shirt as he began to speak softly to a fascinated Brandon.

"Brandon, you mean as much to me as if you were my

own son. I love you dearly, boy, so dearly that I cannot allow you to follow the path you are headed on. As a man, Brandon, you have to learn to control your faults. You are blessed or cursed with my temperament and habits. You like girls and drink much too well. Be that as it may, you cannot hurt others that are weaker than you to serve your pride."

Brandon licked his dry lips, for it had suddenly occurred to him just what Lucas was going to do.

"Brandon, what you did to Steven was a thing that is unpardonable among gentlemen of character. It is the first time in eighteen years that I have felt ashamed of you."

Brandon felt suddenly very ill, not from fear of what he knew was coming, but with guilt and shame at its reason.

"I'm sorry, Uncle Lucas."

"I know, boy, but I want you to taste the feeling so that you know how it is to be shamed as Steven was."

Brandon was about to speak again, but before the words could leave his lips, Lucas' fists flashed, he felt a smashing blow and stars flashed before his eyes. He was knocked from his feet and sat down heavily on the ground. He felt himself lifted with ease and another blow was quick to follow. Lucas could, with his ham-like fists, damage Brandon badly. That was not his aim. He reserved his strength. But the beating was quick and thorough. About a half an hour later, Brandon, both eyes black, nose bloody, lips swollen and bruises all over, blankly refused to try to stand again for he knew those punishing hands would only send him to the ground. He was weary, beyond any weariness he'd ever felt before, and there was no part of his body that did not hurt. He felt himself being pulled up from the ground and crying like a baby, pleading. Lucas led him to a small stream nearby where he washed him clean then he sat with him, and Brandon felt the verbal beating he received far exceeded the physical one.

"I expect you to go to Steven and apologize like the man I know you are. If you hate me, Brandon, I feel it is not too high a price to pay to make the man of you I know you are. You are brave, honest. You have all the good qualities it takes to make a man and I will not let you throw them away."

Brandon looked up at him through his half-closed eyes and knew that not only did Lucas speak the truth, but that his eyes were filled with tears of pain. When the old axiom of his father's, "This hurts me more than it does you," came to him, he tried to laugh, but did not quite succeed. Lucas saw, though, that Brandon had grown in stature both mentally and physically in the past hour. He chuckled.

"You are a mess."

"Only outside, Uncle Lucas," Brandon said through cracked lips. "Inside I think I look a little bit better than I did yesterday. I will never do anything like that again, I swear. I didn't know anything could hurt so bad or leave you feeling so rotten."

"You will apologize to Steven?"

"Sincerely."

"Good."

"Will you help me to my horse. I don't think I can make it on my own."

Effortlessly, Lucas supported him and Brandon realized from the strength of those heavily muscled arms that Lucas could have broken him completely if he had deserved it. He realized then fully the lesson Lucas had taught him, that superior physical strength did not make a man.

He had gone to Steven and apologized to a shocked Steven who could not help gaping at Brandon's battered face. Looking at each other, it had occurred to them both what they must look like. They began to laugh.

"Boy, we look like a couple of Roman gladiators," Steven laughed.

"Yes," retorted Brandon. "The losers."

A friendship began then that was to remain for the balance of their lives. The friendship between Lucas and Brandon had been forged together into mutual love and respect. It made Brandon glow inside himself when he saw the respect in Lucas' eyes.

Life for him after that had been good. Led by the example of his parents and Lucas, Brandon was a happy man. He made friends easily, for he was sincere and honest in his friendship. Girls tumbled for his good looks which, when he went from boyhood into manhood became even more like Lucas.

Then came the announcement that they were moving to the Governor's mansion and would not be back home for two years. He was miserable, and rebelled violently. He reluctantly went with his parents. He had intended to ask them if he could return each summer with Lucas and spend the summers at home. He intended to—until the ball at Clearhaven. He went with his parents out of sheer boredom and then across the room he saw Susan. She had been introduced to him, and from that moment on he found it difficult to keep his eyes from her. He danced with her as often as he could, but she was quite popular. He noticed David's glower but refused to stand aside just

393

because it made one of Susan's suitors angry.

They were dancing together when he questioned her about David.

"Susan . . . are you . . . ah . . . I mean . . . The gentleman over there seems upset with me. Is he your beau?"

"David? David is my dearest friend. We've been friends a long time. He's sort of like a big brother."

Brandon smiled. When a girl referred to a man as a big brother there was no serious interest.

"I could see where he would be jealous. If you were even my honorary sister, I would keep you under lock and key. A girl as beautiful as you must have a string of broken hearts from here to Richmond."

The quick blush on her cheeks made him want to pull her even closer in his arms than propriety allowed.

"Thank you for your compliment, but I really have no beau."

"None! Are the men about here that stupid. I hope I can take advantage before they realize their folly. Could I have your permission to call on you one day soon?"

Again the crimson flooded her cheeks, but he could see also the sparkle of pleasure in her eyes.

"I must speak to my parents first," she said softly. Brandon, at that moment, would have spoken to the devil himself if he had thought it necessary.

"Of course," he grinned. "Let us speak to them together, shall we? That way, I can plead my cause." He tucked her hand in his arm at the close of the dance and they made their way toward Sarah and John, who both immediately saw the flushed faces and shining eyes.

"Are you enjoying yourself, Mr. Monroe?" Sarah asked.

"Immensely," Brandon replied enthusiastically. "It is the best party I've been to in years."

John muffled his laughter. There was not enough years to speak of.

"Father, Mother," Susan began, "Brandon . . . Mr. Monroe, has asked if he could come calling occasionally."

John's eyes snapped toward Brandon and now it was Sarah's turn to hide her laughter. John had become so protective of Susan as though she were his own daughter. He had acquired a family and was not about to give any part of it away too readily.

"You are quite welcome in our home, Mr. Monroe," John replied.

"I . . . I thought I might take Susan riding one day soon, or to visit with my parents."

Under John's penetrating gaze, Brandon wilted. He was quite sure that John was going to refuse to let him see Susan and had already begun creating arguments in his mind. John opened his mouth and Sarah also was sure his words were of refusal. She gently laid her hand on his arm. His eyes turned to hers. She smiled and said softly, "Remember?"

John's eyes softened, so did the words he spoke to Brandon.

"I'm sure if it meets with her mother's approval, it is all right with me."

John was rewarded by Susan's bright smile and Brandon's obvious relief. Now he whistled lightly to himself as he went downstairs to breakfast. He had taken advantage of his first opportunity and had asked Susan to go for a buggy ride today, and he did not want to be late. His parents and Lucas were already at the table. To his parents, Brandon was perfection, but the devilish twinkle in Lucas' eyes told Brandon he understood exactly how he felt. He often wondered about his uncle. He was so wealthy, so handsome, yet he had never made a pretense of wanting to marry. Women had thrown themselves at him, this Brandon knew. Also, he had very seldom resisted their advances, yet he had kept himself away from all permanent commitments. Thinking back over the years, Brandon remembered a time when his uncle had spent two years away from home. "Somehow," he thought, "there was something that had happened to him in that two years . . . but what?" Brandon ate the quickest breakfast he had ever eaten, then asked to be excused. Lucas watched him leave the table with a half smile and unreadable eyes.

"Tell me, Lucas," Crayton interrupted his thoughts, "what do you think of our new acquaintances?"

"Acquaintances?"

"Yes. Mrs. Martin and her family. Especially, those Deverall boys and that Markham fellow."

"Well, it's a little too soon to judge. I'm sure they are good, responsible citizens who can be depended upon to help rebuild what the war has damaged. I like Matt Deverall. He seems very interested in the politics of this country now that she's severed her umbilical cord. I wouldn't be surprised to see him elected to some office one day, perhaps when he's a little older."

"Yes, it's a shame Paul Martin died in defense of his country. I'm sure he would have made a great leader."

"You know all about Paul Martin?" Lucas questioned gently.

"Yes, a much respected man and an excellent leader. I'm sure his wife is devastated at his loss." Crayton went on talking about Paul, telling Lucas all of his known history. But Lucas' mind was not on Paul Martin dead, it was on Margaret Martin very much alive.

"Devastated by his loss," he thought. "No, Margaret did not seem so much grief-filled as she did . . . what? Expectant, or as though something was incomplete and her soul remained suspended within her until something or someone released it." He vowed to find out the truth about Margaret, for she was the first woman in over twenty years that had touched a place within him that he had kept from the knowing eyes of the world. A place that had been held by only one other. His mind shied away from a memory that he had kept locked away for a long, long time. Resolutely and in self-protection he changed the subject and they continued to talk of other less distracting things.

Margaret sat at the large desk in her study going over the household accounts with John. They were just finishing when the sound of an approaching buggy could be heard. Margaret rose and walked to the window.

"It's the young Monroe boy. I suspect he has come to take Susan riding."

"Yes, he asked permission last night," John replied humorously. "I must say it didn't take the boy long."

"Susan is a very lovely child. He would be a fool to dally elsewhere when he could have her company. She's an intelligent girl, John, don't underestimate her. I agree she is a little shy, but I think you need have no fear of her well-being. She'll do credit both to Sarah and to you."

"I never doubted her for a moment," John laughed. "I guess I'm getting old. I . . . I guess I'm trying to hang on to her as long as I can."

"No one can blame you for that, and you're certainly

not old. Why, you're not quite forty yet. You've a long happy life to share with Sarah."

John's answer was interrupted by a knock on the door. "Come in," Margaret called.

Matt opened the door. "Good morning."

"Morning, Matt. How are things at Foxmore?"

"Fine, just fine. Deanna and I are taking a trip to town today. I just stopped over to see if there is anything you might need."

"Deanna mentioned nothing about going to town today. Was it a sudden decision?" Margaret asked.

"She just said she had an appointment and she wanted to go," he grinned. "The lady's word is my command."

"And besides, you'd like to stop in the Boar's Head and have a drink and bend their ears with your version of how Virginia politics ought to be run," John laughed. "I seem to remember a day long ago when someone told me that the last thing he ever intended to do was get involved in this country's politics."

"That was before my poor head was turned and I got led astray by a beautiful patriot."

"Oh," Margaret said solemnly, "poor, poor Matt."

"Yes, I agree," Matt said dolefully. "I discovered there's truth to the old story."

"Which one is that?" John questioned.

"If you can't lick 'em, join 'em," Matt laughed and both Margaret and John joined him.

"Well, Matt, there's really nothing I need, but why don't you and Deanna stop by on your way home."

"All right, if Deanna's not too tired. She hasn't been feeling up to par lately. I think she should see Dr. Morgan, but she insists she is fine. Well, if possible I'll see you later," he waved and closed the door after him.

Margaret and John watched the door in silence for a moment then Margaret began to smile, which dissolved into a chuckle and from there to outright laughter. John watched her in surprise.

"What is so funny?"

"Oh, John," Margaret said as she walked toward the door. She stood in the open doorway for a moment. "I wouldn't be a bit surprised if we did not have any guests tonight. I suspect Deanna will be tired and want to have a quiet dinner at home." She was still laughing softly as she closed the door on John's questioning face. She turned from the door in time to see David coming downstairs taking the steps two at a time, his face a mask of anger.

"David!"

David stopped, somewhat surprised to see his mother there. Quickly he composed his face so that it was unreadable. "Good morning, Mother."

"Where were you going in such a rush, and with that look on your face as though you were angry at the world."

David laughed a little shakily and his eyes refused to meet hers.

"Nowhere really . . . just out for a ride."

"David," Margaret said gently, "I don't recall you ever lying to me before. Is it Susan?"

For a few moments David didn't answer, then his eyes rose to hers. In them she saw the painful despair of first love.

"You needn't be ashamed of loving someone, David. It is too rare an emotion. But you cannot make someone love you in return. It has to be a freely given gift. Jealousy is a destructive and ugly emotion and often leads to more hurt for the one who carries it. You are not a child, David. Nor are you a man who surrenders easily. If you want Susan, you must go to her as a man, not as a child. And if her choice is another, you must also be able to accept that as a man."

For a moment David's anger gained control. "What do you know?" he said sharply. "How do you know how it feels to love someone who doesn't love you, who . . ." he stopped, paralyzed with what he had said. Margaret's face paled and she looked for a moment, as though someone had struck her. What Cat had told him of his mother's love for Mark Severn and of the way he had left the letter unanswered came flooding back. He had never felt so ashamed or miserable in his entire life.

"Mother, I'm sorry. I didn't mean that, you know I didn't mean it. I would never hurt you so." There was such deep anguish in his voice that Margaret reached out for him and drew him into her arms.

"I know, David, I know," she said gently. "Listen to me, David. Stop the irrational thoughts you are thinking. Put away the childish jealousy and think with that calm patience you inherited from your father. I will say no more, for I'm sure that when you have done so you will change your mind about your actions." She released him and stepped back. Her lips curved in a half smile and she reached out and gently touched his face. "You are so like him, you know," she said softly. Then she turned and he watched her slow ascent of the stairs.

Slowly he walked to the bottom of the steps. He was angry with himself now for being the foolish child his mother had mentioned. Susan had only just met Brandon. There was no earthly reason for him to be upset if she went buggy-riding with him. She was shy, and it

400

would be good for her to meet people and go places. David did not realize that his real feeling for Susan was the protective brotherly love. For the emotion he thought he had was a small thing compared to what he would one day experience.

When he had left his room he had been determined to follow Brandon and Susan. Now he laughed at his foolishness and headed for the one place he had always taken his problems . . . Cat's cabin.

He was welcomed there as he always was, both by Deeta and Cat. They urged him to stay for dinner. They were laughing and talking when they heard a rider approach. Cat went to the door and opened it just as Jason stepped up on the porch.

"Jason, you're just in time for dinner."

"I've already eaten, thanks, Cat. If you can, I'd like to talk to you a minute . . . alone."

David stood up quickly and followed the two men off the porch.

"What is it, Jason?" Cat said. "What's wrong?"

"Cat, there's been another abduction."

"Again?"

"Abduction," David said. "What are you talking about, Jason?"

"David, there are a few men drifting through the state of Virginia . . . not men, animals. They have been stealing slaves and reselling them."

"Why does that concern Cat and Deeta? They're free, both of them."

"We know that, but these snakes don't. How would either Cat or Deeta prove they were free if they were miles away with no papers?"

"What can we do?" Cat said gently. "We can't hide in

401

a hole the rest of our lives."

"Matt wants you and Deeta to move back to Foxmore until this is over."

"I don't know how Deeta will take that. This is the only thing she's ever had of her own, and I don't know if I can get her to leave even for a little while."

"You've got to try, Cat," Jason said. "What if they come by some day when you're out hunting and Deeta's alone?"

"Deeta won't be alone," David said firmly. "I'm staying here. Cat and I can take turns. One of us will be with Deeta all the time."

"I guess that settles that," Cat grinned.

"I still think you ought to come back to Foxmore."

"We'll stay," Cat replied. "With David here one of us will be home all the time."

"All right," Jason said quietly. "Matt and I will be up off and on to look in on you."

"Thanks, Jason."

Jason waved and went to his horse. Both David and Cat remained silent until he was gone.

"Thanks, David."

"For what?"

"Being a friend."

"Cat, you and Deeta are two of the most important people in my life. There is nothing I wouldn't do for either of you."

Cat clapped him on the shoulder and they went back into the cabin. David had no idea how soon fate would call on him to prove his words.

Chapter Forty-Four

Margaret moved about her room in the half shadows of early dawn. Lucas was waiting for her. She had actually been surprised when he was announced at such an early hour by an even more surprised maid. Dressing quickly, she went down to meet him.

"Good morning," he said, his admiring gaze telling her how well she looked in her blue riding habit. It was a well-worn habit in which she felt comfortable. Cut severely and completely plain, it did more to accentuate her rare beauty than a more elaborate costume might have.

"You said before the sun came up," she shrugged with a laugh. "And I believe in being punctual."

"Sunrise from Morgan's hill is a beautiful thing to see. I thought you might enjoy it. Shall we go?"

He could tell immediately that Margaret was going to keep him as distant as possible. Although he held her to her word, she intended to keep it impersonal.

"Of course," he murmured. He held the door open for her and she passed him quickly without looking at him, but he was also aware of the deep rose in her cheeks, and he wondered if it were anger or another emotion.

She rode well, easily controlling her horse. It told him that she was well-accustomed to riding. She was a mystery to him, and nothing in the world aroused Lucas faster than the challenge behind her beautiful eyes that told him, "stay away."

They rode for over half an hour and faint streaks of light bordered the horizon as they crested a rather high hill. At the top, she dismounted and stood surveying a scene he felt she had seen a million times before.

Margaret stood still and Lucas dismounted and walked to her side. The view from where they stood, Lucas had to admit, was probably one of the loveliest he had ever seen. The valley spread out before them for a great distance, its lush green touching the base of a ridge of hills behind which the sun was rising. Everything was suddenly ablaze with the golden glow of the sun that kissed the early morning dewdrops, turning them into a million glistening diamonds. He didn't know how long they stood and watched the glorious sunrise, but the sun was just over the crest of the hill when Lucas turned to tell her of his deep appreciation of what she had been willing to share with him. When he looked at her, what he was about to say remained unspoken. Margaret was not watching the sunrise; her gaze was held elsewhere and she seemed to be miles away from him. He let his eyes follow hers and saw, for the first time, a small cabin that sat nestled among the trees. That the cabin held some significance for her was obvious.

"It's a lovely view."

Margaret's attention, drawn so suddenly by the sound of his voice, seemed disoriented. Then she realized that she had been drifting again through the past. "Yes, I come here often," she said softly. "This place always brings me a deep sense of peace. I wish . . ."

"What?"

"Nothing," she laughed. "Nothing. One should never wish for lost things . . . It is useless."

404

"Don't we all wish for any good things we have lost?"

"I suppose. Do you, Lucas? What do you wish for from your past?"

Lucas' face remained still for a few minutes. "There is nothing in my past I would care to relive again. The future is enough for me."

"The future . . ." Margaret repeated softly.

"What about the future, Margaret . . . your future? There's a great world out there to see. A woman with your wealth and beauty should see it all."

"Why?"

"Why? Why not?"

"Lucas, I learned a long time ago that it is impossible to run away from yourself. Whatever you feel, whatever you are, you carry with you wherever you go. If you ever expect to find happiness you must stand still and let it come to you. If it is destined to."

"And if it is not?"

"Then what good does running do?"

"I suppose you are right," he chuckled. "I've not stood still often enough to try your theory." He looked down into her eyes and saw the unguarded loneliness, the longing, the despair in one quick moment before they were veiled against him.

"Shall we go back?" she said quickly, then turned to walk toward her horse. He walked in silence at her side, and when they reached her horse, he assisted her into the saddle. Mounting quickly, he followed her horse down the hill and into the quiet green valley.

The balance of the morning Margaret guided Lucas about the plantation, then asked him if he would care to visit Foxmore and Dartmore.

"We could be at Foxmore by lunchtime. A cool drink

and something to eat should be quite welcome by then," she laughed.

"Quite," he agreed.

As Margaret had said, they reached Foxmore just about noon. It was Deborah who welcomed them and gave orders for two more plates for lunch. "Jason and Matt should be back soon."

"Where have they gone?"

"There's a meeting in town today. Something about stolen slaves. I'm sure Matt can tell you more about it. For some reason it's gotten him quite upset."

"Where's Paul Matthew?" Margaret questioned. "Lucas, you must meet my grandchild. He is a beautiful boy."

"I'm sorry, Mother, I left him with Mada at Clearhaven. I just wanted an hour or so of uncomplicated conversation with Deanna and with Paul around, uncomplicated is an unheard-of word."

Their laughter was interrupted by the sound of approaching horses and soon Jason and Matt came in. Matt extended his hand in immediate welcome to Lucas.

"Mr. Olivier, welcome to Foxmore."

"Thank you, Mr. Deverall. I've not seen it all, but from what Margaret has shown me, you have a lovely and productive place here."

The first-name basis between Margaret and Lucas did not go unnoticed by any of them. "You will stay for lunch, won't you, Mr. Olivier?" Matt asked.

"Yes, thank you, I must admit I'm famished. I do wish you would call me Lucas."

"Well," Matt laughed, "a first-name basis between neighbors is a must. I'm Matt, and the first Mr. Deverall is Jason."

"Come," Deanna said. "Let's go in to lunch."

The meal was a warm friendly affair and Lucas felt included almost as a member. "How fine it would be," he thought, "to settle here and put down roots, to build . . . to forget." His eyes drifted to Margaret in animated conversation with Deanna over some antics of young Paul's. "How very lovely she is," he mused. He suddenly became aware that someone was speaking to him.

"Lucas," Matt was saying. "Do you know if the Governor has any plans to do something about these slave bandits?"

"I think he's doing everything he can, Matt. He's formed a rather large armed group to patrol. He's placed as many armed guards as he can spare on each plantation. The citizens have all been alerted to keep their eyes open for strangers in the area. I think the abductions will cease soon. This area is becoming entirely too hot to operate in any longer and someone is bound to see them and send out an alert."

"I wonder where they could be hiding. I would swear between Vern and us we know every inch of this area."

"They must be a reasonably small group that splits up after each theft. One man can hide easier than a dozen."

"I think," Jason replied, "that there is someone influential in this area that is helping them. There is no other reasonable way that they could remain unseen. Whoever he might be, his name, properly used could sell a lot of slaves . . . anywhere."

"I hadn't thought of that, Jas. If that's the story then how could we ever hope to catch them?"

"Question everyone to find out who sells slaves out of Virginia. Follow one of his group and see if they pick up

407

any more along the way."

"Good idea," Lucas said. "I shall tell my brother-in-law. Maybe he can trace the largest slave sellers easier than we. I'll talk to him as soon as I get home."

"Speaking of home, Lucas," Margaret replied, "I think it's time for me to return. If you leave Sarah long enough she does all the work. Now that John is building their home. She tries her best to do all of mine and all of hers, too. I would like to be back before supper."

Lucas rose immediately. They were escorted to the door and Lucas was urged to come again as soon as possible. When they rode away, there was a moment of silence on the porch, then Deanna and Deborah looked at each other. "Oh, I wish," Deanna said softly.

"Me, too," Deborah answered. "If Mark Severn had not returned nor answered Sarah's letter all this time it is obvious he has chosen not to come."

"I agree," Jason said. "Margaret has been lonely for a long, long time. It's unfair to her to spend the balance of her life alone."

Matt had not spoken but had watched the two riders until they were out of sight.

"What are you thinking, Matt?" Deanna said softly. He slid his arm about her waist and drew her tightly against him.

"I was thinking how much like your mother you are."

"Yes, I've tried to be."

"Deanna, if I were gone," he said, his eyes holding hers intently, "how long would you wait for me?"

"Matt, what a question."

"How long?"

"Forever . . . for as long as it took for you to come back. Love for me will always be you. There is no place in my life for any other."

"Your mother," Matt said firmly, but gently, "will never marry another man. Her heart belongs now and forever to Mark Severn. If Lucas Olivier has any thought along that line, he will be bitterly disappointed." Neither Deanna nor Deborah answered for in their hearts, they knew Matt's words were true.

Margaret and Lucas arrived home only a few minutes after Brandon had brought Susan home. They had enjoyed an early morning ride and gone from there to the Governor's mansion, where a proud Brandon had shown her about. They had lunch with his parents, who watched in amused wonder a different Brandon than they had ever seen before. That Susan was completely captivated by Brandon was obvious to everyone but the boy in question, who was mentally fighting the ghost of David Martin from whom, although he didn't know it, he had absolutely nothing to fear. David had returned from Cat's to gather some of his clothes and explain to his mother why he was going to spend the next few days at Cat's cabin. The fact that Cat thought David was enough protection for Deeta when he wasn't around made David extremely proud and anxious to get back. After Jason had left Cat's cabin, David had taken the opportunity to talk to Deeta about Susan. It was Deeta's clear thinking and gentle considerate words that had again set David on a straight path. He had grown in a few hours and was profoundly grateful to Deeta for her affection. If necessary, he would have given his life for gentle Deeta and huge Cat.

"David," she had said. "The gods of my people believe that man and woman were created as one, then separated by committing sins against the God. For every man born from then on, a woman is born that was meant to be his mate. When I first saw Cat I knew deep in my soul that this was the man from which I had been separated from the beginning of time and the man I was meant to rejoin. If it was not so between you and Susan a long time ago then it is not so now. You are like a big brother to her and she loves you, but maybe this man is her mate and maybe out there is the one woman to which you belong. Do you question the gods, David. Go through life proud and take what they give. If it is meant to be Susan, it will be so. If it is not, then do not try to separate what the gods have joined or only you will be hurt. Do you understand, David?"

"Yes, Deeta, I understand. I know you are thinking of my good, but . . . Susan and I, we were always together. I thought . . ."

"You and she were both lonely and frightened at the time so you clung to each other. That is not surprising. But do not mistake that for love, David. For love is by far a greater experience. I know you, David, so believe me when I tell you it will come in time . . . when the gods please."

Riding back to Cat's after seeing Susan and Brandon together he had to admit to himself that Deeta was right. He was jealous and afraid to lose one of the first close friends he had ever had. But seeing together Susan and Brandon he realized that they were falling in love with one another, and being with them had given him a sudden sense of rightness.

"Deeta's gods," he laughed to himself. Then his face grew still and he looked up and whispered. "I hope you have something in store for me as good and beautiful as

410

Susan." Then he chuckled again at the stern Anglican-raised David Martin praying to the ancient gods of Africa for a mate.

"If Mother hears about that, she would skin me," he thought, nevertheless, deep inside in the shadowy corridors of his heart, the prayer lingered. It was just past dark when he arrived at Cat's cabin. He unsaddled his horse, rubbed him down, fed him and stabled him for the night, then he carried his belongings into the house.

The night wore on, and clouds covered the starless sky. Night sounds were conspicuously absent, heralding the coming of a storm. In the deep blackness surrounding Cat's cabin, no one could have seen the two men who sat on their horses, motionlessly watching the last lights in the cabin flicker and go out. The soft rumble of thunder could be heard in the distance.

The bigger of the two men remained motionless while the other seemed impatient at their lack of action.

"Jake, what the hell are we goin' to do, sit here all night and watch that cabin?"

"Shut up, I'm thinkin'. We didn't make no plans on that boy bein' there. I don't mind pickin' up a couple extra niggers, but I don't want no truck tanglin' with that kid. It will bring the whole area down on us."

"Shit, Jake. He's just a boy. Gimme five minutes and I'll cut his throat for ya and we won't have any trouble with him. I'm anxious to get my hands on that big buck. He should bring a good piece of change. And have you seen that gal. Prettiest little ass I've ever seen. I'm gonna have me a taste of that before she goes on the block."

The bigger of the two men remained silent, but if it could have been seen in the dark, his face would have shown his partner his obvious disgust.

The moon passing between banks of dark rain-filled clouds momentarily highlighted the features of both men. The smaller of the two was a man approximately thirty with as evil a countenance as could be found. His brows were thick and bushy, and covered small beady eyes that continually darted from place to place as if in fear of remaining still. His face was thin and sharp of feature, yet the mouth was thick-lipped and somewhat obscene-looking as he continually licked away spittle that gathered in the corners. The man next to him kept some distance between them, for the smell of him was no better than he looked. He wondered aimlessly if Bib Craton ever took a bath. Although Jake was not the real name of the bigger man, it was the only name under which he would work with the degraded group with which necessity had put him. The pale light of the swift-moving moonlight crossed his face for a moment, and it would have been obvious to any beholder that the man was not the same caliber as his accomplice. His face was one that had seen a better life, better times. He had a kind of dissipated handsomeness. His brows furrowed over eyes that were dark and wide-spaced, and the thin and regular nose was centered on a face that was angular with a square jaw and wide thin mouth that was compressed now with distaste for his partner.

"God, Bib, don't you ever think of anything else?"

"Not while there's a pretty filly like that around to be mounting, and free, too. I like to taste 'em all before we sell 'em."

Jake snorted in derision. "Taste! You damn near ruined that last one we took. It is one thing havin' 'em, but I bet the boss would be real upset if he had any idea how you treat the girls we grab."

412

"Well, now," Bib said softly. "The boss is only worried about the price we get for 'em. He don't give a damn if they's a little bit handled. Besides, a gal with a bellyful sells for more than the girl alone. Two for the price of one pleases the buyer and I aim to see they all get pleased." He chuckled at his own idea of wit. It was clear by his silence that Jake was not so amused.

"We're goin' back to tell the boss about that boy stayin' here. He's the Martin boy from Clearhaven, and that makes him related to those Deverall boys from Foxmore. I don't want them or Vern Markham after us. I sure ain't goin' to kill no man just to get two more slaves."

"The boss wanted these two for the plain and simple reason they ain't slaves. Those Deverall boys are lettin' these niggers think they are uppity by freein' 'em. Boss says there ain't no room in this state for him and those two free-livin' niggers. He wants 'em sold back into slavery where they belongs, and I don't think he'd be all that fired up if we got rid of one of those nigger lovers while we was doin' it."

"Bib," Jake said, his voice cold as ice, "we're not going to do anything for a while. Not until that boy ain't in that cabin. You got that clear or do I have to knock it into your mule head?"

"I don't know, Jake. Maybe we ought to tell the boss you're getting soft for this job. You some kind of nigger-lover, Jake, or do you want that little piece of chocolate cake for yourself?"

Before the last word fell from Bib's lips, it was cut off by his yelp of painful surprise as a huge heavy hand grabbed him by the throat, closing off his wind until he saw sparkling stars before his eyes. Jake gave him a heavy shake and his words crept softly into Bib's ringing ears.

"You listen to me, you crawly little worm, don't you ever say one word about me or I'll rip the skin off you, you understand?" Bib jerked his head in quick assent. "I'm still the boss when we're out here and if I say we don't move yet, we don't move. You got that through your rock head. I don't want to hear your filthy mouth again tonight."

Bib squeaked and writhed helplessly. Then Jake gave a grunt of disgust and released him. Bib was weaving in the saddle and gasping for breath. He was also quite sure that from this moment on, he was going to stay well away from Jake's hands.

He nudged his horse to follow Jake, who was already a black, fading shadow in the trees.

Inside the cabin, Cat and Deeta were in bed talking together in quiet whispers. Although David's room was on the opposite side of the huge living room, they did not want him to overhear.

"David is growing into a wonderful man, Cat."

"Yes, I know. Paul would be extremely proud of him."

"He's a lot like you, you know. He listens to things with both his head and his heart."

Cat pulled Deeta into his arms and held her close to him. "Deeta, do you think for a moment that it was for me he came here. The boy has a love for you almost as deep as his love for his mother."

They lay still for a few moments holding each other in deep peace and contentment. Then Deeta raised himself on one elbow and looked down on the face of the man she loved so dearly. Gently, she bent and touched her lips to his. She felt the hard strength of his arms as they came about her. Her heart overflowed when she felt the hunger

414

in him reach for her, and she knew that she was the food for his hunger that would always appease him.

"Oh, Cat," she murmured. "I do love you so very much. The gods have been good to me. They have not only given me the mate of my soul, they have quickened my body with new life. I will give you a son, my husband. A son to be strong and good like his father, a son to walk this land in freedom."

"Deeta, Deeta what is there in the world to make a man happier than to know that he was joined by a woman such as you to create a new life."

His hands caressed, with more tender care, the softness of the body he knew so well, she yielded to him with a deeper passion than they had ever attained. Her soft body molded itself to his and she murmured words of love that filled his mind until his world contained nothing but her. He felt her move with him and the beat of her heart blended with his until they were one as they had never been before. Even after they had reached a pulsing, blinding release he could not let her go, but held her against him and with his eyes closed let his hands memorize even more fully this woman who carried his life within her.

"A child, Deeta," he whispered, ". . . when?"

"In early summer . . . I think June."

"I must make the things you need. A cradle, another room, the chest for his clothes . . ."

Deeta laughed. "You have a great deal of time, husband. You need not start tonight."

He chuckled and rocked her tightly in his arms until she exclaimed that unless he wanted his child to come out flat he should release her. Then they laughed together like children and talked into the wee hours of the

415

morning, too filled with joy to sleep. When Deeta finally did succumb to sleep, Cat lay awake, his mind forming great thoughts for his family's future. He was, he thought, probably the happiest man in the world tonight. He was still smiling when sleep overcame him and he slipped away to pleasant dreams. Dreams he would need in the black days to come, for fate never gives a blessing so easily without extracting payment.

Chapter Forty-Five

Jeremy bent over the map that lay on Sir Francis' desk and watched Sir Francis' finger glide from spot to spot.

"Time will not allow you to catch up with him at any of these places, but if you were to go straight to Wilmington, you could arrive there before him."

"Wilmington," Jeremy murmured. "So close. If I could catch him there it would not be a long journey to Clearhaven. I thank you, Sir Francis, and I know I can thank you for Mark. You are returning to him the greatest happiness of his life."

"God speed you, son," Sir Francis smiled. After Jeremy left Sir Francis' office he went directly home, where he informed Louise of the possibility of reaching Mark.

"Jeremy, let us go along. If Mark is in time, there will be a wedding, a wedding I have looked forward to for years. I should like to be there when Margaret and Mark are reunited."

"Can you be packed and ready within the week? If we leave any later than that, we'll miss Mark, and he might be on his way to God-knows-where before we could find him."

"Of course. I'll begin immediately."

Jeremy's twin boys rebelled instantly at the idea of leaving home, so the decision was quickly made that they

417

would stay with their older brother Randolph and his wife. Jeananne was as excited about going to America as her mother was. She was just about to reach her seventeenth birthday, and there was nothing exciting to her in the dominantely male household. Jeananne was a pretty girl whose Scotch-English ancestry could be plainly seen in her ivory skin, flame-colored hair and emerald green eyes. She was Mercury's child. All quicksilver enthusiasm. Jeananne bubbled continually and was exuberantly anxious to journey to this new land about which she had heard so many wild stories.

"Mother, what kind of clothes does one take to this wild country?"

"I suppose," her mother laughed, "the same type of clothes you would take anywhere else."

"Are there really savages there, Mother?" she asked, her eyes wide with excitement.

"I'm sure if the people we're going to visit live there that it cannot really be as savage as gossip contends."

"Oh," Jeananne said in disappointment. "Mother, why are we really going there?"

"To visit an old friend of your father's, and with a little good luck to a wedding."

"Oh, Mother, won't you tell me about it. Father never tells me anything. I'm not a child you know."

"Of course you're not. Sit down, Jeananne and I will tell you a romantic fairy tale that will make this whole trip worthwhile for you."

She told Jeananne the whole story about Mark and Margaret while Jeananne sat in rapt silence. From then on, there was no question of urging Jeananne to hurry as she was even more anxious to go than her parents were. The ship they took from London Harbor was a small but

418

speedy vessel, but their trip was slower than the regular three-week journey because they were caught in a severe storm. A frightened Jeananne and a pale Louise were helped ashore in Boston Harbor.

The last place that Mark was to visit in America was a city called Wilmington, in a state named Pennsylvania. From Boston Harbor, they were to engage the services of another ship, but Louise was too ill to continue their journey immediately. Despite her protest, Jeremy found them temporary lodgings where they could spend a few days and allow Louise to recover.

Four days later, after Louise insisted that she was quite well, they boarded a ship and sailed for Wilmington harbor. Once they arrived in Wilmington, Jeremy secured them lodging in the same place that he knew was Mark's final destination, then they settled and waited for Mark's arrival.

Mark Severn travelled with only his personal servant, Stuart, who had been with him for many years. He sat comfortably in a large inn where he had just come from negotiating a very large trade agreement between the firms Sir Francis represented and the American colonists with which they wanted to begin to strengthen the bonds and reunite the two countries.

Stuart entered the room carrying a tray that held a bottle of brandy and a glass. "'Tis a good thing I brought along a few bottles of Severn Hall's best, sir. This God-forsaken country does not seem to have a decent bottle of spirits in the whole of it."

Mark laughed. "It's a young country, Stuart. Maybe they have not had the time to age their wines."

Stuart gave a noncommital grunt which made Mark laugh again. Stuart was wishing every day that they were back among the comforts of Severn Hall. He was distressed that Mark had adopted the more casual dress of the Americans, and it annoyed him even more when the Americans had the audacity to treat his employer in their relaxed easy way and not with the deference he felt one of Mark's position required. "After all," he thought, "Lord Severn is a knight of the realm and should be shown the respect due one in that position."

Stuart kept Mark's clothes in immaculate condition and cooked such meals for him that most of the friends Mark had acquired in America were quite envious. Stuart had had many blunt and straightforward offers to leave Mark and work for them. He was aghast at their nerve, and showed it plainly for all to see. "He," he said regally, "had been part of the Severn family for over fifty years. He was proud of his position and his complete mastery of it and he intended to stay part of it until the day he died, or," he said with a broad smile, "until Lord Severn dismissed him," for he knew Mark considered him part of his life and would never even consider such a thing. Mark sighed deeply and braced his feet on a stool in front of his chair while he sipped the brandy Stuart had handed him.

His journeys had taken him from Quebec down the American coast. They had been travelling for almost six months and he was weary of it. Sir Francis had been right when he had told Mark there would be much opposition to his mission. Other more powerful countries, trying to isolate England from progressive trade with the colonies and from the building of any bonds between the two, had done their best to stop him. Experienced politicians had worked against him in every way. Only his considerable charm and completely honest dealings had worked in his favor. But tonight he was tired of the glib-tongued people

420

he had to battle and had allowed himself one night to himself just to unwind. He came out of his quiet thoughts when he realized Stuart had asked him something. "What?"

"How much longer, Lord Severn, will we be living in this savage country?"

"Our future itinerary will take us at least four more months, Stuart," he chuckled. "So you may as well face it, you will be here and you might just as well try to bend a little. These are a wonderful people, because they are not all as wealthy nor as . . . noble. Although I'm beginning to see that nobility doesn't have quite all the charm it used to have, it doesn't mean they are not a good, honest, hard-working people trying with all their ability to guide a new country's future."

"You sound as though you admire them, sir."

"I do, in a way, Stuart. If you had been here as I was during the war, you would have seen a spirit such as I have never seen before. Farmers, armed with practically nothing, rose up and faced—and defeated—the crack army of England. That is no mean feat. Now they want to guide their nation in the right path which will be no mean feat either. I . . . . I sometimes think I would like to be part of it."

"Are you honestly considering staying here, my lord?"

"I've been tossing that idea about in my mind. What does Severn Hall have to offer me now? Loneliness . . . memories of what might have been? Here I can at least try to begin a new life."

"Milord . . ." Stuart began, then he hesitated and turned away.

"Stuart, say what you think. We've never had any

secrets between us since I was a child. You think I'm wrong don't you?"

"You are Lord Mark Severn. Your country has given you great honors and you have an obligation to fulfill them."

"Aren't I doing that to the best of my ability right now?"

"Yes, but you are talking about the balance of your life, not right now."

"The balance of my life would be hell at Severn Hall."

"Is it that, sir," Stuart said softly, "or is it because here in America you are a little closer to her."

Mark was about to protest that he did not understand what Stuart was talking about, but he knew to lie was useless, for Stuart knew him as no other did.

"Stuart, Margaret is reunited with her husband now that the war is over. There is no place in her life for me. Yes, if I am here I feel a little closer to her, and if I work for the same cause as she, I feel I'm linked with her in some way . . . to her . . . and to my daughters."

Stuart was silent before the anguished look in Mark's eyes.

"It was a mistake, sir," he said gently, "for God to ever let you know those children were yours. Now your heart will never be anywhere else and that will leave you with nothing."

"Stuart, I'm in a morose enough mood, please don't remind me that the balance of my life is a blank."

"It needn't be, sir."

"What do you suggest I do with it?"

"Do what your name and position obligate you to do. Go home, marry, have sons and work for the benefit of your country. You are a man of great strength there and

422

you can guide it from there toward the goals you want. I don't want to hurt you, sir, but the longer you stay here, the worse it will be for you. The closer you get to her, the harder it will be for you to turn back. Someday, the longing will be too great to see her, or to see your daughters, and then you might make a tragic mistake that might ruin more lives than yours."

"Is that what I've been doing, Stuart?" he asked softly.

"Yes, sir. I've seen your moods change day by day and I know it is the shortening of the miles between you and her."

Mark contemplated the brandy as he slowly turned the glass between his hands, but the bitter truth of Stuart's words could not be denied. He was working his way closer and closer to Margaret.

"All right, Stuart," he said softly. "When we have finished our business in Wilmington, we will go home. If Alicia will still have me, I'll ask her to marry me. I guess . . . maybe . . . this is the first time I've really seen the finality of everything. I guess I have always wished deep in my heart that someday she would send for me. That everything that had passed before would be a bad dream. Now, I find myself awake."

"It is the best for all concerned, sir," Stuart answered, but the answer was gentle with the sympathy he felt for a man he loved as a son.

"We leave for Branton tomorrow and go from there to Philadelphia and then to Wilmington, where we will find the first ship home."

Stuart nodded.

"If you don't mind, Stuart, I'd like to be alone for a while."

Again Stuart nodded and slipped silently from the room.

Mark stood and began to pace the room slowly as the words Stuart had spoken pounded within his mind. Suddenly he was blazingly angry, angry with the perversity of fate that continued to dangle just out of his reach. "Damn!" he exploded as he threw the brandy glass against the wall and heard it shatter, watching the brown stains run down the wall.

The next morning Mark and Stuart left early, for the journey to Branton would take them several days since there were several stops Mark had to visit along the way; personal contacts from a list of names Sir Francis had entrusted to him just before they left.

They arrived in Branton just before dawn, ten days later. Stuart and Mark went directly to the room that had been prearranged. Mark discarded his travelling equipment and fell into the bed.

"God, it feels good to sleep in a clean bed for a change. Those past few flea-infested barns you found have left me exhausted. I intend to sleep for a few hours and I don't want to be wakened by anything short of a natural disaster."

"Very good, sir. What time shall I call you?"

"About four. I might be able to make myself decent enough to call on Mr. Regan. Once my business is concluded with him you can pack and be ready to leave for Philadelphia."

"In the meantime, I shall prepare you something edible. I shudder to imagine what this place has to offer."

Mark was already wrapped in a blanket and half asleep by the time Stuart left the room. The business he expected to spend a day on cost him, to his annoyance, an entire week. Then they were finally on their way again. They had been travelling with a rather large retinue with two wagons to hold their cooking equipment, tents and medicines. Stuart rode in one of the wagons because he had adamantly refused to mount a horse. He sat on the wagon seat now and watched Mark riding a few feet ahead. "His lordship," he thought, "was a fine figure of a man even in the atrocious clothing he had adopted." He was at ease in the saddle, riding ramrod straight. The tight leather pants and high boots he wore accentuated his lithe figure. His shoulders were broad, and there was not an ounce of fat on him. Not like some of the other lords who had come to make their fortunes here for one reason or another.

When they finally reached Philadelphia, Mark was quick to take Stuart aside. "Stuart, we will probably be here over a week. It might be wise for us to skip Wilmington altogether and make plans to leave for home at the end of that time."

"But sir . . ."

"What's the matter now, Stuart? You were the one that was so anxious to go home. Have you changed your mind?"

"No sir, but there's a matter of honor, sir."

"Honor?"

"Sir, no Severn has ever gone back on his word in his life. I should not like to see it begin with you. We agreed to certain things, and I don't believe we should do anything short of what Sir Francis expects of us."

Mark was trying his best not to show the combined emotions of exasperation and plain hilarity. He coughed to cover the laughter that slipped out at the continual reference to "we," as though he and Stuart were bound together as one by some invisible bond. He sighed deeply.

"All right, Stuart, Wilmington next and then home. Or do 'we' have any further obligations on our honor that 'we' have to see to?"

"No sir. Wilmington, sir, then home on the first ship with a clear conscience that we have done everything to Sir Francis' satisfaction."

"Good," Mark said dryly. "I wouldn't want 'our' reputation to carry such a blemish."

"Right, sir," Stuart beamed, as though Mark was an errant child to which he had succeeded in showing the right path.

The frustrating days in Philadelphia were relieved by Mark's acquaintance with several leaders of America who were definitely interested in binding up the shattering wounds of both countries and tightening again the broken bond between them. His interest in and admiration for General Washington, who was now the first president-elect of this new country, was unbounded. But his much deeper enthusiasm was for another acquaintance he made. He made the meeting seem accidental, but he had maneuvered it purposely arranging to be introduced by President Washington.

It was only by chance overhearing a conversation not made for him to hear that he heard Benjamin Franklin mention not only the Deverall name but the Martin name as well. Slowly, not noticing the interested gleam in Franklin's eyes, he maneuvered the conversation toward Virginia, its patriots, and in particular his friendship with several influential families there. "The Deveralls," Franklin said softly. "I have made their acquaintance only once, but I was quite favorably impressed with both gentlemen. At the time of our meeting, the younger, Matthew, I believe his name was, was about to leave England for America. He'd purchased a piece of property there. Foxmore is the name. I must say for a while there he had us quite worried, for one of our best operators and most loyal patriots lived on the adjoining plantation." He went on to tell Mark of the entire episode and the entire family's involvement in it. His astute eye and his uncommonly alert instincts noticed Mark's much deeper interest in the Martin family, especially the twin daughters. He filled Mark's hungry heart with stories of the girls. It was an unhappy thing that Franklin himself did not know of Paul Martin's death, because if he had been able to tell Mark it would have put the sun back into his life.

"Tell me," Franklin said gently, "you are acquainted with Paul Martin?"

"No . . . no I knew Mrs. Martin . . . slightly in England, many years ago."

"I see," Franklin answered. He knew further questions were useless, but his romantic turn of mind told him there was much more here than he was told. Mark let the conversation slip into other channels, not because he was satisfied with what he had learned but because his desire to know more of Margaret and her daughters was insatiable, and he did not want to be responsible for having the breath of scandal touch Margaret in any way. On the last night they were to be in Philadelphia, Mark breathed a sigh of deep relief. He was only too aware that the journey from Philadelphia to Clearhaven was not very long.

They departed for Wilmington the next day. This would be the last of his obligations to Sir Francis. He was determined to conclude his business rapidly and leave the area as soon as possible. There was no use tempting fate. He knew he would make the drastic mistake and try to see Margaret, so he promised himself that he would be on board the first boat that left for England. His mood became darker and darker as they neared Wilmington, and even Stuart hesitated to say anything to him lest his head be snapped from his shoulders.

Finding their pre-arranged quarters was done quickly by Stuart. Their baggage settled in, Mark paid and dismissed the men he had hired to drive the wagons and move their baggage about.

Before they went to their rooms, Mark and Stuart found the best accommodations for eating and shared an early lunch. Then, to Stuart's dismay, Mark purchased two bottles of whiskey before they returned to their apartment. Once there, Stuart was dismissed gently but firmly.

"I can take care of all I need for tonight, Stuart. Go out for the evening. Find some new friends and enjoy yourself and," Mark chuckled, "don't worry about me like an old mother hen. I shall take care of business as usual tomorrow. As for tonight, if you don't mind I'd like to just relax and be alone."

Stuart eyed the two bottles of whiskey and this brought another amused chuckle from Mark. "Don't worry, Stuart, I can handle that, too. Please allow me a little forgetfulness. Once we're on our way back to England, I will never dwell on these memories again. Is it too much to ask for one night to be allowed to feel sorry for myself?"

"Of course, sir," Stuart said miserably as he backed from the room and closed the door after him. Taking off his jacket, Mark hung it carefully over the back of a chair.

He removed his boots and sat down in a rocker near the window placing the two bottles of whiskey on the floor beside him. He rolled up the sleeves of his shirt, lifted both feet, and crossed them on the ledge of the window. Then he slowly reached down, lifted one of the bottles and uncorked it. He held the bottle up to the light and looked through it at the amber liquid.

"Good-bye again, Margaret," he said softly, then raised the bottle to his lips and drank.

Slowly, methodically, he drank from the bottle. One sip for every memory he pulled from the depths of his soul. They had laughed together freely and happily over the smallest things. The way her eyes sparkled across the room when she had read the unspoken thought in his mind. The way they had walked together without speaking for long moments, then suddenly began to talk of their future and their love. The soft feel of her skin to the touch of his fingers. The fine threads of her black satin hair against the white pillow as he bent above her taking her body and making her part of him.

He dragged out every thought, every moment, because they were to be for the very last time. He did not love her, but he would not cheat Alicia by bearing with him the ghost of Margaret. He was and always would be a man of honor. So he took the memories one by one and relived them, mourned them . . . and sent them to their death. He was over three-fourths of the way through the first bottle when the knocking on the door disturbed his thoughts.

"Go away, Stuart."

"Mark! . . . Let me in. Mark! It's me, Jeremy."

Mark looked at the closed door for a few minutes not quite believing the voice on the other side.

"Mark! Goddamn it, Mark, open this door or I'll break it down. I have some good news for you."

Still disbelieving what he was hearing, Mark rose unsteadily to his feet and made his way toward the door. It was only when he opened the door that complete realization entered his foggy mind.

"Jeremy? What are you doing here?"

"I have made this trip just to rescue a friend and I see I made it just in time."

After Stuart was called they spent the next few hours sobering Mark up, then Jeremy told him about the letter.

"Come with me, Mark. I want you to read the letter for yourself. Louise wouldn't let me bring it. She wanted to see your face when you read it."

Mark's face was pale. "Jeremy, when did this letter come?"

"Most likely a few days after we came home, why?"

"All this time," he whispered. "All this time, I've not answered, Jeremy . . . she must believe . . . she must believe I've chosen not to come."

"Mark, get hold of yourself. You'll never know until you go and find out. Louise and I have a cottage on the edge of town. Come with me, read the letter, then go to her."

Mark nodded his head in agreement for words would not come to him to express the fear that again . . . he might be too late.

As rapidly as Mark's unsteady movements would allow, they began to make their way to Jeremy's cottage. At the door, Jeremy was about to reach for the latch when the door was pulled open and Louise stood framed in the light.

"Oh, Jeremy, thank God you're back," she gasped.

"Louise, what's the matter?"

"Jeananne and I were waiting for you when we heard this funny thump from the back door. We went to see what it was . . ."

"And?"

"We found this young man. He's badly hurt, Jeremy. I believe he's been stabbed."

Mark became suddenly sober as they rushed to the open bedroom door.

"Oh, my God," he whispered as he looked down on the boy in the bed that hovered so close to death.

"Do you know him, Mark?"

"Yes . . . It's Margaret's son . . . David Martin."

Chapter Forty-Six

Deanna yawned and stretched, then turned toward Matt's still figure. His slow, even breathing told her he was in a deep sleep. The first pale light of dawn made its way through the closed shutters in thin beams of sunlight. She could hear the birds as their trilling filled the air. "How beautiful," she thought. Anything that morning would have made Deanna think so for she was so very happy she felt about to burst. She thought back to the day when she had first seen Matt. That eventful, rainy day when he had opened the door that threw her into his arms. All the days and nights that had passed since then came back to her. Over some, she mourned the death of her father and the terrible time when she thought Matt was going to die of his wounds. Wounds received in a cause he barely understood, but to which his love for her had taken him. But other thoughts made her head swim in dizzy happiness. The first time they had ever made love on this very bed. The dangerous time when they were separated and his daring rescue of her.

She looked down on him. In sleep his face seemed younger, more vulnerable. Taking hold of the long braid of her hair that she wore to bed against Matt's wishes, for he loved nothing more than to tangle his hands in her hair and make love to her, she tickled the end of his nose. He turned his head away from the annoying touch and

432

murmured something unintelligible. Again she tickled his nose and laughed as his hand brushed at the consistent annoyance. She bent forward to touch him again and suddenly shrieked with surprise as two strong arms bound her and pulled her body across his, holding her prisoner.

"Caught you, my lovely nuisance," he laughed. "Now you must pay the price for rousing a man from some very beautiful dreams."

"Were you dreaming of me?"

"You conceited little witch," he chuckled evilly. "What makes you think I was dreaming of you. Maybe it was another with long, golden hair and green eyes."

Deanna smiled, then slowly she raised her arms and slid her hands through his hair. She lowered her lips to his and gave him a searing kiss that would have burnt him to a cinder had he been made of wood. But he wasn't, he was flesh and blood, both of which burned with the desire to possess her. She released his lips and smiled again.

"Will that banish those dreams, love?"

"Deanna, love," he grinned. "That banishes everything but one thought."

She laughed again and flung her arms about him, pressing herself as close to him as she could get, enjoying the hard feel of his body close to hers. He took immediate advantage of her gay mood and caressed the smooth curves of her body.

"Every time I'm with you," he murmured against her throat, "is a rare and new experience. I never know what you're going to be, seductive gypsy or mysterious lady. But no matter what you are, I have enough love to include them all."

She chuckled throatily and in her exuberant happiness

433

began to kiss him wherever her lips would fall. Taken by surprise by the quickness of her attack, he began to laugh. Then he took her by the shoulders and held her a little away from him. The beauty of her deep blue eyes against the midnight black of her hair had always drawn his admiration, but today there was a special beauty in her flushed pink cheeks, in the tremulous moist lips and in the sparkle of her eyes.

"God, but you're lovely. You are happy, aren't you, Deanna?"

"Oh, Matt, if I were any happier the world would not be able to contain it."

"I hope I'm the cause of some of this, for the past three years it has been my one goal in life."

"You are love, oh you are," she said as she laid back against the pillow. "It is such a lovely day and I feel as if I own the world."

He turned to face her watching her out of questioning eyes. "He'd seen Deanna in every kind of mood," he thought, but never had he seen her like this.

"Can I take all the credit for this," he grinned, "or is there something special that makes you happy today?"

Deanna reached up and lay her hand against the side of his face. Her eyes were tender as she said softly, "You, love, you and the child I carry within me."

For a moment he was stilled both by her extraordinary loveliness and the words she had just spoken. Then he turned his face and kissed the palm of her hand that rested against him. Words to tell her how he felt left him completely, but she knew, for the depth of love in his eyes told her.

"What can I say to tell you how complete you have made my life, Deanna. There was a time a few years ago when everything I saw in the world was black. Then you came like the sun on a summer day, and you let me find a place for all the love I have. Now everything is perfect, everything is whole. God has given me everything in the world a man can ask for."

"Oh, Matt," she whispered, "I do love you so." His arms gathered her to him and his lips found hers in a kiss so passionate, so possessive that it rocked the foundations of her soul and sent her careening into a world where only they existed.

He wanted to draw her within him, to make her understand the depths and the heights to which her love had taken him. The hands were strong that searched her body, and the fiery kisses travelled in seeking desire that lifted her and carried her along in the torrential stream of his magic.

He sheathed himself within her and moved in slow, easy movements that drove her wild. Her body arched to meet his and she clung to him as they moved together as one. Slowly they spiralled upward, aware only of the heat and the touch of each other . At that final moment, when he blended their bodies together, she clung to him and whispered his name over and over.

They lay still, she contented and he unwilling to leave the sanctuary of her body.

"Deanna," he whispered, "if we were to never love again, I would still feel blessed. This magic you and I have shared would be enough to sustain me."

Tears filled her eyes and the thickness of the love in her throat left her unable to speak. Slowly he lay back against the pillows and drew her to him until her head rested on his chest. They held each other for a time in silence, knowing that no words were necessary, that no words could touch what they felt.

"Matt?"

"Uh-humm?"

"What will we name the baby?"

"Do you have anything special in mind?"

"I've thought of millions of names, but I want you to like it too."

"Well . . . let me see . . . How about Joshua if it is a boy and Lauren if it is a girl."

"They're both beautiful names. Good, it will be Joshua."

"Just like that," he laughed. "Don't you consider the baby's gender might be female?"

"I've given that some thought, but I feel you would really like a boy first then a girl next time," she giggled. "And you must remember, Matt, I always try to please you."

"Well, let me inform you, madam, that it can be either one as long as you're all right. In fact, I think having a little girl might be nice. Of course my one stipulation is that she look like you."

"I'll keep that in mind," she said solemnly. They lay together and talked for over another hour. This had been a habit since their marriage. It was the time they both enjoyed the most, for they shared all their thoughts and all their problems then.

"Matt, do you have a great many plans for today?"

"Well, it's time we began to repair of the fences. Cat and Jason offered to help when the time came. By the way, did I tell you that Jason has the plans completed for their own home?"

"No, when do they begin?"

"In early spring, just before we plant. Jason wants to

begin everything at once."

"I'm going to miss them being here. The house will seem so big again after they're gone."

"They'll be close. I gave them a nice-sized piece of ground between us and the borders of Dartmore Hall. Having Vern for a neighbor on one side and us on the other was quite pleasing to both Deb and Jason. Besides," he turned and looked down into her upturned face, "I like the idea of having you all to myself."

"Is Deeta coming with Cat today?"

"Both Deeta and David. Neither Cat nor David will let Deeta out of their sight."

"There haven't been any signs of the thieves for a long time."

"I know. Over three weeks. Maybe they've moved along, but for a little while longer, we'll take precautions."

"Deeta told me just a few days ago that she's also expecting a baby. I'm glad she's coming today. I can't wait to tell her. I hope you're not angry, Matt, but I told Mother first, or at least I tried. For some reason, I think she already knew."

"Who knows a child better than its mother? No matter how old you grow, you're still her child. I'll bet she knows you almost as well as you know yourself."

She slid her arms across the broad expanse of his chest, down his ribs to rest on his hip. "Like I know you."

"Yes, love," he whispered gently as he touched her forehead with his lips. "As we know each other. Every heartbeat, every thought," he held her against him and they remained quietly held in this rare moment.

As they sat at breakfast later they heard the horses approaching that heralded the coming of Cat and Deeta who, when they entered, were invited to share the balance of breakfast. "We've eaten already," Cat said, "but I will have some coffee. Where's Jason?"

"Still abed," Matt laughed. "Seems he has a strange attachment to it in the last few years."

"Where's David, Cat?" Deanna questioned.

"He'll be over a little later. I told him to go home and share a little time with his mother. The boy's been our shadow for the past three weeks, and he's due for a break."

"Cat," Deanna asked, "how is he now? How does he feel about the situation between Brandon and Susan?"

"He'll be fine, Deanna. The boy is like the father. Paul would have been proud of him. He'll go home and neither of the other two will hear a word from him. As far as Susan is concerned, he'll always have a special place in his heart, for her, but . . . well, it's kind of like your feelings for David, love . . . but different."

"I understand."

"I wouldn't be surprised," Deeta said, "to be hearing some kind of announcement soon. It's so obvious that Brandon and Susan are deeply in love with each other. I think it's their combined shyness that's kept him from asking her long before this."

"Yes, I wouldn't be too surprised either," Cat laughed. "Things around here look brighter every day. Happiness seems to be contagious."

"Don't say that, Cat," Deeta said, and it surprised everyone to see that Deeta was actually frightened. She laughed a little in a flustered effort to hide her alarm. "It is not wise to call the attention of the gods to one's happiness. They are quite jealous."

Cat eyed her steadily while the others began to talk of

other things to ease Deeta's confusion. When the men had left, Deeta and Deanna sat over their coffee and happily discussed the future birth of their children. Jason was the next to appear.

"Where's Matt?"

"He and Cat have gone to repair the fences. They said you were to join them as soon as you've eaten."

"I'll just have a quick cup of coffee. I can eat one of those muffins on the way." He gestured toward the three remaining blueberry muffins. Deanna wrapped all three in a napkin.

"You need more than one."

"Deb should be down soon. Paul is up and she's dressing him. I'd best be on my way. See you later." Grabbing up the napkin filled with muffins, he headed for the door. The door slammed behind him and soon the sound of hoofbeats faded away.

Matt and Cat labored for quite a while in silence before it occurred to Matt that Cat was not usually so quiet. "Something bothering you, Cat?"

"Yeah . . . it's something I've been wanting to tell you for years. Up until now, it never made any difference. Your father called me Cat, and at the time no other name seemed necessary."

"And now?" Matt said gently a smile lighting his eyes. "You're going to have a child and you want to give him your name."

"That's right."

"What's so difficult about that?"

"Matt, there's a little story that goes with it that I think you of all people should know."

"Cat, you listen. You can tell me or not, that's up to you. You are the closest friend I have, and I don't think

439

anything could change that."

"I guess I want to."

"Whatever it is, Cat, it's between you and me unless you say different."

"Thanks, Matt. The story goes back a long way. When your father found me I was running away from a terrible situation."

Matt waited in silence. He knew Cat would continue when he was ready.

"I was born a slave, Matt. My mother and father were slaves before me. I was about twelve, a boy filled with hatred and bad memories. Memories of the way my mother was abused by our white master, memories of how my gentle and wonderful father's pride was slowly destroyed. It would kill him a little each time my mother was sent for. She was so very pretty. One day he could take no more. He fought back. For his efforts, he was tied to a stake and beaten. Within me grew such a hatred that my twelve-year-old mind could hardly bear it. I waited, dreamed of the day when I could do something about it. And it came . . . it came."

Cat's voice faded as his eyes looked into the past. Matt remained silent still.

"My mother was a gentle creature . . . like Deeta. She named me Jessie Luke after my father. They loved each other so much it was a beautiful thing to see. And they loved me . . . they loved me. My father was big, even bigger than I. By the time I was twelve my head reached his shoulders. To me, he was like a god. Then one night the master got drunk with all his friends. They came and got my mother. When my father tried to interfere, he was shackled and dragged along. Dragged along to watch what they did to my mother in their drunken orgy. It killed

440

her . . . killed the sweetest, most beautiful woman . . .

"I watched my father. He was dumped back into the cabin we shared. He was quietly insane, Matt. He sat for hours that next day sharpening his knife. I sat beside him and listened to his silent hatred as it flowed about me. That night, I followed him to the master's house. There were only three of them home, the master, his son, and his wife. I will not tell you what I watched him do that night, Matt. It is a thing almost unbearable even for me to remember. He knew he would be caught and killed but he didn't care, his life had already gone with my mother. His only goal was to save me. We walked until the dawn and reached the harbor. Before he was caught, he had me safely stowed away on a ship leaving for England. I damn-near starved to death on the trip over. The night we docked, I found a way to slip ashore. I'll never forget it, it was raining and I stood there, a lost, hungry, black child. Just as I was about to collapse, through eyes bleary with tears and dizzy with hunger, a tall stranger found me."

"My father?"

"Yes. I'll never forget how he cared for me, Matt. Overlooking everything that I was or might have been, he took me in, in his house to be raised with his sons, educated beyond anything I could dream of. Offered the one thing I never knew, friendship."

"Why are you telling me this after so many years, Cat?"

"I guess it's because I want to name my child, if he is a son, Jessie Luke, and I want someone besides me to know the honor and self-sacrifice that goes with the name. I guess it's because I want you to be my child's godfather, and because of that I feel you have the right to know."

Matt was choked with emotion as he held his hand out

and Cat took it.

"I feel honored, Cat. Deanna and I will be proud to stand as Jessie's godparents. If the time ever comes that it's needed, we'll see he gets the best."

They both turned at the sound of an approaching horse and watched Jason ride up. Then they put in an exhausting day's work, stopping to eat the small lunch Deeta had packed for them.

"Jason, I've got the men working to thin out that stand of trees on Grist ridge. I thought we'd season the wood and you could use it to help build the house."

"Good idea. I was wondering if we were going to have to ship lumber in."

"This country is remarkable. Everything we might ever need we can get from the land."

"We've decided where to put the house."

"Where?"

"You know that flat green meadow about four or five miles on the west side of Cat's cabin. We took a ride up there yesterday. It's beautiful and just the perfect place for the house. If you and Deanna will part with it, Deb and I would like to build there."

"It's yours," Matt laughed.

"What's so amusing?"

"We sure are populating this side of the river aren't we? When I first came here, Clearhaven was the only nice place. Foxmore was a disaster, and Dartmore Hall was only half remodeled. Now, Dartmore is a showplace and Foxmore's coming along well. John's building, and Cat's place is getting bigger and bigger, and now you."

Their laughter echoed across the valley and was heard by the two riders that kept out of view while they watched the comings and goings of Cat. They wanted him just the way he was now, relaxed and happily unaware of what they had in store for him. When they arrived at Foxmore several hours later, they found David sitting on the front porch steps.

"I swear I think the boy's chained to us. He ain't takin' no chances. I doubt if the President gets any more serious protection than we do."

"It's been weeks since anything has happened," Jason replied. "I'll wager those bucks have gone on to greener pastures. The Governor has tightened things around here so they've probably given up."

"Yeah, I tend to agree with you, Jason," Cat replied. "Another week to satisfy our young gladiator here and we can all relax."

They dismounted in front of the porch and gave their horses' reins to the young stableboy who would see to their care. David rose and came down the steps to meet them.

"Evenin'," he grinned. "You got another guest for supper. My presence isn't exactly appreciated at home right now."

"Why's that? You been up to some kind of mischief lately?" Cat asked.

"Nope, been a good boy for such a long time, I think I've forgotten how to be anything else."

"Then why'd you get tossed out?"

"Not tossed out, Cat," David grinned. "I just used my better judgment. Mother's putting on a nice supper and the Governor and his wife have been invited. I kind of thought something was up and my absence would be the easiest way."

"Well," Matt laughed. "Looks as though young

Brandon has gotten up enough nerve to propose to Susan. Maybe we'll be having another party soon."

"Suits me," Jason said. "I'm all for parties. Any excuse is good enough," he clapped Matt on the shoulder as they went in and joined the women for supper.

They were right about the reasons for Margaret's preparations. Brandon had formally asked John and Sarah for permission to become engaged, so formally that it took every effort on John's part not to laugh when Brandon, pale-faced and visibly trembling, had faced John and launched into a speech that John would swear he had practiced for weeks. It would have surprised Brandon to know that John and Sarah had talked the matter over long before he decided to speak. "She's just a child," John had said firmly. Sarah had laughed.

"She is not a child, my darling, she is very much a woman and if you would only stop seeing a little girl in pigtails you would see that for our shy little rose, Brandon is the perfect match. That he loves her is known by everybody. It's as obvious as the nose on your face."

"I know you're right, Sarah. But I love her, too, and it's hard to part with her."

"In this case, my dear, I don't think we are losing a daughter, we are gaining a son. If Brandon comes to you soon, and I'm sure he will, please at least listen when he talks to you."

"All right," John said gruffly. "But if it is an engagement, it is going to be a long one."

"Oh, John," Sarah said, a mischievous smile in her eyes. "I've often heard that long engagements breed trouble." She leaned close to him and kissed him slowly and quite thoroughly. "Don't you remember how you felt when you were that young?"

444

John put his arms about her, but by that time he was laughing.

"Woman, are you by any chance telling me I'm getting old?" he questioned, and he could hear her answering chuckle as his lips found hers in a resoundingly forceful kiss. He held her a little away from him. "You have a way with you, Sarah. No matter what path I start walking on, I always find myself being led down the path you've chosen. I don't know even where I go astray. I think it's somewhere between here," he slid his arms about her, "and here." He kissed her again, only this time the kiss was a searching one that found in her as it always did the answers.

To Brandon and Susan's delight, the supper went well and the engagement was formalized. As everyone left the table to have brandy, Brandon took the opportunity to get Susan alone for a few minutes. Quickly taking her hand he drew her out the door and they walked across the stone patio and through Margaret's garden.

Chapter Forty-Seven

Finding a stone bench in the shadows of a great tree that grew at the edge of the garden, Brandon and Susan sat together. The pale light of the moon made Susan look even more fragile than usual. Brandon looked at her in wonder. She seemed like a soft rose, almost too delicate to even touch. He could smell the fragrance she wore and was filled with the same deep, aching desire to hold her and tell her how much he wanted her. He had vowed that he would not lay a hand on her until they were married, but he had to admit to himself just how thin his self-control was getting. He took her hand in his and gently kissed it.

It was better for both concerned that he did not know the thoughts that were running through her mind at the moment. She watched the moonlight sparkle across the thick blond hair, felt the strength in the hand that held hers. Susan sensed the depth of desire in Brandon as he sat near her and held back with supreme effort the desire to kiss him. Her mind and body were in a confused turmoil. Susan was not as unwise as Brandon thought. Although she had never been with a man, she had discussed her feelings with her sister, Caroline, who had openly told her all she should know. Caroline had urged her to be open and honest about her feelings for Brandon, and Susan awaited only the reaching out by Brandon to let him know how deeply she loved him and that she wanted to be his wife in every way.

"I'm so glad your father agreed to our engagement, Susan. I don't know what I would have done if he had refused."

"I know what I would have done."

"What?"

"Packed my bag and run away with you," she said calmly. He looked at her now not only in complete surprise but with the sudden suspicion that there was much more to Susan than he knew.

"Would you really, Susan? I mean . . . leave everything and everyone to be with me?"

Susan turned toward Brandon. He held one hand in a tense grip, with the other she touched the side of his face.

"I love you, Brandon. I want to be your wife. To me, that means completely, without reservations. From now on, there is no one more important in my life than you."

Brandon took hold of both hands and kissed them.

"There is another thing you should know," she added.

"What?"

"I've seen so many people marry, then a day comes when the man searches elsewhere for affection he might not get at home. I am not that kind of a woman, Brandon. I'm a very possessive woman. I want you for myself alone. I want to make you happy. You must have patience with me for a while. I'm a little frightened, but not frightened enough not to realize that I love you beyond reason."

Although Brandon had kissed Susan several times, they had been as chaste a kiss as he could manage, so he was quite unprepared for the soft half-parted lips that touched his, searching for the beginning of what was to be. Lost to any self-control he might have had, Brandon's arms closed about her and his lips took hers in a fiery answer to her unspoken question. Slender white arms crept about his neck and he pulled her into his arms, feeling the soft round breasts against his chest and the supple body in his arms. Brandon surrendered completely to the passion that flamed through him.

Susan was still enjoying thoroughly the light, random kisses that fell on her cheeks, eyes and lips, and his lips drifted down her throat to the valley between her breasts. He heard the soft sound of pleasure and realized, happily, he was going to have a wife as passionate as he. Now, he was frustrated by the knowledge that they were in the wrong place to go any further and that there were too many articles of clothing between him and what he wanted. Susan was also aware of the same situation. Soon they would have to go back in the house. She laid her head against his shoulder and he held her without moving, both of them aware that for this time, they must regain control, yet elated by knowing that a day was coming when they would not have to.

"Brandon?" she said softly.

"Yes?"

"There . . . there have been others for you?"

Brandon nearly choked searching for an answer. He had other women but he was certainly not as experienced as Susan thought he was. Besides, at the moment, he realized that anyone else had faded even from his memory. "I won't lie to you, Susan."

"I'm glad there were," she laughed lightly. "I'm so . . . so new at this, that it is probably better that one of us knows. Brandon, I want to make you happy. You will tell me if I do anything terribly stupid? You won't become angry with me?"

In her innocence, Susan touched exactly the right key that brought forth every gallant instinct Brandon possessed. "Darling, you couldn't do anything drastically stupid if you tried, just as I couldn't be angry with you. I love everything about you. The way you tip your head up, and how your eyes sparkle when you laugh. The way you have of looking at me as if I had all the answers to everything. I like the soft feel of your skin and the way it smells like jasmine and your hair is so pretty I'd like to loosen it and feel it in my hands. Don't you see, Susan, anything before you is unimportant for, just as for you, this is the first time I've ever really loved someone. So we'll travel this road together for the first time. We'll have each other and no one has to lead the way. We'll do it together, learning from each other, sharing with each other, and best of all loving each other."

That she was silently crying he knew, for he could see the silvery glistening of tears on her cheeks. But they were tears of complete happiness. He stood up and drew her to him, and again she felt his arms about her, holding her close to him. He bent his head and gently kissed the tears away. Her lips were salty and moist, and he tasted lightly of the intoxicating nectar of love that held all the promise of complete beauty.

As the days went by, things fell into a pleasant kind of order. The plans for Susan's wedding began. Deeta was often at Foxmore or Clearhaven, but never was she unescorted by either David or Cat. Despite both of their protests, David was determined to stay until he felt sure there was no danger to Deeta. All evidence seemed to say that the people who were stealing slaves had gone on. There was no sign of them for weeks. Even the Governor

449

was about to lift the restrictive force he had covered the area with. Days turned to weeks and the day for the large engagement party that John and Sarah had planned for Susan drew near. Margaret insisted it be held at Clearhaven which was, by far, the bigger and better equipped to hold such an affair.

Susan would have been ecstatically happy except for one flaw. It had suddenly occurred to her that David had gone from Clearhaven at the same time she had found her love for Brandon. She worried the thought over and over in her mind, wondering if David's reason for leaving the comforts of his home was her. Finally, she could bear the doubt no longer. Early one morning, she had her horse saddled and rode alone to Cat's cabin.

She found David atop Cat's cabin, stripped to the waist and laboriously repairing a leak. He heard her approach and waved to her, then began to climb down the ladder.

"Good morning, Sue! What are you doing out so early?"

"I came to see you, David. I . . . I wanted to talk to you."

"Is something wrong, Sue?"

"No, not really. David you aren't angry with me are you?"

"Angry, why should I be angry with you."

"I thought . . . well you left Clearhaven so abruptly that I thought . . ." her voice died helplessly. He took hold of her shoulders and smiled down into her pleading eyes.

"Do you love him, Sue, really love him?" he asked gently.

"Oh, I do, David. Brandon is so wonderful and I love him more than my own life."

"Then that's enough for me. A big brother should see to the safety of a sister as sweet as you. If you love him and he loves you, then I'm happy for you and I wish you every good thing there is."

Her eyes clouded with tears and she threw her arms about his neck. Laughing, he held her tightly in his arms.

She was still there chatting happily with David, seated on the front porch of Cat's cabin, when they saw Brandon riding toward them. At that moment, David knew for certain Susan's love for Brandon was all that she said it was. He watched her face brighten and her cheeks grow pink.

Brandon dismounted and strode toward them. "Good morning," he grinned. "Sue, your mother told me you were up here so I decided to come up and ride back with you."

"Why don't you both stay and have lunch with me? Cat and Deeta probably won't be back and I hate to eat alone. I have a nice bottle of wine cooling in the stream over there, and Deeta's kitchen is always filled with something good."

"Sounds great to me," Brandon replied. "How about you, Susan?"

"Wonderful, I'd love to. Why don't we take some food out under that nice shady tree?" It was agreeable to all three and soon they were seated on a blanket eating Deeta's fresh crusty bread, large slabs of ham and cheese and washing it down with the cool wine. Although he tried to hide his thoughts, David was aware of Brandon's relief. It was obvious to David he had come to make sure that David knew both that Susan was his, and that he would do whatever necessary to protect his interests.

The next hour passed rapidly, with a lot of laughter

451

and amusing stories. Susan helped gather the balance of the food, put it away, and tidied up Deeta's kitchen. Then she and Brandon mounted their horses and waved good-bye to David, who was already atop the cabin again hammer in hand.

Brandon and Susan rode along in silence for quite a while. Susan was aware that he seemed to be in deep thought about something. Suddenly he brought his horse to a stop and she reined in her horse and sat looking at him both in surprise and curiosity.

"What's the matter, Brandon?"

"Susan, can we go somewhere and talk. I have something to tell you?"

"Where?"

Brandon stood up in his stirrups and surveyed the area. Then he pointed. "Let's go over there."

A thick stand of trees about a half mile away stood just on the opposite side of a small creek. They left the road, crossed the wide grass-filled meadow and rode into the shaded depths of the trees for a good distance before Brandon stopped his horse, dismounted and walked to her side.

He reached up to lift her from the saddle, then he hobbled both horses so they would not drift away.

"Brandon, what in heaven's name is the matter with you?"

"I lied to you," he said bluntly.

"What?"

"I lied to you," he repeated.

"About what?"

"Your mother never told me you were up at Cat's. I passed one of the Dietrick boys when I was headed toward your house and he told me he'd seen you this

452

morning riding toward Cat's cabin."

"Well, what is the difference who told you where I was? You found me and the morning was quite nice. I'm glad you did."

"You don't understand."

"Well, then, for goodness sake, explain."

"I knew Cat and Deeta were already at Clearhaven."

She was quiet for a moment while what he was trying to say finally registered on her.

"And," she said softly, "you thought I was coming here to meet David when I knew no one else was at home."

"That's right," he said miserably.

"Oh, Brandon, how could you think such a thing. After that night in the garden when I told you how I felt about you. Do you think I'm the kind of girl that gives her love freely to any boy she sees?"

"God," he groaned. "I'm sorry, Susan. You know I love you and you know I don't think of you like that. It was just that I was suddenly so jealous and afraid."

"Afraid?"

"I guess I've always been afraid. When you love someone as much as I love you, it's easy sometimes to get carried away by jealousy. He's known you so much longer than I, shared so many things with you. I created all kinds of monsters in my mind. I could see him taking you away from me. When I started up here, it was with the decided urge to beat him."

"What changed your mind?" she asked gently.

"You!"

"How?"

"I don't really know. I looked at you and it suddenly all melted away, then when we were all together I saw the

453

easy way you two talked together and for the first time I guess I knew that you two really are family. I felt like a fool. I wouldn't blame you if you were mad as hell at me. But I had to tell you."

Susan stepped close to Brandon and slid her arms about his waist. Tipping her head up, she smiled at him. "How can a woman be angry at a man who loves her so much. Brandon, you must know for sure, once and for all, that there is no man now, nor will there ever be, who makes me feel as you do. I love you," she added softly.

"Then I'm forgiven?"

"Not quite," she laughed. "I think you had best prove to me you're sorry and that you know I love you."

He smiled as he pulled her against him. "What does my lady have in mind?"

"The matter is in your hands," she murmured as his head lowered toward hers. "I'm sure you have enough ingenuity to think of something."

The last words were stopped by the hard mouth that took possession of hers. His arms tightened about her until she could barely breathe, and his mouth parted hers in a kiss that searched her soul. She felt dizzy with the sudden burst of flame that suddenly exploded somewhere in the depths of her and flooded through her, leaving her weak and clinging to him. When he lifted his mouth from her and looked down into her half-closed eyes, he knew it was too late for either of them to turn back. He cupped her face in his hands and kissed her forehead, eyelids, cheeks and touched her lips lightly again and again until he heard her soft murmur of protest. He slid his hands into her hair and worked it loose from the pins that held it. From there, he let his hands drift down over her shoulders and gently caress the slender waist. "I want you Susan," he murmured huskily.

"And I want you, Brandon," she murmured against his throat as she laid her head against him. He could feel her tremble and he knew she was afraid. He tipped up her chin with his hand and looked at her.

"You know it's all right, my darling. I'll wait. If you're afraid, I understand."

"Oh, Brandon," she whispered. "The only thing that I am afraid of is that I will be a disappointment to you. Please have patience with me Brandon, but don't leave me now, for I need you as much as you need me."

"A disappointment," he groaned. "God, you're the loveliest thing in the world!"

"Then," she said gently, "make love to me Brandon. Make me belong to you for now and for always."

Brandon quickly looked about him, then taking her hand, he led her to the base of a huge tree whose roots stood two feet above the ground. Between two of these he found a deep grassy hollow and drew Susan down with him.

If Brandon had learned nothing else in his sexual encounters, he had learned that waiting for his partner's pleasure gave him more pleasure. His hands were slow and gentle as, amid several long, seeking kisses, he removed the blouse she wore and slid the straps of her chemise off her shoulders to her waist. Her skin glowed like pale ivory. He marvelled at the rare and delightful beauty of her small breasts crowned by the rosy pink nipples that were hard and erect from the bubbling force of the desire for him that flowed through her. He cupped them in his hands, then gently kissed each one. Capturing a hard up-turned nipple, he sucked gently, hearing her gasp of pleasure and for the first time felt her fluttery hands reach for him to hold her closer. She felt the soft grass beneath her bare back as he lowered her to the ground. He bent above her now, his hands sliding the skirt down off her hips. The balance of her clothes followed and he drew her into his arms. Feeling the long, slender length of her against him, his hands caressed her now, and he felt her stir and waken in his arms as he found spots that elicited deep sighs from her. Amid delicate touches and many kisses, he removed his clothes too. His body, warm and strong against hers, added fuel to the inner fire that was threatening to consume her. Guiding her hands and speaking softly, he led her to discover him as he was discovering her. She touched him freely, feeling the hard muscle of his chest that narrowed at the waist, the flat ridge of his belly, then lowering to the pulsing manhood that frightened her both with its size and its throbbing life.

Very few men would have taken the care to arouse her even further. The foolish man would have possessed her then and might have lost her forever. Brandon was no fool. Touching her lightly, he allowed his kisses to roam down the length of her body, stopping here and there when he felt her quivering response increase. Soon, under his gentle touch, she began to move against him, her body instinctively searching for the release from this blinding need.

His hands caressed a silken thigh then slowly pushed her legs apart and found the soft moist warmth of her. With the delicate circling motion of his fingers, he lifted her to a plane of blinding passion. It was only then that he rose above her. He saw her half-closed eyes and moist, parted lips, felt her hands drawing him closer within her. Trying to hurt her as little as possible, he made the first deep thrust hard and quick. He heard her whimper softly and saw the glistening tears, but felt also the urgent hands and writhing body pull him closer.

Now he allowed himself to give in to the crying demand of his own body. He moved with a slow rhythmic motion, sheathing himself completely within her with each thrust. She moaned soft, unknowing words of love that filled his heart with the joy of knowing she was as lost in the beauty of their love as he.

After a climax so shattering that even he was shaking, they held each other in silence. Lying side by side, facing each other, legs entwined, Brandon caressed her sweat-moistened face, brushing strands of hair away. "I don't think you can even imagine how very much I love you, Susan."

She sighed in the deepest sense of contentment she had ever known. She buried her face in the hollow of his throat and felt him gently caress her hair.

"Oh, Brandon," she murmured softly. "Will it always be like this for us? So very beautiful I thought I would die?"

"It will be better," he promised. "When I learn what pleases you the most, when I discover all the secrets your body holds. After we're married and we can have all the time together that we want, when we don't have to watch for the eyes of others, we will share such a beauty as there has never been before."

"Now you make me impatient for that day."

"Now," he laughed, "maybe you will understand how I feel when I say the days and weeks are too long."

"Brandon?"

"Yes?"

"I cannot stay away from you until the day we're

457

married. Am I so very terrible to say such things?"

"My precious, you are the greatest thing for a man's ego to come about. Whether it is terrible or not, I hope you continue to say such things for many, many years."

"Do you remember what I said in the garden?"

"About what?"

"About not sharing you with any other. That was before I knew you. Now . . . I think I should kill any woman that tries to take you from me."

"You needn't worry, love," he said teasingly. "Believe me, you are enough woman to satisfy the demands of the most hearty man. And with something like you around, I'll be spending time protecting my home and not have any time to go roaming about outside of it."

"Brandon, do you think we could convince our parents to move our wedding day up a little?"

"I doubt it. They were certainly be suspicious. Then they would concentrate on keeping us apart. I have a much better suggestion."

"What?"

"Why don't we make this place ours. We could meet once in a while."

"What a lovely idea."

Brandon sat up and began searching through his jacket pockets.

"What are you looking for?"

"Found it," he laughed, as he held aloft a small knife whose blade folded back into the handle. He rose to his knees and began to carve into the bark of the huge tree. She knelt beside him and watched. In a few minutes, he heard her soft words of approval. He had carved into the tree "Brandon and Susan—their first home."

458

He looked down into her eyes and his face became serious.

"I love you, Susan, marriage vows or no. This is the first we have found each other. It is as sacred to me as though we were already married. If I ask you, will you come here with me again?"

"You need only call me, Brandon. I will come. Someday we will build a house here and share it. Until then, we will keep this special place to share the love we have."

"Susan," he whispered.

She looked up into his eyes and saw the mirror of her own. "Would she always know this feeling when he looked at her so," she wondered. She closed her eyes as she felt him reach for her. They knelt facing each other, completely aware of each other's needs. His hands slid down her silken skin and rested on her hips holding her hard against him. They kissed, gently at first, but the memories of the past flame was too much for both of them. His arms surrounded her and they seemed to blend together. The length of her body held tightly to the length of his. She laid her head against his chest and closed her eyes to savor more deeply the feel and the taste of him. She did not need to be led now, her hands caressed the broad muscles of his back and slid downward until she held him as tightly against her as he was holding her. She heard the thunder of his heartbeat, felt the wild heated need for her that flew between them like a current. She wanted to cry for sheer joy, to shout to the heavens in exuberant happiness. She might have called out his name, but she wasn't sure, for a hungry mouth captured hers in a blinding kiss that sent whatever senses she had left reeling off into oblivion. She was no longer Susan, she was no longer the gentle creature she had always been. Brandon released the woman from the little girl and now he was surrounded by a blazing whirlwind of woman. He laughed in sheer, deep pleasure as he lay back on the ground and pulled her with him.

It was over an hour later before they mounted their horses and headed back toward Clearhaven. Susan had braided her long hair because the pins were irretrievably lost. They rode along slowly, holding hands and talking together in soft whispers as lovers do. He was reluctant to leave her, but rode home with the happy feeling that one day the waiting would be over and he could keep her with him. Thoughts of having her in his bed for the balance of their lives, of having her all to himself for long nights, sent him home on a cloud of pleasure.

Chapter Forty-Eight

Lucas did his best to spend as much time with Margaret as he could, although he knew she was trying her best to stay away from him. He did not know what troubled her mind, but he was making a determined effort to find out. Whatever memories she was chained to, he intended to release her from them. At every social occasion, he was at her elbow. He arranged chance meetings with John, or Matt and Jason and accepted every invitation to Clearhaven.

The day after their first ride, he went alone to the cabin that had drawn her interest. He pushed open the door and went inside. The place was nearly empty, and looked to him as though it had not been occupied for a long time. He drifted through the rooms, saw the long-extinguished fire in the fireplace and the tangled covers on the bed.

"Why Margaret?" he wondered. "Why here; what drew you here?"

He was about to leave when he saw something gleam near the fireplace. He bent to pick it up. A button, a gold button . . . military. "But," he thought, "the only military people about here had been without uniforms." He had heard the stories so often. No, the only military with fine uniforms were British.

Shadowy pieces began to form in his mind. Margaret had been born in England. Determinedly, he put the button in his pocket, left the cabin, and went to town to inquire into the cabin's ownership. He found that the original owner had long since died and that the house now belonged to the city.

"Has it ever been rented out?" he asked the clerk.

"Off and on for years."

"Can you tell me the names of the people who leased the house for the past . . . let me see . . . about five or six years."

"Could," the clerk said slowly, eyeing Lucas' rich suit and obvious affluent condition, "but that would mean a lot of searchin', take a lot of time."

Lucas grinned and pulled a twenty-dollar gold piece from his pocket. "Will this make the search a little easier?"

The clerk smiled and took the coin without a qualm. Then he reached into a drawer and drew out a book and quickly thumbed through the pages. Finding what he wanted, he replaced the book and went to a shelf that contained several cartons. Lifting down one, he searched through the pages until he found one. Laying it aside, he continued his search until he had a small stack on the table beside him. He replaced the carton and brought the stack of papers to Lucas.

"This here is all the people who've had the place since the owner died."

Lucas took them and began to go through them. There was one name and former address on each slip. None of the names meant a thing to him. Then he reached the next to the last paper and his breath caught. Colonel Mark Severn, Occupation-forces. He read slowly and Margaret's interest in the small house became evident. He could not bring himself to believe Margaret would have a casual affair. There was still much more to this, but he was now at a loss as to who to ask. He could not ask part of her family if Margaret was having an affair with a British officer while her husband was away fighting the same army.

As the weeks moved along, Lucas tried in every way he knew to make Margaret's life more pleasant. He began to notice that he was impressing John and Sarah more favorably. He expertly questioned them and found them quite open on all subjects except Margaret. There they shied away from direct answers. It did no more than increase his desire to learn what was being kept such a deep dark secret.

Margaret stepped down from her buggy. She was doing some last-minute shopping for the engagement party of Brandon and Susan. It would have been a job left for Sarah, but Margaret had insisted. She wanted to get away not only from Clearhaven for a day but also from the always imminent threat of the unannounced appearance of Lucas. That Lucas was falling in love with her was obvious. She did not want to hurt him, but she knew she could not give what Lucas wanted. That he was a kind and gentle man only made matters worse. She felt he deserved something much better. There was no way for her to tell him that she loved another man. A man she would never see again. That when she slept, she dreamed of Mark, that she could close her eyes in the middle of the day and feel the touch of his hands or the taste of his lips on hers. She had found it completely impossible to erase Mark from her heart and she would not give herself to another man knowing that part of her would always be locked away from him. It was not fair to Lucas and she vowed it would never be allowed to happen.

She spent over three hours going from store to store, making her purchases and delivering orders for the foods to be delivered the day of the party. Purchasing her last item on her list, she walked back to her buggy, only to stop a few feet away as she saw Lucas leaning against it, watching her approach. Lucas came to her and took the packages she was carrying.

"I'll put these in the back of the buggy for you." He did so, then helped her inside. "You know, it will be close to dark before you get home. I'm going to tie my horse to the back of the buggy and ride out with you."

"That's not necessary, Lucas. I'm not afraid. Besides, I have something I have to talk to John about and this is as good a time as any."

Before she could raise any more protests, he walked to his horse, brought him to the buggy, tied him to the rear and climbed in beside her. He lifted the reins and expertly wheeled the buggy around and headed it toward the road to Clearhaven. They rode along in silence for a few minutes. He had waited patiently for the opportunity to get Margaret alone, somewhere where she could not run from him. "Are you all prepared for the party," he began. It was nothing remotely resembling what he wanted to say.

"Yes. I think we're quite prepared. I'm happy for Susan. Brandon seems to be a nice young man."

"He is. Susan would have to look far to find a better man than Brandon. I'm proud to say I've had a little to do with his upbringing."

Margaret looked at him. His profile against the early evening sky was softened. "He is a very handsome man," she thought. "It would be easy to care for him. I truly wish the best for him. I wonder why no woman before this has brought him around to thinking of marriage."

Again several minutes passed before they spoke. Now they had left the town. About a half mile from town the road separated, and one road led to Clearhaven and the other was a narrow, untravelled dirt road that had once been used to service a mine in the hills. Since the mine had petered out, the road had not been used for years. As they reached the "Y"in the road, Lucas quickly pulled the reins and in a minute they were headed down the deserted road.

"Lucas, what are you doing? I must get back to Clearhaven."

"I want to talk to you and I can't get you alone anyplace else. You," he smiled at her, "have been hiding behind your family. I guess I have to make it temporary kidnapping just to get you alone for a few minutes."

There was nothing she could do outside of leaping from the carriage, and she was entirely too proud to do that. There was no way she was going to allow him to have any idea that her heart thudded nervously and that she was actually a little frightened of him. They went a good distance down the road before he pulled the buggy off the road beneath the shade of a tree, tied the reins carefully and turned to look at her. The half shadows of early evening cast across her face. The wide eyes and tremulous mouth told him without words that she was afraid. Her hands clasped tightly together in her lap and he reached out and covered them with his huge hand.

"For God's sake, Margaret, don't be frightened of me. You know I wouldn't hurt you."

She lifted her eyes to his and they held for a moment, then he said softly, "It's not me you're afraid of, is it? . . . It's yourself?" He cupped her face in his hand and

465

lifted it so she could not look away.

"I want you, Margaret," he said softly. "I want you to marry me. I want to try to erase that lonely lost little girl look from your eyes, I want the chance to try and make you happy."

She closed her eyes and the hot tears stung them and fell down her cheeks. "Don't you understand, Lucas. You are a fine man and I do not want to hurt you, but I cannot . . . I cannot."

"Why, because there is someone else?"

"No."

"Then why?"

"Because I do not love you, Lucas and a man as warm and loving as you should have a woman who loves him, who can give him herself completely."

"I didn't ask you to love me, Margaret. I asked to let me love you, to let me help you through whatever it is that has caused you such pain. In time maybe you could learn to love me a little. At least give me the chance to try."

"Lucas, how very unfair, how very unkind. To take comfort from you, to expect you to give without expecting a return."

"I've never expected fairness from the world, Margaret, just as I've never expected kindness. I have enough love to last the both of us and enough confidence that, given a chance, I think I could make your life happy, and that would make me happy."

"Everything is so confused in my mind. I must have some time to think."

"Fair enough. But while you're thinking it over, I want you to remember this." His hands spanned her waist and he lifted her on to his lap, ignoring her sounds of protest.

Her arms were pinioned to her side as he put one arm about her. With the other hand, he held her face immobile as he kissed her. Surprisingly, Lucas' lips were gentle on hers. There was no doubt that he was an expert in this field for despite Margaret's firm efforts, the kiss stirred her. He knew she was a woman of deep passions, just as he knew it had been a long time since she had been able to vent these passions. Slowly, his mouth grew more demanding and forced hers apart.

His large hand caressed her body gently. She began to fight him and it pleased him for he knew she was not immune to the feeling he was getting from the kiss. It was enough for him for now. He lifted his head from hers and looked into her eyes. There he saw the knowledge that she was also hungry for love.

Gently, he deposited her back on the seat beside him, for he knew that if he held her any longer he would not stop until he possessed her, and that, he knew, would destroy all his future plans.

He kissed the corner of her lips and smiled, "I'll be patient. You think about it, but try to remember how much I care for you. We could have a lot of good years in our future or we could both spend them alone and lonely. I'll wait until after Susan's party. After that, there is no reason we can't begin to plan a future of our own. Will you answer me then?"

"Yes, Lucas, I'll answer you then."

He smiled as he released her. Just before he picked up the reins, he said softly, "Remember, Margaret, I love you."

He slapped the reins against the horse's rump and they rode in silence back to Clearhaven.

At Clearhaven, Margaret immediately went to her

room while Lucas went in search of John, who seemed to be nowhere on the Clearhaven property. Finally, he was told by one of the workers that John was at the location where he was building his house. Asking quick directions, Lucas mounted quickly, for with the questions he had to ask, it suited his purpose that he talked to John alone.

He found John packing his equipment into the wagon in preparation for coming home to Clearhaven. It was close to dark and for a moment John couldn't tell who was approaching. Then, he became a little curious as to why Lucas Olivier would seek him out. Deep inside, he felt he might know his reasons.

"John, I'm glad I found you before you left for Clearhaven. I have something to talk to you about and I'd rather it be kept between the two of us."

"Step down," John smiled as he waved his hand toward the house that was almost three-quarters finished. "Come on in and I'll show you around the McMahon Mansion."

Lucas followed him from room to room as John escorted him with deep pride through the house he had built with his own hands. They sat on the steps of the front porch. "Lucas, I know you didn't just come over here to see the house. What's on your mind?"

"John," Lucas began hesitantly, then he resolutely continued, "I've asked Margaret to marry me."

John looked at him in silence for a moment then he said softly, "Did she accept?"

"Not exactly, but then she didn't refuse exactly either."

"Lucas you didn't come over here just to tell me this. I'm sure you could have told me any time. What is it you want from me?"

Lucas sat contemplating the night for several minutes, while John remained silent and waited.

"Who," Lucas said, so softly that John could barely hear, "is Colonel Mark Severn?"

John jumped in surprise. "How the hell did you know about Mark?"

"Suffice it to say I have ways of finding out what I want."

"Then why didn't you find out about him yourself?"

"Because others might have told me all about the man, the officer, the career . . . I just want to know what he meant to Margaret, and . . ." his voice softened, "what he still means."

"At any other time I might have told you to mind your own business, but I know what Margaret has been through these past few years. She deserves a little happiness if she can get it. I'll tell you the story, Lucas." John proceeded to tell Lucas everything, and Lucas sat in silence and listened until John was completely finished. When he was done, Lucas cursed violently . . . passionately.

"If he were dead, I could defeat his memory. But he's a ghost. How does one go about fighting a ghost that might reappear some day and steal his life?"

"Listen to me, Lucas. Sarah wrote to Mark a long time ago and she even followed that letter with another. Neither received any response. In the letter she told Mark if he chose not to come, she would understand. It is obvious he has chosen not to return. Sarah never told her about the letters, but for the sake of Margaret's happiness, she will if you think it is necessary. Mark Severn, as far as I'm concerned, is a stupid man to have made such a choice, but now at least you no longer have to be afraid of him. He will never return."

"No, don't show her the letter. If he does not come back, I will one day convince her to marry me. I'll make her happy, John, that I swear. And we need never mention Mark Severn's name again."

"I won't lie to you, Lucas. I know, better than anyone, how much Margaret loved Mark. The shadows of that love will remain a long, long time. I would even have sworn that he loved her as much. I couldn't quite believe he did not even bother to answer, but it fills me with anger to think he discarded that letter so easily. From now on Margaret's welfare is my utmost concern."

"And mine, John. Time will help heal some of the wounds and I will help heal the others."

John didn't know for sure if he had done the right thing or not, but as he rode back to Clearhaven beside Lucas and listened to his plans, he tried his best to push aside the elusive shadow of worry, but it still nagged him as he watched Lucas ride away from Clearhaven.

The day of the party finally came. The family gathered resplendent in dress and overflowing with wishes of happiness for Susan and Brandon, who gave evidence of being completely in that state already. That Brandon and Susan had shared stolen afternoons in the shade of their tree was a secret of beauty that made them both glow.

Matt and Jason were the first to arrive with Deborah and Deanna. It was John who played host, for neither Sarah nor Margaret was ready. Susan had been in her room all afternoon preparing, for she wanted to look her absolute best when Brandon arrived.

"Come and have something to drink," John invited. They were sipping drinks and talking when Vern and

Caroline arrived, and it was only a few minutes later that Cat and Deeta appeared, accompanied by David. Deeta's creamy beauty had been enhanced both by her obvious glow of love and her ability now to dress as the others. Her long dark hair had been braided and wrapped about her head in a shining coronet. She wore a dress of deep wine color. Its simplicity accentuated her amazingly beautiful figure. Only the soft full roundness of her breasts gave any evidence of pregnancy, and only Cat knew for certain. When they came in, it was Jason who remarked to the rest of the group "Deeta is truly a very beautiful woman."

"She certainly is, Jas," Deborah agreed. "I'm glad she is free, happy . . . and has Cat."

"Yes," Matt agreed. "This slavery business is getting out of hand. The whole institution of slavery upsets me, not to mention the idea of Cat and Deeta ever being one."

"Speaking of that, is there any more news of our thieves?" Jason asked.

"No," John responded. "The Governor, along with the rest of us, think they've moved on. He lifted the ban today and called all the guards in."

"Do you really think they're gone?"

"It's been a long time since anyone was taken," John replied. "I think we're safe now."

"Sold," mused Jason. "I just could not imagine people the caliber of Cat and Deeta being sold like so much cattle. It's a touchy idea and I wouldn't be surprised if one day it didn't brew into a kettle of trouble for this country."

"I shouldn't want to be a part of it. It could turn into a nasty affair."

Cat and Deeta came over to join them and heard the

471

last remark.

"What nasty affair?" Cat questioned.

"We were thinking about our thieves," Matt replied. "And that brought up the whole subject of slavery."

"Well, you're right about one thing. Slavery is a nasty affair. But there are different circumstances to it," Cat replied. "I never really thought of myself as a slave, either to your father or to you, Matt. But Deeta has seen a different side of it. So I guess it's not only in ownership, but in man's inhumanity to man."

Their conversation was interrupted by the arrival of Sarah and Margaret. Immediately after their entrance the guests began to arrive. Susan was nervously watching out her window for the Governor's carriage and her heart leapt into her throat when she saw it coming up the drive. She ran to her bedroom door and down the hall to the top of the stairs, and there she stopped and composed herself until she felt in control of her wayward body's remembrance. Slowly she walked down the stairs to meet Brandon, who, as always, marvelled at the cool beauty who had been a woman of intense flame in his arms only a few hours before.

Armed with the knowledge of Margaret's past, Lucas became more patient and relaxed. By hard and painful experience, he knew that one could not forget a love that easily. When his presence became less forceful, less demanding, Margaret relaxed more too, and it pleased not only all her family but Lucas as well when they saw the smile reappear and even heard her laughter, unrestrained and without fear. Susan gloried in this very special night as guests from near and far came to wish her and her future husband well.

Margaret and Lucas were dancing together and for the

472

first time Lucas saw her smile at him hesitantly, as though she were thoroughly enjoying herself. Lucas chuckled as he looked around the room.

"What is funny?"

"David seems to be enjoying himself. I imagine Cat and Deeta are going to have to carry him home, and I'll bet he isn't laughing so heartily tomorrow."

"Lucas, do you believe Cat and Deeta are safe now?"

"Oh, I think so. There's been no sign of anything and the area has been searched pretty thoroughly."

"Maybe I should just insist that David stay here at home tonight."

"I wouldn't do that. Let him make the decision on his own. The boy is proud. You wouldn't want him to think he's hiding behind mama's skirts, would you?"

"No, of course not."

"That works in reverse to you, you know," he said softly.

"Meaning," she replied, "that you think I'm hiding behind my family . . . that I'm afraid of life."

He shrugged, "I didn't say that."

"But you implied it."

"Yes, I guess I did. Why don't you answer it . . . honestly?"

Margaret looked both at Lucas and into herself, something she had refused to do since Paul had died. Her guilt at being with Mark when Paul should have had all her faith and devotion still ate at her. Now, in the two years since Paul's death, she had dedicated herself only to the welfare of her family.

"Maybe you are right, Lucas," she said gently, "but I can't help myself right now. I need the safety of my family."

"Margaret, it is meant to be in life that children leave their parents and make a life of their own. That is the way it should be. David will marry one day and no matter how much they love you, it does not fill an empty house or an empty bed. I told you before that I have enough love for both of us. Why don't you give me a chance to prove myself. What have you got to look forward to in the future that is better than what I have to offer."

"You said you would give me time."

"Time is a friend or time is an enemy. With children, like Brandon and Susan, it is a friend, but when you stand on the threshold of your golden years it is an enemy. It will steal everything away from you one day when you're not looking and you'll be left with emptiness. You are too sweet and too valuable for me to let that happen."

Lucas stopped dancing and tucked Margaret's hand under his arm and led her outside where they could be alone. "Margaret, let me try to fill the empty places."

"Lucas, what do you want of me!" she cried softly.

"I want you to stop fighting me. I want you to reach out to me. I want you to stop looking backward and face the future with me."

"I'm so confused," she said gently. "I don't know anymore what is right or wrong. What have you done to me, Lucas. I was fine until you came into my life. You have upset everything. All the rest of my life was organized, I knew where I was going. I knew what the future would be."

"Good," he said with a smile. "At least I've shaken you from that cold little shell you were hiding in. Maybe . . . maybe with time you'll come out into the sun again."

He put his arms about her and hesitantly, she put her arms around his neck and lifted her lips for his kiss.

Lucas had known too many women not to know that Margaret was a warm, passionate one. His kiss was a gentle thing, a kiss that told her he would wait for her for as long as it took. Without the demand and the pressure, she relaxed in his arms and he felt his blood flow thickly through him as her body blended against his. There was a hesitancy there, as if a fear still existed, but it was a good beginning. Slowly, he parted her lips with his and his hands caressed her. She stirred in his arms and stepped back from him. "Lucas," she began, her voice thick with tears.

"Shhh," he said softly as he reached out and touched her face with his fingertips. "It is all right, my dear. I understand. I'm happy to know you are not completely insensitive to me. It's enough for now, and we will go on from here. I am a patient man, Margaret and when I find everything I've always wanted, I will do nothing to jeopardize it, nor will I stop until I possess what I want."

"You are a devil in my life, Lucas," she smiled.

"Oh, madam," Lucas laughed heartily, "you have not seen the devil in me, yet. Prepare yourself, my sweet, for one day you will meet the devil aroused and you will understand that you are the only one who can contain him. Come and kiss me one more time, then I will let you escape temporarily to see to your guests," he grinned, then changed his expression to an evil lear as he reached for her. She laughed as she felt the firm strength of his hard arms gather her to him. His mouth was hungry for hers and the kiss almost drove him to the edge of precipice he was not as yet ready to see.

He released her, and with a gallant gesture offered her his arm. She took it, grateful that he did not know how her body trembled in sudden want, in remembrance of the passionate woman she had always been.

They rejoined the party that was now at its best. Everyone had partaken both of food and drink until they were in mellow moods. Even Cat, who usually abstained from drinking too much, was in an exuberant mood. He danced with Deeta, holding her close and whispering suggestions in her ear until the light sound of her laughter could be heard.

David was past any other feeling but complete euphoria. "Tonight," he thought expansively, "I am pleased with everything and everyone." He toasted the engagement of Susan and Brandon so often that everyone was laughingly betting he would not last through too many more. They were right. When the last guest left, Cat, weaving on his own feet, carried David to his buggy and collapsed within. Deeta lifted the reins, bid everyone good night and headed their buggy toward home.

Chapter Forty-Nine

Deeta drove the buggy slowly toward home while David reposed in the back seat and Cat sang her love ballads and tried to kiss her.

"Cat," she giggled, "will you behave. You're going to frighten the horses with your wailing and moving about."

"Wailing!" he cried and pressed his hand over his heart. "You have wounded me fatally, woman of my life. I am singing you my love song and you laugh."

"I wouldn't be laughing at your love songs if you weren't also acting like a bear in heat."

Cat tightened both arms about her and nuzzled her throat while she helplessly clung to the reins to keep the horses from bolting.

"A bear in heat," he said against her throat. He deposited several random kisses while his hands found delectably soft parts of her body. "If a man didn't come in heat around you, he would have to be dead."

His hands slid down over the small roundness of her belly and caressed it gently. "My child, he lies there asleep," he laughed. "When we get home I think I shall awaken him."

Deeta laughed, but reserved her thoughts on what Cat would be capable of doing once he lay down. They arrived at the cabin and Cat urged David out of the buggy and inside, where he proceeded to collapse on the love couch in front of the fireplace. Cat and Deeta stabled the horses and put the buggy away then half supporting half guiding Cat, they made their way back inside.

"Cat," Deeta whispered, "shall we get him up and make him go to bed?"

Cat was, at the time, more interested in getting Deeta to bed than he was David. Taking her by the hand, he drew her toward the bedroom. "Let him sleep where he is. In his condition, it really doesn't matter, and in the morning he's going to be miserable wherever he is."

Once inside the bedroom, Cat closed the door behind him. There was no light, but neither of them cared at the moment for Deeta was enclosed in his arms and being kissed rather thoroughly by a man she had thought too drunk to accomplish anything.

"Ummm," he murmured. "You taste sweeter every day." He held her face between his huge hands and tried to see her in the pale shafts of moonlight that came through the window.

"Do you know what you mean to me, Deeta. You are the center of my world. You are the beat of my heart, the flow of my blood. I love you more than my own life. If I had to sacrifice it to spend an hour with you, I would. I want you to know how very much you've changed my life. Existence without you would be an unthinkable thing now."

He touched her lips with his over and over again until the magical heat of him blended with hers and began to lift her with him. Her arms slid about him and he rocked her gently against him savoring the sweetness of the lips that seemed as hungry for him as he was for her. He removed her clothes, and bathed in the pale light she

478

seemed to him to be a goddess of beauty. He lifted her in his arms and held her for awhile, and amid her sighs of pleasure his lips touched one passion-hardened nipple and then the other. He laid her on the bed, and joined her there. Deeta gasped in surprised pleasure as his mouth began a slow discovery of her body. She was like bitter-sweet honey and he wanted to taste. He found places on her body that stirred her so that she groped for him with her hands to hold him there. But he eluded her and his lips travelled on to more sensitive areas until with a pounding heart he heard her irrational and passionate words of love and felt her body lift in search of him. He touched the soft inner flesh of her thighs with lips that seared her flesh, then lifting her slender hips in his huge hands, he held her writhing body while his lips found the center of her need. Moaning, whimpering sighs sounded softly in the night.

Deeta knew nothing except the hands that held her and the lips that drew forth a fiery need for him that she could not control. Her body was a hot searing flame; a flame of pale yellow, brilliant red, deep blue that licked at her soul and sent it winging away into the night leaving her ablaze, twisting her body in search of the fulfillment that would quench it. He heard her call out his name, felt her seeking hands and body that cried out with a fire as deep as his own. With superhuman control, he slowed himself, and again his hands and lips moved over her body. Her hands grasped him and he did not even feel her nails as they clung, trying to pull him within her. Her body trembled like a leaf in a hurricane. He lay back on the bed and pulled her over him, and a deep sense of sensual pleasure filled his mind as the dark cloud of her hair fell about him and he buried his face between her breasts and lowered her until their bodies joined. For one heart-rending moment, they were both stilled with the tremendous wave of blinding passion that devoured them. Then their bodies began to move in easy stroking motion. Completely in tune with each other. Their rhythm increased until they reached a peak of blinding completion. Deeta gasped and lay upon him, and neither of them had the strength to move. Cat kept his eyes closed with one arm binding her to him and the other gently stroking her sweat-slicked body.

Cat chuckled and murmured softly, "If that didn't wake my son, he is past waking."

Deeta giggled and curled herself even tighter against him, her head against his chest. They drifted off into sleep so, each of them too content to move. The night lengthened and the moon crept lower and lower in the sky. Then came that moment of total darkness, that moment when the moon was gone and the sun had not risen. The moment when evil lifted its hand to strike.

None of the occupants of the small cabin heard the stealthy footsteps on the porch nor the gentle touch of experienced hands that opened the door. Three shadowy forms crept inside. Two of them went toward the bedroom and the other went to David's side. He stood beside the couch and leveled his gun at the sleeping form.

At the bedroom door, Jake and Bib stood for a moment and listened. Assured that no one was awake, they gently pushed the door open and went inside. Then they moved quickly, efficiently and with deadly purpose. Jake struck a flint to light the lantern at the same moment Bib grasped Deeta and jerked her from the bed, holding her slender half-awake form with one arm while he held his gun to her head and looked with an evil grin on his face at a rousing Cat. Cat blinked his eyes open at Deeta's sudden withdrawal and saw her being held.

With a half-wild roar, he jerked upright, preparing to attack.

"I wouldn't be too hasty, friend," Jake drawled. "Unless you want your pretty little woman smeared all over the walls."

Cat froze, his cold eyes closely watching Bib. He licked his dry lips when the full realization came upon him. "Deeta," he thought. "Deeta in the hands of these two animals."

Jake could see that despite his warning, Cat was steeling himself to attack. He took the step that separated them, for Cat's full attention was on Bib and Deeta. With a quick movement, he raised his gun and struck Cat a blow that knocked him to the floor completely senseless. Deeta screamed once before Bib's hand closed over her mouth.

David struggled up from a deep, heavy sleep. Some shrill sound reached his consciousness. He blinked his eyes open and looked in blank disbelief at the man who stood beside him grinning and holding a gun just inches from his face. With the combination of his drinking the night before and wakening so suddenly, it took a few minutes for what was happening to register. The realization that it was Deeta's scream jolted him into action, and he began to rise from the couch. His head pounded furiously and his stomach churned with nausea. Still, he managed to get on his feet.

"Stay put, sonny," the man laughed harshly. "Your friends will be out in a minute."

"Deeta!" David shouted ignoring the man. "Deeta! Cat! One of you answer me, are you all right?"

481

No sound came from the other room and David's fear grew. Then the door opened and Cat staggered out, his temple dripping blood over the side of his face and his hands and arms tied firmly with enough rope to hold ten men. Deeta was pushed out behind him followed by Bib and Jake.

David went to Deeta's side and put his arm about her. She was shaking so badly he could feel the vibration in his arm, but her eyes were on Cat, who was still dazed from the blow. "What do you want?" David snapped. "This is the stupidest thing you will ever do in your lives. You're going to have every man in the area after you."

"Don't you fret none, sonny," the man who'd wakened David replied. "We'll be long gone from here before your family even knows what happened."

"They'll follow you. You'll never get away with this. Cat and Deeta have a lot of friends around here."

"We're about to teach your friends not to be nigger-lovers, and make a nice piece of change too. We'll sell the big buck to some cotton grower who will teach him what work is. And the gal . . ." he laughed. "There's a nice house in Louisiana that will be glad to buy a gal that looks like her." Cat's huge frame trembled in a burst of rage and David's face went white. "He would die," he thought, "before he would let Deeta be used so."

"We have to take you along for a ways. We was hopin' you'd finally give up, but since you ain't got the sense to give up, you'll just have to travel with us a ways."

"For a ways?" David questioned softly.

"Well, you ain't very valuable to us. Before we get where we're goin' we'll set you free."

David smiled, for he knew they had no intention of

him ever being freed. His hands were tied. They were taken outside and forced up on horses. Both his and Cat's hands were bound to the pommel. Deeta was put in front of Bib on his horse and the other two, mounting, took Cat and David's reins and moved away.

Cat's eyes never left Deeta, who was directly in front of them. He watched with gritting teeth as Bib took the opportunity to fondle Deeta leisurely. The other men paid no attention to Deeta's muffled sounds of protest. At one time, the sound of ripping cloth came to them.

The first break of dawn found them already far from the cabin. They rode swiftly. There was no pause to eat at noontime and they only stopped for seconds when Bib insisted he had a call of nature. They were all taken aside to find comfort, Bib drew Deeta into the bushes and soon the sounds of a struggle were accented by a yelp of anguish and the sound of a hard slap. "Get that girl out here, Bib," Jake called. "We have to put more distance between us before they find out they're gone."

Bib came out dragging Deeta, his face red and angry. The outline of his hand was raised in welts across Deeta's face.

"Damn bitch, kicked me, right where it hurts most."

Jake laughed. "Serves you right. Leave her alone before that big buck breaks those ropes. The way he's been lookin' at you, Bib, if he got loose, I wouldn't give you two cents for your life."

Bib gulped and cast a quick look at Cat. Assured his ropes were tight, he remounted and drew Deeta up in front of him. The front of the cotton dress they had forced on her in the cabin had been torn open. As if to push Cat, he watched Cat's face as he slid his hand inside her dress and slowly caressed her. Deeta writhed in his arms and Cat's eyes blazed in a look of deep hatred that Bib could see. He withdrew his hand and urged his horse forward and they were on their way.

Except for occasionally resting the horses, they ate while they rode, and they travelled all that day, the following night, and all the next day. Satisfied that they had enough of a start, Jake called a halt the second night. They lit a fire and ate the first cooked meal. David was still too angry and too afraid for Deeta to eat until Cat nudged him.

"Eat, David," he said softly. "We'll need the strength." David saw his logic. If they were weak and an opportunity arose they would not have the strength to get Deeta away. He choked down as much of the ill-cooked food that his stomach would tolerate.

Cat looked at Jake, who returned his gaze without a sound. "You, you're the boss here?"

Jake shrugged. "Second in command. The boss will meet us later to take you off our hands."

"My woman," Cat said softly. "She's carrying a child. Don't let him hurt her. Let her lie next to me when we sleep," he watched the flicker in Jake's eyes. "I'm beggin' you," he added softly.

"You can have her," Jake said.

"Jake! Damn you!" Bib said. "I'm keepin' her with me."

"Jesus, Bib, the girl's pregnant."

"Who the hell cares. I've ridden some with rounder bellies than she's got."

"I said," Jake commanded in a cold hard voice, "put the girl down next to him and go to bed. We got a long

484

hard ride for the next two days."

Bib had never had the courage to go against Jake. Angrily, he thrust Deeta down beside Cat. She immediately pressed herself as close to Cat as she could get.

"Deeta," Cat said, "loop your arms over my head." Her hands, bound together, came up and she put them over his head, laying her head in the hollow of his throat with a deep trembling sigh. The strain she had been under all day was too much for her, and although she made no sound, Cat could feel the hot tears fall against his skin.

David lay down on the other side of Deeta just to make sure Bib could not get near her for the rest of the night. David slept fitfully, Deeta slept from exhaustion, but Cat lay awake, a cold burning hatred glowing in his eyes that never left Bib for a moment.

The next morning they were awakened just before dawn. Bib gloatingly pulled Deeta away from Cat and amid her silent tears, he drew her up on the horse in front of him. Another day, another night passed. On the fifth night they were camped and settled when Jake began to make preparations for leaving. He ordered the third man to come with him and they rode away from the camp.

Bib sat in front of the fire and ate slowly. Deeta lay a few feet away from Cat because Jake had not had them placed together before they left. Cat, his eyes watchful, knew without a doubt he was reading Bib's mind. He knew what an evil course the man's mind ran in. Sweat beaded his body as he strained against the bonds. Bib wiped his greasy hands on his shirt and slowly rose from the fire. He walked toward Cat and squatted down in front of him. He reached out and tested the ropes that held the huge man. Secure in the knowledge that they were tight, he went over and tested David's. They too were secure.

Bib chuckled as again he squatted down in front of Cat. "Too bad you're all tied up like that. Your little girl over there's probably all hot and ready for a man. Now," he said in mock sympathy, "since you can't do anything about it, I feel it's my duty to make the little lady happy."

Cat writhed helplessly against his bonds. "You bastard, if you lay a hand on her, I will let you take a long long time to die."

"Bucko, you ain't goin' to do nothin'. When Jake gets back we're splittin' you up. You go one way, the girl goes the other. We'll have her sold to a place where those pretty round curves of hers will be appreciated."

Cat went to reply, but the words were cut short as Bib stuffed a rag in his mouth. Bib rose and went to David. He jerked his head back and stuffed a rag in his mouth.

Bib walked slowly toward Deeta, who lay in deep exhausted sleep. With one foot, he nudged her. Slowly her eyes blinked open and she looked up at the face that hovered over her. With a cry of terror she tried to crawl toward Cat, but felt herself lifted bodily from the ground and held in a strong grip. Her hands bound in front of her and Bib's arm about her waist, she twisted helplessly in his arms. With deliberate pleasure he tore the dress from her, watching Cat's face. He let his hand roam over Deeta with slow leisurely caresses. He reached around and took hold of Deeta's arms and jerked them above her head. Moving around in front of her, he smiled at her. Deeta kicked out at him and he slapped her so hard that had he not been holding her, she would have fallen. "You, my pretty, are going to learn your first lesson in obedience.

Where you are goin', they are goin' to want you well trained, and I'm just the one to do it."

He gripped Deeta's face with one hand and planted a kiss that ended in a yelp of pain as Deeta sank her teeth in his lips. Now Bib was furious. He released her arms and she almost fell. While she was still unsteady, he slapped her again and again, until she sank to her knees. She looked up at him, her body weaving back and forth. He reached down and gripped her by the hair and struck her again. With a soft moan, Deeta collapsed on the ground. Bib knelt beside her, his brutal hands moving over her with feverish haste, squeezing and pinching. Then he stood up and grasping the rope that held her hands together, he lifted her up. Her efforts to battle were feeble now, but that was not what brought the tears to Cat's eyes nor the moaning sounds from his throat. It was the thin red trickles of blood that were running down Deeta's legs.

Bib dragged her to the limits of the fire's light, then threw her to the ground and tied her arms to a small tree over her head. David closed his eyes, the hot tears falling, for he could not bear to see Deeta's loveliness violated.

Bib fell upon her, thrusting himself deeply within her with a satisfied grunt. The thin, mournful wail that escaped from Deeta's throat was echoed by Cat. The sound was an eerie and mournful scream that sounded like a wild animal dying. Temporarily satisfied, Bib stood up. He walked away, leaving Deeta where she lay. She was still, like a broken doll . . . and deadly quiet.

Bib looked across the leaping flames of the fire at Cat and David, and for the first time felt a real fear that began deep in his vitals and blossomed out through his body,

487

leaving him weak. He walked back over to Deeta's side and saw the small pool of blood that was forming beneath her. Panic struck him then. If the girl died, Jake would kill him. He went back to David. "The girl needs tending to. If I untie you, you see to her. One false move out of you and I'll kill your friend."

David nodded, frantic to get to Deeta's side. The ropes cut loose, he crawled over to her. There was no doubt in his mind that she was losing the child she was carrying. He tore off his shirt and tried to stop the flow of blood. Then his heart came to a shattering stop as he looked at Deeta's face. Her eyes were wide open and blank of any expression. "Deeta," he said softly. She gave no answer. He laid his head against her breast and heard her heart beating heavily. "Deeta," he repeated, but there was no reaction. It was as if she existed in another world . . . a world safe from the pain and shame that had been inflicted on her. He knew Cat was watching him and he felt so inadequate, so helpless. Two people that he loved more than life and he did not know what to do to help them. He crawled back over to Cat, a Cat who seemed cool and unemotional.

"Cat," he whispered frantically, "she's losing the baby. What can I do?"

There was a slight quiver of the muscle in Cat's cheek but it was the only sign of anger that he showed. In a quiet controlled voice, he began to give David instructions. Through the night, David labored and sweated to save Deeta, and when the morning came, she slept and David fell down exhausted by Cat. Cat remained motionless, his eyes never leaving Bib's face for a second as though he wanted to imprint on his mind everything about the man. Bib retied David and went to Deeta's side. She lay curled in a small ball, covered with a blanket.

"Not much of a woman who can't take a little riding. She'll probably die young. Where she's goin', they'll get a lot more from her than that." He spat and walked into the bushes to relieve himself.

David crawled to Deeta's side and called out her name gently . . . but still no answer . . . he called out again, bending a little closer. She remained quiet and still. Pulling back the blanket from her face, a small cry of pain escaped him. She lay as she had the night before, with her eyes wide and unseeing, while her breathing was low and regular. He was frantic to reach her in some way. Gently he shook her shoulder, but he might as well not have existed. Deeta had escaped into a quiet world and he did not know how to find her. The sound of approaching hoof-beats drew his attention, and in a few minutes Jake came riding up alone.

Jake dismounted and looked about him, a puzzled frown on his face. "Where's Bib?" he asked David.

David's pain, rage and helplessness boiled to the surface. "Damn you, you unfeeling bastard. You left her alone with him last night. You knew what he'd do, what kind of a pig he was. I'll kill you," he shouted, and ignoring the fact that his hands were tied together, he attacked Jake, who calmly struck him with his fist and knocked him on the ground. Beyond reason now, David leapt to his feet and flew at Jake again. Jake stepped aside, and this time he struck David with all the force he had, knocking him to his knees. Another blow and David fell unconscious. Jake looked at him lying in the dirt, then walked over to Deeta. Kneeling beside her he looked at her for several minutes, then he stood up and went to Cat, who had not said a word since the minute Deeta had lost the baby. "I gave Bib instructions not to touch the girl. What went on here last night?"

Cat's voice was controlled and even, yet it was a voice so filled with death that even Jake moved back from him despite the fact that Cat was tied so firmly.

"The beast that you left unchained last night took the life of my child and the soul of my wife." The voice was so frozen and calm that Jake felt a shiver of icy fingers up his back. "For this he will pay a price his mind cannot imagine. You are the one who unchained him. You are the one who knew what he was. It is you that must pay the greater price." Cat's voice had softened and his eyes held Jake's in a mesmerizing grip. "You will pray to die long before I finish with you."

Jake was afraid. A man tied and helpless, and he was afraid and he knew it . . . Worse, he knew Cat knew it, too.

Bib reappeared and Jake rose to face him. "Bib," he said softly, "you son-of-a-bitch. I told you not to touch the girl. What the hell's the matter with you?"

"Chris' sake, she's only one nigger in a bunch. What does she mean to you, anyhow? We'll sell 'em both and get rid of them. You gettin' soft again, Jake?"

Jake was at his side in a minute. He grabbed Bib by the front of his shirt and shook him as a dog would shake a small animal. He spoke in a low guttural voice between clenched teeth. "I ought to kill you. What do you think she's worth to any buyer that way?"

"Then sell her with the buck. He can take care of her." Jake looked at him in disgust and shoved him away from him so violently that Bib sprawled on the ground. Jake

490

turned back to Cat, followed by a glazed look of pure hatred from Bib. Jake knelt again in front of Cat. "I had no intention for anything like this to happen. It was a mistake to leave him here with her, and I'm sorry, but there ain't nothin' I can do about it now except sell the two of you together. You can keep her with you and take care of her. She'll be all right."

Cat said nothing and his haunted eyes simply looked at Jake in remorseless hate. Jake felt a new kind of fear. David, who had crawled over to Deeta and sat holding her hand, watched him unblinkingly. Cat's eyes never left him, and he already knew Bib could turn on him at any time. All he wanted to do was to get rid of them all as soon as possible. He turned to Bib. "Get up and pack our things. We'll be just outside Wilmington tomorrow night. We'll slip past it and they'll be waiting for us. We'll sell the both of them to Glazer and he'll take 'em on the three rivers. They'll hold them there for a couple of weeks then ship 'em down the river."

"Glazer gonna give us our money?"

"Yeah, and you're gettin' one-third instead of one-half. You forced us to sell her cheap so you take the loss."

Bib glared at him but did not answer. Both Cat and David absorbed everything that was said. It wasn't much but at least they knew where they were, where they were headed, and the fact that they could keep Deeta with them. Then David's thoughts came to an abrupt halt. "What are you gonna do with that kid?"

"We don't have no choice, he knows too much. We got to get rid of him. Tomorrow night before we cross the border, you can dump him."

"Good. I'll take care of him and bury him deep. They'll never find a trace of him."

Cat and David looked at each other. The deep lump in his throat kept David from speaking, but he saw the look of understanding in Cat's eyes.

He closed his eyes and held Deeta's hand while he silently prayed . . . first to his God . . . and then to Deeta's.

Chapter Fifty

Cat refused to let his mind think of his and Deeta's future. His body was one deep, flowing pain from the loss of blood circulation. He could barely move. He knew that if he wanted to be of help to David or Deeta, he had to get his body under control. Somehow, he had to get these ropes off of him.

"Jake," he called. Jake came over to his side.

"What do you want?"

"You've got to loosen some of these ropes. My blood is stopping. I won't be of any value to anyone in the condition I'll be in tomorrow."

Jake contemplated the truth of this statement. Cat had been tied for days. "I'll tell you what. Bib is goin' to sit right by the girl with his gun against her head. I'll take some of those ropes off. If you try anything, we'll kill her."

"No," Cat said gently, "I wouldn't leave Deeta with you. It's not time yet, but when the time does come," he laughed a mirthless laugh, "you will be the first to know."

"Bib," Jake said, angry that he was still afraid of Cat. "Sit by the girl. If he makes one false move, kill her."

Bib did as he was told and Jake pulled a knife from the top of his boot and cut all the ropes except the ones that held Cat's hands together. Cat gasped, and with supreme

493

effort he kept himself from crying out at the pain that flooded his limbs as the circulation began again. He staggered to his feet and rubbed his legs with his hands and stomped his feet until he could feel the strength flow through him.

Jake contemplated his words while Cat waited, his heart thudding painfully within him as he prayed silently.

"You," Jake called to David. "Get over here." David dropped Deeta's hand and moved away from her.

"You have a couple of minutes. Try anything at all and I kill the girl and your friend both." Cat went swiftly to Deeta's side and dropped to his knees beside her. Gently he lifted her hand in his and pressed it to his lips, feeling its cold lifelessness. His heart broke within at the agony of seeing her so helplessly lost. The wide eyes gave no sign of seeing him or hearing his voice. He wanted to lift her, to hold her close to him and breathe some form of life back into her, but his hands, tied together, left him unable to do anything but hold her hand and soundlessly mourn.

"All right," Jake snapped, "get away from her." Cat turned. He would beg . . . crawl on his knees to rescue Deeta from any more harm.

"Jake, you know I wouldn't leave Deeta or David. Tie me if you want, but let David hold Deeta in front of him. You cannot put her on a horse in her condition. Please," he added softly, "I beg you. Please. I don't want her to die."

Cat didn't know what he had said that touched off some deep memory in Jake, but he could tell by the flicker of some unknown thing in his eyes that he had. He pursued the fleeting thought. "You can take the reins of

David's horse. He won't do anything foolish. But let him carry her." Cat's voice was pleading.

"All right," Jake said. Bib had made everything else ready. Jake walked to him and untied his hands. Without a sound, David mounted his horse. Bib went toward Deeta.

"No!" Cat said furiously. "Don't you touch her! Jake, for God's sake, you put her in David's arms. I will die here before I let him touch her again!"

Jake nodded as if he understood exactly how Cat felt. Bib was ordered to keep his gun on Cat. He walked over and lifted Deeta's limp form from the ground and handed her up to David, who cradled her gently against him. Cat was retied and they began their journey. Again they travelled the whole day and it was just past sunset when Jake called to halt and they built a fire and cooked some food.

David had held Deeta against him, cradling her so that her body would not take the force of the horse's motion. He was stiff and sore, but he would have ridden forever before he would have shown any sign. He felt a deep sense of guilt at being half-drunk when Cat and Deeta needed him most. He felt, in some measure, to blame for the position they were in. He knew his time was running out, but he promised himself he would not give his life up easily.

Cat's mind was in motion also. They took off the heavy ropes that bound him, leaving his hands tied. Deeta lay close beside him, her condition unchanged. He rolled on his side and lay close to hers. Gently he touched her face with its unseeing eyes.

"Deeta," he whispered softly, "I'm here. I'm strong enough for both of us. I love you, Deeta. Don't hide from

495

me. Let me help you. We can put our lives back together. Someway I'll get us out of this. We'll start all over, and everything will be all right, I swear, Deeta, come back to me," he sobbed softly. There was no sound from her still body and no flicker of knowledge in her eyes. With a deep sigh he pressed himself close to her and closed his eyes against the pain that almost defeated him.

The night was an ominously dark one with low rumbling thunder in the distance that told of an approaching storm. David lay awake, knowing that the morning light would be the last for him. Suddenly, he no longer felt afraid and his mind seemed to recall everything in his life with more clarity than he'd ever had before. He found the values in things he had overlooked before. He thought of his father, his mother, all the people who suddenly seemed so much more precious to him. He rolled over to try to sleep and something sharp penetrated his shirt causing him to jump. He felt about him on the ground until he found what it was. It was the broken rusted blade of an old knife, its handle having long ago disappeared. David wondered wildly if it was strong enough to sever the bonds that held him. Slowly, he looked about. Cat and Deeta lay together and both Bib and Jake were asleep. He twisted the blade about in his fingers, almost losing it in the process, then laboriously began to saw back and forth on the ropes that bound him.

Predawn light streaked the sky that was heavy with rain clouds. The ropes that bound David were three-quarters of the way cut, and he sawed frantically for he knew with daylight his time was over.

Jake and Bib began to stir and David felt the panic rise in him. He strained and pulled at the ropes, then suddenly they gave and his hands were free. He lay still, not knowing for sure exactly what to do. If he had been able to slip over to Cat, he could have freed him too. Slowly, he got to his knees and crawled quietly toward Cat, keeping an eye on Bib and Jake. Inch by inch he worked his way over until he was beside Cat. He reached out and touched him gently. Cat was awake instantly.

"Shhh," David whispered. With a motion he showed Cat that he was free. Cat kept silent as David began to saw on the ropes that bound him. Before he could even begin to cut the ropes, he heard the sharp shout from Jake. "Hey! What the hell . . ." Jake was on his feet and David knew there was no way out for him. He had to face the two of them without help from Cat. Quickly, he slipped the piece of blade inside Cat's shirt, and he reached out and gently touched Deeta. Then he turned to meet Jake, who was rushing toward him. David leapt to his feet and met Jake's attack. They grappled and fell to the ground. It was Bib who drew his knife and circled around the thrashing men, trying to find an opening to finish the battle off. Cat watched the one-sided battle with a deeper feeling of misery than he'd ever felt before. David was slender and wiry but Jake was by far the stronger. He got to his feet somehow with David right behind him. David was clinging to him, striking as many blows as he could, but Bib was right behind him. Suddenly David stiffened, and Cat saw Bib jump aside with a gleeful look of satisfaction on his face. Then as Bib moved from between them, he could see the knife protruding from David's side.

"David!" Cat screamed as David slowly sagged to his knees. His eyes held Cat's for one long, stricken moment. "I'm sorry, Cat," he whispered. "I'm so damn sorry." He fell face forward and lay still in a small pool of his own blood.

Cat could only stare at David's limp form and feel the blade he had slipped inside his shirt. "David sacrificed his life for us," he thought. "I'll repay them, David. For you and for Deeta. I'll repay them."

Jake climbed to his feet, panting.

"Well," Bib said jubilantly, "that takes care of him."

Jake nodded. "Leave him and get everything together. Check his ropes and make sure they are tight."

Bib checked the ropes closely, and it never occurred to him to search Cat. When they mounted, Jake carried Deeta and Bib held the reins of Cat's horse. Cat looked back over his shoulder at David's still form in the dirt and vowed silently his death would not go unavenged. They rode along, Jake setting a rapid pace. Cat had shouted angrily at him for not letting him bury David. "Let me bury him. You just can't leave him lie there for wild animals to find."

"Can't I?" Jake said coldly. "He'll lay right where he is. Maybe you'll learn a little lesson about gettin' smart. One wrong move out of you and we drop the girl too."

Cat remained silent but he marked another memory in his mind for which Jake must pay. Cat made no move toward using the knife blade. He would wait for the shadows of night.

They worked their way around the city of Wilmington and camped that night about three miles away from the town. The next morning, a man named Glazer would come for them and pay Jake and Bib. Whatever Cat had planned to do he must do tonight, for in the morning Jake and Bib would be gone.

As soon as they checked the ropes binding Cat's arms, they both lay down beside the fire. "Bib, one of us should stay awake and keep guard over that buck."

"He ain't goin' nowhere. He knows the girl would pay for it. I got half a mind to get her over here and have a try at wakin' her up." Bib laughed, and Cat began to tremble in a combination of fury and fear that he just might do it.

"Forget it, Bib. We'll have some money tomorrow and you can go buy yourself one with a little more life in her."

They curled up by the fire and soon both of them slept, while, stealthily, Cat began to saw at the bonds that held him. It was just after midnight when the ropes fell away and Cat was free. He lay still, intently listening, but there was nothing except the night sounds and light snores from the two who lay asleep by the now-dead fire, unaware of the terror that began to crawl toward them in the night.

Mac Glazer and two men rode through the first morning light toward the place where they were to meet Jake and Bib. They were laughing among themselves when they came out of the woods to the meeting place and were upon it before they realized that something was wrong. Jake would not have let them get that close without hailing them. They urged their horses forward, then suddenly stopped. Their faces froze when they realized how still the two men by the fire were. They came up closer and their eyes widened in horror. Both men were close to the fire. In fact they were securely bound, and both of them had their bare feet in the fire burnt to blackened cinders. Their mouths gaped open, tongueless and filled with congealed blood that was already attracting flies. Their eyes had been forced from their sockets. It was clear to all three men that the two lying on the ground had died in terrible agony.

"You goin' after 'em Glazer?" one man spoke.

Glazer's face was a green sickly color and he was trying his best to control the urge to run. "Hell no," he gasped. "I don't want no part of a man that could do a thing like that. Whoever these two they caught and wanted to sell to us must be crazy. It's better we get out of here."

It was ironic that Jake and Bib were denied the burial in the same brutal way they had denied David.

Cat held Deeta in front of him and led another horse. He was on his way back to find David's body if he could. He could not bear to go home without it and tell anyone what had happened. There was not another emotion in him, and he was drained as dry of feeling as a dead man. But he was sure of one thing: he would never regret what he had done to the men that had hurt Deeta and killed David, and he would do it over again and enjoy it.

Cat came to the place where David had been, only to find it empty. David's body was gone. Obviously someone had found him. Cat was faced with a terrible dilemma. In Deeta's condition, he could not just travel about looking for David. He had to get Deeta home, somewhere where she was safe, somewhere where he could nurse her and hope she would recover. Reluctantly, he headed toward Clearhaven, but he promised himself to come back to Wilmington to find out where David's body had been taken, by whom, and where he was buried. He would not rest until David's body was returned to Clearhaven for burial in the family plot. He nursed his grief in silence as he moved toward home.

David slowly regained consciousness. Coming up from a deep black well of intense pain, he couldn't move and he felt icy cold. Lying still, he tried to orient himself, and the full flood of memory came rushing back. "Deeta," he moaned softly. "Cat." He tried to get to his knees and cried out at the pain that streaked through him. Fumbling with his hands, he reached to find the source of the pain. The handle of the knife still protruded from his body. It burned like fire, but he was afraid to move it because at the slightest touch he wanted to scream. Slowly, painfully, he worked his way to his knees. He had to find help. He was dying and he knew it, but his fear for Deeta and Cat overcame his fear of death. Grimly, he forced himself to stand erect. He was sweating so badly that he could barely see, and was panting heavily. The loss of blood made him weak and dizzy. He knew in which direction Wilmington lay, but doubted if he would ever have enough strength to get there. He began to stagger in that direction. Each minute was a black, pain-racked hour. He staggered on and on until his mind and body became disconnected. His brain screamed for him to go on while his body shook with pain and wanted to lie in the grass and cease to move forever.

On and on and on. He began to cry, heavy rocking sobs that tore at his lungs, for he knew in his heart he was not going to make it. He fell, and rose again. Fell for the second time and staggered to his feet, but the realization came that if he fell again he would not be able to get up. He blinked his eyes when he thought he saw a faint yellow glow of light ahead. The sweat blinded him and he moved forward, only to fall again. He sobbed as he pushed himself to his knees, and his body would not rise again. He began to crawl toward the pale light that flickered ahead.

He was leaving a trail of blood as he crawled up the

three steps to the back porch of a small house, and a heavy black cloud was pressing him to the ground with an unbearable weight. With all the strength he had left, he slapped his hand against the door, then he laid the weight of his body against it. He was already unconscious when the door opened and he fell in a heap at Jeananne's feet. Jeananne shrieked at the bloody, dirt-covered man that lay before her. Louise came running and stopped in shock at the sight of David. Once the shock was past, Louise ran to his side. She laid her hand against him to see if he was still alive and was rewarded by a faint erratic pulse.

"Jeananne, we must help him; he is still alive. Your father will return soon with Mark. In the meantime, help me and we will get him into a bed."

"Mother," Jeananne gasped, "that knife . . . it's all bloody . . . he's all bloody . . . Mother."

"Jeananne!" Louise said sharply. "Help me." They managed to get David face down on the bed. Louise tore away his shirt, then turned to her daughter. "Boil some water and fetch me one of your petticoats. We must remove that knife and clean that wound. It is already beginning to fester."

Jeananne ran to do her mother's bidding, then watched in wide-eyed fascination as her mother began to sponge away the dirt around the imbedded blade of the knife. She gently touched the knife to see if it was movable, and the touch brought an anguished cry both from David and Jeananne. Louise knew that if David was to live the knife must be removed and the wound had to be cleaned. Grimly, she took hold of the knife handle, catching her lips between her teeth and mustering every ounce of strength she possessed, she pulled quickly and was surprised how easily it slid from his body. She wet pieces of Jeananne's petticoats in the hot water and washed the wound until fresh red blood spurted from it. Unsure of whether she had it clean enough, she formed a pad and pressed it over the wound. It took both of them to work the strips of cloth beneath him and get the wound bound. Once it was tightly bound, Louise sent Jeananne to watch for her father, then she undressed David, washed the dirt from him, covered him with a warm blanket and joined Jeananne to wait for Jeremy and Mark.

It was over an hour before she heard their footsteps on the porch. She threw the door open and tried to explain as quickly as she could what had transpired since he had been gone. Both Mark and Jeremy ran to the bedroom. Jeremy looked at the boy on the bed and frowned, then he looked at Mark and was surprised to see that Mark's face had gone white and he was staring at the boy.

"Do you know him?"

"It's David . . . Margaret's son . . . David Martin."

"My God, what's he doing here, and in this condition?"

"Something must be terribly wrong at Clearhaven. David is not the kind of boy to leave his family. I know how much Margaret loves him, she talked of him and his future so often."

"Jeremy," Louise said, "you must get a doctor immediately."

"Yes, I will go at once."

"I'll stay with him," Mark said quietly.

It was only a short while before Jeremy returned with the doctor. They were all excluded from the room while the doctor worked on the unconscious boy.

Mark paced the floor while the rest of them sat in silence, not quite believing what was happening. Time ticked by slowly. The silence of the room was broken by

Mark's despairing laugh. "I wonder if God has never intended for Margaret and I ever to be together to have any happiness."

"What do you mean Mark? You'll be with her soon," Jeremy replied.

"Can I go back to her bearing the body of her dead son? Haven't I caused her enough grief. Is it always to be so, that every time I come into her life I bring her pain, when all I want is to be with her to try and make her happy?"

"Mark," Louise said, "stop this. That child is going to live, and you two are going to know each other. You can go back to Margaret together. Maybe God is testing you now to see if you are worthy to be a husband and a father. At least," she added softly, "you can pray for that."

Mark sighed and smiled at Louise. "You are right, I suppose. Here I am blaming God for all the things I've done in my own stupidity. I'll tell you this, if David lives, there will not be such mistakes again."

Louise smiled at him. "Don't tell me," she said quietly. "Tell God. I'm sure he's been listening for your admission that you need him, have needed him for a long time."

Mark rose and left the room. He stood on the porch and watched the millions of stars blaze in the heavens. For the first time in his life, Mark Severn, the independent, strong soldier, reached with his whole heart for the strength and the help he needed. His heart became humble as he silently prayed for David's life and Margaret's love.

The time passed slowly, then the doctor came out of David's room. Mark was immediately at his side.

"How is he? Will he live? Doctor . . ."

"I've done everything for him that can be done. I

504

believe he is going to live but he must have a great deal of care. I don't think he will regain consciousness for quite a while and when he does, he will be extremely weak."

"You needn't worry, doctor," Mark replied with relief thick in his voice, "he will have all the care he needs."

True to his word, Mark barely left David's side for the next two days. He kept him clean and cooled his fevered body by continually replacing cool cloths upon him. He sat and listened to David's fevered rambling and heard first-hand of his love for his father, his mother, whom they both loved, and of the tragedy that had struck Deeta and Cat.

David rambled on and on until Mark was despairing that he would not survive. Then, two days later, he opened the door to see David, weak, but lucid for the first time.

"Well," he smiled, "good morning. You had us all worried. We thought you were never going to wake up again. How do you feel?"

"I'm thirsty," David croaked hoarsely through dry lips.

"Good. I'll send for something for you to drink." He opened the door and called into the next room. "Jeananne, our patient is awake. He's thirsty. Would you bring him a cool glass of water?"

Mark sat down on the chair beside David's bed that he had been occupying for the past three days. He leaned forward and rested his elbows on his knees. "We know all about your ordeal, son. You talked a great deal in your fever. When you are able, we will gather men and search for your two friends. People who look like them cannot be that hard to find."

"How . . . how do you know what they look like?"

"I've seen them before. I've seen all of your family, David."

"You know me? I've never seen you before."

"I know you, but even if I hadn't seen you before I would have known you. Except for your eyes, which are exactly like your father's you look like your mother."

"I don't understand. You know my family? What is your name?"

"Severn," Mark answered. "Mark Severn." He watched David's eyes turn from grateful questioning to amber glass.

"You! How can you sit there and smile at me and talk of my family when you have caused my mother so much pain? Couldn't you have even had the decency to answer Sarah's letters so my mother could be free of you?" David was panting in his weakened anger. "Cat told me all about everything, how they had written you a long time ago and hoped you would return and you couldn't even take the time to write, to tell Sarah that you wouldn't come. I don't want any help from you. I hate you, Mark Severn, and when I get out of this bed, I'll find my friends alone."

"Well," Mark said gently, "you are incapable of getting out of that bed, and while I have you helpless I intend to explain everything for I don't want to have to defend myself against you when you are well." David glared at him in helpless belligerence. Mark chuckled softly, then began to talk. He told David why he had not answered the letters and that he was headed toward Clearhaven when David found him. He was pleased to see the angry look begin to fade.

Then he was shaken when David said, "I hope you're in time."

"In time?"

David explained Lucas' presence and his feelings toward Margaret. He was even more surprised when Mark smiled. "Margaret is mine," he said gently. "She is now and always will be. I was a fool to let her go the first time. I didn't want to hurt her more while your father was alive for your mother is an honorable woman and refused to leave him. Now it is our turn to find a little happiness, and nothing or no one is going to take it from me again."

"I know my mother loves you, Mark, but she is terribly alone and Lucas may find her one day in a weak and lonely moment."

"No," Mark laughed. "I'm going to have faith in a friend I spoke to the other night. He's granted part of my request. I believe he will grant the other."

The door opened just as David was about to answer. His open mouth snapped shut and his eyes grew wide in admiration as a beautiful flame and ivory vision stepped inside and closed the door behind her.

Chapter Fifty-One

Margaret slept late the day after the party and she was annoyed with herself. It was usual for her to rise early and see to the household herself and not let everything to her housekeeper and Sarah. Today she felt lazy, as though she could find happiness just walking alone through the high pines or riding along the riverbank. She lay back against the pillows and thought about the party last night. It had gone well. Susan and Brandon were so completely happy with each other, and she could tell that David's happiness for them was genuine.

When her thoughts turned to David, she chuckled aloud. "I'll bet," she thought, "that David isn't feeling quite so well this morning." She thought of the way David laughed and toasted Susan and Brandon as often as he could with as many appropriate limericks as he could remember. They were all good enough to recite in front of guests, and she wondered how many he kept inside that would have turned people green with shock. "So much like Paul," she thought. And Cat was no help the way he encouraged David. She hoped that Deeta got them both home safely last night. "Maybe," she thought, "I should take a ride up there today just to check."

She rose and sent for a bath. Luxuriating in the warm water, she allowed herself the freedom to do a thing she always kept in check. She thought about Mark and she remembered what Lucas had said to her before. Could she marry Lucas without love? Was it enough for him or would he one day realize that her heart was lost to another. Her love for Mark was as clear and warm today as it had been twenty years ago. If she closed her eyes and allowed the tentacles of her mind to reach out and touch him, she could still hear his laughter, the gentle voice that spoke words of love, and feel the touch of his hands on her that made her warm with the secret depth of pleasure only he could reach. Mark, whose magical kisses could make the core of her melt until she was soft and pliable in his arms.

It was a useless thing to think of marrying Lucas. She would not come to him as a cheat and a liar. It was best that they understood now that it could never be. She dressed with infinite care and slowly left her room.

As she walked down the stairs, she could hear voices from the dining room. She went in and found Sarah and John enjoying breakfast with Deanna and Deborah.

"Where are Matt and Jason?"

"Matt went into town, Mother, and Jason decided to ride along with him," Deborah replied.

"And where is my beautiful grandchild?"

"Still asleep, I hope," Deborah laughed. "At least he was when Deanna and I left. We wanted to have breakfast with you."

"Well, did you enjoy yourselves last night?" she inquired.

"The party was beautiful, Margaret," Sarah said. "I thank you for Susan and John and me. We are grateful for your kindness."

"Sarah, it was a pleasure for me, also."

"Well," Deanna said, "I think the two who enjoyed

509

themselves the most were David and Cat."

Deborah laughed. "Did you hear some of those atrocities David toasted to? They were hilarious."

"I'll wager it's not so hilarious today," John said. "I'll bet there are a couple of whopping big headaches up at Cat's cabin today."

"Don't worry," Sarah answered. "Deeta will make them them heartily regret the fact that she had to drive them both home in that condition. Especially Cat. I can see that big one now, feeling miserable and not having a sympathetic Deeta to lean on."

"I don't know if I have time to go up there today," Margaret said thoughtfully.

"I wouldn't, Margaret," John said. "I'd give Cat and David enough time to get themselves back in shape. I'll take a ride up tomorrow and very graciously tell them both that you've forgiven them."

She laughed. "All right, John. If you think it best, I'll stay here and wait for them to come home."

"David should be coming home to stay now. Everyone is sure the scare is over."

"I'm glad. I was quite worried for a while, but I'm glad everything will be back to normal soon."

John rose. "If you lovely ladies will excuse me, much as I'd like to stay in this beautiful company I've a lot of work to do and I want to get busy."

"How is the house coming along, John?" Margaret questioned.

"Fine. It's under roof now, and in about a month we'll be able to move in."

"Are you going to have a house-warming party?" Deanna laughed. "You know Matt and Jason. Any excuse for a party is a good one."

"Yes, I think it's a good idea. Only this time, we'll make sure David is not the closest to the punch bowl."

"Don't worry," Deborah said wickedly. "I'll bet young master David is sorry today for each sip he took last night."

They laughed together and the sound pleased Margaret, for she could hear the flow of contentment beneath it.

Deborah and Deanna were the next to leave. Then Sarah and Margaret sat together and sipped their coffee in companionable silence.

"Margaret?"

"Yes?"

"Can I ask you a personal question?"

"Of course, Sarah."

"What is between you and Lucas?"

Margaret rose from her chair and walked toward the window. She looked out but was thinking over the answer she would give.

"You needn't answer me if you don't want. I know it was a bad question to ask now, but John and I, we worry about you, about your future."

"I don't mind answering you, Sarah. I'm only trying to find the words to make you understand. I like Lucas."

"Like?"

"I'm genuinely fond of him, Sarah. He is a kind and loving man, but . . ."

"But?"

"But I don't love him."

"Margaret, what you and Mark had, it will never be again."

"I know that."

"Then why not try to enjoy what happiness Lucas can

511

give you?"

"Because it is a terrible thing to do; to try to live a lie is impossible. The day would come when he would realize he's been cheated."

"I don't think so. I think he loves you enough that he will live with what you can give. Margaret, maybe time will free you from your past. Maybe you will be able to turn to him one day and see that you really can learn to love."

"Don't you understand, Sarah, I do not want to learn to love. If I cannot have Mark, if I cannot have the vibrant beautiful love we shared, then I want nothing. I will not stand in between, wishing for one and living the other."

Sarah stood up slowly, and walked to Margaret's side. "Margaret," she said gently, "I think deep inside you halfway believe that someday Mark may come back. I think that hanging on to that dream is what keeps you from turning to Lucas."

Margaret was silent for several minutes, then she said softly, "Maybe you are right, Sarah. I suppose that somewhere inside I feel that he will be living with the same need as I and that he will find it as empty as I and will come back. Maybe you are right about that, but you are wrong to think it is the only thing that keeps me from marrying Lucas. It is because I truly do not want to hurt him and I feel that a small hurt now is better than a tragic hurt later."

Sarah stood and looked at Margaret for a minute while she decided what words to say. For she intended to sever the connection once and for all with Mark's memory. A small hurt now, she repeated in her mind. She would hurt

Margaret now by telling her she had written to Mark and that he had a chance to return and chose not to come. Maybe then Lucas could pick up the pieces and help Margaret put her life together again.

"I have something to tell you, Margaret."

"What?"

She was about to speak when the door opened and Lucas walked in.

"Good morning. I was told you were finishing your breakfast. I came to ask you to go riding with me today."

Margaret smiled. "Yes, it sounds like a lovely idea." She turned to Sarah, "You were about to tell me something, Sarah?"

"It will wait until tonight."

"Good," she walked toward the door. "Give me a minute to dress, Lucas."

"One minute," he laughed. "I'm an impatient man."

Margaret's laughter floated back to him as she climbed the stairs.

The day drifted by for all of them and it was not until dinner that Margaret realized none of them had gone to Cat's cabin that day, nor had there been any sign of Cat, Deeta or David. It was Matt who laughed at her sudden, uneasy feeling. "Don't worry about Cat. That's how he got his name. He can take care of himself. In a couple of days you'll see them laughing and making fun of you for worrying about them."

"I suppose you are right."

The daily routines went on uninterrupted for three more days, then Margaret became seriously worried. "Jason, you and Matt ride up and make sure they are all right, just to ease my mind."

513

"Of course we will."

They left immediately and rode toward Cat's cabin. They were laughing about something as they rode up but the laughter died on their lips as they saw the door of Cat's cabin slowly swinging back and forth with the breeze. Quickly, they dismounted and ran inside. The obvious evidence filled their hearts with fear, for they could tell no one had been there for days. They rode their horses at a wild pace back to Clearhaven. Immediately they sent riders to Vern Markham's and to John's unfinished house to bring them back. Then they went in to tell Margaret.

"They're gone. It's clear they haven't been in the cabin since the party. The fire has been cold for days, the door was open and the house had filled with dust. You know Deeta would never have let that happen if she had been there. She was too proud of her home."

"Matt, what are we going to do?"

"First we're going to get together and try to find some trace of the trail they took. John is good at that. Then we'll follow them."

Lucas had been called and was going along. He went to Margaret's side. "We'll find them, my dear," he said softly. "We'll bring your son home."

Margaret nodded, unable to speak because of the fear that threatened to choke her. "David," she whispered then she covered her face with her hands. "Please God don't let him die. I could not bear it."

It took John almost three-quarters of the next day to find traces of the trail they had taken. Food and equipment were packed and they started. It was a quiet group of men who worked their way, slowly following the

514

almost negligible traces the kidnappers had left. Two days later, they found their first camp. Another day and a half before they found the second. They had just left the second camp, travelling slowly while John traced their trail. They worked their way in silence, none of them knowing and all of them fearing what they might find.

John shouted and they crowded around him. He pointed. Working his way up the trail was a horseman who was obviously carrying something heavy. He reeled in the saddle but clung to the horse.

"It's Cat!" Matt said, and kicked his heels into his horse's side. It took them about ten minutes to get to Cat's side, and they were shocked when they reached him. Cat was as near exhaustion as he could be. For a minute he even refused to let them take Deeta from his arms. It was only when Matt spoke to him softly and promised to take good care of her that he released her.

They took them home as rapidly as they could. But it was frantic women who met them six days after they had gone. Margaret had Deeta taken to her own room and called the doctor. Cat refused to sleep or to even sit down until the doctor reappeared. He shook his head.

"She is in a severe state of shock. She had, of course, lost the child she was carrying, but her body is young and healthy, and it will heal. Her mind . . . well, that is not such an easy thing."

"Will . . . will she recover?" Matt asked.

"Matthew, I'm sorry, but I don't know, I really don't know. She may stay this way a week, a month, a year . . . perhaps forever."

Cat groaned like a wounded animal and sat in the chair burying his face in his hands. There were no words anyone could say at the moment to comfort him. Then Margaret went to him and knelt in front of him.

"Cat," she whispered. "Where is David?"

Cat lowered his hands from his face and she looked into his bleak despairing eyes . . . and knew. "How?" she choked out.

Cat began to talk and the words welled up in him, bursting the gates. He told them everything, the words tumbling over one another as if in a hurry to get out. A darkness struck Margaret so deep and so filled with pain that she did not realize that Lucas had lifted her from the floor and held her while she cried brokenhearted, rending sobs. He took her to another room and had the doctor give her something to make her sleep, then he sat and held her hand until the drug began to work.

She lived in a shadowed world for days. Cat was forced to rest, but he slept a little and then returned to Deeta's room. There he sat for hours, and watched for any sign that Deeta might recognize him. After several days, Cat rose and said quietly and firmly, "I'm taking Deeta home."

For a while, they tried to stop him. "Maybe if she is around familiar surroundings, she might find comfort. Maybe if she feels that she is finally safe, she might find her way back from wherever she is," he said.

Matt and Jason helped him get her to the wagon then rode with him to the cabin. Cat walked in slowly, remembering the last night they had shared here. The three men worked to clean the cabin. Cat put Deeta to bed, then came out and sat in front of the fireplace with Jason and Matt. They could feel the urgency in him to talk, so they quietly sat and listened while he rambled on and on. It was a need now, a need to wash some of the misery away. He talked of David's bravery, his sacrifice. They let him go on until the weariness overcame him. His voice died to a quiet whisper, and it was then that he unfolded the horror of what he had done to the two men responsible for Deeta's condition and David's death. If they were shocked at Cat's merciless violence, they were wise not to show it. At the end, they put Cat in bed with Deeta and closed the door. "I'm afraid to leave them alone here," Matt said.

"I agree. It's going to affect us all like this for a long time. God, Matt, I wonder if Deeta will ever come back."

"I hope so, Jas. I don't know what Cat will do if she doesn't."

"I think we had all best take turns staying. Cat will need all the help he can get."

It was agreeable to all of them when Jason returned and told them Matt was staying the first three or four days. Cat cared for Deeta like a loving parent would a helpless child. He bathed her, dressed her, forced food, which she obediently swallowed. He filled her room every day with wildflowers. "She always liked flowers around. The house was always filled with them," he said.

When Matt could bear the quiet misery no longer he went home and Jason came, but it affected Jason also. The pain was a thick heavy blanket that smothered all the joy in life.

Deeta would stay wherever Cat would put her, so he sat a chair on the front porch facing the setting sun. It was a view that Deeta loved most. At the end of each day, he would take her to bed, cradle her in his arms and cry

517

silent tears while she slept. Several weeks passed before Margaret felt she had enough control of herself to go to Cat. They sat together and talked of the boy they both had loved. It helped both of them, giving each other the strength to face the future.

The day of their return was a black one for Susan also. At the news of David's death, she had run from the room crying. When Brandon came later and was told what had happened, he asked for Susan, but no one seemed to know where she had gone.

"She just ran," Margaret said.

"I don't know where she has gone to." Sarah was worried for fear some harm might come to her in her distraught state.

"Never mind," Brandon said gently. "I know where she is."

He mounted his horse and rode to the only place Susan could be: a place that was a comfort to her, a place where she had found love. At first he did not see her and wondered if he had been wrong, but then he saw her small form, curled tightly in a ball at the base of the huge tree. He went to her, knelt beside her, not quite sure of what to do in the face of her crying. Then he lay beside her, pulled her close in his arms, caressed her and let her relief herself of all the pain. It was a long time before she got her grief under some control. Amid sobs, she talked of David. David her brother. David her friend.

Brandon could only listen and try to soothe her as best he could. When the tears were gone, she lay still in his arms, clinging to him, allowing his love to surround her and bring her some peace.

They talked together softly and Brandon was happy to

518

feel that another new bridge had been built between them. She had turned to him in grief and need and he had been able to give her the comfort she needed. Now she knew that Brandon's love was a thing of strength they could build on. "You really never got to know David well, Brandon."

"I know," he replied grimly. "I was too busy being jealous of him to make a friend of him. I'm sorry for that."

"Brandon, I guess there was a little childhood love between us, but nothing to ever compare with what I've found with you." She looked up at him, her eyes deep pools of love into which he immersed himself. "When I know," she continued, "how much I love you and when I think of Cat and Deeta, I wonder how he can be so strong. I would be unable to cope with life as he does. If I lost you, I don't know how I could continue . . . Cat is like an iron mountain. His love for Deeta seems to grow larger and larger every day."

"Susan, considering all the times we've come here, all the beauty we've shared, I think I would feel like Cat does. He feeds on his memories, of the good times together. And hopes that one day a miracle will happen."

Her eyes held his and she lifted both hands and held his face between them. The tears that fell now were tears of joy. "Yes, you would be like that. Strong, and always there to help me. You have given me so much, Brandon." Her voice died to a whisper. "And I love you so very much." She pulled his face down to hers and touched her lips to his. His arm came about her and she lay back against the tree, drawing him with her. "Love me . . . love me," she whispered.

"Oh, God, I do, Susan, more than my life," he whispered softly in her ear.

Words were no longer necessary things. With gentle and infinite care, he removed both her clothes and his, then pressed her body close to his so she could feel the warmth, let it surround her, let it speak the words he had held inside. It was not a fiery demanding thing, this love they shared today, but it was the very best time they had ever been together. Their bodies blended in a slow and gentle merging. Brandon's face was also damp with tears when they finally lay together, clinging to each other in silent wonder of the beauty they had shared.

It was an amazingly quiet time for all of them during the next few days. It seemed as if everything hung in the state of suspended animation. Life seemed to slow, and flow about them like a deep river. There seemed to be something unfinished, something that hung in the air waiting, and no one knew what it was. Sarah did not get the opportunity to talk to Margaret again, for Lucas was there all the time. He was trying to make Margaret's life a little brighter.

Margaret, Sarah, and all the other women took turns going to Cat's cabin to clean and to make Cat a little more comfortable, a thing Cat did not seem to care about these days. His only waking thought was Deeta, and Margaret wondered just how much he slept, or if he did. No matter how early they would come, Cat was awake. He would talk to them and let them help him with everything but Deeta. He seemed to grow frantic when someone else tried to do anything for her and they found that it was better for Cat's peace of mind to leave Deeta entirely to his care. Margaret began to worry about Cat's state of mind. One night, just at dusk, they sat on the porch of Cat's cabin talking. Cat had put Deeta to bed, but he seemed restless, and Margaret felt she should stay with him for a while. They spoke in quiet voices.

"Cat you need some rest. Why don't you let me spend a day with Deeta and you go to town with Matt. The time away will do you some good."

"No."

"Cat?"

"No, I won't and it's no use of you arguing with me. Deeta needs the strength to get back from wherever she is. She needs my strength."

Suddenly Margaret became aware that Cat was harboring some deep feeling of guilt. She could not believe for a moment this was true, but after a few more quiet questions, she felt sure. "You have always been Deeta's strength, Cat," she said in a gentle, patient voice.

"Not always," came his muffled reply.

The truth of his deep feelings, feelings no one else had questioned came clear to Margaret. Maybe it was because she had felt them before because she had lived with guilt and grief that she understood. She had to get Cat to speak about it, to take it out of the deep shadows of his mind before it drove him to the brink of madness.

"I'm sure," she began softly, "that you have always done your best, Cat. No one could expect more of you than you have given."

Cat bent forward and put his elbows on his knees, holding his head between his hands. "I was drunk the night we were captured. I should have known better. I should have been protecting her." His body shook with a grief he could no longer contain. Margaret remained silent. "She never said a word to condemn me for the fool I was. The whole time we were held she never said a word. But I knew, I knew she felt in her soul that I was strong enough to protect her. My strength failed her than, but it will never fail her again. I'm to blame for what she has become. I have killed the only beauty that ever existed in my life."

"Cat! That is not true. You were helplessly tied. How could you have done anything?"

"Don't you understand, Margaret. She never should have been put in that position. I sleep like the Cat after which I am named. There never had been a time in the past few months that I had not been aware of every sound around this cabin. Always awake, always aware, except that night. When she needed me I was drunk."

"Then David is to blame too," she offered softly.

"No . . . David was a friend, a child to her. I was the one that should have known."

"So you will remain strong . . . until you break."

"I will not break. For as long as she needs me I will be here."

"Oh, Cat, what can I say to help you. Don't you know we all love you. It hurts everyone, especially Matt, to see you in such pain. And not be able to share it with you, to help you in some way."

"You can only help me by leaving me be. Someday she will reach out for me, and I want to be there. I cannot fail her again."

Margaret knew it was useless to argue with Cat. He closed off every argument she might have. She rose slowly and went to her horse. Although it was past dark, she was not afraid. She had ridden the paths too often to be frightened.

She rode slowly, her mind grasping for ways to handle the terrible problems that her family had. Unaware that she was allowing her horse to pick his own way, she was finally aroused from her deep thoughts to see where she was. A startled cry escaped her. The horse, having gone this way often, had found his way to the cabin that she and Mark had shared so long ago. She dismounted, tied the horse, and slowly walked up the steps, crossed the porch and pushed open the door.

It was dark inside but she did not need a light. She knew the cabin too well. Slowly she made her way to the bed. She sat down for a minute then slowly lay back, allowing her mind to drift into the past.

It was over two hours later that Margaret closed the door behind her. The Margaret who mounted her horse and left for home was a different person than the one who had entered the cabin. She had made her peace with the past and saw her plans clearly before her. She had made final and irrevocable decisions about her future. She wondered just how her family would take it. There was one person she knew would understand and that was Cat.

She arrived home and although she was questioned about where she had been, she only responded by explaining she had spent some time with Cat. She could not explain what had happened to her in the cabin, for she felt no one would understand. She went to bed and slept dreamlessly and at peace. The next morning she had a message sent to ask Lucas if he would come to Clearhaven that night, that she had something very important to talk to him about.

She went about her household duties that day in an aura of quiet contentment. Everyone sensed it, but no one questioned. They were grateful that after all the grief

Margaret had suffered, she was beginning to smile again.

Lucas arrived just after dinner. Margaret had him shown to the library where she joined him. She went in and closed the door behind her. She crossed the room and she and Lucas stood facing each other in front of the fireplace.

Chapter Fifty-Two

David gritted his teeth to keep a cry of agony silent as Mark, as gently as possible, rolled him on his side to check on his bandages. Mark chuckled to himself when he realized that David held back the cry because Jeananne stood on the other side of the bed, her face filled with fear.

"You're healing well, In a couple of weeks, you should be out of that bed."

David rolled back gasping, the sweat beading on his forehead. He closed his eyes as her cool hand rested on his brow.

"I'll go get you something cool to drink and some food," she said gently. "You need to eat to help you regain your strength."

She left the room, closing the door behind her. David watched her slender figure until the door separated them. He was still involved in thoughts of her when he heard Mark's soft laugh. He turned questioning eyes to him. "Skinny little thing, isn't she?"

"Skinny! She's beautiful . . . she . . ." His words stopped and he could feel his face turning red, but he refused to drop his eyes from Mark's amused ones.

"You're absolutely right, boy, I was just testing your health. Any man who could not see Jeananne's beauty would have to be dreadfully sick."

Now David laughed. "I'm not that sick."

Mark pulled up a chair and sat beside David's bed. He had spent most of his waking time there in the two weeks since David had regained consciousness. They had talked long hours and established a tentative rapport between them. Mark had first made it clear that he was not trying to take Paul's place in his life, that he knew the deep love and respect in which David held his father. But he had also firmly announced that he was going to marry Margaret and try to make her happy, no matter what David thought. David had a lot of hours to think, and he realized that after all his mother had been through, she deserved some happiness. He just wondered, deep in his heart, if she had already found it with Lucas.

"David, I think we'd best get you on your feet tomorrow. I feel the sooner you're out of that bed, the sooner you'll get well. The wound is closed nicely."

"It can't be too soon for me. I'm going crazy lying here all day not able to do anything."

"In another week or so, you'll be a different man. You're young, and you bounce back easily. There are a few things I'd like to discuss with you."

"Like what?"

"I told you I would help you find your friends, and I'm not usually a man to go back on his word. But I think we should go to Clearhaven first so your mother will know you are alive. She must be frantic with worry about you."

"You are right, but the thought of where Cat and Deeta might be tears me apart inside."

"We'll find them no matter where they are. Besides, we'll have added help from everyone at Clearhaven. They might even know more than we do by this time."

"All right," David sighed.

"We'll get you up in the morning. It will be a painful experience but it is best for you."

"I'll be all right."

"I'm sure you will," Mark responded dryly. Jeananne had just re-entered with a tray and David's eyes had brightened. "I'll run along and let you eat. You need," he said in straight-faced humor, "a lot of good food and tender care."

Jeananne looked up at him through innocent eyes. "Uncle Mark, I'll see to it that David gets all the care he needs."

"Good. You are just the medicine he needs." She was surprised when she heard Mark's soft laughter as he closed the door behind him. Jeananne gave David her brightest smile as she set the tray down beside his bed.

"Let me put another pillow behind you so that you can eat comfortably," she said. She bent over him to arrange the pillows behind him and the soft scent of her and the warmth of her closeness alarmed him with a sudden and violent reaction of his body. She wore a dress with a square neckline. There was only two or three inches between him and the soft, rounded skin above the neckline. He clenched his fists and firmly held down the urge to pull her into his arms and press his lips to that velvety skin. He was so frantic that, despite her obvious innocence, she could see his heated arousal. He felt himself swell, and prayed she would not notice.

"Jeananne," he said softly, "sit down with me while I eat." He knew that if she did not move away, if she continued to bend near him as she was, he would not be responsible for what he did. She handed him the tray and he set it abruptly on his lap. They sat together and talked while she urged him to eat. Question after question

527

bubbled from an enthused Jeananne. In her short life, she had never met anyone with such a romantic aura as David. From the night he fell at her feet, Jeananne had been lost in a dream of David. She questioned him now about what had happened, and he was quite aware of her bright, admiring eyes.

"Jeananne, tell me about you. I've been talking away about myself, but I don't know anything about you."

"Oh, David, I've never done anything or gone anywhere except here." She bent forward again and put her hand on his. "We have heard so many stories about your country. Are there really savages here?"

David contemplated an answer. "Depends on what you mean by savages. The red-skinned people that live in the western part of our country are referred to as savages. But lately, I've seen more savagery around here among what we refer to as 'civilized man.' The men who hurt Deeta, they are savages in my opinion."

"You must have a very special love for these two people."

David nodded and began to tell her about the place Deeta and Cat held in his life. Jeananne was a very bright girl. It took her no time to sense the sensitive and loving nature that was part of David.

"You must have been raised among a great deal of love."

"Yes," he smiled. "I'd like for you to meet my family. You would love them, and they would love you, you're so . . ."

"So what?" she said softly. Her lips slightly parted, she looked at David with wide green eyes. He reached out and touched her lips lightly then let his fingers caress the side of her face. "Perfect," he finished softly.

Jeananne's heart began to beat furiously and her cheeks pinkened under his intent gaze that she did not understand.

"I don't think I've ever seen a girl anywhere that is as pretty as you. Your hair is a miracle, like fire gone wild. I've always liked green eyes, but yours are more like . . . like emeralds."

She leaned toward him, enchanted by the gentleness of his touch. His fingers had slid into the softness of her hair. They gazed at each other, completely aware of some magical force that drew them to each other. Applying a small amount of force, he drew her toward him. He would have kissed her then, but a knock sounded on the door. Jeananne blinked as though some spell had been broken. She sat back and looked at David with eyes he could not read. The door opened and Jeremy came in. "Mark tells me you're doing quite well, young man, that you'll be getting up tomorrow."

"Yes, I'm anxious to get out of this bed, sir."

"You had us quite worried you know. It was nip and tuck there for a while. I'm happy you'll be up. I know Mark is anxious to get to Clearhaven and I suspect you are also anxious to get home."

"I certainly am, sir. You and your family will spend some time with us, won't you, sir?"

Jeremy's eyes twinkled at the hopeful sound in David's voice, he nodded. "I expect we'll stay. It's a wedding we've looked forward to for twenty years. I'm anxious to see your mother again. It's been so long, and she was such a beautiful woman."

"She still is, sir," David replied.

Jeremy nodded again as though he had always felt this must be so.

"I have to go into town and pick up some things. Is there anything you need?"

"Well, sir, if I'm getting up tomorrow, I'd best have some clothes to wear. I imagine the ones I was wearing are beyond repair."

"They are," Jeremy laughed as he rose. "Worry not, young man. When you arise tomorrow, you will be dressed. Is there anything I can get you, Jenna?"

"No, Papa," she smiled, "thank you."

Jeremy waved and left the room. David turned to her. "Jeananne, what did he call you?" Jeananne blushed prettily and laughed.

"When I was born my brother could not say my name so he called me Jenna. It seems to have stuck. Now all three of my brothers and my mother and father sometimes call me Jenna."

"Could I? Would you be upset if I did? I like it."

"If you would like, I . . . I would be pleased."

David held out his hand to her, but Jenna rose swiftly. She was all too aware of the magnetic attraction David had for her.

"I must go help my mother."

"Well, you can take this tray back to the kitchen." She reached out for the tray, keeping her eyes downcast but still was not prepared when his hands gripped her arms. She was forced to look up at him. He smiled. "Come back and sit with me later. I like talking to you . . . please?"

"All right,' she whispered. Then she gripped the tray and moved toward the door. Looking back over her shoulder just before she left the room she said, "I like talking to you also, David. You're not like any other boy I've ever met before."

She closed the door while David was still searching for

some gallant, flowery reply. David relaxed against the pillows. Suddenly he felt so exuberant he wanted to shout, but a sharp pain brought him back to earth with a reminder of what he had to do.

True to her word, Jenna came back late in the afternoon. They sat and talked together for over an hour. Laughing over each other's minor childhood problems, listening with sympathy to each other's likes and dislikes, moods and temperament. David slept well that night. His young body was rapidly regaining health and his young heart leapt up in dreams of flame-colored hair and crystal green eyes.

Mark appeared early the next morning with clothes for David. It took the two of them to dress him, and when he sat on the bed with the clothes on he felt sure he would never be able to move again. He was panting with effort, and sweat ran down his back in rivulets.

"Come on, David. Today we make it to the chair and back again," Mark said determinedly. Jenna came in at that moment. Immediately she went to David's side.

"Let me help you. Between me and Uncle Mark, you'll be able to do it."

David stood slowly with grim determination which almost fled him when a slender arm went about his waist and he could feel her slender body pressed against him.

"Lean on me," she said, not realizing that David would have collapsed before he did. His arm went around her and Mark supported him on the other side. He moved slowly toward the chair. Once there he sat helplessly exhausted while Jenna changed the bedding on his bed, then they helped him back. He sat on the bed, his back propped against several pillows. "Now," Jenna said happily, "you are ready for a big breakfast."

531

She left the room and returned with another tray. David groaned. If she was going to hover over him again, he was in no position to hide the condition he knew he would find himself in. Mark was laughingly aware of David's thoughts by the look of sheer panic in his eyes. Deftly, he took the tray from Jenna and set it on David's lap, causing him to blush furiously by winking at him as he did.

Mark's work every day got David on his feet, but Jenna's constant nearness almost put him back in bed again. Every day he moved a little easier, walked a little farther and was less and less tired. His strength was growing in leaps and bounds, and so was his desire for Jenna. The first day that he left the room and remained up for the whole day was a victory for him. From then on, he regained his health rapidly. To keep his mind away from Jenna, he concentrated on plans to find Deeta and Cat. Once they got home and assured his mother that he was fine, he would return and try to trace Jake and Bib. No matter how he tried to control it, the black rage hit him again. Once the door to his memory was opened, he could not erase the picture of Deeta's blank eyes or Cat's painful look when he slid the blade inside his shirt. It was probably what triggered his wild dream.

In the dream, he was running, he did not know where and he did not know why. There was a mist about him and he could not see where he was or where he was going. Then he heard the sound—a mournful agonized wail. It was Deeta, echoed by Cat. The sound went on and on, and though he tried to follow it, he could not seem to get any closer. He ran, arms outstretched, tears hot on his cheeks. Then suddenly his feet seemed to be sticking and he looked down to find himself in a thick dark ooze that prevented him from running. He forced his legs forward one after another, using all his strength but barely moving. He called out to Cat and Deeta, his voice thick with pain and tears and still the cry of pain seemed to echo all about him until he could not bear it.

"Stop it!" he screamed. "Cat! Deeta! Please stop it! I can't run any faster . . . please . . . stop! . . . stop! . . . stop!"

Jenna lay half asleep, dreaming of David. She had done so for many nights. She could not explain to herself the feelings he roused in her. She only knew that when he looked at her something deep in her moved, and when he reached out to touch her she felt all hot and melting as if her bones were turning to hot water. Parts of her body seemed to change when she was near him, as they were now, and when she dreamed of him she touched her breasts, wondering at the hard erectness of the nipples. Sliding her hands over her nightgown she pressed them between her thighs feeling the warm, pulsating beat. Jenna was not entirely stupid. She had seen animals mate before, and from the giggling confidences of some of her girlfriends, she had heard the words, but no one had ever told her of the wildly delightful feeling. Her body moved restlessly on the bed.

The sound that finally drifted through her light sleep was like someone crying. She sat up, listening intently. Finally, the words came clear to her. Someone was crying, heartbrokenly, the words "Stop . . . stop . . . stop." She rose from the bed and left her room. Standing in the hall, she listened again until she realized the sound was coming from David's room. She went to his door and opened it. David lay on the bed thrashing back and forth and calling out in a strangled sob Cat and Deeta's names and begging them to stop.

She went over to him, pity in her heart at the broken sobs that emanated from him. Bending over his bed, she took hold of his shoulders. David came awake from the dream, grasping at who he thought was Deeta. He pulled her down on the bed beside him and was rocking her in his arms and holding her close to him when awareness hit him. He realized first that he had been dreaming and second that Jenna was in his bed, in his arms and calling his name softly to quiet him. He lay paralyzed for a moment. Her flame-colored hair fanned out on his pillow picking up the pale strands of moonlight that filtered in. She was warm and soft. He could barely make out her face, yet he could sense the emerald green eyes that looked up at him.

"Jenna?"

"You were dreaming," she answered simply. She did not move, but lay there realizing if even David did not, that this was where she really wanted to be.

There was a soundless moment as David continued to look down on her. His eyes, growing accustomed to the pale moonlight, could make out her pale ivory face and the half-clad body that lay beneath his. Very slowly, he bent his head and touched his lips to hers. They were frightened lips, trembling under his. His hands slid under her body and pulled her against him. Since this was a new thing for Jenna, she followed her instincts. Slowly, her mouth parted and accepted him. He felt her small tongue flick lightly against his lips, searching for something she did not know but that her woman's soul told her was there. It was enough to set David's mind and body on fire. His lips took command of hers and his tongue thrust deeply, answering the pressure of hers.

His hands found and eliminated the small scrap of clothing that lay between them and he felt the long silken length of her body against his. Her small breasts pressed against his chest and her arms about his neck sent his need for her exploding in his loins. A hunger in him drove him and he caressed her gently while his mouth moved from her lips to her throat then down to the round silken breasts. Catching one in his mouth, he sucked it while he felt her writhe in passion, and a soft murmured sigh of his name escaped her lips. It was only at the sound of her voice that realism hit him.

What in Christ's name was he doing? In the home of people who had saved his life, he was thanking them by seducing their daughter. He rolled away from her with a low gasping sob of sincere regret.

"David," she whispered. Her body moved in its urgent need to press against him and she clung to him.

"Jenna, this can't be. I can't do this to you, here in your own home. Your parents will kill me, not to mention your Uncle Mark my soon-to-be father."

She trembled in his arms. The need was so great that she did not understand how to cope with it. She began to cry softly, ashamed now that she had seemed to him to be so wanton.

David drew her against him, aware that her body had needs as great as his.

"Shhh, don't cry, love," he said softly. "I'll make it all right, don't cry. I love you, Jenna. Everything will be all right."

As he rocked her against him her crying gradually stopped, and she whispered haltingly, "David, what did I do wrong? Why don't you want me? I want to be with you."

"Jenna, I probably want you more than I have wanted anything in my life. We cannot dishonor your family by our needs. Believe me when I tell you this hurts me more than it does you. There are ways I can relieve your needs a little, and we will save the better part for one day soon when we have the right to each other.

"I only wanted to please you," she said and he could sense that she was about to cry again. He stopped it in the only way he could—he took her mouth in a gentle kiss.

"Lie still, love. I'll make it easy for you," he said gently. She obeyed, and felt him slide his hands down her body until they rested on her hips. She could barely make out his dark form over her. She felt him gently push her legs apart. She did not know what he was doing, nor did she care any longer. Suddenly she felt his lips touch gently the core of her urgency, flicking tiny fingers of flame through her body. She caught her lips between her teeth to keep from screaming out the sheer exotic pleasure she felt. Her body arched to meet him and he continued to hold her hips in his hands while he tortured her with the fiery pleasure. Then suddenly she felt as though her body exploded and she quivered in his arms and lay still. David rose and lay beside her, holding her close.

"Oh, David," she whispered softly. "Can we do that again, it was beautiful."

David choked with silent laughter. "Listen my sweet little innocent," he said. "You have got to get out of this bed and out of this room before I do what I really want to do and ruin everything for us. I almost deflowered you this time and I don't think I have the strength to go through that again without finishing it."

He jerked to alert surprise when her hands slid over his

536

body and found his throbbing, enlarged manhood. "Then can't I do for you what you did for me? If it makes me feel so much better, surely it will make you feel the same."

"Damn it!" he said, "don't do that!"

She jumped as though he had struck her and immediate regret filled him. "I'm sorry, darling, but if you touch me again, I think I'll burst."

"David, you are unfair. I simply want to share with you the beautiful feelings you gave me. I don't care what anyone thinks. Even if they knew—which they won't."

"There's only one way you can share that with me and that is if I make you completely mine. Do you know what I'm talking about?"

"Yes, I think I do. I've been told you . . ." she stammered. "You want to put us together, and David I want you to. I want to be part of you. I almost felt that way before but you stopped, but I want to feel that oneness again with you. I don't want it to ever be anyone else but you."

"It will hurt you for a minute, Jenna," he said softly.

"I love you," was her only whispered reply. David took her face in his hands.

"Jenna, if I ask your parents tomorrow if we can marry, will you be my wife when we get to Clearhaven?"

"Yes, oh, yes, David."

This time David did not try to hold back, and when he took her in his arms, he slowly and purposely began to arouse her. He wanted her to climb with him to the heights—and she did. She had never known such a beautiful emotion in her life. His hands traced magical pictures of love across her skin and his lips, searching for the vulnerable parts, drove her to a wild and frantic desire. No matter how much she tried to pull him against her, he held back, building her need higher and higher. This time when he knelt above her he spoke to her soothingly and softly while his hands found her and opened her to him. At that first moment of pain she pressed her lips together and clung to him. If the pleasure she had felt before was immense, this was even greater. He filled her, reaching deep within her to a well of ecstasy she had never even dreamed of. Her body arched to meet his deep thrusts and they moved together in slow rhythmic motion. She heard him breathe words of love in her ear as their bodies blended and she held him close, wanting to pull him deep within her and hold him forever. If the fiery explosion she felt before gave her a glimpse of the beauty of their love, this opened the door wide. When they finally lay together legs entwined and their bodies stayed joined as though they could not bear to separate.

"You are mine, now, Jenna Mackenzie, for now and for always. I'll not let you go now that I've found you. I've never known anything like the way you make me feel in my life. Do you remember you promised to marry me?"

"Yes, I promise. Oh, David, I'm so glad you didn't send me away. Something might have happened and I might never have been lucky enough to have known you like this."

"I love you, my flame-haired beauty, and when we get to Clearhaven, we'll stay together forever."

Jenna sighed contentedly and David held and caressed her until she dropped her head against his shoulder in a light sleep. David rose from the bed gently so as not to disturb her sleep. He wrapped a blanket around her and carried her quietly to her room. There he kissed her and returned to his own bed. He was about to get in when he noticed the stains of blood on his sheets—something he hadn't thought of. For a moment he panicked, then he gently removed part of the bandage about him, he rubbed them vigorously over the sheets, staining them also. If the stains were noticed, he would only claim that there was a little blood from his wound while he slept, but nothing that would cause any harm.

He went to bed and almost immediately he slept and this time, there were no nightmares, just pleasant dreams of flaming hair, soft skin and very willing lips.

Chapter Fifty-Three

David's body was so relaxed he might have slept most of the day away if he hadn't heard the quiet opening of his door. He turned his head toward it and opened his eyes. Jenna stood just inside the door watching him, with a bundle of fresh clean sheets in her arms. He sat up on the edge of the bed and looked at her. Her eyes fell and her cheeks turned flaming red, and David rose and went to her. Taking the sheets from her hand, he put them aside. Gently, he tipped up her chin to look at him and was more surprised to find her eyes swimming with tears. "Jenna, love," he said gently, "what's the matter?"

"I . . . I was working in the kitchen with my mother, and we were talking about . . . well about men and women. She said . . ." her words stopped in a choked sob.

"She said what? Does she know about us?"

"No! I never told her that," Jenna said in a shocked voice. "We were just talking."

"Then what did she say that upset you so?" he said tenderly while he brushed away the tears.

"David, Mother said any girl who gives herself to a man before they're married is bad . . . wicked . . . a . . . a whore. David," she said tearfully, "I'm not, I'm not bad. I love you. I didn't feel anything bad about last night. I felt so good this morning I wanted to run to you and feel you hold me. But Mother said . . . David, I'm not a whore, am I?"

If it hadn't been such a serious matter to Jenna, David would have laughed, but he contained his laughter and drew her into his arms holding her tightly and caressing her hair. "Jenna, what happened with us last night was the best, most beautiful thing in the world. There was nothing bad or wrong about it. You," he said quietly, "are the most perfect, most beautiful woman and nothing bad could touch you. What we shared was good, Jenna and don't let anyone else's words tell you any different. If a woman gives herself to any man, every man, then she can be called a whore for there is no love in it. It's just a need of the body. With us, it will always be just you and me. Do you love me, Jenna?"

"Oh, David, I do. Just thinking about being with you makes me all warm and soft inside."

"Well, I love you, too," he laughed, "and I feel warm all over, inside and out, and far from soft. We'll go to your parents today, tell them how we feel about each other, and ask permission to marry as soon as we possibly can. I'm having a difficult time resigning myself to waiting, but for you, I'll try."

She murmured something, but with her body pressed so close to his, he did not hear what she said. Taking her shoulders, he held her away from him. "What did you say?"

He was rewarded by another blush and she lowered her eyes, "I said," she repeated softly, "I won't try." Her eyes raised to him, "I want to be with you, David. Why should I deny what I feel to you. You said last night we were like one. Well how can I keep the other half of myself from knowing how much I want it?"

"Bless you," he said fervently as he put both arms

541

around her and held her so tight she could barely breathe. "You certainly know how to make a man feel good, but it's dangerous, Jenna. Making babies before we get married would bring down the wrath of both sides of the family on us and I for one wouldn't want to be on the wrong side of your Uncle Mark's anger—much less your father's."

"What can we do?"

He kissed the tip of her nose and grinned at her. "I'll think of something. In the meantime, you'd better change those sheets, and to keep anyone from asking questions, I suggest you get rid of them somehow. They're covered with evidence of what we did last night."

Jenna nodded. She picked up the clean sheets and carried them to the bed. David sat in the chair and watched her work. It was a pleasure to see her young curvacious body move, and it renewed the hunger for her within him. If she were his wife now she would not have been changing the sheets, but lying on them.

Mark knocked lightly and stuck his head around the door. "Breakfast is at table this morning, David. There will be no more spoiling you. It's time you got up and out. I don't suppose you can climb aboard a horse yet, but a good long walk will do you some good. Fresh air to put a little life in your blood."

"All right, as soon as Jenna is finished I'll get up and dress and be right with you." David acknowledged Mark's words with a silent laugh. If there were any more life in him, he would be fair toward bursting his britches.

David and Jenna sat down to the breakfast table together. During the meal, David could feel Mark's eyes upon him. He looked up once to catch a small flicker of amusement, and he wondered worriedly just how much Mark knew. David and Jenna had agreed that they would speak to her parents that night after dinner, for Jeremy and Mark were too busy that day and David wanted time, in case there was any argument, to convince them.

By the time dinner came around, David was so nervous he was pacing the floor, and Jenna flitted from one job to another until her mother was exasperated with her and sent her to market just to get her out from under foot.

David created every type of argument in his mind and formed his defenses. "They were too young," he thought. "I'm twenty, sir, soon to be twenty-one. I know Jenna is only seventeen, but I love her and I feel confident that I can take care of her." Argument two: They had not known each other long enough. When you loved someone as much as he loved Jenna, there was no difference between a week, a month or years. He would always feel the same. Argument three: What of his family?

He was sure his mother would love Jenna as much as he, and as for his sisters and their husbands, they were not much older than Jenna herself and would welcome her with open arms like another sister. Argument three eliminated! he thought happily.

He was sure he had everything in his mind straight, knew exactly what he was going to say . . . until the moment came. They sat at the dinner table and tried to eat, but neither David nor Jenna had much of an appetite. When the long excruciating dinner was finally over, they retired to the large living room for brandy, cigars and some quiet talk before bedtime.

Jenna sat on a small stool beside David's chair. She wanted to be as close to him as she could. Conversation was erratic and light, like the pale gray smoke that curled around Jeremy's head. Several times David tried to steer the conversation toward them but each time it seemed to get away from him, until finally he could bear the suspense no longer. Their eyes were all drawn to him when he reached down and took Jenna's hand in his. He touched it to his lips gently, then looked toward Jeremy in grim determination. It silenced all of them, but David and the others missed Mark's smile that he rapidly buried in his glass of brandy. "Mr. Mackenzie, I have something very important, both to me and to Jenna, that I have to talk to you about."

Jeremy, of course, took in the meaning of David's words and the way Jenna was clinging to him, it took him only a moment. He had suspected that there was an attraction between David and Jenna for quite a while, but he did not realize it had grown to these proportions. "David, I must say some words to you both that I'm not sure you will appreciate, but they must be said. When you came to us, it was during a very traumatic and emotional thing, both for you and for Jenna. You are grateful for the care she has given you and she is a very romantic girl, overwhelmed by the adventure and the chivalry surrounding what happened to you, but this is hardly enough to build a whole life on."

"I don't mean to argue with you, sir, but there is much more to our relationship than gratitude. Of course I am grateful to her, but," he smiled, "I'm grateful to you and your wife also."

Mark laughed. "He's got you there, Jeremy."

"I don't mean to treat this lightly, sir. What I feel for Jenna goes far beyond gratitude. I want to take her to

544

Clearhaven; I want her to be part of my life, my future, I love her . . . very much."

"I see."

"I can make Jenna's life good. She'll never want for anything. I'm a hard worker, sir, and I'm sure my mother would give Jenna and me a piece of property, and we could build a house and make a good life."

Jeremy looked at Louise whose eyes were wet with tears. "You will be so far away from us, Jenna," she whispered.

Jenna rose from her stool and went to her mother. Kneeling in front of her chair, she took her mother's hand in hers. Their eyes met, and Jenna remained silent, but Louise knew the day had come when she must relinquish her child. "I love him, Mother," Jenna said gently. Louise took her in her arms and held her for a moment. Then she held her a little away from her and looked at her half smiling, half crying.

"David," Jeremy said, "this is a shock to both her mother and me. We must have some time to think. We will put off the decision until we reach Clearhaven."

David was disappointed, but knew he could only make matters worse by arguing. He felt since they actually hadn't refused that he could do more to win them over to his side at Clearhaven than here. Jenna looked at her mother, the distress clear in her green eyes. Louise put her arms about her daughter for a moment, then she rose to her feet. "It is best we all get some sleep now," she said, extending her hand to Jenna.

When they had both left the room, there was a deep and poignant silence. Then Jeremy said gruffly, "David, it is not long from here to Clearhaven. If you want to be on your way soon, you'd best put some effort into riding tomorrow. As soon as you are able we will leave."

"Yes, sir," David replied.

"Well, I'm to bed," Jeremy said, disturbed at David's hurt look. "You'd both best be too. We will begin to pack and start making preparations, and by the time David can sit a horse for a day without pain, we'll be on our way."

"Good night, Jeremy," Mark said.

When the door closed behind Jeremy, David rose to his feet. He paced the floor for a few minutes, almost forgetting Mark was there.

"David," he said quietly, "would you like to go out for a walk. We need to talk, you and I, and here is not the place for it."

David was surprised that Mark felt he could not talk for fear of being overheard by his closest friends, but he silently nodded.

They walked along in silence for a while, and David could see that Mark had something he wanted to say to him and was searching for the right words.

"David, without doubt I would say that Louise and Jeremy are two of the dearest, best friends I've ever had. They have stood beside me through good and bad, most of my life, but . . ."

"But what?"

Mark turned to him and they stood facing each other. "You really love Jenna, David?"

"I do . . . I don't believe for a minute what I feel for Jenna could be misconstrued as gratitude."

"You're quite sure?"

"Mark, what are you getting at? If there's something you want to say to me, why don't you just say it."

"All right, David, I will. I once made the worst mistake in my entire life by letting the woman I loved slip away

546

from me. It has cost me everything. I've known loneliness, the kind which you can barely imagine. I've lost the chance to have a son like you, daughters like your sisters. I don't want anything like that to happen to you, so I'm going to give you the best advice I can. Don't let anyone or anything take Jenna from you. Don't listen to arguments about your age, gratitude, Jenna's innocence or anything else. If you want her, fight for her, take her and to hell with everyone else in the world. Make your way through the world with whatever you have, but don't let anyone take from you the one thing that completes your life, the woman you love. If anything happens and you need help, I want you to know you have a friend in me."

David was silenced by the depth of Mark's emotion. It was only then that he fully realized how much Margaret meant to Mark. "No one will take Jenna from me, Mark. I decided that at the beginning. I respect your friends, Jenna's parents, but I will not let them ruin our lives. I know Jenna loves me. I've made all the arguments in my mind, that I'm the only man she's known, that she's too young to make such a decision, but they're all unimportant. She loves me and I love her, and that's the end of it."

Mark clapped him on the shoulder and laughed, "I'm glad. Now I can sleep easier."

David realized suddenly that Mark had tried to offer him something more valuable than just the words. He offered him the first tentative reaching of a father toward a son. He wanted to find a place, not just in Margaret's life but in her children's lives as well. He wanted them all to try to find the empty places in their lives and begin anew. He extended his hand to Mark, who took it in a strong grasp then pulled the boy into his arms and held him for a moment, neither of them ashamed of the tears that wet their faces. They walked back to the house in a silence that was comforting and easy.

David found his bed and lay there with his arms folded behind his head waiting for the sound he wanted to hear.

It came—the soft click of his door as it closed behind her and the faint sound of her bare feet as she crossed the floor and stood by his bed not knowing if he were awake or asleep. Unsure of whether he wanted her there or not.

He stood up from the bed and lit a candle, then turned to look at her. She looked like a child with her slender body in the long, full nightgown and her hair in braids. "I hoped you would come," he said softly.

"I'm frightened, David."

"Of what?"

"That my parents might take me home. That we might be separated, even that someday you could find someone else."

He went to her and held her against him, listening to the fluttering of her heartbeat. "You are wrong on several things. First I will not let your family or any other person in the world take you away from me. Second, we will never be separated if I had to go to the ends of the earth to prevent it, and lastly, but most important of all, I love you, Jenna, you and only you. There is no one in the world who could take your place. Tell me, love, if you had a choice . . . would you go with me?"

"Anywhere, David. I would wander the earth like a gypsy if I knew I would always have you."

David held her a little away from him, and without a word he began to unfasten the buttons at the neckline of her gown. She blushed pinkly and raised fluttering hands to stop him. "Don't you want to put out the candle?"

Slowly he shook his head negatively. "I want to see you. I want to know you, to memorize everything about you. I want my eyes to remember what every other sense I have already knows." He slid the nightgown down to a pile at her feet. He wondered how anyone so small could be so perfect. Removing his own clothes, he reached out and drew her body against his. She felt cool to his heated skin, and he closed his eyes for a moment to savor the sweet softness of her as she rested confidently against him. He felt the texture of her skin under his gentle touch and marvelled at the creamy glow. His lips touched the silken fragrant hair and wandered in slow lingering kisses to her forehead, her closed eyes, her cheeks then found the soft half-parted lips that awaited his.

He felt the blood begin to surge through him as his heart picked up the pounding beat of his desire. With a slight bend of the knees, he lifted her from the floor. Their eyes held as he took the two steps to the bed. "David," she whispered, "your wound, you will hurt yourself."

"There's only one place on my body that hurts right now," he laughed softly, "and you my dear have the cure for all my pain."

He lay beside her and drew her against him sliding his hands down over her body until he held her hips tightly against him. Tonight there would be no hurry. Tonight he intended to discover everything about the tiny beloved form that trembled beneath him.

Jenna was to become aware of a passion so deep and demanding that it carried her away to a world where she only knew of David's existence. David, whose gentle touch turned to fire; David, whose hungry mouth devoured her and lifted her on a turbulent sea of ecstasy. Words tumbled from her lips unheard by her, but David's heart swelled with joy to realize that with him, Jenna had abandoned the world about them and was glorying in the beautiful pleasure of their loving in a blending of their bodies so perfect, so attuned to each other's rhythm that they moved as one. His teeth nibbled gently on the soft skin of her belly, down to the curve of her rounded hips. He dove to a depth of her that Jenna could not believe existed. She wanted to cry out, to tell him of her pleasure, but caught her lips between her teeth. Her legs opened to him and she revelled in the hard deep thrusts of his body as he entered her. Her body arched to meet his, and twining her legs about him and pulling him to her, they reached a peak of ecstasy that left her sobbing and trembling in his arms. He remained within her, not wanting to leave the warmth of her body. Legs entwined, bodies joined, they lay together. In gentle quiet words, they spoke of love, of the future, of the joy they shared. He held her close until the gentle regular breathing told him she slept. He hated to let her go when he could hold her through the night, waken her with kisses and share her moments of waking to find them still together.

He carried her back to her room after carefully checking the dark hallway to see that no one else was about. He stood over her bed after he had safely deposited her under the covers, and looked down on her peacefully sleeping form. A feeling of warm belonging filled him. No matter how lonely his past was, he realized now he had found the one person who would always fill every empty spot within him. He bent and brushed her lips again in a light kiss then returned to a bed that had never felt emptier.

True to his word, Mark was up early the next morning urging David to dress rapidly. "The horses are ready. We'll got for a short ride today, then stay out longer and longer until your body is accustomed to strenuous activity."

David kept his chuckle of amusement to himself, but wondered gleefully if his body would be faced today with any more strenuous activity than the previous night. They rode for the entire morning and David claimed no effects from it, so after a nice leisurely lunch, Mark had him back in the saddle again. David knew that Mark was containing his urgent need to get home only because he felt that David was not yet physically prepared for the journey. David fell asleep that night so soundly he did not hear Jenna come, nor did he hear her soft throaty laughter when she could not waken him. It gave her ammunition for some subtle teasing later.

She asked Mark if it was all right if she took his place and accompanied David on his ride. "Of course," Mark agreed, smiling at Jenna's mischievously glowing eyes. Once they were on their way, David talked happily for a while before he realized he was chattering away and Jenna was silent. He could not think of anything he had done or said that could have made her angry with him. He pulled his horse to a stop and she turned questioning eyes to him. "Let's walk the horses for a bit to rest them," he said.

Obediently, she dismounted and walked beside him. The day was bright with golden sunlight that filtered through the trees as they walked along the forest path. Finally David could tolerate her silence no longer. He put out a hand to touch her arm and she stopped, looking up at him with eyes he could not read. "Jenna, you're upset with me for something. Whatever I might have done to offend you, I'm sorry, but I just don't see what you could be angry about."

Jenna wanted to laugh and throw herself into his arms when she saw the distress in his eyes, but keeping her face expressionless, she said softly, "I have just begun to understand what position I am in."

"What position?" he said, his brow furrowing in a frown as he tried to puzzle out just what she was getting at.

She sighed deeply. "It's all right, David, I understand, but you could have made it a little easier for me."

David had reached the end of his patience. "Jenna, what the hell are you talking about?"

"A man like you, you have been every place, seen so much, had lovers before." David reached out and grabbed her shoulders shaking her.

"If you don't tell me whatever it is you think I've done, I'm going to shake your head from your shoulders."

"If you were tired of me, you could have told me so."

"Huh?" he grunted dumbfounded.

"To pretend to be asleep, David, to let me stand by your bed shivering in the cold . . ."

David realized now what she was saying, but still he could not see the humor in her averted face.

"You . . . you actually think I was pretending? Jenna, I swear, I didn't know you came, I don't even remember falling asleep. You've got to believe me. I would never do such a thing to you. It was only . . ." He had been speaking in a rapid pain-filled voice until she lifted her eyes to him. Suddenly he stopped, "Why you little brat," he said with a muffled laugh as he pulled her tight in his arms. He could feel her body shake with laughter also. "Well, your revenge should be complete. You had me scared there for a minute. I thought you were really angry with me."

"David," she laughed, "you were so sound asleep last night. I touched you . . . all over, and you lay there like a man dead. It is a terrible blow to a woman's pride not to be able to rouse a man who claims he loves her."

"Claims he loves her!" David whispered against her hair. "Try that same trick tonight, if you dare, and see what happens."

Her eyes sparkled as she put her arms about his neck and looked up at him. "Will you be awake and waiting for me?" she said in a teasingly doubtful voice.

"You're tempting fate, woman. A man can only take so much fun being poked at his virility, then he has to prove himself so there are no doubts left."

She slowly drew his head down to hers as she murmured against his mouth, "I await your proof, my darling, with a great deal of anticipation." Her gurgling laughter was drowned in the searing, demanding mouth that took hers and the strength in the arms that held her.

There were no doubts left in either David's or Jenna's minds about the love they shared the next morning. Mark was the only one who noticed David's self-satisfied grin and Jenna's soft dreamy look as he announced that they would be ready to leave the following day. It was only because Mark had shared the same feelings David had and had seen the same look in Margaret's eyes after they had made love that he realized what had happened. "It's obvious," he thought, "that our two young birds have found each other. I'd best work toward getting old

553

Jerry's permission for these two to get married before we have a real problem on our hands."

All their baggage packed, the coach they had hired was ready to leave. Mark and Stuart, having their own paraphernalia, had arranged it so that Mark's coach carried most of the baggage, and Jeremy's carried Louise, Jeremy and Stuart. Mark had chosen to ride and David and Jenna, being young, vital and enthusiastic, had decided to ride also. They rode along at a pace much faster than the coach could go, and stopped to eat lunch under the shade of a tree and wait until the coach caught up with them.

That Jenna was completely happy was obvious to everyone who saw her. Her eyes glowed, her cheeks were pink and her usual enthusiasm was magnified. She asked both Mark and David so many questions that they finally collapsed in helpless laughter, professing they had no more strength to answer questions with. Mark's heart was singing Margaret's name over and over, praying she would accept him back into her life and her heart. As for David, his face was turned with joy toward home.

Chapter Fifty-Four

Matt lay very still, cradling Deanna against him, enjoying the way she curled against him for warmth. She slept, completely confident of her safety in his arms. Early morning light was just beginning to streak the night sky. He thought back on how good life had been to him, of all that he had, and was grateful. He took the treasured memories one by one and enjoyed them. Now he was to be a father. "Would he be able to be as good a father to his child as his father had been to him?" He wondered. He remembered Paul Martin, who had made the ultimate sacrifice not only for his family, but for all the families. The floodgate of memory, once opened, released the bad memories along with the good.

The tragedy of what had happened to Deeta and Cat created a black void in their lives. He and Jason had been to the small cabin in the hills so often, yet still could not reconcile themselves that this terrible thing had happened to Deeta. Cat remained, solemn and quiet now. More withdrawn into himself than he had ever been. Still he refused any help with Deeta. He stood, like a man of granite, prepared to care for Deeta the balance of her life with love and tenderness.

He thought of the pain and misery that struck with the news of David's death. He had held Deanna while she sobbed out her grief in his arms and felt the same pain for the loss of a young brother. For Deanna and Deborah there was each other, but for Margaret, there was no one. Matt profoundly admired the amazing control and strength Margaret had shown. Matt was probably the only one who felt there was no chance for Lucas and Margaret. He watched with sympathy as she slowly stood up from the wreckage of her life and turned toward the new day. She had become a strength in the family to which they all clung.

It was weeks before Deanna could speak of David without crying. She began then to relive the pleasant times they had shared, hoping the good memories would help heal the grief. Susan had been devastated at the loss of the one person, outside of Caroline, that she loved and felt was like family. With Brandon's strength, she struggled through the quiet, dark days and nights that had struck Clearhaven.

They had never spoken of the revenge Cat had taken on their abductors. Questions that were asked were met by a united front of silence. They felt Cat had suffered enough. Somehow, no matter how he tried to ignore it, Matt felt that there was something to come. Something seemed to be hanging thick in the air, making everyone quiet and subdued as though it were a live thing to be felt.

Deanna stirred restlessly in his arms as though she were having a bad dream. She rolled a little away from him and lay on her back. Matt rolled gently on his side and looked at her. "She is so damn lovely," he thought, and the wonder struck him, as it always did, that this beautiful raven-haired creature loved him and at this moment was carrying his child within her. He reached out and laid his hand gently on the soft roundness of her belly.

"Are you listening, child of mine," he whispered. "I love you. No matter boy or girl, I love you, and I will try my best to give you the best life I can. I have given you already a lovely mother. I want us to be more than father and child, I want us to be friends. I want us to know and understand each other. How can I tell you of the hopes and dreams I hold for you. If you are a daughter, I can pray that the qualities of your mother and grandmother are given you. If you are a son, I want to give you the great gift of honor and pride from your grandfather. Whatever comes, I will guard you and guide you to the best of my abilities. If I fail, I ask now for your forgiveness, because I am unsure of my way yet, but before God, I will try, I will try."

He bent his head and touched Deanna's lips with his. He felt her stir awake, then gently she rolled into his arms and he pressed her against him.

"I was dreaming," she said softly.

"Of what, love?"

"I dreamt that you were talking to our child."

"I was. It was no dream."

"And did he answer you?" she laughed softly.

"Of course, madam. I want you to know that my child and I are establishing a beautiful relationship." His face became serious as her blue eyes lifted to his. "It's a relationship I intend to nurture and care for as long as there is a breath in my body."

"Oh, Matt, do you know how many times I have thanked God for that rainy day on the 'Destiny.' The day a stiff-necked royalist was thrown into my arms to be made a patriot?"

"Am I never to be forgiven for not rallying to your cause that very day? You had no business hiding from me

557

all that time. I could have told you it was no use. I knew you would belong to me the first time my arms held you. That is a frightening thought. It was like buying a pig in a poke. I had no idea then what you looked like, all wet and bedraggled. You could have been as ugly as sin."

"Well, I have a surprise for you, my handsome pirate. I saw you quite clearly and I was in love with you then. I'm really," she leered, "a wicked witch in disguise, and if you are not careful, I shall steal your heart and eat it."

"Impossible."

"Why?"

"I no longer have it."

"Oh?"

"No, my witch, it is in the safe keeping of a lovely blue-eyed, raven-haired lady who," he chuckled and kissed the tip of her nose, "cares for it very well. I'm afraid, wicked witch, your cause is lost, for I would not retrieve it from my lady if I could."

She sighed contentedly and nestled closer in his arms, satisfied with the unconscious caresses he gave her.

"Deanna, I'm going up to Cat's today. I want to try again to get him away for a while. I know he wants to care for Deeta but he cannot do that if he falls apart himself."

"Do you want me to go with you, Matt?"

"If you would. Maybe if you offer to stay with Deeta, he'll agree to leave for a few hours."

"We can at least try."

"Do you want to ride over to Clearhaven first? Maybe your mother would like to go along?"

"Yes. That would be a good idea. With John and Sarah moving, Mother has too much time alone. I want to keep her from memories too much."

"I know she's good for Cat and for Deeta."

"Deeta?"

"I know, she doesn't move or talk, but for some reason she seems to be more relaxed and content when your mother is about. It's more a feeling than anything else. But it does give Cat peace of mind when she is there, too."

Matt rolled over and got to his feet. It had always been his habit to sleep without clothes, and he had not changed since he married. In fact, Deanna claimed that his heathen ways had rubbed off on her, for she preferred to sleep with her body close to his.

She watched him now, the lithe movements of his tall, muscular body as the rays of early morning touched his sun-bronzed skin. She felt a delicious warmth fill her. "He looks like a Greek god," she thought. She lay back against the pillows and closed her eyes, only to snap them open when with an evil chuckle he snatched the covers from her.

"Up woman, the day is wasting."

"Ah," she mourned, "it is terrible to lose one's beauty and charm. There was a time when I could have kept you in bed 'til noon with a crook of my finger."

He laughed and bent over her, one hand braced on each side of her and his eyes smiling into hers. "You haven't crooked your finger."

She stuck her hand up between them and wiggled her finger under his nose. He slid his arms under her and drew her up against him. The mouth, of infinite tenderness and blinding passion, took hers in a deep and most satisfying kiss. She sighed deeply with her eyes closed and twined her arms about his neck. "Lose your beauty and charm," he said softly against the throbbing pulse at the base of her throat. "It should be forbidden

559

for one woman to be supplied with so much. What is a poor mortal like me to do when he's seduced by a goddess?"

"You can do nothing mortal," she whispered, "but surrender."

"Willingly . . . most willingly," he murmured. His hands were already caressing her softness, seeking the touch that elicited sounds of pleasure from her. It was quite a while before they descended the steps together and were greeted by muffled sounds of laughter coming from the breakfast room.

Young Paul Matthew, having reached the age of three, was a beautiful child. He had the deep, midnight color of his mother's hair, but they were combined with pale crystal blue eyes, eyes that absorbed everything about him. His bright, inquisitive mind found and questioned everything. His continual questioning, "why?" to all things was sometimes looked upon with delight and sometimes by cries of anguish, depending on how many times in an hour it had been asked. As soon as he saw Matt, who, next to his parents, was his favorite person in the world, he lifted his arms with an insistent cry to be lifted up. The strong arms of his Uncle Matt had tossed him happily in the air often before and he desired it to be done again. Only this time, he was sticky from trying to devour a bowl of porridge. Matt laughed, "Next time, young man. I've no desire to draw flies all the way to Clearhaven."

They sat for a while enjoying breakfast, but enjoying even more the bright-eyed child. Afterwards, Matt and Deanna slowly rode toward Clearhaven. The day was clear and beautiful with a soft breeze rustling in the trees. Thick piles of white clouds lay overhead tied to the earth by thin beams of sunlight. Matt drew a deep sense of strength when all about him he saw things that belonged to him: from the lovely vision that rode beside him to the beautiful place through which he rode.

At Clearhaven two people stood facing each other. "You wanted to see me about something important, Margaret?"

"Yes, Lucas," she replied. A small tingle of expectant fear coursed through him as he recognized a new depth to her voice that he had never heard before.

"I want to talk to you about us."

"You seem to have been giving it a lot of thought."

"I have."

"Why do I get the terrible feeling that I'm not going to like what you are about to say."

"Because you know as well as I that we can never marry. You, because you are too proud and strong a man to be able to spend the balance of your life loving a woman who cannot return your love. I, because I cannot lie or pretend with you. All that I am, all that I have been, all that I will ever be, I gave away once. I have nothing left to give another. It is wrong to say I will come to you, Lucas, when a ghost from my past refuses to set me free."

"Is that enough for you, Margaret, just to live with this ghost?"

"I don't know. I only know that I cannot make a promise to you or to anyone that I know deep in my heart I cannot keep. To stand before God and know that I am lying both to him and to you is impossible."

Lucas stepped close to her and took hold of her shoulders. Margaret did not move, and her clear blue eyes looked up at him with calm pride and a complete

561

absence of fear. "It's not enough, Margaret. We are both passionate, warm-blooded people. You won't deny that you feel what I feel when I touch you."

"To try to deny that you are an attractive man, Lucas, is foolish. To try to deny that you can make my body respond to you is also impossible." She pressed her closed fist between her breasts. "But what of me, what of the woman who exists in here. Just possession of my body is not enough for either of us, and you know that is so. You would look in my eyes one day, Lucas, after we had been together, and you would see the shadow of another man. You would learn to hate me then, for I cannot give you what you deserve."

Lucas drew her gently into his arms and she laid her head upon his chest. "Margaret, I know about Mark Severn. I have known for a long long time. I have wanted to ease the pain for you. To see you smile, hear you laugh. At first, that was all I wanted. Then as time went on I realized that was not enough for me. I wanted you. I still want you."

"And you have just said the very thought about which I'm speaking. As time goes on it will not be enough, as time goes on from today it will not be enough. You will reach again for more, only to find me empty of what you seek. The love you have for me would slowly turn to ashes."

Lucas tipped up her chin and looked down into the calmness of her eyes. He was not ready yet to give up. He bent his head and touched his lips to hers, trying to draw from her some sign of weakness, some sign that he might one day win. Margaret remained immobile. She did not fight nor try to withdraw, but she did not respond either. Her lips were soft beneath his, but they gave him nothing. When he lifted his head and looked again into her eyes, Lucas knew he was defeated. Slowly, he released her. "Margaret, can we go through the rest of our lives alone? Do you think you are the only one who has lost someone, who has been hurt, who carries around the ghosts of the past? You are not. Let me tell you of love. Love that burned with a flame so bright we thought it never could be extinguished.

"I was young, so very young. My parents and I travelled to Spain. Oh," he laughed, "I was the gay blade, enjoying all the excitement court life in Madrid had to offer. Then I met Maria." His voice softened. "God, there never was a woman as beautiful as she. She had hair like a night without a moon and large gold brown eyes. I often used to tell her that her eyes looked like whiskey. She was already promised to the son of a great house in Madrid. I never knew, or perhaps I didn't want to know, how much the women of Spain were controlled by their men. She never went anywhere without a dueña. At first I took it as a dare to find ways to meet her. But the first time we were alone we both discovered that we were falling in love. We tumbled into it recklessly, passionately. Then I made the mistake of asking for her in marriage. I had grossly insulted both houses.

"That night we were together as we had never been before. I loved her so very much. I held her, made love to her, promised her everything forever. She cried and begged me to take her away then, but not me," he said harshly. "I was sure there was nothing we couldn't conquer. I told her not to fear, that I would find a way and take her home with me. I will never forget," his voice died to an agonized whisper, "the tears in her eyes nor the tragic words she spoke to me that night. 'I love you,

563

Lucas, mio. Please never forget that. I love you and want to be with you always. No matter what happens, remember I will never hold another man as I have held you. My heart, my body, my soul, they are yours, Lucas, until the day I die.'

"I held her and kissed away the tears. We loved with a beauty beyond reason, beyond thought. I would give my life now to change what I did. I left her alone that night to go and prepare my family, to make arrangements to take Maria home with me. I went the next day to her parent, Don Manolo Alverez. I still cannot believe what happened.

"'Maria,' he said, 'is gone.'

"I was ordered to leave his house and never return. I was wildly angry and for the first time I was afraid. I cursed, I threatened and in the end, I begged. Where they had taken her, I never knew. She vanished from Madrid so completely she was never seen in public or anywhere again. I spent two years trying to find her. I met with closed doors and silent faces everywhere I turned. It was as if the ground had opened and swallowed her. There has never been a woman who touched my heart until you. I had put aside all thought of marrying for every time I looked at another woman I heard her tear-filled words, 'Remember, Lucas,' and I did. I could not run far enough, drink enough, love enough to wash her lovely despair-filled cries out of my heart or my mind. So you see, Margaret, you are not alone with your ghost. Cannot we console each other for the balance of our lives? Can we not find some kind of happiness?"

"Lucas," Margaret whispered. He looked down again into her tear-washed blue eyes and felt the leaden weight of his heart at what he saw. "I'm sorry, I'm sorry for your pain and for mine. I see now you do understand what I

564

feel, but it is not good for us. We would destroy each other. It is better that we end it here and now before we create a greater disaster than we have already had."

He knew with a deep feeling of certainty that he and Margaret would never share the rest of their lives, and he realized she was right. Before they hurt each other worse than they had already been hurt, it was best that he go. He reached out, and with gentle fingers, brushed the tears from her cheeks. Then he put his arms around her and held her close to him for what he knew would be the final time. He raised her face so their eyes met and held.

"You are a beautiful and compassionate woman, Margaret. We will always be two people who can reach out to each other if the need ever arises. I will go. I will leave the area for I cannot stay here. Kiss me good-bye, love, for all the times we can never be together, for all the love we will never share." His voice died to a whisper as he put his arms around her and drew her close. Their lips touched, blending lightly. Then his arms encircled her and with a whispered sob he pulled her close, bound her to him with arms of steel and took her mouth in a passionate kiss of farewell.

Suddenly he was gone and Margaret remained with her eyes closed and the hot tears flowing down her cheeks.

Matt and Deanna crested the hill overlooking Clearhaven just in time to see Lucas mount his horse and ride away.

"Lucas Olivier," Matt said. "He's certainly in a hurry."

They urged their horses forward and in a few minutes dismounted in front of Clearhaven and went in to find Margaret calmly and quietly seated in the living room. She raised her eyes when they entered the room. When

565

they met his, Matt knew instantly that Lucas was riding away from Clearhaven for the last time.

"He's gone?" Matt questioned gently.

"Yes . . . he's gone."

"Are you sure, Margaret?"

"Yes, Matt, I'm sure. It could have been no other way. You see, I have lived yesterday. Today I find I have the strength I need so I am no longer afraid of tomorrow."

Both of them accepted her words with the finality with which they had been spoken. Matt went to her and took her hand in his. Raising it to his lips, he said softly, "you are a remarkably wonderful woman. I don't think I would have had the courage to do what you have done."

"I wouldn't cheat him, Matt. I don't think I would have had the courage to have lived like that. In the long run, we have both found the easy way out."

Deanna put her arms about her mother, but Matt knew that Margaret gave solace instead of taking it. "We were going to Cat's for a while. Would you like to ride with us?"

"Yes, yes I would."

Within the hour they were on their way. When they stopped outside the cabin, Margaret sat for a moment contemplating it. "It is so terrible," she whispered. "Whenever we approached this place before there always seemed to be a feeling of warmth, of welcome. Now it seems so cold and unhappy." A hot burning tingled in Matt's eyes when he thought of the deep well of grief in which Cat lived.

The house was well kept, for Cat found release from some of his tensions in labor. Deeta sat in a chair in front of the fireplace. They could not believe how well Cat cared for her. She was thinner, yet her body was rounded and soft. Her eyes were still as always, as if they were looking inward instead of out. Her skin, flawlessly beautiful, glowed with health, despite her mental condition. When they walked in, Cat was in the process of brushing her long, thick black hair. He did so with a gentle touch of loving care. Cat smiled his greeting.

"Sit down. I've some cool wine to refresh you after a long ride." He finished the brushing of Deeta's hair, checked to make sure she was seated comfortably in the chair, then went to pour them each a glass of wine. Matt went over and kissed Deeta's cheek, followed by Deanna, who knelt in front of her and took her limp hand in hers. She talked to Deeta just as though there were no problems.

"Deeta, you are looking well today. I can't wait until you can come down again to Foxmore. Jason and Deborah will be leaving soon and it will be lonely. I do hope you'll visit me soon, I . . ." Her voice choked on a sob and she moved away from Deeta, turning to the warmth and safety of Matt's strong arm.

They sat close to Deeta and sipped their wine slowly. "Cat, I came up to ask you to ride to town with me today. It will only be for a couple of hours."

"No, there's nothing I need in town, and if you don't mind, Matt, I'd just as soon stay as far away from those not-too-sympathetic people."

"Something's happened, Cat?" Matt said gently. "What is it?"

"It's not important, Matt."

"It is to us, to the friends who care for both of you. If you have trouble, so do we."

Cat remained silent for a minute then he said softly, "It seems there are some people in the town who don't know Deeta and I are free. It seems they think you should sell off the uppity niggers you got on your property. It seems they think if Deeta can't do something to earn her keep, you should get rid of her."

Matt's face went white and he heard the angry sounds from both Margaret and Deanna. "Who, Cat? I want to know which of my *friends* would say such a thing?"

"No. That I will never tell you. When the time comes, I will do whatever needs to be done. I don't want you to say or do anything that will cause you any problems later. It's my battle, and I'll handle it."

"Damn it, Cat! I thought we were friends? What are friends for if they can't depend on one another. Why do you feel you have to be so strong all the time! Why won't you let someone reach out and help you? Why can't you admit that you need someone too? You're not made of stone, Cat, you're mortal just like the rest of us." Matt was angry with Cat for the first time he could ever remember. He wanted to somehow pierce the stone wall Cat had built protectively about himself and Deeta. Matt had stood up as he spoke and both Cat and Deanna's eyes were upon him. But Margaret was looking at Deeta, for a shadow had passed over her eyes when Matt had mentioned Cat's strength.

Had she seen a flicker in those wide, lifeless eyes? Had she seen a faint tremor in that still form?

Margaret's eyes froze on Deeta's face as Matt talked, but there was no sign now that Deeta saw or heard the angry words that broke over her. "It's not that I don't want or need your friendship, Matt," Cat answered. "You know I do. It's just that there are some things in a man's life he has to face alone. The fact of people's feelings toward slaves, the way everyone turns their back on people because of their color, the fact that Deeta and I have to live in this world the best way we can, that is something a man has to have the strength to face. I won't let them reach Deeta, Matt. No matter how they batter against me, I won't let anything hurt Deeta again."

Margaret sucked in her breath quickly and held it. There it was again. The soft whisper of movement behind those eyes. She not only knew what brought forth the awareness, she also knew why Deeta was hiding behind the window of her eyes.

"Matt," Margaret said softly, "it is useless for you two to argue. Both of you already know the other would die for him if necessary. Have patience with each other now. This anger will pass."

Matt sighed deeply and held his hand out to Cat. "She's right. I'm sorry Cat. It's just that I feel so helpless, and we care for Deeta so very much."

"I know. Have patience with me, Matt. It's hard not to reach out, but I have to stand alone this time."

Matt nodded. "I'm going on into town. Margaret are you coming too?"

"No, you and Deanna go along. I want to stay here. It's about time this cabin had a woman's touch in its cleaning. And no sass from you, young man," she laughed as she shook her finger at Cat. "I'm staying and I'm having supper with you."

"Perish the thought I should send you away when you offer to cook a meal," Cat laughed. They stood and watched from the porch as Matt and Deanna rode away, then Margaret turned to face Cat.

"Cat, can we just take a few minutes alone? I'm sure Deeta will be all right for just a minute and I have something very important I have to say to you."

569

"All right. Just let me check and see that she's comfortable." Margaret watched through the door as Cat knelt beside Deeta's chair. "I'll be right back, Deeta," he said softly. He kissed her cheek and rose slowly and went to the door.

Margaret and Cat walked under the trees. She was searching in her mind for the right words to say to Cat of something she knew. Finally, she turned to him. He waited in silence.

"Cat, you want Deeta back? Well, I know where she is . . . and I know why she is there. I am wondering now if you are strong enough to do what needs to be done to open the doors for her. Are you Cat? Are you?"

Chapter Fifty-Five

Cat looked as surprised as if a good friend had turned on him and struck him. His eyes registered the hurt, but he said nothing. Margaret studied Cat's face, from the almond-shaped eyes, black as pieces of coal, to his ruggedly handsome features. Ancient Egyptian ancestors had erased from him some of the African features, leaving traces of the fine cut lines, high cheekbones and a straight nose slightly widened about the nostrils. His mouth was wide and firm and his jaw broad and stubbornly clenched.

"What have I not done to prove my strength to her, Margaret?" There was a proud pleading in his voice. "Have I failed her in some way. If there is a path that I cannot see to follow, tell me."

"That is just the point, Cat. Day by day you have shown Deeta just how strong you are, how proud you are, and day by day you have pushed her farther and farther away from you."

"I do not understand," he said desperately grasping.

"Cat," Margaret began slowly searching for words. "Deeta is a proud and beautifully sensitive woman. She carried in her heart the knowledge that you loved her for her beauty, her pride. She was the woman of your choice, and it created a world for her she had never known before. When Deeta first came to us, she was a very

frightened child. Life for her had been difficult."
Margaret continued brutally, watching the pain ripple
across Cat's silent features. "She was used by men and
none too gently. Then you came, with your gentleness,
your kindness, offering her something she had not had in
a long time . . . pride. She was proud of what she was
becoming. Then the day came when she found she was
carrying your child. She was blindly happy, for she
thought now she could return to you some measure of
love, some gift to thank you for what you had given her."

Margaret became aware that the huge man was silently
crying but she could not, would not stop for their very
lives depended on making Cat understand.

"Deeta did not say anything to you when you were
captured because she thought you expected her to be
strong. She felt she would shame you, damage your pride
in some way if she were weak. Then came the moment
when her body could not take anymore. She felt herself
weakening, felt herself losing the baby . . . your baby.
The one thing she could not bear to lose. Her mind could
not accept this and it ran to a deep dark place to hide.
Hide not from the world, Cat, but from you. She felt she
had failed you, failed the strong man who had given her
so very much."

His shoulders were shaking now with uncontrollable
grief and his huge hands were clenched together in front
of him. Margaret's voice filled with deep pity and died to a
whisper. "Every time you come to her with strength, Cat,
you make the world more unbearable for her. She recedes
a little farther where the light of your strength cannot
find her."

"God," he sobbed, "what can I do? How can I tell her
that my life is nothing without her? If there is a way tell

me, how . . . how?"

"Are you strong enough to be weak, Cat? Are you strong enough to beg. To tell her that you no longer are strong, that you need just as she needs, that you are suffering just as she is? Are you Cat?"

Cat turned his back on her for a moment to try to gain control of the heavy sobs that racked him. Margaret put her hand on his back.

"I know you are, Cat. I've had faith in you too long to lose it now."

Without another word, she turned and mounted her horse. Cat did not move until the sound of hoofbeats faded in the distance and the stillness surrounded him. Slowly he turned and walked toward the cabin. His steps echoed across the porch and he pushed open the door. He looked across the room at Deeta who sat quietly. He did not wipe the hot tears from his face as he crossed the floor and knelt in front of her. He reached out and gently took her hands in his. His voice was cracked and hoarse, barely above a whisper as he began to talk. "Deeta . . . all my life the only thing I've ever had to help me survive is cold pride. It was my only shield against everything I had to face. I never let anyone inside it, I never let all the hurts they had to fling touch me. I was strong and I hid behind it. I built a great wall out of that pride and strength behind which I hid all the misery and pain I've known." His voice broke and he drew Deeta' hands to his lips. "Deeta," he cried, his huge body trembling and rocking back and forth, "Deeta, I cannot go on any longer. I don't have the courage or the strength to face a life without you. Help me, Deeta. Come back to me and help me. Don't leave me to wander through the balance of my life alone. You are the only ray of light that has ever given me warmth."

He bent forward now, laying his head in her lap as the unrestrained tears fell, clung to her. "Deeta, I need you. There is no strength left in me. It is all spent. I face only a black existence. Come back to me, take my hand, give me back what I have lost . . . Deeta, please?" he whispered softly, "come back to me. Don't let me die alone in the dark." He lay with his head in her lap for a time during which he sensed no existence. There was nothing in him now but the burning need for Deeta to know that she was the only part of him that lived.

Something moist and warm touched his cheek. He could not for a moment, realize what it was, then his heart gave a tremendous leap. Tears! Deeta was crying. He lifted his head to look at her. The tears fell down her cheeks, but he was no longer aware of them. He only saw her large dark eyes fill once again with love and warmth. "Deeta," he whispered. He raised his hand and touched her cheek with his fingers, afraid that it was all a terrible nightmare and that he would waken and find her gone again. "Please stay with me . . . I need you so very desperately. Don't ever go away again, for the world is very dark without you and I cannot find my way."

"Cat," her voice was a soft murmur, "I'm sorry," she sobbed. "I'm so sorry. Our son, he is gone." Cat pulled her gently into his arms while the tears, once started, could not stop. He comforted her and she comforted him as they mourned together for what they had lost. The tears were the best thing for Deeta, he knew, for she had contained her grief all this time.

Gently he picked her up and carried her to their bed where he held her against him and began to talk to her of their life together, of the promise of the future and most of all of the deep and abiding love he had for her. They slept, and for Cat it was the first quiet, dreamless sleep in many months. Yet he clung to her even in his sleep.

How long he slept he did not know. He wakened with a start to find his bed and his arms . . . empty. A blank wave of panic washed through him and he leapt from the bed and ran to the small parlor. There was no sign of Deeta.

The sun was setting behind the hills bathing everything in a soft rose glow. This all went unnoticed by Cat as he pulled the door open and ran out on the porch. The sigh of relief was almost a cry as he saw Deeta standing there looking out at the beauty around her. He came up beside her and put his arm about her waist and drew her against him. She rested her head against his chest. "I never realized how truly beautiful it is here until now," she looked up at him. "Beloved husband, I never really knew before the extent of my love for you. It is more than just a woman's love for a man. It is joining all you are and all I am to make one complete person."

Cat bent his head and touched his lips to hers. "From this terrible thing I too have learned. We will go on, you and I, and begin again. But this time we will be able to know and to feel for each other, and there will be no hidden emotions, no false pride to build walls. Deeta, when I thought I'd lost you, when all of my world had turned black, I hid behind my walls. Instead of turning to you as I should have done I built up my strong fortress and hid. That will never happen again." He held her close to him. "I want you to know in your heart now, that my need for you is even greater than yours for me."

"Oh, Cat," she murmured as she held him against her. The steady throb of his heart reassured her that he would be there always and the words he spoke were truth. "I'm home . . . I'm home and I will never leave again."

He held her close as they walked back into the house and closed the door on the world that had tried to destroy them and failed, and they opened another door to a bright new future.

Instead of going home, Margaret went to Foxmore. She wanted to explain to Matt exactly what she had said to Cat. She was worried now about the effects of her words and if she had been right about what she had seen in Deeta's eyes.

Matt and Deanna had not come home yet, but Jason and Deborah were there. She tried to explain what she had done and felt relieved when both Jason and Deborah had assured her she was right in trying anything that might bring Deeta back to Cat.

Deborah asked Margaret to please stay for supper and see Deanna and Matt before she went home.

"I'm sure you will rest easier when you have spoken to Matt."

Margaret agreed, for spending an hour or so playing with Paul Matthew relaxed her and she could forget for a few minutes all the problems this day had wrought. When Matt and Deanna did return and she had told them all what had happened, Matt agreed to go to Cat's the next day to find out if he was all right.

Matt insisted on taking Margaret home. "It's too late for you to be riding about by yourself."

Too tired to argue, Margaret let them tie her horse to the back of the buggy and take her back to Clearhaven. When she arrived there, she was in a mild state of exhaustion. She sent for a hot bath and afterwards fell into bed and instantly to sleep. The exhaustion had been deep and she slept late the next morning, which was a very rare thing for her to do. She enjoyed the beginnings of the day and often was up to watch the rising sun.

She ordered her breakfast in bed, which surprised her entire staff and within an hour brought a worried Sarah to her bedside. "Margaret," she said alarm sounding in her voice, "are you ill?"

"Good heavens, Sarah, I've never been sick a day in my life."

"Then . . . breakfast in bed . . . at ten o'clock?" Sarah could not keep the disbelief from her voice.

Before Margaret could answer, a breathless Susan was at her door accompanied by Brandon and John. They stood, looking so worried that Margaret lay back against the pillows and laughed until the tears came. When she could control her laughter and had noticed their relieved smiles she said, "I want you to know that today is my thirty-ninth birthday and I feel I should be able to celebrate it by having breakfast in bed if I choose."

"Your birthday!" Susan said, aghast at their failure to remember, "Oh, how terrible to have forgotten it! Aunt Margaret, I'm sorry."

"Well," Margaret said humorously, "I would just as soon forget it myself. Thirty-nine. Good heavens, I'm getting old."

"Old!" scoffed John. "No woman as beautiful as you are should even give a thought to the years. With each one you seem to get more beautiful."

"Thank you, John."

"Since it is your birthday, I suspect your girls will be here soon. We'd best let you eat your breakfast and get dressed," Sarah said.

When the door closed behind them, Margaret sat for a few minutes in deep thought. Her mind drifted across the span of her thirty-nine years and as a result brought to life again the vision of Mark. She allowed herself, "for the last time," she thought, to let Mark walk through her mind. She singled out each memory one by one and held it close to her heart. She was fifteen again. The day she had first met Mark. She had thought him so mature then at eighteen, a new graduate from the military school, tall proud and beautiful in his uniform. She thought of their year together, of the laughing, happy times they had. She thought also of the magic she had found the first time they had been together. Now she realized they had both still been children. When she found herself pregnant, she had refused in her stubborn pride to tell him. She had merely insisted that he give up his military career and stay and marry her. Mark's whole career would have been over, and she knew now he never would have been happy. Looking back now she could see how wrong it was to try to force him into a mold he did not fit just for her own selfishness, and to keep from him the fact of his children's birth was worse. She imagined him now, happily married to someone. A sense of peace pervaded her and she made a decision then. Mark had a right to his children and they had a right to know him. She would tell Deanna and Deborah and they could go and see Mark.

Her mind drifted to Paul. Paul with his kindness and strength. Paul who had held her through the years and made her life good. He knew, but had never once asked about the girls or their father. He had accepted them as his own. She wondered how many men would be as strong as Paul.

No matter how she tried to hold it away the memory of

David came. "David," she whispered, feeling the hot tears sting her eyes. She remembered Paul's excitement at David's birth, his love for David over the years. His undivided care for his children. Again the deep sense of guilt struck her. Would it have been different if she had been able to give Paul the love he needed? She felt she had cheated him and closed her eyes against the harshness of her thought. As though to ease her pain, the memories of Paul Matthew's birth came and Susan and Brandon's happiness with each other. Life gives and life takes away and in the sum of it, it balances the two. She was grateful for the good things and would bear the memories of the bad within her without complaint.

She set aside her tray almost untouched, rose, bathed and dressed, and went downstairs to hear voices from the parlor.

Matt and Jason were there with Deanna and Deborah. All of them were talking excitedly. "It is a miracle," Sarah proclaimed.

"It is, a beautiful miracle," Matt answered. "You should see the two of them together. Cat seems to be afraid Deeta will vanish, and she laughs at the continual way he keeps reaching out to touch her."

"It's a beautiful thing to see," Deborah added. "I felt like crying this morning."

"You did cry," Jason replied with laughter dancing in his eyes. "Did you think you could hide such happiness, love?"

Jason sat holding young Paul on his lap. The boy seemed content to stay and watched intently the words and feelings that passed between his parents. Not understanding but feeling the warmth that seemed to come from that, he lay back against Jason's chest and

579

listened with deep contentment to the rumble of laughter that made him feel happy.

"Good morning, everyone," Margaret smiled. "You all seem so excited this morning, what has happened?"

Deanna and Deborah went to their mother and kissed her, "Happy birthday, Mother," Deanna said.

"Yes, Mother," Deborah said as she kissed her cheek, "a very happy birthday. You deserve it and many many more."

"I agree with that," Matt said as he too kissed her soundly. "Cat and Deeta will be here soon."

"Cat *and* Deeta," Margaret exclaimed happily. Matt still stood beside her with one arm about her shoulder.

"Cat *and* Deeta," he repeated. "I don't know what words you used but you are responsible for a miracle. Cat looks upon you as something close to a saint. He's bringing Deeta down soon. They want to thank you together."

"Oh, Matt, I'm so happy."

"Well," Jason said as he stood up. He went to Margaret and handed Paul into her willing arms. "I think," he laughed, "we ought to turn this into a celebration."

"Jason," Deborah giggled, "you would turn just about any occasion into a party, wouldn't you?"

Jason chuckled. "When you have as much to celebrate as we do, sure. The birthday of one of the greatest ladies I know. The return to us of two friends like Cat and Deeta. All the good things we've got, starting with this little gift," he reached out and tousled Paul's hair. "And the future one Deanna's carrying. Don't you all agree with me it's a cause to celebrate?"

"Matt, will you please tell me what happened at Cat's?" Margaret begged.

"Well, I went up this morning because Cat had said he had made something for your birthday and wanted to come down with us and bring it. When I got there, I was not only greeted by a wildly happy Cat, but a conscious, beautiful and amazingly happy Deeta. They were both laughing and talking at once, trying to tell me what happened. All I could really make out of it was that," he waved his hand toward her and bowed slightly laughing, "Lady Margaret had performed a miracle. And Margaret, when I looked in Deeta's eyes, I agreed. You have. She is radiant."

The laughter and warmth filled the room. Margaret cast aside any regrets she had from the past and opened her heart to enjoy the future. Their gaiety was interrupted by the sound of an approaching buggy. Cat and Deeta were met at the door and showered with kisses, hugs and laughing tears.

Cat helped Deeta down from the wagon and amid all the clamor made his way to Margaret's side with Deeta's hand in his. He stood before her now, silenced for a few minutes by the depth of the emotion he felt. "What can a man say to someone who has given him back his life. I can only say that my life is yours. There is nothing you could ask of me I would not gladly give."

"And I, too," Deeta said softly.

"Oh, Cat, I'm happy for you both. It is not me but your own love for each other that has done this."

Cat and Deeta both shook their heads negatively. "We would still be drifting away from one another if it weren't for you."

Margaret leaned forward and kissed both Deeta and Cat, her tears too close to allow any more speech.

"I've something for your birthday. Deeta and I started

to make this a long time ago."

"Thank you, Cat."

Cat went to the wagon and lifted down what seemed to be a very heavy large square object. It was covered with a blanket. It was the size of a large trunk and even Cat's strength found it quite heavy to carry. He placed it in front of Margaret and pulled the blanket away. Margaret and all the rest gasped at the beauty of Cat's gift. It was obvious that a great deal of time and affection had gone into its making.

It was a large chest made of burnished wood that had been polished to such a shine that Margaret could see her face reflected in it. The whole top had been laboriously carved with an intricate design of vines and flowers. In the center was a large flat oval space that had been indented into the wood. Into this "Margaret Martin" was carved with scroll-type letters.

Margaret went down on her knees in front of it and lifted the lid. The inside had been lined with cedar wood. In the bottom lay a book, large, with the outside cover made of some soft leather. She lifted it out and gently opened the front page. Here the scroll writing was repeated more delicately. Her initials lay in an oval intricate design, three M's connected by curled letters.

"Cat, Deeta, it is so very beautiful. How can I ever thank you? What can I say?"

Deeta knelt beside her. "There is nothing that needs be said. We give this to you with all our love. Cat killed the deer from which we made the leather for the book. We hope it will, from now on, hold all your memories, contain all the births and deaths that touch the family."

The two women embraced each other and this was a signal for all of them that the celebration begin. They all brought gifts and Margaret exclaimed joyfully over each one. The chest was carried into the house and put in Margaret's room where, she claimed, it would remain the rest of her life and would one day belong to her family. The book was put in the center of her writing table. She wanted today's joy to be the first thing recorded in it.

Cat and Matt stood a little aside. "Matt, have you decided about what we talked about this morning?"

"Yes, and I've talked to Jason and John. They agree that what you want to do is the right thing. I just don't think we can bring up the subject today. Not while she's so happy."

"It's going to be a hard thing at any time. But I think the sooner we tell her the sooner we can be on our way. David's body should be brought home and buried in the family plot. We cannot rest while one of your family is lying so far away in a lonely grave that no one cares about."

"All right, Cat. When the party is over tonight we will talk to Margaret. We could make plans to leave tomorrow. Do you have any idea where he is buried?"

"No. But the only place someone could have taken a body from where David died was Wilmington. I cannot stand the thought that the boy lies in an unmarked grave. That no one has been there to care for it."

Matt nodded in silent agreement. The party began then and the rest of the day stretched forward for them to enjoy. Margaret had tables set up under the trees and soon they were laden with food. Large hams were baked, crisp fried chicken served on huge platters, cooled bottles of wine, freshly cooked vegetables from Clearhaven's huge gardens.

The party, by the time night fell, was filled with

laughter and gaiety. Even young Paul had been allowed to stay up, and was happily going from person to person enjoying the spoiling he was getting. A small bonfire had been lit and they sat around it now in comfortable quiet relaxation. Paul lay asleep in Jason's arms. Matt sat on the ground resting his head against Deanna's knees while her hand lightly caressed his head. John and Sarah sat side by side in quiet conversation. Cat and Deeta sat near Margaret.

"Margaret," Cat said quietly, "I hate to bring an unhappy note into your day, but I have to have permission to do something I feel needs doing."

Margaret looked up into his anxious face. "You want to go back to Wilmington and bring my son home?" she stated softly. Both Cat and Deeta were so surprised that she knew their intentions that they were momentarily speechless.

"I'm grateful that you feel so, Cat. It was a thing I intended to do myself."

"No, please, Margaret, let me," Cat requested. "I want to do this. I feel we owe David at least that much. He gave up his life for Deeta and me and I want to do something."

"All right, Cat. When do you intend to go?"

"Matt and I were going to leave first thing tomorrow if you agreed."

"Very well, I will make all the arrangements here. David . . . my son . . . he should be home among the people who loved him."

All of them were far enough away from the main entrance to the house so that none of them heard the approaching wagon and riders. The sound of hoofbeats were muffled on the soft gravel of the drive. David dismounted, and accompanied by Mark, Jeremy and the tired women they went into the house, only to find it practically empty.

One of the young servant girls exited the kitchen at that moment carrying a tray. When her eyes lit on David, her hands began to shake and her face went white. The appearance of what she thought was the ghost of David Martin frightened her into immobility. David went to her, controlling his laughter, and assured her he was both alive and well.

"Where's Mother?"

Stammering painfully, David could finally piece together the story of his mother's birthday party that was in progress. "It's all right," he soothed her. "I think I've brought her the best birthday gift I've ever given her."

"David," Mark said nervously. David turned to him in surprise at the tension in his voice. "I'd like to see Margaret alone."

"All right, you go into the study, I'll send her to you."

Mark agreed. He closed the study door and then laughed a little to himself at the remembrance of the last time he had stood in this room and blackmailed her into meeting him. He leaned against the fireplace and waited.

David asked Jeremy and Louise if they would be patient and wait for a few minutes, and when they agreed he took Jenna by the hand and led her toward the back of the house. They were shrouded in darkness as they moved toward the fire. David's gaze devoured the scene of his family all in one place. Then his gaze fell on his mother and Cat in conversation. He was only a few inches from them when he heard their words. They were, "My son should be home among the people who loved him."

"I am, Mother," he said softly.

Everyone was frozen to a stunned stillness as David

stepped into the light of the fire, drawing Jenna with him. Margaret was the first to regain her senses as she ran to him and he caught her in his arms, holding her close and crying with her. "David! David, oh God, my son. You are alive, you're well!" She was feverishly touching him, trying to reassure herself he was all right.

"I'm fine," he laughed through his tears. "Did you really think I could forget your birthday?"

Pandemonium broke loose as everyone, especially Cat, welcomed him and overwhelmed him with questions.

"I'll answer everybody's questions as soon as I can breathe," he laughed. "Mother," he said gently. "This is Jenna Mackenzie . . . the girl I'm going to marry. Her parents are with me, and I've got your birthday gift in the study. Won't you come with us so I can give it to you?"

Chapter Fifty-Six

With Jenna on one arm and his mother on the other, David led the way into the house. There he introduced Jeremy and Louise. Although Margaret had only met Jeremy once long years before, she felt there was something very familiar about him. Jeremy did not enlighten her because he did not want to diminish David's surprise. "I will answer all your questions," David said, "but not before I've given Mother her birthday gift."

"David, a gift can wait," Margaret said impatiently. "I'm sure everyone would rather know what happened to you. Please, we've been mourning your loss and now you turn up alive and well. We have to know, especially Cat. You have no idea what that poor man has been through. You owe us an explanation."

"Oh no, Mother," he said firmly. All of them were surprised at this new, and older David. "This is the most important gift I have ever given you and I will not explain one thing until you go to the study and collect the gift that has been long overdue."

Margaret looked about her at the faces and gave up the argument. They wanted to hear David's story and her quick reception of his mysterious gift was their only way.

"All right, David, I surrender. But as soon as I see this 'gift' you will tell us all what has happened?"

"Of course, I will, Mother. Now go. This gift has been waiting long enough." He put both his hands on her shoulders and propelled her toward the closed study door. At the door, she turned to argue with him one more time, but was stopped by the glint of laughter in his eyes and the gentle touch of his fingers against his lips. "Shhh, Mother. Just humor me. It isn't every day a man brings his mother a gift like this. I think it will make you happy. Please, Mother?" he added softly, "remember I love you and I want to see you happy." His eyes, so like his father's, smiled down into hers and killed any objections.

"All right," she sighed.

He reached around her and turned the knob of the door, then gave her a gentle shove toward it. As she turned to go in she could hear his light laughter.

Margaret turned and closed the door behind her, unsure of what she was to look for as a gift. Her eyes flew to the tall form of a man standing beside the low burning fire.

"Mark." It was so quietly spoken. Still he turned when he heard it.

"It seems we've been in this position before, haven't we, my love?" he said gently. "Only this time I have nothing with which to bind you to me except my love. Will you accept that, Margaret? May I stay?"

She never knew whether she moved toward him or not, whether she called out his name or not, but she suddenly knew she was in his arms. With her eyes blinded with tears she reached for him. It was all he needed. With a few quick steps he was beside her, lifting her against him, capturing her willing lips with his while she clung to him desperately.

When he had finally reluctantly released her lips, she said brokenly, "How did you know I needed you so? I was too blind and filled with self-pity to write?"

"Sarah wrote me, told me how you felt, and left the rest to me." He went on to explain everything that had happened. From missing her letter, to David tumbling into Mackenzie's door. "How I wish I had found that letter sooner," he whispered against her hair. "Too many years have been wasted." He tipped her chin up to look at him. "I will waste no more Margaret. I have a lot of years to catch up on."

"No, Mark, we will waste no more."

"We will send for a reverend. Tomorrow, you will marry me," he said firmly.

"Yes, Mark, oh, yes," she said as he took her lips again in a kiss that warned her he would accept no other answer. He held her against him in an embrace so fiercely possessive she could only cling to him. Then she felt his chest rumble with laughter and looked up questioningly. "It is a shame to waste tonight," he said, wickedness glittering in his eyes. "I know a little house not far from here. It's empty and a most perfect place for lovers."

"Ah," she said teasingly, "you sound as though you have been there before?"

"I have, with the most seductively beautiful woman God ever created. She was a creature of love and we shared something very wonderful. I have missed her."

"And you would find her again?"

"I never should have let her go. I should have dragged her away with me, and I will tell you now, once we meet again, my midnight goddess and I, I will never let her escape me again. Tell me," he said softly, "you will go

589

back with me, back to where we left our love, back to find it again."

"Gladly, my darling, gladly," she smiled.

Mark cupped her face in his hands and searched her eyes. He must have found some deep satisfaction there for he smiled, then kissed her gently. "Come, I want to shout it to the world. Do you know my love it has taken me twenty-five years to catch you. You won't mind if I tell everyone just how happy I am to have accomplished this feat?" He took her hand and drew her to the door.

David rubbed his hands together gleefully. He sent for some champagne. Now everyone was puzzled as he set out a glass for each of them and poured. Setting the bottle down, he turned to face the study door. Bracing his feet apart and clasping his hands, he stood smugly grinning, rocking back and forth on his heels and watching the door to the study.

It was only Jeremy and Louise who knew what was happening beyond that door. The doorknob turned and at that moment David and Jeremy began to pass the glasses about. As the door opened and Margaret and Mark appeared, David raised his glass and toasted them in a firm masculine voice. "I give you, my mother, the most beautiful woman in America and Mark Severn, my soon to be step-father. Let us wish them all the happiness they have so long deserved."

Everyone shouted in surprised happiness and raised their voices and their glasses in a salute. Margaret, tears falling unashamedly down her smiling face, went to her son and put her arms about him.

"You will agree, Mother," he laughed, "it is the best birthday present I've ever given you."

"Oh, you young devil. To frighten me so and then to

bring back to me all my happiness in one moment. What can I expect of you next?"

"I'll tell you," he said. He turned and held out his hand to Jenna who went to him. "I've asked Jenna's parents if we can be married. If they agree, I would like to have the wedding here."

Now that Mark was here, Margaret remembered just where Jeremy fit into his life. She had remembered Mark speaking of Jeremy often as his closest and dearest friend. She turned to Jeremy and Louise. "I imagine this is the most bizzare reception you have ever had to a country or to a home. Please," she extended one hand to each, "let me welcome you to Clearhaven."

"Thank you," Louise smiled, but Jeremy stepped closer and kissed Margaret on the cheek.

"Do you know," he laughed, "I have always wanted to do that. All through the years Mark and I were together, I have been told of Margaret. Margaret's beauty, Margaret's charm, Margaret's smile. It was all the man could ever think of. It's no wonder Britain lost the war. Mark's mind was not on what he was doing."

They all shared Margaret's laughter. Then she said to Jeremy and Louise. "Our children, they want to marry?"

"Yes. So the young man has said," Jeremy replied.

"You have an objection, Jeremy?"

"Not really, Margaret. I felt that Jenna was too young and a father worries about the kind of man his daughter will marry. But I can see from tonight that my worries were unfounded. I'm sure her mother and I will agree that when we thought of marriage for Jenna, David was exactly the kind of person we had in mind."

"Good heavens," Sarah said, "do you know that we will have three weddings?"

"Brandon and I would be pleased to share our day," Susan offered. "Why don't we have them all at once."

"Marvelous idea," David replied.

"A mother getting married on the same day as her son," laughed Deanna.

"Well," Deborah supplied, joining in on the fun, "I'll bet it's something this town has never seen before. Please Mother, do say yes. Let's let the whole area know just how happy we all are."

Mark drew Margaret against him and smiled down into her eyes, "Well, my dear?"

She nodded and suddenly everyone was laughing again. "Listen everyone," Margaret said. "I have something to say." They watched her as she lifted her glass again. "I know that my daughters have everything in the world to make them happy. God has blessed me with men like Jason and Matt to care for them, to love them and make them happy. Jason is building a new home, and Matt and Deanna have Foxmore. Tonight I want to give to Paul Martin's son what his father lived for and died for." Her voice lowered and they could hear the sound of the tears in her throat.

"Mother," David began.

"Wait, David," she smiled through the tears. She held out her hand and Mark enclosed it in his, then she turned back to her son. "I give you Clearhaven, David. It was the legacy left to you by a father who loved you and was very proud of you."

"But you, Mother, what about you and Mark?" Mark smiled for he knew what Margaret meant to do.

"It's all right, David," he said gently. "There is a place near here where love was lost once, and we are going back there to find it again. We will live in the small house on the old Sutter road. We intend to make a new start without any of the past that might make it difficult. Clearhaven is yours by right, by love, and that is how it should be. But this little house will be ours and ours alone. Do you understand?"

"Of course I do," he said softly, then he turned to Jeremy and Louise. Gone was the boy, and in his place stood a strong, determined man. "You and your wife must be tired, as we all are. Tomorrow is a better time for talk and for plans."

"You're quite right," Jeremy agreed. "It has been a long journey and a very exciting night." At the door, David held Deeta against him for a moment then he said to Cat. "I'm coming up tomorrow if it is all right with you. I'm bringing Jenna and we'll spend the day. We have a lot to talk over and I want Jenna to know how wonderful my whole family is." Cat nodded and shook David's hand silently.

Slowly the house became quiet. Matt and Deanna were almost the last to leave followed by Brandon. Susan kissed David good night. "I'm so glad you're home and safe, big brother." She smiled, "Nothing is the same without you here."

"I wouldn't have missed your wedding for anything," he laughed.

She lightly ran up the stairs, her heart bubbling with joy.

The lights were extinguished, the house was quiet, and the time ticked slowly by. David sat in the parlor alone thinking of all that had happened and how rapidly the world seemed to change. He could hear the soft chime of the clock as it struck one. He had been sitting in the dark room for a long time. He rose slowly, knowing that the deep hunger that gnawed within him could be appeased by only one. He walked up the steps quietly and stood in front of Jenna's door. Slowly he turned the knob and pushed it open. She sat on the edge of the bed, his little girl-woman, her hair in braids and in the same long nightgown. He closed the door behind him and with a small smile on her lips, she reached for him.

No one heard the soft click of the front door as it closed. No one saw the slender figure that ran across the lawn to the stables. No one heard the soft muffled hoofbeats as the horse was guided out along the drive and across the meadows toward a small house.

The door to the house opened as soon as she pulled her horse to a stop. Mark was at her side, lifting her down from the saddle and holding her in his arms. "Minutes are like hours," he whispered. "Welcome home, love . . . welcome home."

Cat helped Deeta down from the buggy, but to her surprise he let go of her as soon as her feet hit the ground. She went inside and waited while he put the buggy away and cared for the horses.

Seated in front of the fireplace she loosened her long dark hair and brushed it, humming lightly to herself. She heard Cat's footsteps cross the porch and looked up expectantly. He opened the door and their eyes met. Her smile faded as his eyes left hers quickly and he said quietly, "I thought you would be in bed by now. You must be tired."

He hung his coat on the hook behind the door then sat

down in a chair as far from her as he could get. To keep his hands busy, and to keep from looking at her, he began to remove his boots. He stood them in the corner then went to the kitchen. She could hear him moving about. She knew he was not hungry, for he had eaten at the party. There was no doubt in her mind. For some reason he wanted her to go to bed before him. She sat still as the worry gnawed her mind. Was it because he could not touch her? Was it because he felt she was too weak to become his wife again? Deeta knew now of the weeks that had passed since their ordeal. She knew her body and her mind were well, just as she knew that Cat would not rush her. He would wait until he was sure that no harm would befall her.

He walked back to the room and she smiled to see the nervous movements of his hands. Her smile broadened as she read the hunger in his eyes he could not hide. She rose and went to him. She could tell now just how hard it was for him not to reach out to her. His enforced celibacy left him completely unprepared to handle her nearness.

Moving nearer she slid her hands about his waist and laid her head against his broad chest. She could hear the rapid pounding of his heart and feel the tremor in the muscles of his chest and arms as he valiantly resisted putting them about her.

"Cat," she said softly, "hold me."

"Deeta," his voice rasped, "I can't."

She looked up into his eyes and smiled. "Why?"

He gulped heavily, "If I put my arms around you now it'll kill me."

Slowly she moved against him, feeling the length of his body against hers. She could feel the desire rise in him.

"Don't you want me?"

"Want you! Woman what are you trying to do to me?" He lifted her face in his huge hand. "I don't want to hurt you. I'm . . . I'm afraid."

"Don't be. My body sings out to you. I need your love now as I have never needed it before. Show me that you need me too. Love me Cat. Please?"

"Are you sure?" There was an agony in his voice.

"I'm sure."

He bent his head, and touching his lips to hers he closed his great arms about her and enfolded her in the warmth of his desire. "Deeta," he whispered. "I have been so long without you. I have dreamed of you day after day, night after night until I can hardly stand it." He lifted her in his arms and rocked her against him while his mouth searched for familiar spots that tasted sweeter than he had even remembered. He carried her to the room they had last shared so long ago. With an infinite gentleness, he removed her clothes and caressed her slender body. His huge hand cupped her breasts while he discovered the rosy tips with his mouth. He felt her stir beneath him, her need forcing her body to search for his. He heard the soft whispered words of encouragement. Her hands clung to him pulling him closer, and Cat pulled her against him. He wanted their joining to tell her that it was more than the seeking of her body. That he wanted the Deeta within. He chained them together body, heart, soul, and Deeta felt the power of his love in a magical fire she had never known existed. Nothing they had ever shared had prepared her for the flowing heat of his body as he joined with hers. He held her gently in his hands like something fragile while his body claimed hers in a spiralling flame of ecstasy that left her gasping and clinging to him.

He touched her face with his lips only to find it wet with tears.

"Deeta . . . I've hurt you?" he said a tone of deep alarm in his voice.

"No, Cat. I am crying because I am so happy my body can no longer contain it. It is overflowing."

He lay beside her, contented now, holding her to him gently. As she drifted off to sleep she could still feel the gentle touch of his hands.

The days of preparation for the combined weddings ran first like the sands through the hourglass. It seemed to be the social excitement of the season for the small town. "The Governor's son was marrying," was the talk. "Who?" was the question. "Who was she and where did she come from?"

By the time the gossips began to find out that there would be three weddings at once, they had a field day, and when they found out that Margaret Martin was marrying Lord Mark Severn, royalty from England, they sat back licking their whiskers at the stimulated conversations.

"Where had Lucas Olivier gone? The Governor's brother-in-law. Wasn't he enamoured of the beautiful Margaret?"

"Who was the young lady David Martin had chosen. A pretty fiery-haired girl from Scotland. After he had courted and bedded," they whispered, "quite a few ladies."

"Brandon Monroe could have chosen any eligible girl in the area. Why in heaven's name did he pick the shy little rose from the gardens of Clearhaven."

To make matters worse, the dressmakers who were chosen to make the wedding gowns were sworn to absolute silence and no matter what kind of bribery was extended not one word of the style or material of the gowns was given out. The day of the wedding dawned clear and bright. The church, to the pastor's amusement, was filled to overflowing. It seemed that every woman in town wanted a glimpse not only of the two pretty young brides but of the beautiful Lady Margaret and the oh-so-handsome Lord Severn. To them it was like a fairy tale come to life.

The first carriage arrived bearing all the men. David, Brandon and Mark were immediately ushered inside the parson's rectory so that they would not see the arrival of the brides. To the amusement of both Brandon and David it was Mark who showed the most pronounced case of nerves. He grinned amiably at a little fun from Brandon and David then said resolutely, "I will make this the best job that I can for I swear I could not go through it again."

So that Margaret would not detract from the younger brides, she had insisted that their ceremony be first. After it was completed she and Mark would go alone to the altar with as little fuss as possible.

The carriage carrying the women arrived at the church and the people left standing outside waited with bated breath for the door of the closed carriage to open. When it did, Sarah was the first to appear. She stepped from the carriage and moved a little aside. Susan was the first to descend. Her gown caused a soft sighing to ripple through the spectators. Satin *peau de soie*, *alencon* lace and satin rosebuds styled her gown. She wore a matching fingertip

598

illusion veil piped in satin and gathered to a lace cap. She carried a small prayer book that had belonged to Sarah's mother. It was covered in satin and lace and adorned with pink roses.

The expectancy grew a little more when Susan, accompanied by Sarah, and Caroline walked slowly up the steps. Jenna appeared next, slowly stepping down from the carriage carefully maneuvering her full-skirted gown. Her gown, styled with a victorian basque bodice and accented with *alencon* lace, pearls and crystals. A matching jeweled lace jubet cap held her cathedral-length veil. She carried a bouquet of lilies of the valley, roses and daisies.

When she had climbed the steps and stood at the church door, Margaret stepped out of the carriage. A murmured sound escaped each onlooker, a sound of deep respect and pleasure, as Margaret was a pleasure to behold. She had chosen a gown of palest rose. Its neckline was high around her throat and the sleeves long and fitted. The very full skirt was touched here and there with tiny pearls and a deep fringe of heavy lace trimmed the hem. She wore no veil, but had coiled her long black hair atop her head. Nestled among the thick rope-like coils were tiny seed pearls. Small pearl earrings were her only concession to jewelry. She wore no rings, but that day she wanted to wear only the plain gold band Mark would put on her finger. They stood in the back of the church in silence, then the soft strains of the organ began. David and Brandon came to the altar from the pastor's chambers and stood waiting. Jeremy kissed Jenna gently and then offered her his arm. Slowly they walked down the aisle toward David. John, silent because he could not speak past the heavy lump in his throat, offered his arm to Susan.

Margaret stood alone in the back of the church. After several minutes the faint words of the pastor came to her.

"I . . . love, honor, cherish," she closed her eyes and whispered, "I love you, Mark." The sound of the organ signalled Margaret that the ceremony was over. In another moment she was joined in the back of the church by the newly wedded couples and the family. David went to his mother and her eyes registered her surprise. She was to go in alone. He kissed her on the cheek and said gently, "Give your arm to me, Mother. I want to walk with you."

". . . but Jenna?"

"She understands. She gave me the idea. Let me walk with you, Mother," he repeated. Her eyes filled with tears. She went to Jenna first and kissed her.

"Thank you, my dear," she whispered.

"No," Jenna whispered back, "I thank you for giving me David."

Margaret turned to David and put her hand under his arm. They began the walk down the aisle to the soft sound of the organ.

Mark watched her come, his heart thudding over the sound of the organ. "Was there a woman as beautiful as she?" He remembered a sixteen-year-old girl whose first love he had been. He saw her as she was then, young and vibrantly expectant, giving her love to him freely and unashamed. The time unfolded before his eyes as he drifted back through the memories of Margaret.

Margaret, too, was remembering. Tall and handsome young Mark, resplendent in his uniform. Young Mark whose fiery kisses then and now could set her heart beating furiously. He saw the faint flush on her cheeks and the half-parted lips. His eyes grew warm with the deep surge of love that pulsed through him. David proudly felt his mother was at that moment the most beautiful lady he had ever seen. Jenna carried his heart, and her youth gave her a different beauty, but his mother was a woman of strength, pride and honor. He thought also of his father and lifted his chin even higher. Paul Martin had left a legacy to be carried down through the years and David vowed at that moment he would do his best to keep that legacy intact for his sons and grandsons.

There was a Grand Ball at the Governor's mansion after the wedding. It was resplendent with hundreds of lighted candles, soft music and flowing champagne. It was a gay and lively party that extended long after the married couples had gone.

Mark and Margaret had told no one that they intended to go back to their small house; everyone expected them to go on a honeymoon and they saw no reason to inform them any different. They shared a late supper there and with infinite love and care, Mark took Margaret to their bed and made love to her . . . for the first time as his wife.

"Well," Margaret chuckled, "I know one thing for certain."

"What's that, my dear?" he whispered as he kissed the top of her head and hugged her close to him.

"It really is no different married or unmarried. You can still shake the foundation of my world."

"Did you expect it to be?" he laughed. "I told you once a long time ago that our love was a very special song. There's only one thing new that I'm overjoyed about."

"What's that?"

"You don't have to leave me. I can hold you here tonight and know you will be here in the morning."

"Yes," she whispered as his mouth closed possessively on hers. "Tomorrow," she thought, as his warm loving arms gathered her to him, "and all of the tomorrows to follow."

Chapter Fifty-Seven

A black carriage rolled down a long road throwing up huge clouds of gray-brown dust as it went. The road wound its way toward a huge white pillared mansion that stood on a hilltop five miles away. The hot Georgia sun was merciless, and not a breeze moved to ease the heat. The carriage rolled on and on, its one occupant swaying with the rolling movement. He was preoccupied with thoughts and did not even notice when the carriage stopped and the driver climbed down and went to the door. He pulled it open and spoke to the man inside. "Mr. Olivier, we're home, sir."

Lucas' attention was brought abruptly away from his dark thoughts. He had left Clearhaven and went immediately to the Governor's mansion where, amid the protests of his sister and brother-in-law, he had packed his things and headed back to Fallon Hall. He knew he was not yet needed there and admitted readily to himself alone that it was a place to run, to be alone, to sort out his life and head it in a more constructive direction. He climbed down stiffly from the carriage. He'd been travelling for over two weeks and his muscles complained of the unaccustomed sitting in one place. He stretched his arms above his head.

"God, I need a hot bath," he said. He moved slowly toward the door. Opening it, he stepped inside the large cool front hall. It was an immense oval-shaped room, and on the far end of the room a large stairway covered in deep red carpet disappeared in a curve lighted by a huge window. It had always surprised Lucas how the hall remained cool in the midst of the hottest summer. He cared deeply for Fallon Hall. It belonged to his brother-in-law, but since Lucas seemed to have the ability to make it prosper, he'd been made a partner in its running and a partner in its profits.

He took the steps two at a time, walking down a long hall to a room at the end. It was obvious that the room belonged to a man. There were no feminine touches anywhere. He threw his jacket on a chair and went to a closet and drew forth some clean garments. These he threw across the bed. He began to disrobe as he walked to the door and threw it open. "Ben!" he bellowed.

There were rapid footsteps in the hall and a slender man of about fifty came in. "Mister Lucas. We didn't know you were comin' home today. We would have had everything ready."

"I don't need anything except a hot bath, something to eat and about forty hours sleep. I'm so stiff I can barely move."

"Yes, sir," Ben grinned. "I'll see your bath is brought up right away."

He left and Lucas went to a table that sat near his bed. He lifted a decanter of whiskey and poured a glass. Bolting it down he poured another before he sat down in a chair. He refused to think. It was too soon to think, and he did not have the strength right now. He sipped the whiskey and willed his thoughts quiet.

Soon he heard Ben coming back. With him he brought two boys who carried the huge metal bathtub. After several trips, the boys had the tub filled with hot water and Lucas sighed with relief as he eased his body down and lay back to enjoy it. Two hours later, he came down, freshly shaven, dressed in clean clothes and carrying an appetite as big as a horse. The meal was served to him by a huge black woman who clucked over him like a mother hen over a straying chick.

"Mars Lucas, you been gone all dis time an you ain't been carin' fo ya self proper."

"I'm fine Esther," Lucas grinned. "All I need is some of your good food in my belly and a lot of sleep."

"Ya'all call that takin' care of ya self. Travelin' day and night like ya was in a powerfa hurry ta get home an sleep."

"I was in a powerful hurry, Esther, my love, for some of your good cooking. A man could travel for years to get a sample."

"Shoo," she laughed. "Yo still is sweet talkin' ain't yo. But that don make no never minds. Yo got to take better care."

Lucas dove into the plate she set before him and ate heartily. She grinned from the doorway before she left the room. Lucas was Esther's favorite person, although she spared nothing in calling his attention to any faults she found. "He's a good kind man, with somethin' eatin' his heart out. I just wish I knew what was chewin' at that boy."

Despite the fact that Lucas was almost forty, to her he was still referred to as a boy in her mind. Mostly because she felt he had never had enough boyhood. "He needs sometin' to turn the young man loose in him again."

Satisfied, Lucas pushed the plate away and drew a cigar out from his pocket. Lighting it, he blew out a soft ring of gray smoke and leaned back in his chair. Now was the difficult time. Now he stood to do battle with the memories that crowded toward him. He rose and went out on the porch to finish his cigar. The sun was just beginning to set and he relaxed, sitting on the top step and leaning back against a huge white pillar.

"He would handle it day by day. One thing at a time." Tomorrow he would start some piece of work. Something strenuous to tire him enough to sleep. If he took care of just tomorrow, maybe all the other tomorrows would become easier. The sun was gone and the soft night sounds could be heard before he stood up, threw the stub of his cigar away and went back into the house. Again he climbed the stairs, this time more slowly, and fell upon the bed. He was so exhausted that it was only a few minutes before sleep overtook him.

He became aware that someone was shaking his arm and he lifted his head groggily from the pillow. "Ben," he mumbled, "what is the matter?"

"You got a visitor, Mr. Lucas."

"A visitor . . . who?"

"I don't know her, sir."

"Her?"

"A young lady, Mr. Lucas."

"Young?" Lucas smiled. "How young?"

Ben smiled back, "Too young for you, suh. I knows you like your ladies a little more experienced. This one looks like a little baby not too long away from her mama."

"What time is it, Ben?" he questioned as he began to struggle into his clothes.

"Gettin' close to noon."

"Noon! You let me sleep fourteen hours?"

"You sure was tired. Esther thought it best you get the

sleep you need."

"Ummm," Lucas murmured humorously. "If I left her alone, Esther would be diapering me and feeding me with a spoon."

"Yes, sir," Ben chuckled, "she sure would at that."

"What's my visitor like and what does she want with me?"

"She's a pretty little thing, scared silly about something. She just clings to that book she's holding and says she'll only talk to you."

"Okay, Ben," Lucas sighed as he walked toward the door. "Let's go see what our little lady wants."

Lucan whistled lightly through his teeth as he went down the stairs. He opened the door to the small sitting room and looked across at the girl who sat nervously on the edge of her chair looking at him.

"I'm Lucas Olivier," he said gently as he walked toward her slowly. "You wanted to see me?"

As he walked toward her he was overpowered by the strangest feeling that he had seen this child somewhere before. She was strikingly beautiful. "A girl," he figured, "somewhere around sixteen." Her hair was an odd color of gold that hovered near brown. As he drew closer he could see her wide, dark eyes, a vibrant amber color with sparkling gold flecks. He stood quite close to her now and realized how very tiny yet perfect she was. Her oval face was dominated by the large eyes. Her lips were full and rather sensuous for one so young, her nose straight and her brow wide. Her skin was a creamy color. Standing very straight and proud she had watched him come down, then she looked up at him and said softly, "Yes, Mr. Olivier, I had to see you. I am Theresa Alverez."

"Alverez," he said gently as the shock of that

607

forbidden name came to him. A floodgate of memories crashed open, almost blinding him with the memories of seeing her face again. "May I sit and talk with you?" she asked. Her voice had a light accent that told him she spoke Spanish more often than English. "I have a story to tell you and a secret to share." He motioned her to a seat and sat opposite her.

"A secret?" he questioned gently.

"Will you bear with me, Señor, hear my story first?"

"Of course, Señorita Alverez," he smiled and leaned back in his chair.

"My name is Theresa. I would like to hear you call me so."

"Thank you . . . Theresa," he replied, amused at her regal behavior.

"Your story?" he prompted.

"Yes. I am sixteen years old. All my life I have been told my parents were dead. For a long while I accepted that. But as I grew older and began to ask questions, I realized that there was some mystery about my birth, some dreaded thing about which I was supposed to have no right to ask. But ask I did, over and over again, only to find walls where I should have found windows. I," she laughed a little, "have a very stubborn nature, Señor. I was determined to discover why I had a past I was not allowed to speak about. A few months ago, my grandfather died. There was much confusion, for my grandfather was a very important man." She said the words with a lift of her head and a proud smile that was so familiar he could feel his heart begin to race.

"I wanted to help if I could as I am a very organized person. I was set to the task of organizing some trunks my

608

grandfather had stored away. I believe," now her smile flickered, "that it was to keep me out from underfoot and to silence temporarily some of my questions. No matter, it was a task I was set too, and I wanted to do it well. So I went through the trunks article by article, paper by paper and . . . I found my past."

Lucas felt suddenly breathless and could feel an expectant quivering within him, but he said nothing.

"I had always cared for my grandfather no matter that sometimes he was a rather cold and often a little heartless. He was to me the only link to what I was or what I expected to be. He was a domineering man who always . . . always had his way. There were always a set of rules by which he lived and he would bend them for nobody . . . nobody.

"The day that I reached into that trunk and took out this book is a day I shall never forget. At first I was going to take it straight to Tia Inez, for I realized it was some kind of family record. It was a gray unpleasant day and instead of giving it up I opened it and read, and as I read, Señor Olivier, my heart broke and I cried. First for my grandfather whose stiff pride and arrogant rules took away from him the one thing he loved the most, then I cried for myself, for what I had been cheated of, and at last I cried for two people who had loved each other and never were allowed to share that love."

Lucas sat quietly looking at her, "Of course," he thought, "those whiskey-colored eyes."

"I read," she continued, "of my mother and father. I found that . . ."

"You found that," he interrupted gently, "they had made the mistake of announcing that they loved each

609

other instead of clinging to each other as they should have done. You found that you had been born illegitimate."

"Yes," she replied softly.

"And you want me to fill in the empty places. Tell you of the things not recorded, for they cannot be recorded. You cannot record all the love your parents felt for each other, nor can you record the heartbreak and grief the arrogant pride of your grandfather caused."

There were tears in her eyes now as she set the book aside and came to him, kneeling in front of him. "You are my father," she said softly.

He looked down, not on Theresa Alverez, but into the eyes of his beloved Maria. "Yes," he said gently. He put his arms about her and held her gently against him as she cried. When she regained control of herself, she looked up at him. "I must know, Theresa," he said and she could feel the pain emanate from him. "I could never find her. I searched and searched. For two years I looked for her. I would have taken her away," he cupped her chin in his hands. "I would have cared for you, loved you. Do you know that?"

"Yes, but there is so much more to this story that you do not know. You see . . . my mother is still alive."

Lucas was numbed for a moment and stared at her, disbelieving what he was hearing. "It seems that the family that you and my mother insulted were quite prominent. By the old and very stiff rules, they insisted that my mother be punished. The sin she committed had to be paid for."

"Sin?" Lucas said, fresh anguish in his voice. "Is it a sin to love?"

"They would allow the rules to be broken for no one. A woman is the chattel, she is the negotiable thing in a family. To break her promise to be wed was one thing, but to become pregnant before she was married was quite another. It was unforgivable by all of them, so they took her to a convent in the mountains. A high-walled forbidding place. There they locked her away from the world and let her suffer all these years. They took me away from her as soon as I was born to make her atone for her great sin. It was not loving, Señor, for they did not know the word. It was disobedience. I told them I was leaving the day of my grandfather's funeral. I would not even stay to see him buried, for I had a hatred burning in me and if I had gone, I would have cursed him for all my years of not knowing. I have come to you to see if you still remember."

"Still remember," Lucas said, and there were tears in his eyes as he replied. "I have held your mother in my heart all these years. Locked in this forbidding place all these years, can she still be alive? Maria was so delicate, so very beautiful."

"She is alive, I feel it here," she said as her small closed fist pressed her breast. "I am going to her. I came to you because I felt you had a right to know, but with or without you, I will go to her."

"Not without me. We will have to break more rules, batter down some walls, but this time I will find her. This time they will not stop me from taking her away. I am only afraid . . . afraid a woman as sensitive and loving as your mother was she might have broken in all the years she was locked away from anyone who cared."

"Whatever we find," she said softly, her eyes meeting

611

his straight and steady, "don't you think it only fair that we should care for her, make the balance of her life easy after all she has suffered?"

Lucas looked down into her eyes and smiled. "You are not a child, but a woman. Sweet and loving-hearted as your mother was. You have her eyes, you know. Like whiskey. I knew them the minute I walked into the room."

"I want to know you," she whispered gently. "I want you to tell me of all the years I have missed. I want to know of you and my mother. Would it bring you too much pain to tell me?"

"No child," he said huskily. "You have no idea what a pleasure it would be to take the old memories out of my heart and share them with you. You," he said in wonder, "are a part of my body and blood. You were conceived in love. I want you to know that. It was not a light, careless thing. I adored your mother. All these years, I have thought her dead. I never dreamed that she and I had produced such a lovely thing as you are. We will talk, you and I, and tell each other all the things we have missed. Theresa," he said her name softly as though he still could not quite believe this miracle that occurred in his greatest time of need. "We will make plans tonight and begin our journey tomorrow. Do you know our destination?"

"Yes, the names and locations are all in this book," she handed it to Lucas who received another severe shock. It was a small, black diary and on the front page in simple delicate feminine writing was the name Maria Alverez. He looked up into his daughter's eyes. "Your mother's diary."

"Yes, I brought it because I thought you would want to read of the love she had for both of us. It will help us to be strong."

He was speechless, his throat too constricted to say anything. He held the diary in his hand, staring at it, feeling some kind of warmth from it, some kind of link to the woman he had loved for so long. Suddenly he brought himself back to the present and looked at his new-found daughter. He could see the tired lines about her mouth and the stiffness of her body that told him how tired she was.

Lucas went to the door and shouted for both Esther and Ben. When they came, he laughed at the open curiosity of their faces. He stood behind Theresa and put his hands on her shoulders. Ben waited expectantly, but it was Esther's eyes that widened with the sudden recognition. Her smile broadened and she said softly, "My, my."

"She's my daughter, Esther," he answered. "Mine and Maria Alverez."

"Of course she is," Esther said, and with a quick laugh she went to Theresa's side. "Child, you couldn't belong to anyone else but my Lucas and your pretty mama. You are just like the two of 'em melted together."

"She's tired from her long journey, Esther. She needs some of your tender loving care."

"I'll see to her," Esther replied. She put her arm comfortingly about Theresa's shoulder and led her from the room.

"Your daughter," Ben said in wonder.

"Ben, I want you to get us packed and ready. We are going to Spain. This time we're going to bring back a bride."

"Yes, sir," Ben grinned. He left, closing the door behind him.

Lucas sat slowly down in a chair and opened the small book in his lap. He read slowly aware of the delicate handwriting of a very sensitive and lonely young girl. The book must have been started when Maria was fourteen. She was always under the restrictive eye of her domineering father and Tia Inez. Lucas began to develop a slow, burning hatred for these frozen-hearted people who had planned to use an innocent young girl as pawn in a game of intrigue and wealth. Then he came to a place that held him and brought the sting of tears to his eyes.

". . . Today I met Lucas Olivier. Dear Diary, he is the most beautiful of men. His smile makes me warm. It is forbidden to speak to him, but oh, I wish I could do so . . ." Lucas read on. "Lucas and I have met. He held my hand and told me of so many exciting places and things he has seen. I felt so good being with him and the strong feel of his hand holding mine gave me strength for the battle to come for Tia Inez has seen us talking . . .

"Father has threatened to lock me away in the convent of San Lucia if I ever see Lucas again. I know what is expected of me, but my heart belongs to Lucas. To hear him laugh at the problems facing us. I have faith in him. I know Lucas will find a way to make everything right for us . . .

". . . I belong to him, to my beloved Lucas. Not only has he possessed my body, but my heart and soul as well. I will never belong to another man as long as there is a breath in my body . . .

". . . Can I tell him that I am expecting his child? No, I

614

will wait until he has set me free, then we will be happy together . . .

". . . I am frightened. Tia Inez, who knows me so well, is suspicious, I have been so ill in the mornings. But I cannot remain afraid. I must remember that Lucas has promised to come for me. Soon all this fear will be gone. Lucas will come. Lucas will come . . ."

Here the diary ended. He closed it and sat for a long time, remembering the vain promises he had made her. The agony that for sixteen years she had borne the pain for what they had done tore him apart. "How will she be?" he wondered. "All these years shut away from the world. You will suffer no more, my darling." He swore, "The balance of your life will be gifted with all the love and devotion I can give you."

Theresa and Lucas became friends, then father and daughter on the long trip from America to Spain. They sat on the ship for hours and talked. He was in a rage that the arrogant Alverez' were going to use Theresa the same way they had her mother. The urge to kill rose up strong in him, only to be eased by his daughter's soft voice.

"They can do us no more harm. Once we take my mother from there we will stay together as a family and they can never reach us again."

In Madrid they hired a carriage and began the last leg of their journey over rough mountain roads toward the convent. It sat high in the mountains far from any village or town. It was a tall gray structure surrounded by high stone walls. Iron gates twice as tall as Lucas were their first barrier. Without stating a name, Lucas informed the sister that came that it was urgent that he come in. When asked why, his mind searched for a reason. He knew he had to get inside the gate.

"My father wishes me to join the order, Sister," Theresa said timidly.

Lucas sighed with relief when he heard the lock slide open and the gates swing inward. They were over the first barrier. Lucas watched everything about him as the sister led him toward the huge front door. The austerity, the complete lack of any sign of comfort, left him weak with wonder as to how the mind of a girl as young as Maria had been, had kept its sanity in these surroundings. Maria had always loved music and flowers, and had appreciated the beautiful things around her.

Once inside the door, they walked down a deserted hall, their feet echoing sharply through the corridor. There were no words spoken as the sister led them to an oak door where she rapped lightly. A soft "Come in" and she pushed the door open. Quietly, in light whispers, she explained Lucas' and Theresa's presence. Lucas wanted to shout, to curse, anything to break the strong oppressive silence. The younger sister faded away and Lucas was left to face the Mother Superior. He was at the end of his ability to stand this and was filled with fear as to the condition in which he would find Maria. His voice cracked in the still air.

"I have come for Maria Alverez," he said firmly, his eyes flashing his rage and his jaw clenched in firm determination. Maybe that is why he was surprised into speechlessness when he heard her muted reply, "Thank God."

Lucas looked at her blankly for a moment then he and Theresa exchanged looks.

"I have prayed many prayers for the deliverance of

Maria. No matter what powerful force keeps her here, I have always felt it .was wrong. Now my prayers are answered. Who are you?"

"My name is Lucas Olivier. We would have been married if she had not been stolen from me. This is our daughter Theresa." Lucas went on to explain partially what had happened though he was too anxious to go into details. "Where is she . . . how is she?"

The Reverend Mother could see the worry in his eyes. "She is well physically, my son, but she has had so many days of lonely grief. Let me take you to her." She led the way out the door, down the same corridor to another set of double doors. She pushed these open and they entered a small chapel.

Lucas' breath caught at the sight of the slender figure in white that knelt there. He took several steps toward her, then said her name in a broken cry. "Maria!"

She turned startled eyes toward the sound. They widened first with disbelief then with wild joy as she realized who it was that stood before her. She was so much thinner and smaller than Lucas had remembered. Her wide amber eyes filled with tears and she ran toward him. He held out his arms and gathered her against him, rocking her in his arms and whispering her name over and over. He caught her face in his hands and kissed her again and again while their tears blended and mixed with the sobbing sounds she made. "Lucas, my love, my dear Lucas," she whispered.

"I'm here," he cried. "Oh, Maria, I'm so sorry, so terribly sorry. I'll make it up to you, all these long, long years you've suffered. I'll make it up to you. Forgive me, Maria, forgive me!" She clung to him with her eyes closed absorbing the feel of the strong arms of her dreams.

"It is over, Lucas? You've come to take me away? I have prayed and dreamed so long I no longer know what is real and what is fantasy."

"I've come to take you home, Maria, to our home. I'll never let you go away from me again."

He slid his arm about her, holding her close to him and began to walk toward Theresa, who stood with her face wet with tears. "I have another great surprise for you. One that I'm sure will give you more happiness. You were imprisoned here because you had the courage to love me and to bear my child. I have brought her to you, the child of our love."

Theresa stood facing her mother for a heart-stopping second, then Maria held out her arms and Theresa fled to them, to the only real love she had ever known.

Arrangements were made immediately, and within an hour Lucas put Maria and Theresa in the carriage, climbed in beside them and held both their hands as they began their journey home. The trip from the convent to Madrid seemed to be almost too much for Maria. She was frightened of everything. Lucas acquired a small house far from the city, secluded and with a high wall around it. There he settled them until Maria could accustom herself to the changes about her and the fact that she had at last found safety in Lucas' arms.

They were married quietly so that no word of the event could reach the ears of the rest of the Alverez family, for Lucas knew his anger was on a thin thread and that he would kill anyone who interfered with them now. Several nights after they had been married, Lucas woke to find Maria sitting up in bed crying softly. He sat up, then realized she was still asleep. Gently, he took her in his arms and soothed her until the tears ceased and he felt her waken and cling to him.

"You were dreaming?" he questioned gently.

"Yes, but the dreams are gone now. I am safe with you. Lucas, let us leave this country and go to yours. I want to walk in the sun again as we used to do."

Lucas had not tried to possess Maria, for he felt she was not emotionally ready. It was difficult to hide the burning need for her. He held her and caressed her, then spoke words to her he had needed to say for a long time.

"Maria, I love you with every beat of my heart. You know that, don't you?"

"Yes, Lucas."

"Then I must tell you that I am deeply ashamed, ashamed that I have had other women since you."

"Had them Lucas?" she smiled, "or loved them?"

"All but one, I had. I will tell you of Margaret. I want no secrets, no barriers between us. She reminded me somehow of you. I asked her to marry me and she was wise enough to see that I was only half a man. That the other half of me was lost to her. Can you understand and forgive me?"

"For the women you possessed for a night, I have no thought, for you are a man of strong passion and you need a woman. For the other, I am glad she was understanding and kind. I am also grateful that she returned you to me. Yes, Lucas I can forgive for I love you also."

He kissed her then, a gentle, seeking kiss, and his heart began to pound as she softened in his arms and he began to feel the welcome within her. With a throaty laugh she raised her arms and drew his mouth firmly against hers.

"Love me, Lucas, for all the years we have lost. Love me!"

He pulled her against him joyously, for he knew he was welcomed and cherished. There was no restraint, no fear, no barriers. Lucas was home.

Epilogue

Deanna stood up from the soft, grassy ground, her hair and clothes disheveled and a sparkling laugh on her lips. She had been carelessly in play with her two-year-old daughter, Lauren. Now she stood up and shaded her eyes, watching the tall man walking toward her.

"Papa's coming, Lauren," she laughed. "I guess play time is over."

Lauren climbed clumsily to her unsteady feet, then began to run toward Matt, who grabbed her up, tossing her into the air and catching her in his strong arms. He held her as he went to Deanna.

"Well, Matt?" she questioned.

"A boy, a big healthy baby boy, and Cat and Deeta have named him Jessie Luke. We are to stand as godparents."

"Deeta is well?"

"She's fine, and Cat is fair bursting at the seams with pride."

"I firmly suspect that Jason and you will find it an excellent excuse for another party," she said dryly.

"Of course," he laughed.

They stood together on the front lawn of Foxmore looking out over the James River. Matt put his arm about her. "Happy?"

"Oh, Matt, I couldn't be happier. The future for us is so bright. Surrounded by family and having you and

Lauren. Sometimes my heart fills so I can barely stand it."

"Well, with Jason and Deborah expecting another child and Cat's baby, not to mention the other increases in the family, we are probably the luckiest people in the world. I always felt, before I came here, that somehow everything was planned. When the ship *Destiny* brought me you and all this beauty. We'll do our best to hold on to it no matter what the future brings. We're strong and building. We have the world to hand to our children."

Deanna smiled at Matt as he bent and touched her lips lightly with his until his daughter, unhappy that she was not getting all their attention, gripped him by the beard and turned his face toward her.

"Daddy . . . take 'auren home."

"Yes, love," he said gently, and kissed her, then he smiled at Deanna. "All the Deveralls and Martins are home."

FICTION FOR TODAY'S WOMAN

THE LAST CARESS   (722, $2.50)
by Dianna Booher
When the news that their daughter might die transforms Erin's husband into a distant, isolated man, Erin learns that there is more than one way to lose someone you love—and few ways to win them back. . . .

TO SUFFER IN SILENCE   (748, $2.75)
by Patricia Rae
The back ward of Harwell State Mental Hospital is a place no one will discuss. And Daniel, an invalid without the powers of speech or movement, is imprisoned there. Unable to convey his sanity, he is alone. Powerless, he is forced TO SUFFER IN SILENCE.

THE VOW   •   (653, $2.50)
by Maria B. Fogelin
She was an exquisite bride-to-be, with the vigor and determination to make her dreams come true—until a devastating accident destroyed her future. Still, she found the courage to live, and searched for the courage to love.

CELEBRATE WHAT IS   (764, $2.50)
by Doris Standridge
The true story of a mother's tragic inability to accept the invalid state of her once strong and athletic son—and of a young man's courageous battle for life!

SO LITTLE TIME   (585, $2.50)
by Sharon Combes
Darcy's love and courage are put to the test when she learns that her fiance has only months to live. And the most important test of all, is the test of time. . . .

Available wherever paperbacks are sold, or order direct from the Publisher. Send cover price plus 50¢ per copy for mailing and handling to Zebra Books, 475 Park Avenue South, New York, NY. 10016. DO NOT SEND CASH!

ENTRANCING ROMANCES BY SYLVIE F. SOMMERFIELD

ERIN'S ECSTASY (656, $2.50)
by Sylvie F. Sommerfield
When English Gregg Cannon rescued Erin from Lecherous Charles Duggan, he knew he must wed and protect this beautiful child-woman he desired more than anything he ever wanted before. When a dangerous voyage calls Gregg away, their love must be put to the test . . .

TAZIA'S TORMENT (669, $2.50)
by Sylvie F. Sommerfield
When tempestuous, beautiful Fantasia de Montega danced, men were hypnotized by her charms. She harbored a secret revenge, but cruel fate tricked her into loving the very man she'd vowed to kill!

RAPTURE'S ANGEL (750, $2.75)
by Sylvie F. Sommerfield
Angelique boarded the *Wayfarer* in a state of shock, just having witnessed a brutal attack of her best friend. Then she saw Devon—whose voice was so tender, whose touch was so gentle, and they both knew they were captives of each others' hearts . . .

REBEL PRIDE (691, $2.75)
by Sylvie F. Sommerfield
The Jemmisons and the Forresters were happy to wed their children and thus unite their fortunes and plantations. But when Holly Jemmison sees handsome but disreputable Adam Gilcrest, her heart cries out that she has always loved him. She dare not defy her family, but she dare not deny her heart . . .